Tree-House Comix Proudly Presents

DOG MAN
TWENTY THOUSAND FLEAS Under the Sea

WRITTEN AND ILLUSTRATED BY **DAV PiLKEY**

AS GEORGE BEARD AND HAROLD HUTCHINS

WITH COLOR BY JOSE GARIBALDI & WES DZIOBA

graphix

AN IMPRINT OF

SCHOLASTIC

Library of Congress Control Number 2022944016

978-1-338-80191-0 (POB)
978-1-338-80192-7 (Library)

10 9 8 7 6 5 4 3 2 1   23 24 25 26 27

Printed in China   62
First edition, March 2023

Editorial team: Ken Geist and Jonah Newman
Book design by Dav Pilkey and Phil Falco
Color by Jose Garibaldi and Wes Dzioba
Color flatting by Aaron Polk and Corey Barba
Creative Director: Phil Falco
Publisher: David Saylor

CHAPTERS

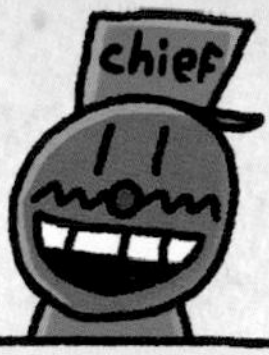
chief

Meet the Cast

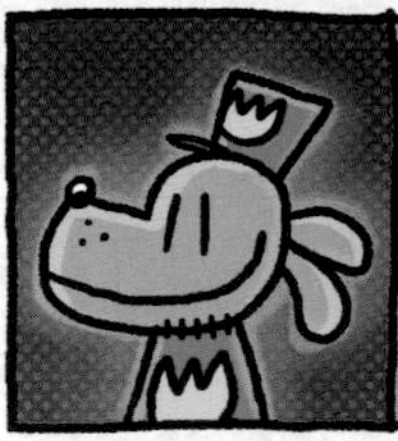

DOG MAN: He's part dog, part man, and ALL HERO! Sometimes he dresses up as a superhero named "The Bark Knight," although he has no superpowers.

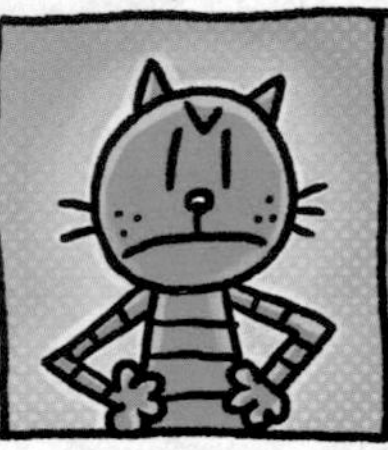

PETEY: He used to be an irritable, impatient bad guy. But when his son arrived, Petey became determined to change his ways. Now he's an irritable, impatient Good Guy.

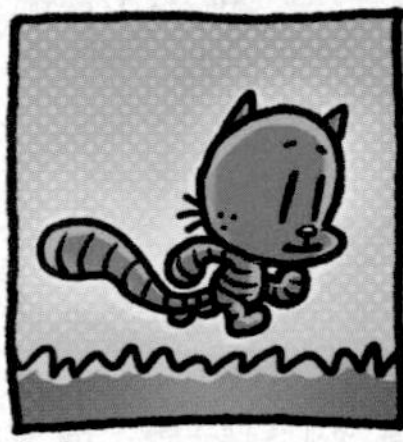

LI'L PETEY: Petey's pure-hearted son. He loves making comics and telling jokes. Sometimes he even saves the world as a superhero named "Cat Kid."

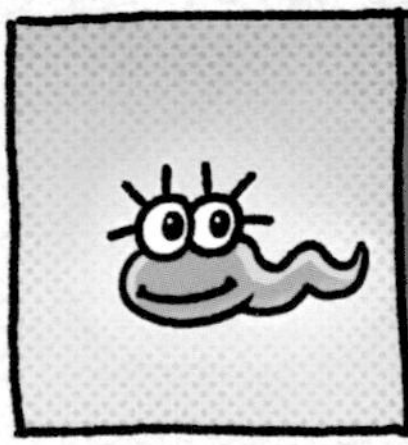

MOLLY: She may *look* like a tadpole, but she identifies as a baby frog. Her superpower is *psychokinesis*, which means that she can move things with her mind.

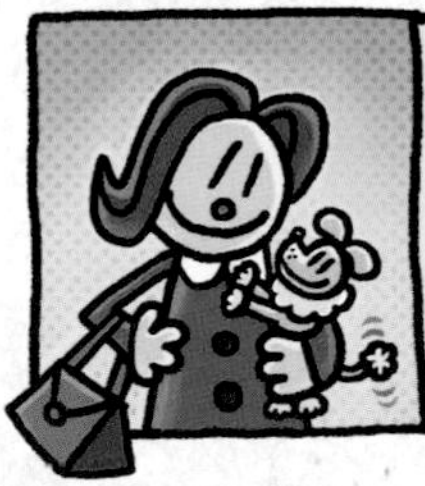

SARAH HATOFF & ZUZU: Sarah is an investigative journalist from Australia who adores her pet poodle, Zuzu. Sarah always carries a purse, too, except when Harold forgets to draw it.

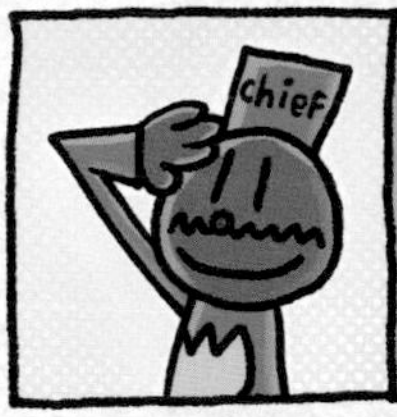
chief

CHIEF: He's Dog Man's brave boss and loyal best friend. Chief also has a HUGE CRUSH on Nurse Lady. Don't tell anybody!!!

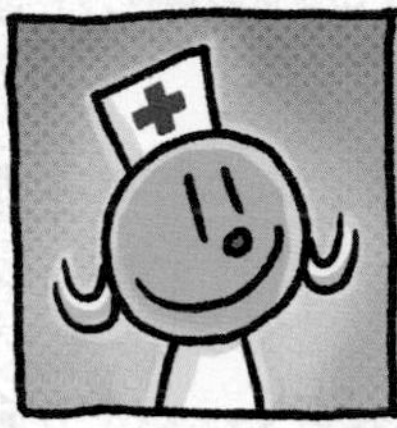

NURSE LADY (a.k.a. Genie S. Lady, RN, BSN): She's a smart and brave health-care professional, and her quick thinking saved Dog Man's life. She also has a MAJOR CRUSH on Chief. Shhh!!!!

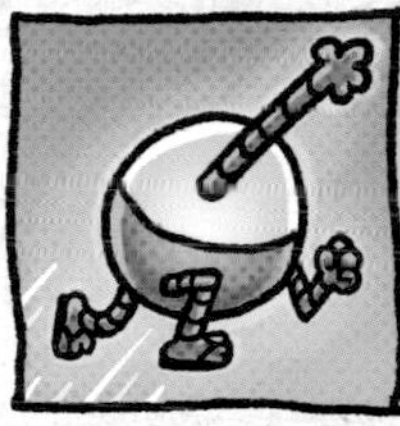

80-HD: A robot designed by Petey and rebuilt by Li'l Petey. Although his exoskeleton houses a limitless supply of helpful gadgets, his greatest superpower is CREATIVITY.

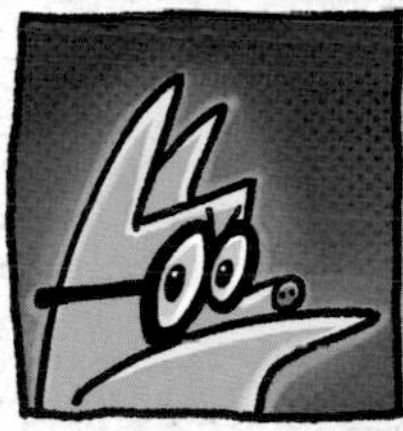

PIGGY: He's the ruthless leader of the FLEAS, which is an acronym for "Fuzzy Little Evil Animal Squad." Recently, Piggy got shrunk by a shrink ray, and was locked up in Mini Jail for "crimes and stuff."

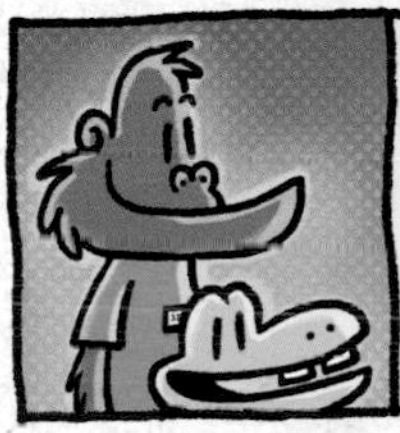

CRUNKY & BUB: Piggy's sidekicks and members of the FLEAS. Crunky (the gorilla) and Bub (the crocodile) also got shrunk and locked up in Mini Jail, but unlike Piggy, they're both pretty good guys.

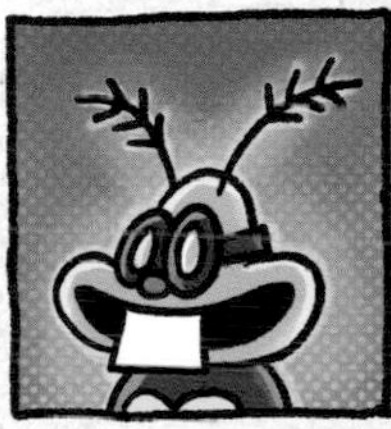

DARYL: He's a friendly moth who founded a superhero club called "The Friendly Friends." Daryl is a loyal friend to Piggy, even though Piggy is mean and rude in return.

for my brother,
Steve Aragaki

CHAPTER 1

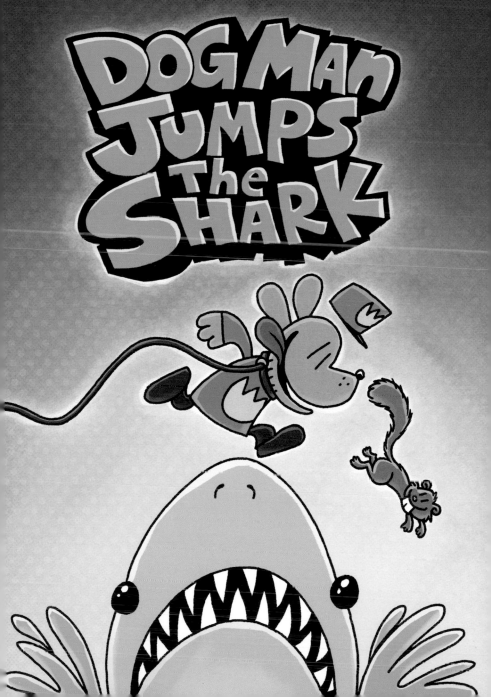

DOG MAN JUMPS THE SHARK

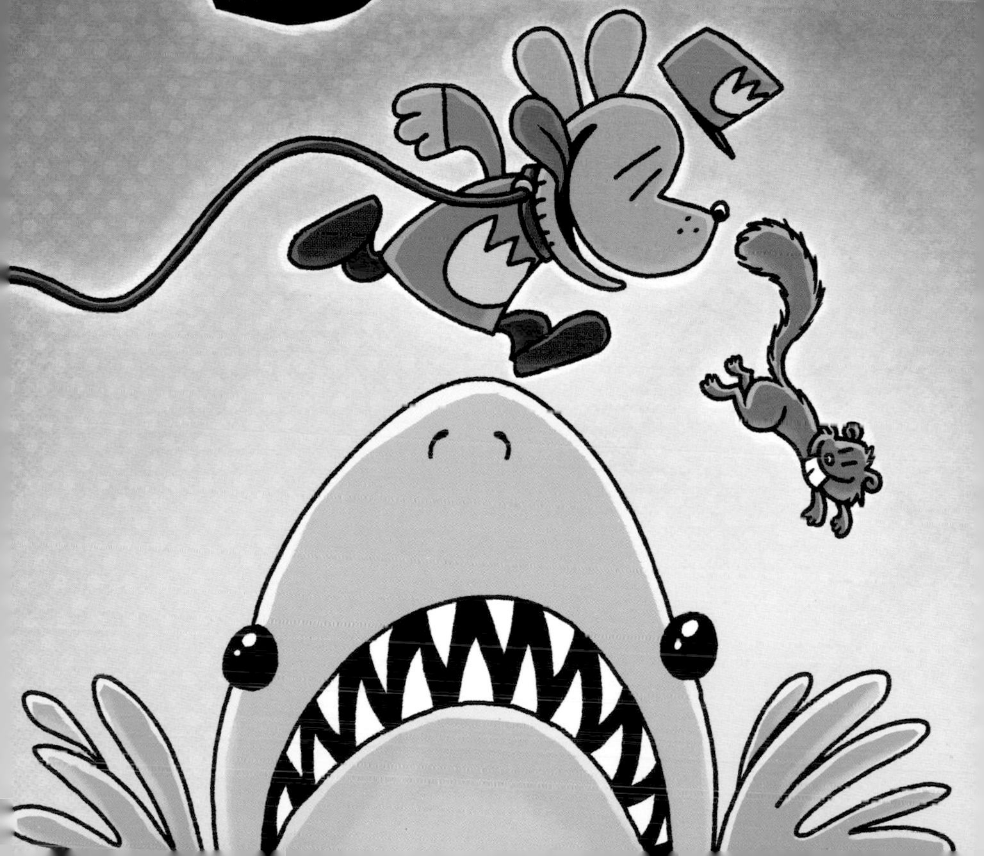

We're almost there!

Thanks for coming with me on my date, DoG Man!!!

I'm a little **nervous!**

Is my breath okay?

sniff sniff

Oh, boy! This is Gonna be...

...GREAT! She's already HERE!!!

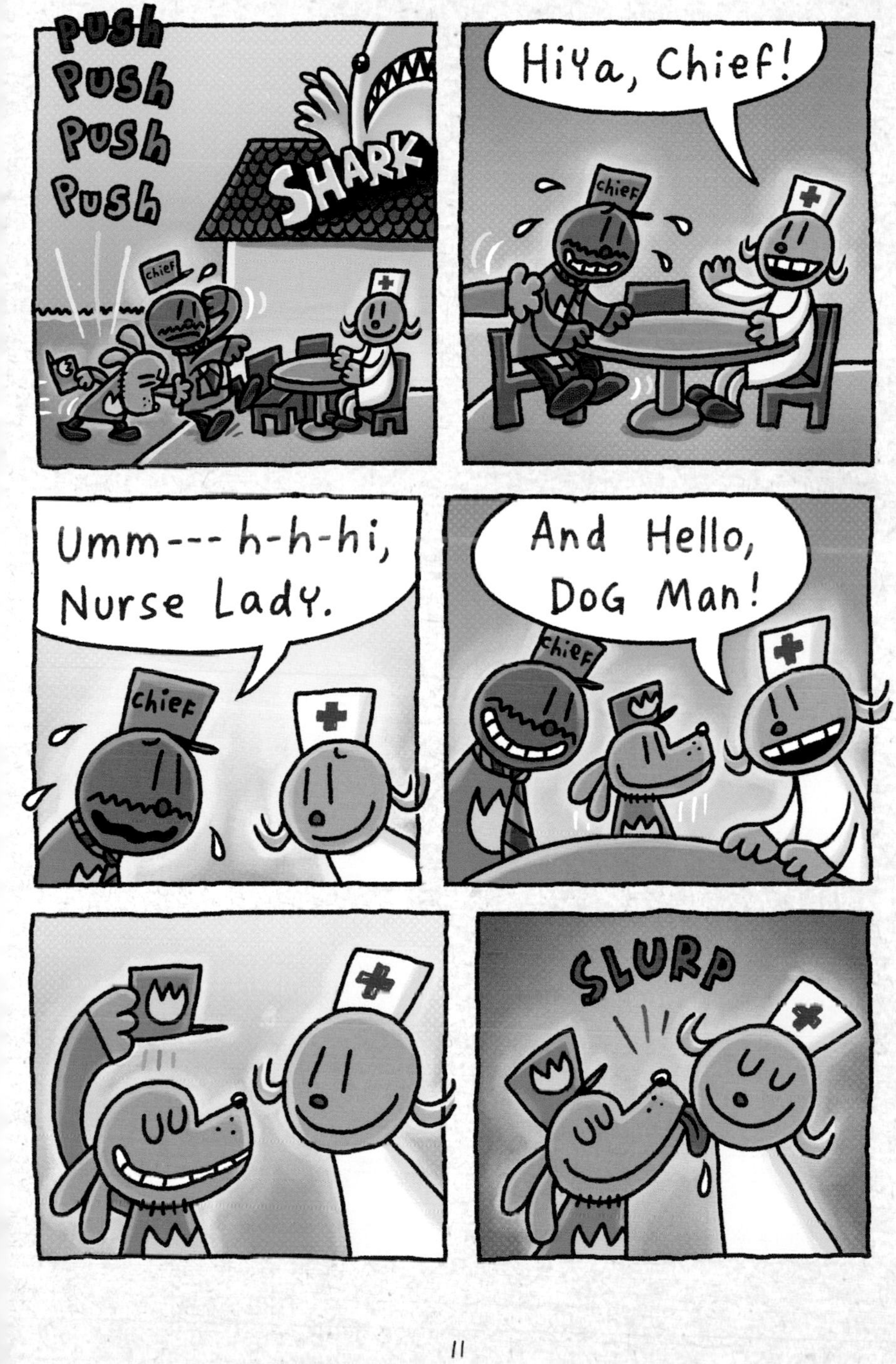
PUSH
PUSH
PUSH
PUSH
SHARK
CHIEF
Hiya, Chief!
CHIEF
Umm--- h-h-hi, Nurse Lady.
CHIEF
And Hello, DOG Man!
CHIEF
SLURP

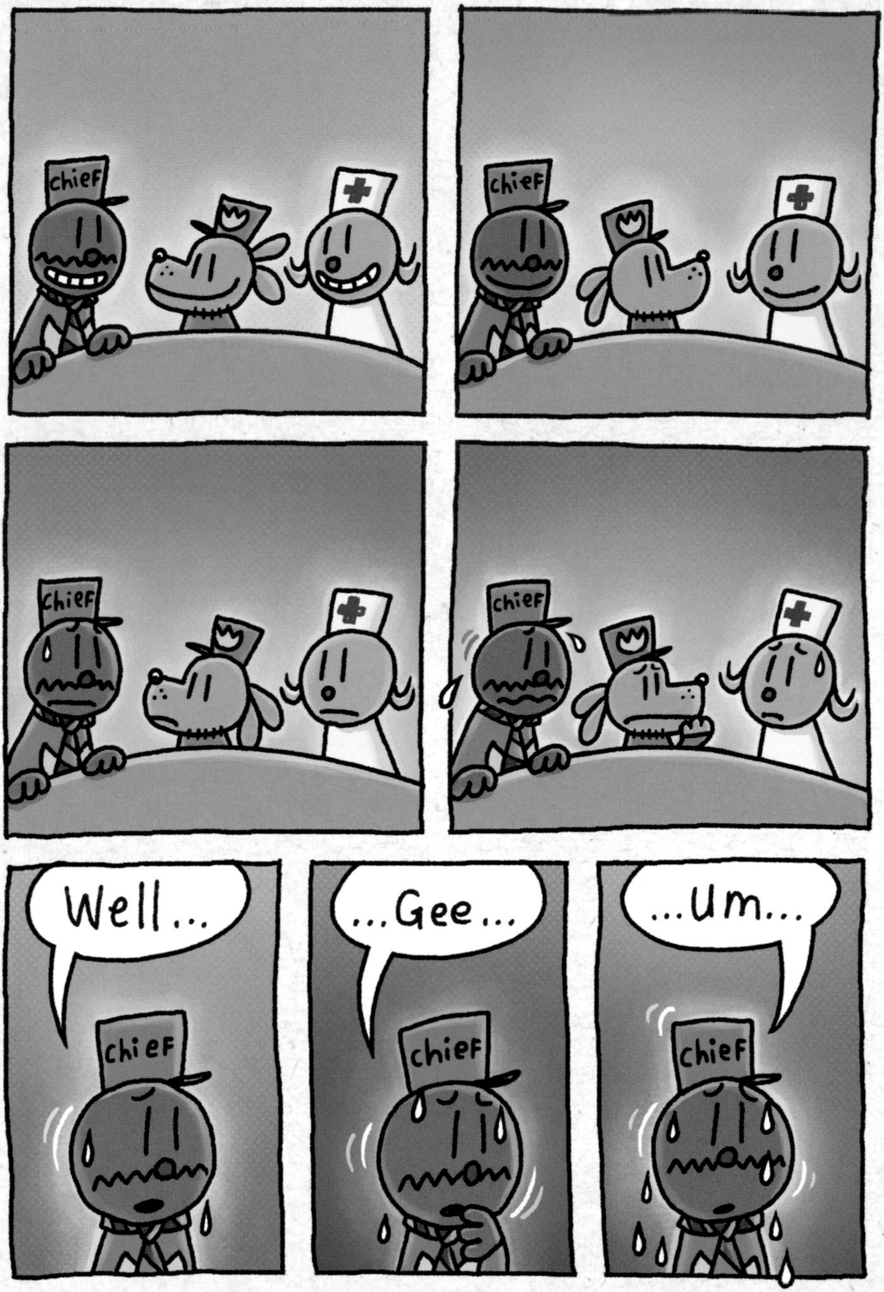
chief
chief
chief
chief
Well...
chief
...Gee...
chief
...Um...
chief

He's not a DOG.

He's DOG MAN!

Well he looks like a DOG to ME!!!

And we don't ALLOW DOGS!

Oh, Yeah? Well I don't see a SIGN!!!

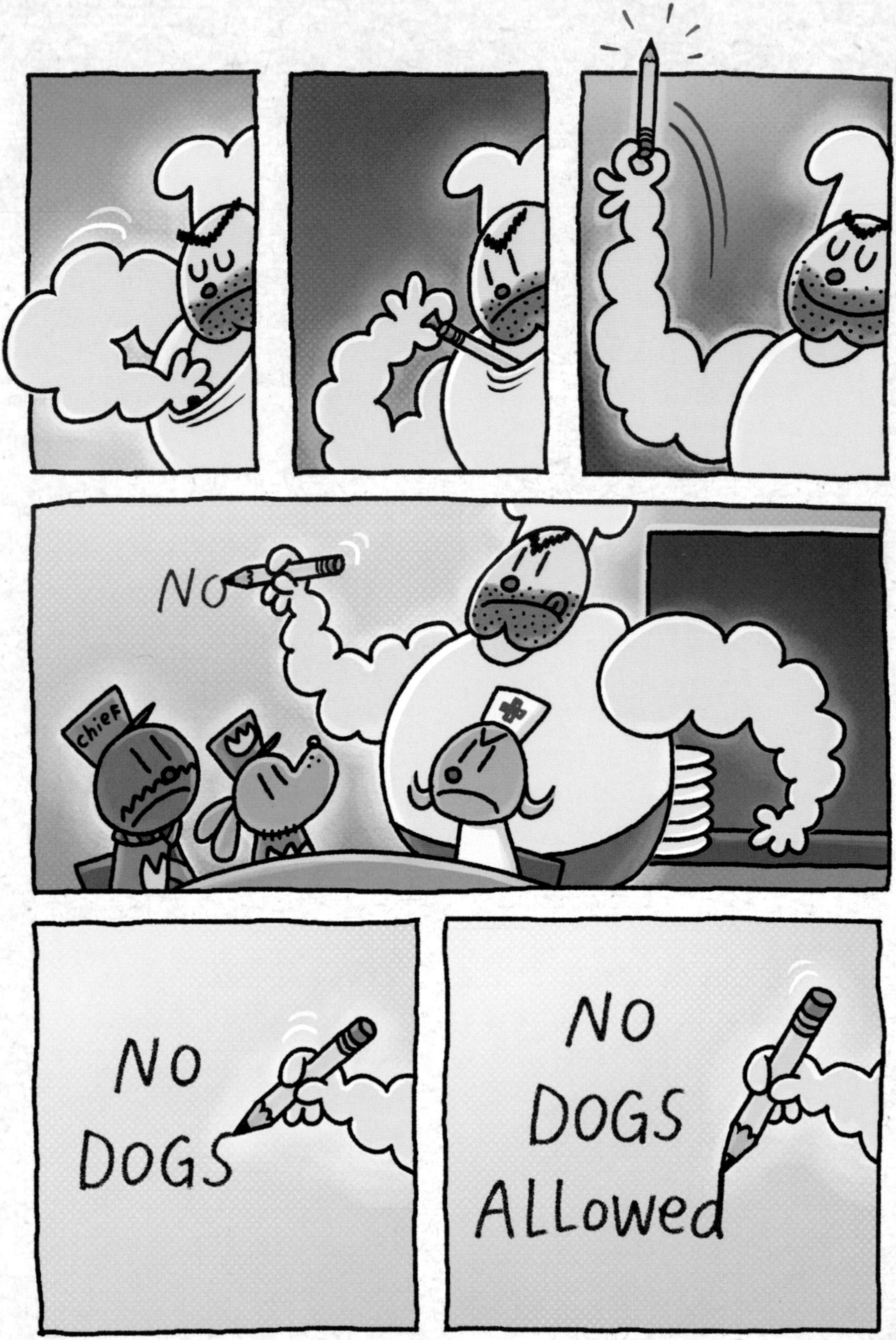
NO
chief
NO
DOGS
NO
DOGS
ALLowed

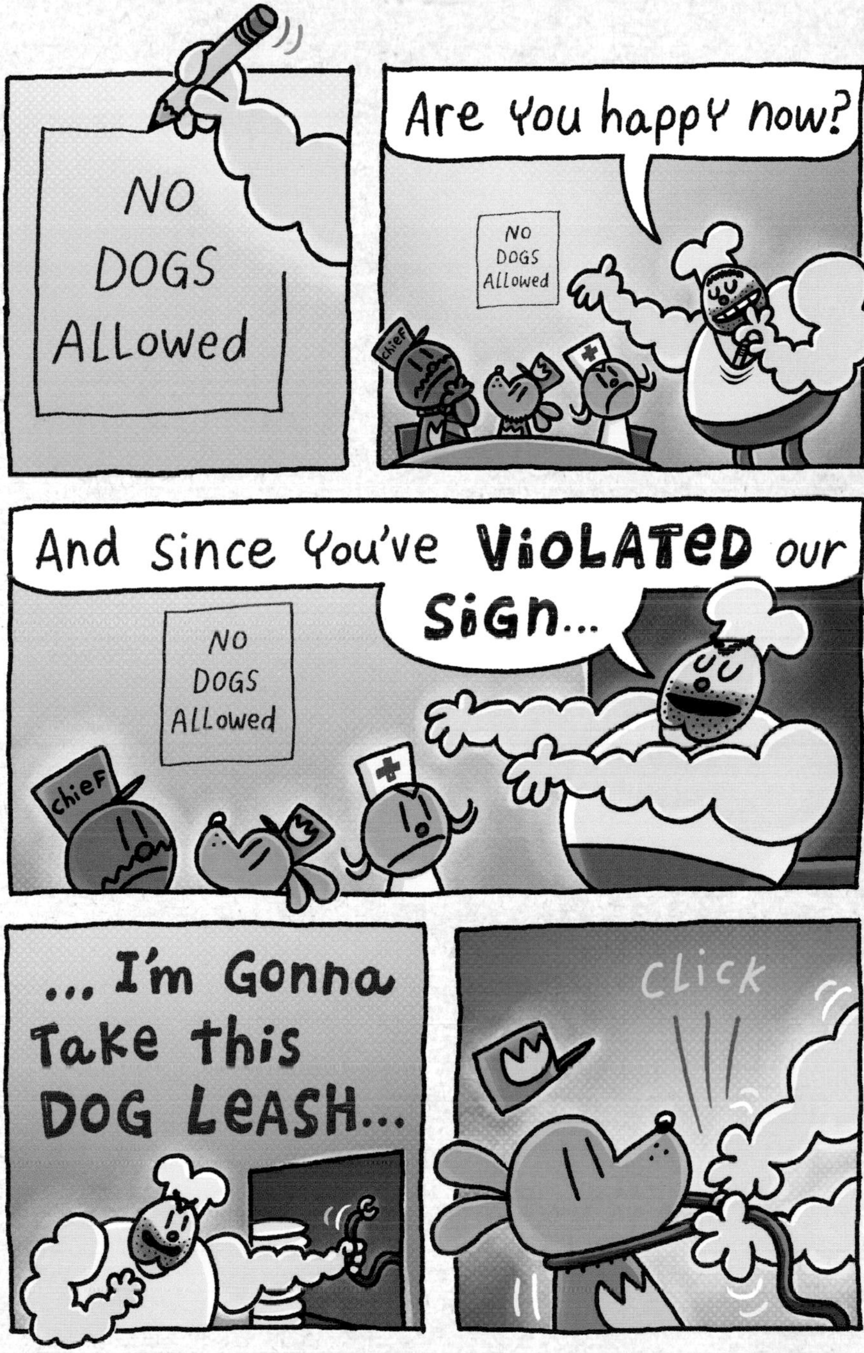
NO DOGS ALLOWED
Are you happy now?
NO DOGS Allowed
chief
And since you've VIOLATED our sign...
NO DOGS Allowed
chief
... I'm Gonna Take this DOG LEASH...
CLICK

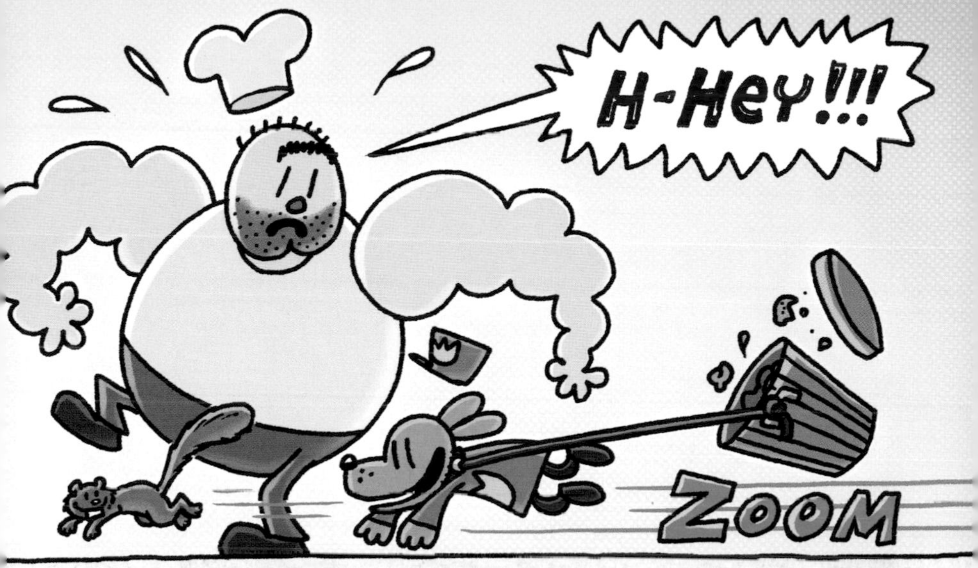
H-HEY!!!
ZOOM

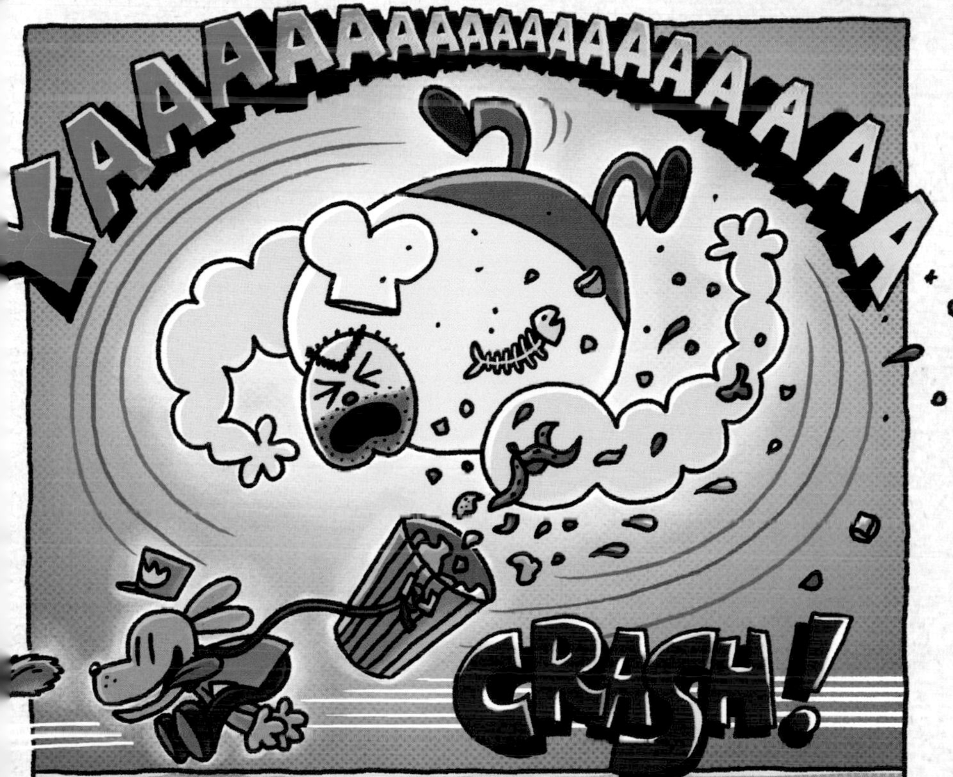
YAAAAAAAAAAAAAAAAAAAA
CRASH!

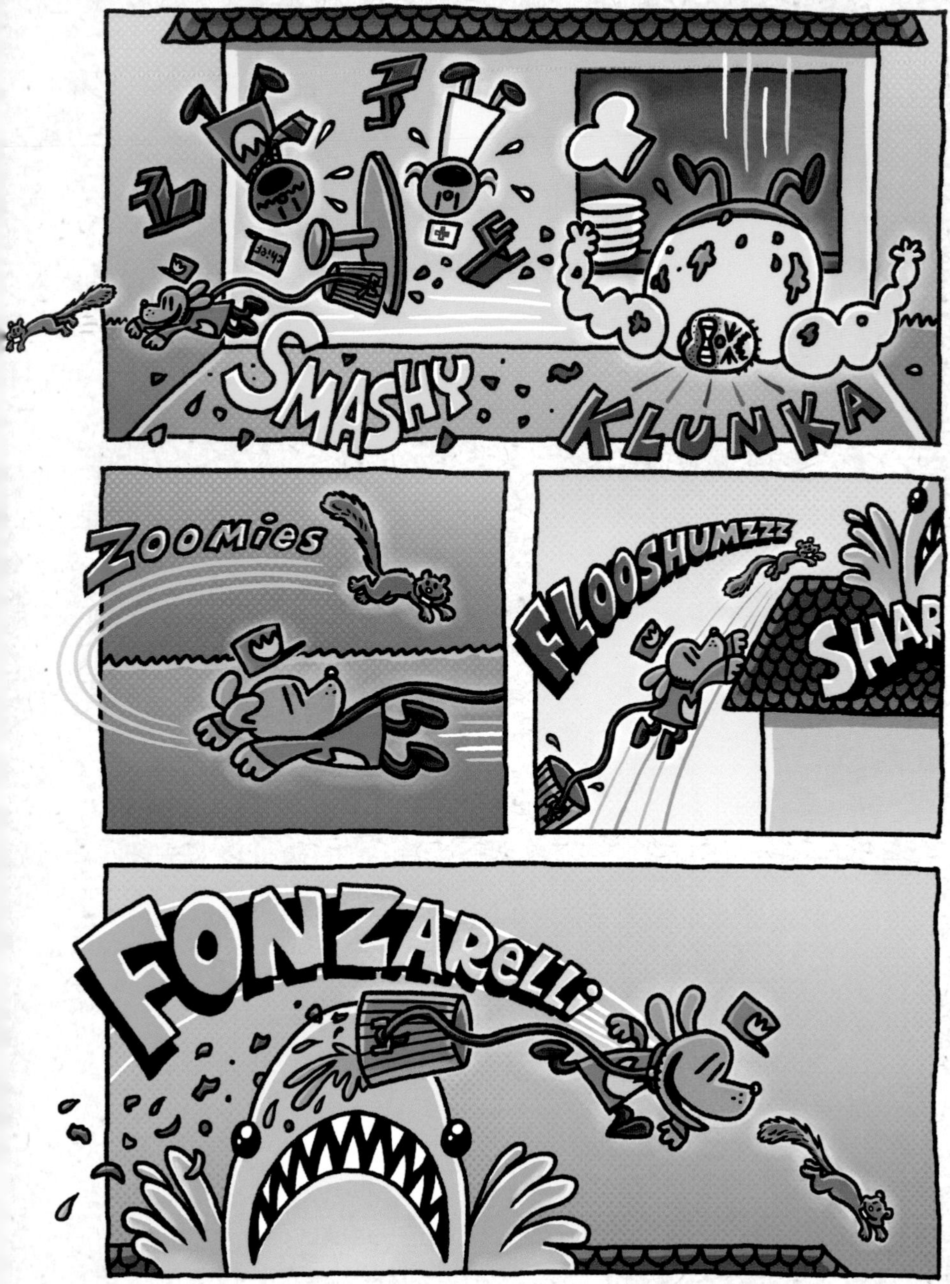
SMASHY
KLUNKA
ZOOMIES
FLOOSHUMZZZ
SHAR
FONZARELLI

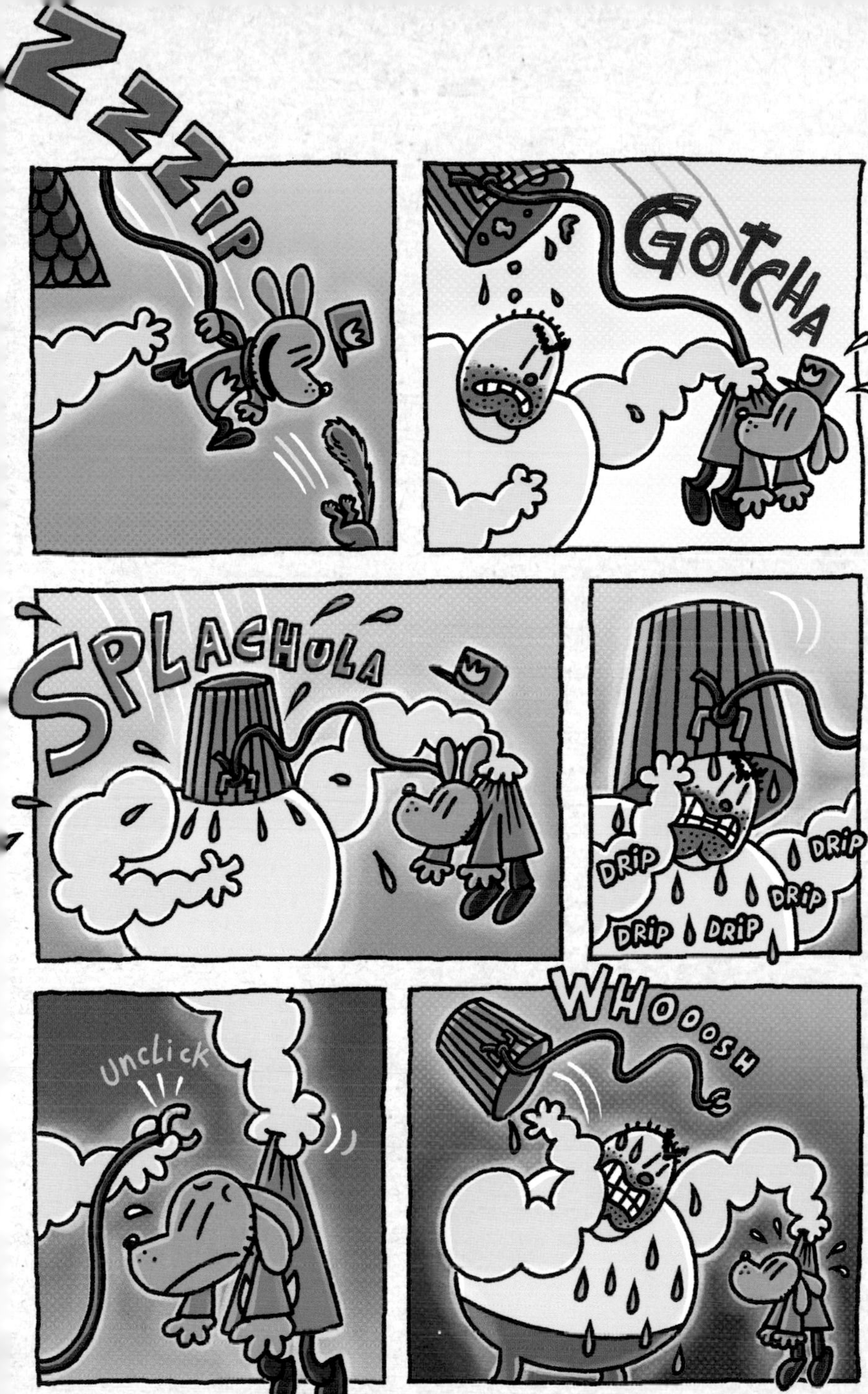
ZZZZiP
GOTCHA
SPLACHULA
DRiP
DRiP
DRiP
DRiP
DRiP
unclick
WHOOOOSH

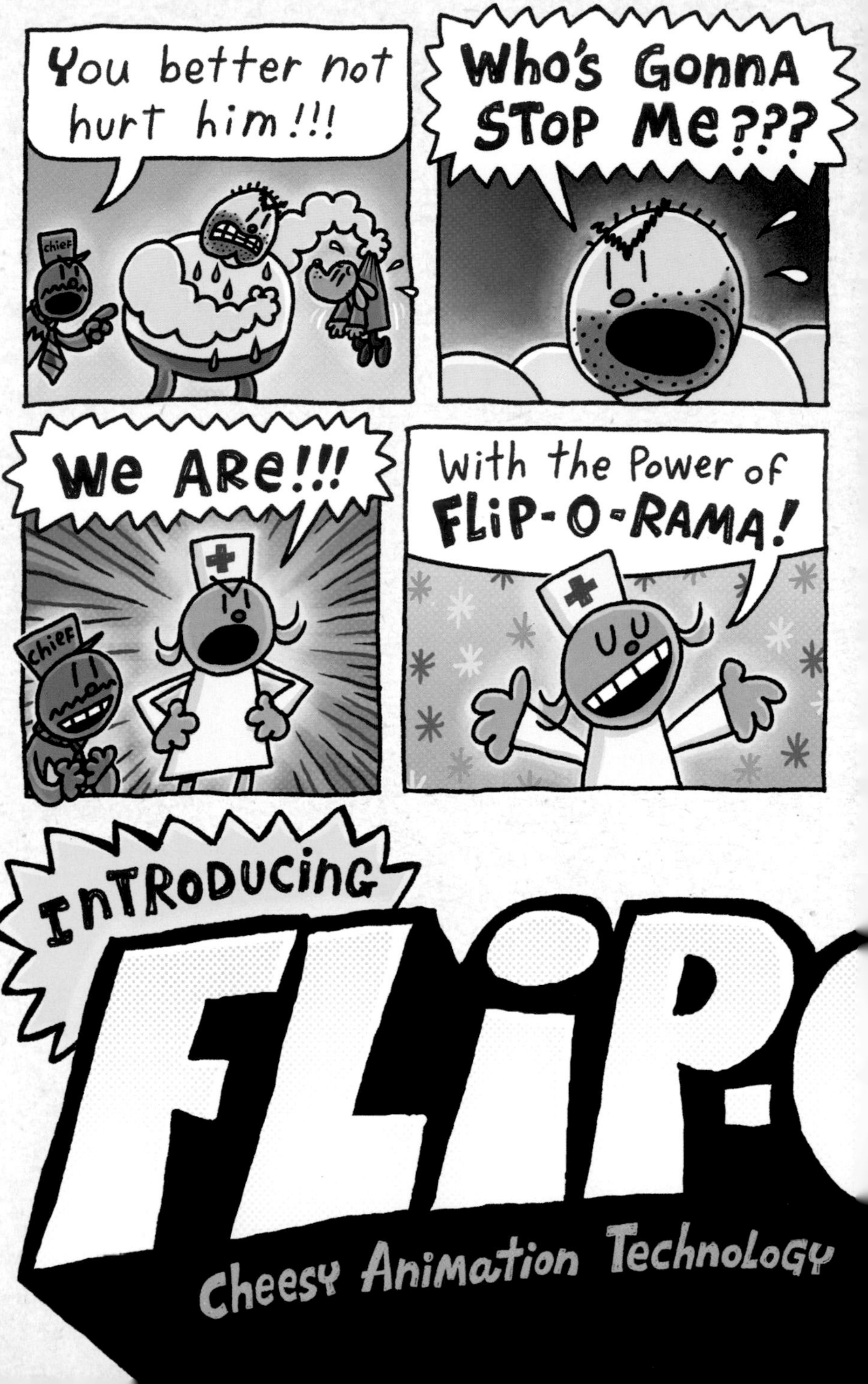

STEP 1.
First, place your left hand inside the dotted lines marked "Left hand here." Hold the book open FLAT!

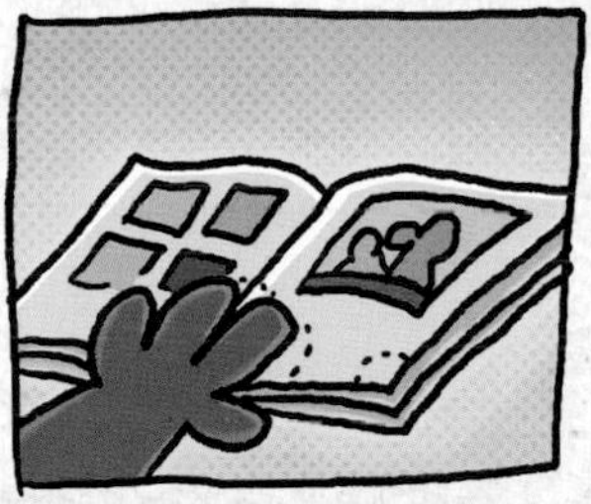

STEP 2:
Grasp the right-hand page with your thumb and index finger (inside the dotted lines marked "Right Thumb Here").

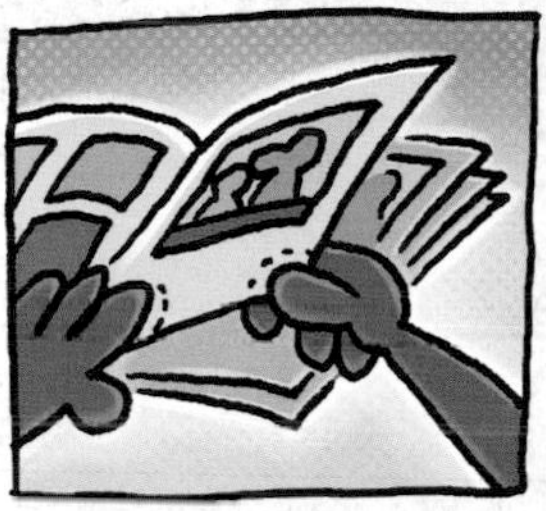

STEP 3:
Now QUICKLY flip the right-hand page back and forth until the picture appears to be Animated.

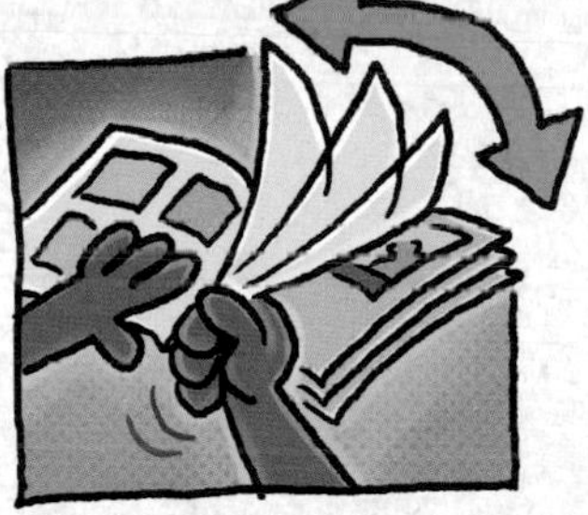

(for extra fun, try adding your own sound-effects!)

RAMA

...FOR A BOLD, NEW WORLD

Left hand here.

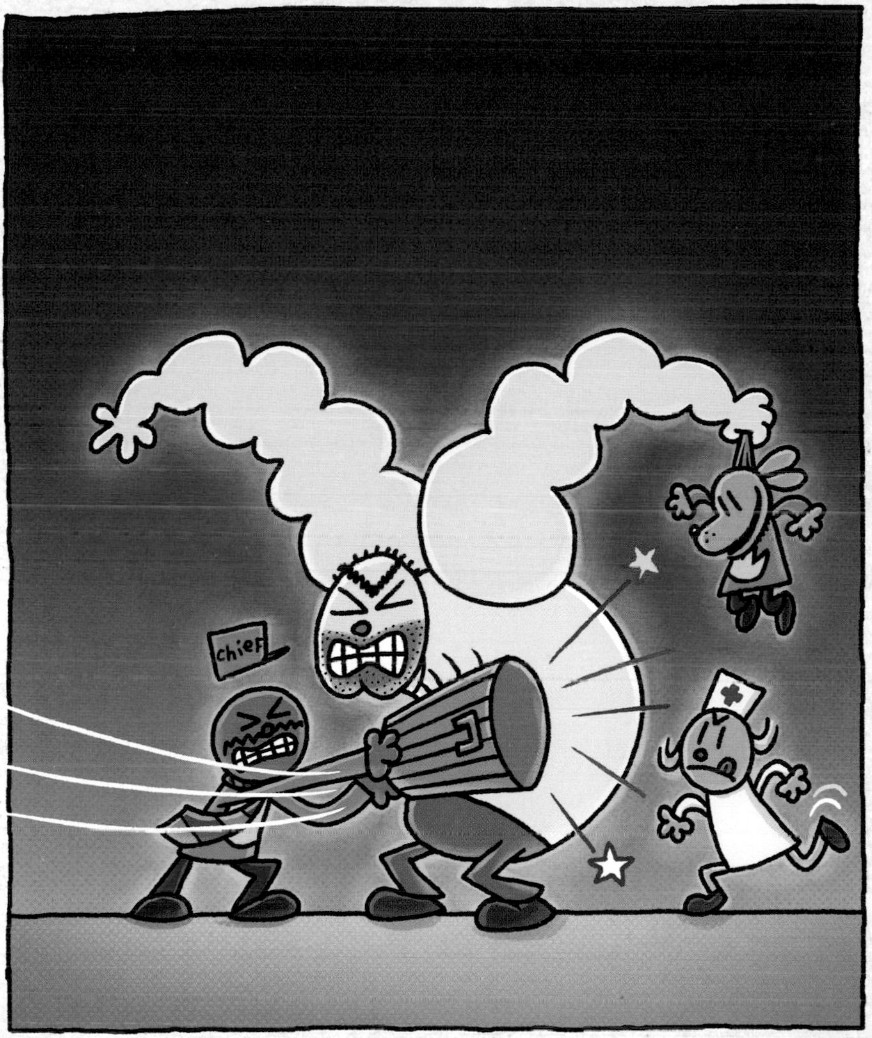
chief

Date Fight

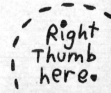

Right Thumb here.

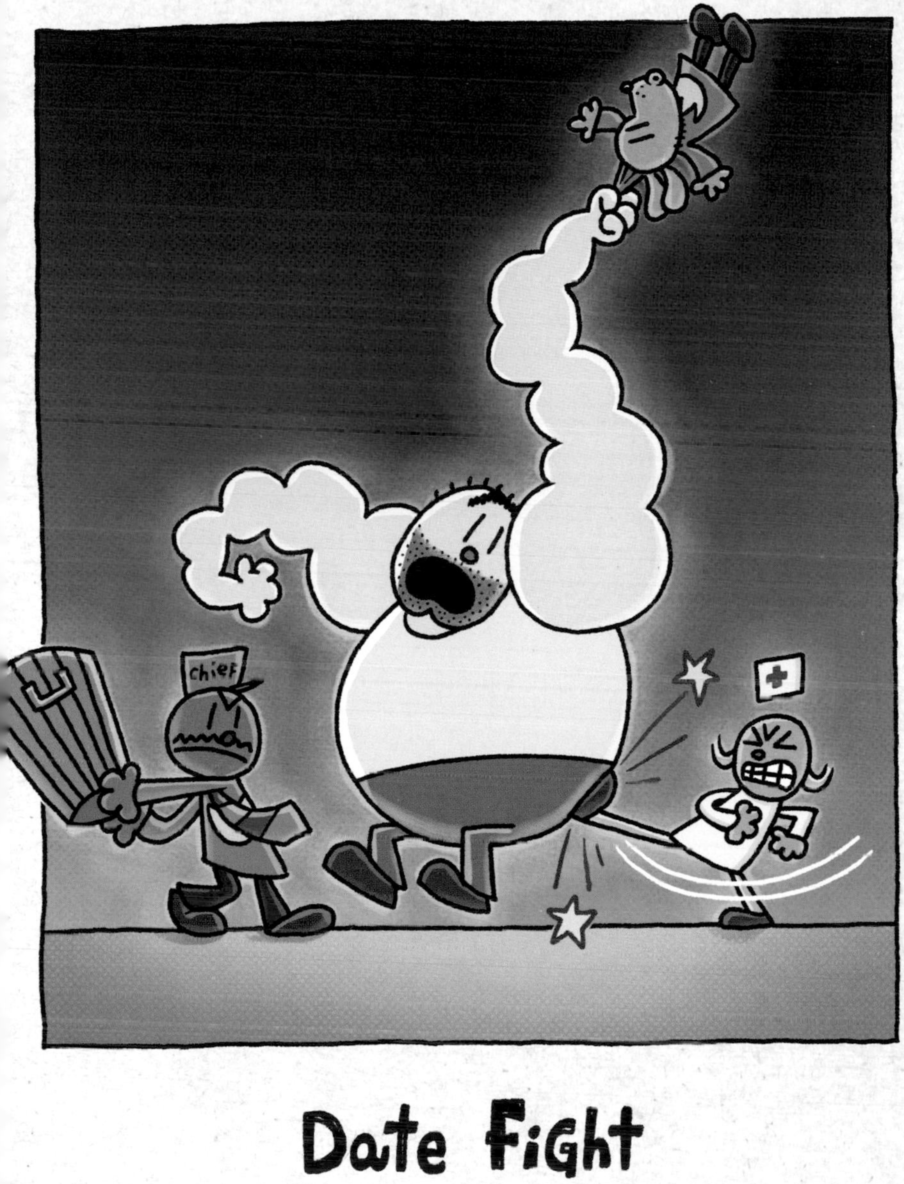
chief

Date Fight

And so...

Are You okay, Dog Man?

Welp, I Guess We better Go!!!

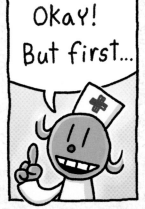

Okay! But first...

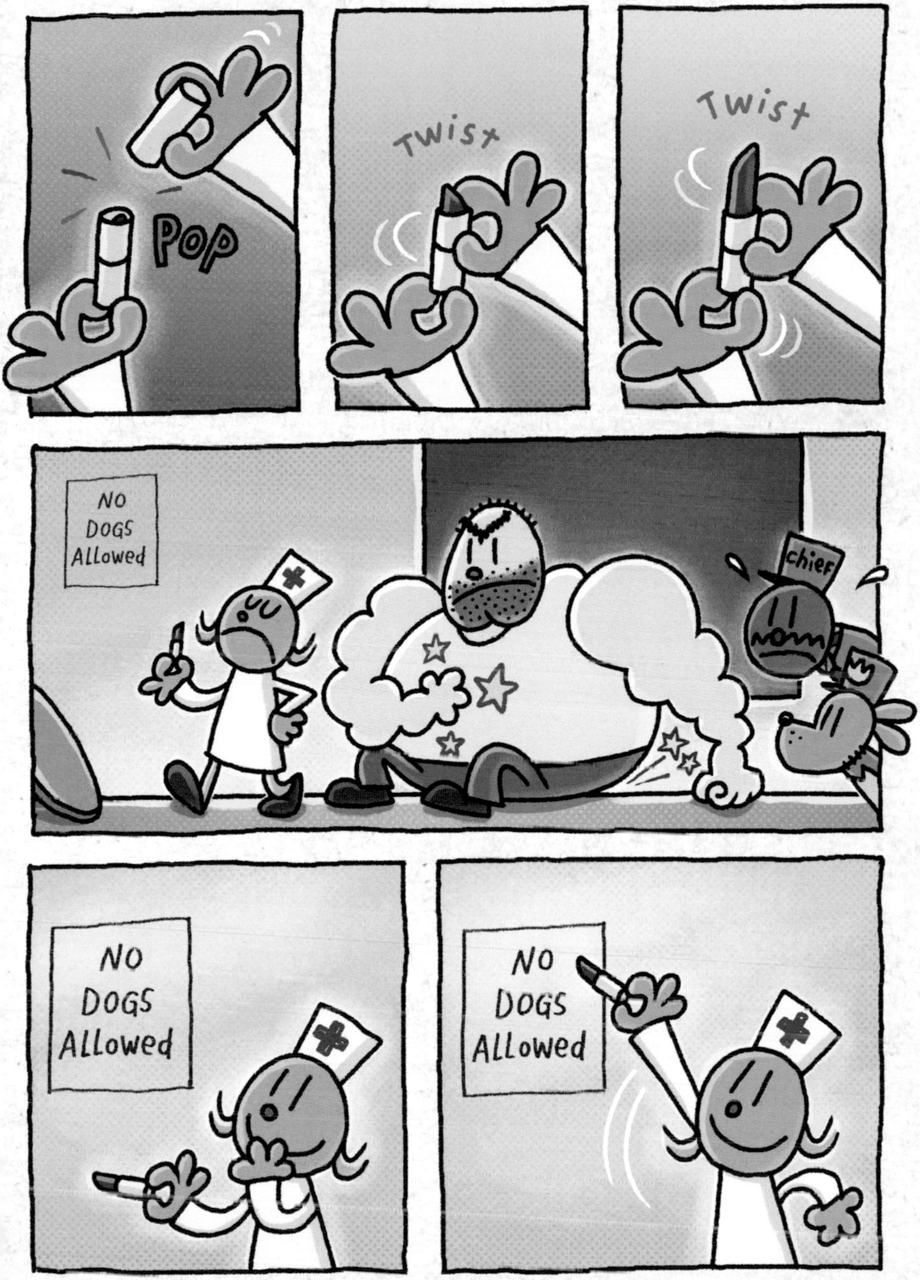

POP
Twist
Twist
NO DOGS Allowed
chief
NO DOGS Allowed
NO DOGS Allowed

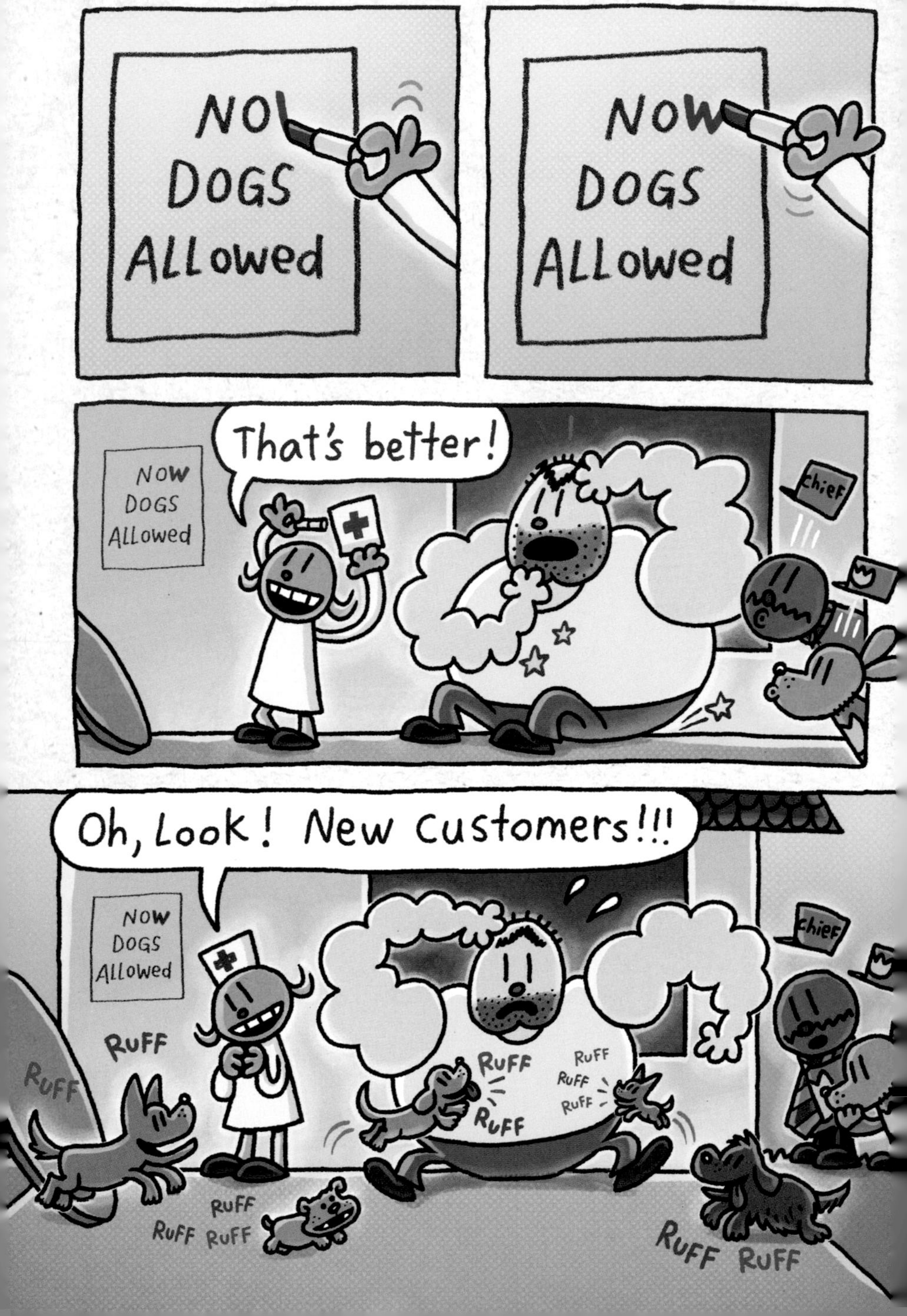
NO DOGS ALLOWED
NOW DOGS ALLOWED
That's better!
NOW DOGS ALLOWED
CHIEF
Oh, Look! New Customers!!!
NOW DOGS ALLOWED
CHIEF
RUFF
RUFF
RUFF
RUFF
RUFF
RUFF
RUFF
RUFF
RUFF
RUFF RUFF
RUFF RUFF

CHAPTER 2

Mini Jail

By George Beard and Harold Hutchins

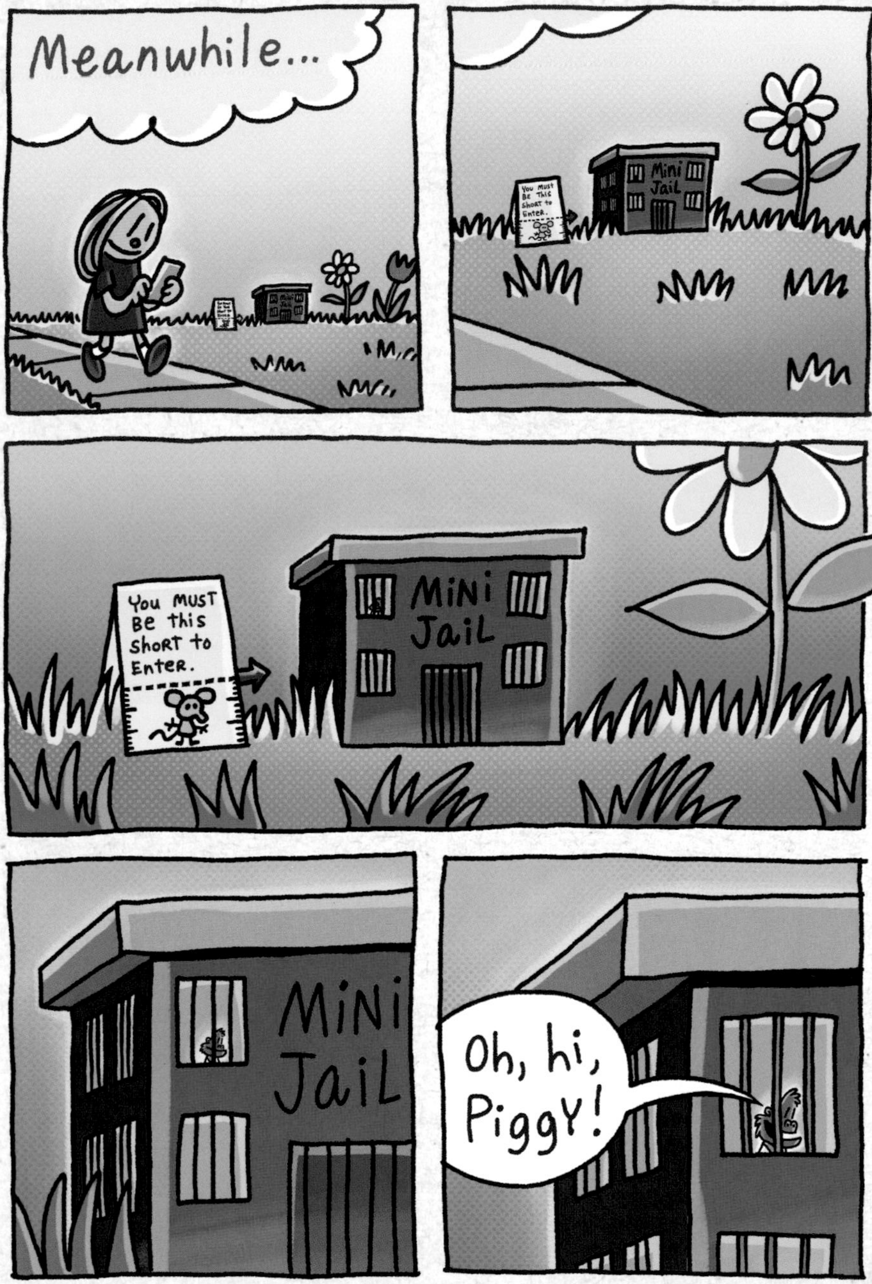
Meanwhile...
You MUST Be this SHORT to Enter.
MiNi JaiL
Oh, hi, PiggY!

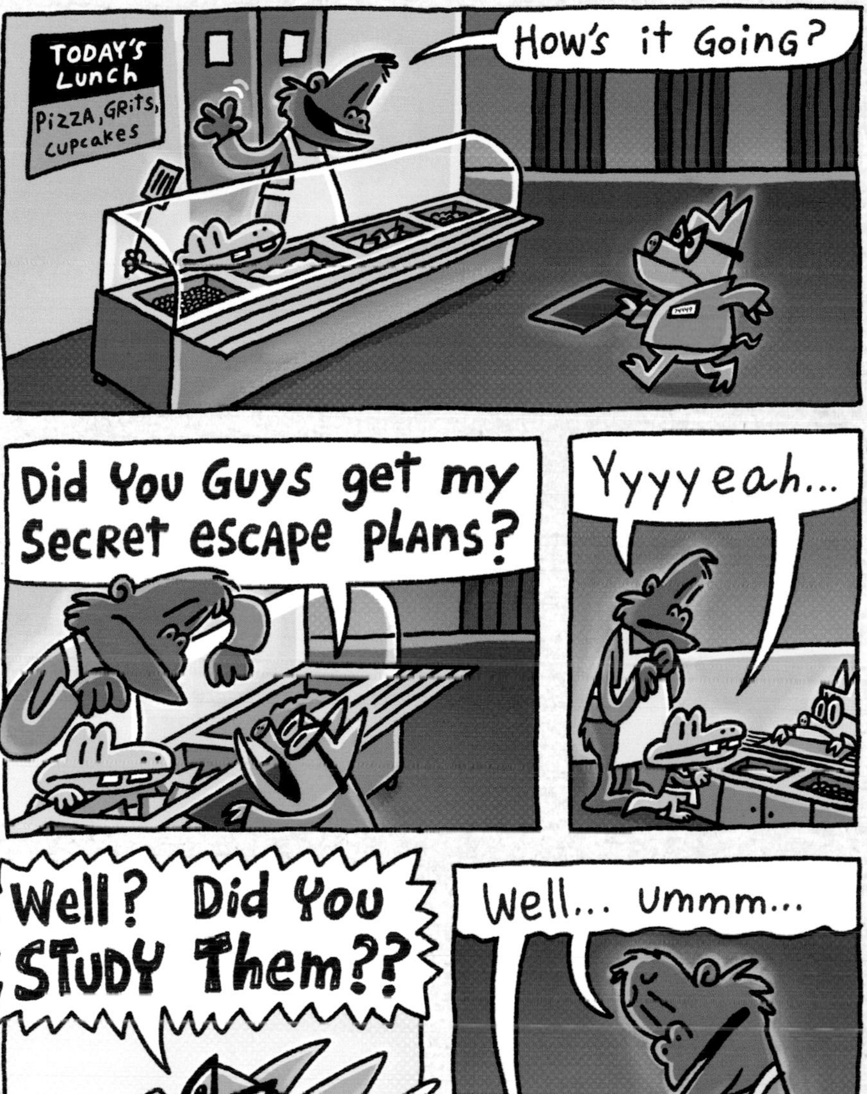
TODAY'S
Lunch
PiZZA, GRits,
cupcakes
How's it Going?
Did You Guys get my Secret escape plans?
Yyyyeah...
Well? Did You STUDY Them??
Well... ummm...

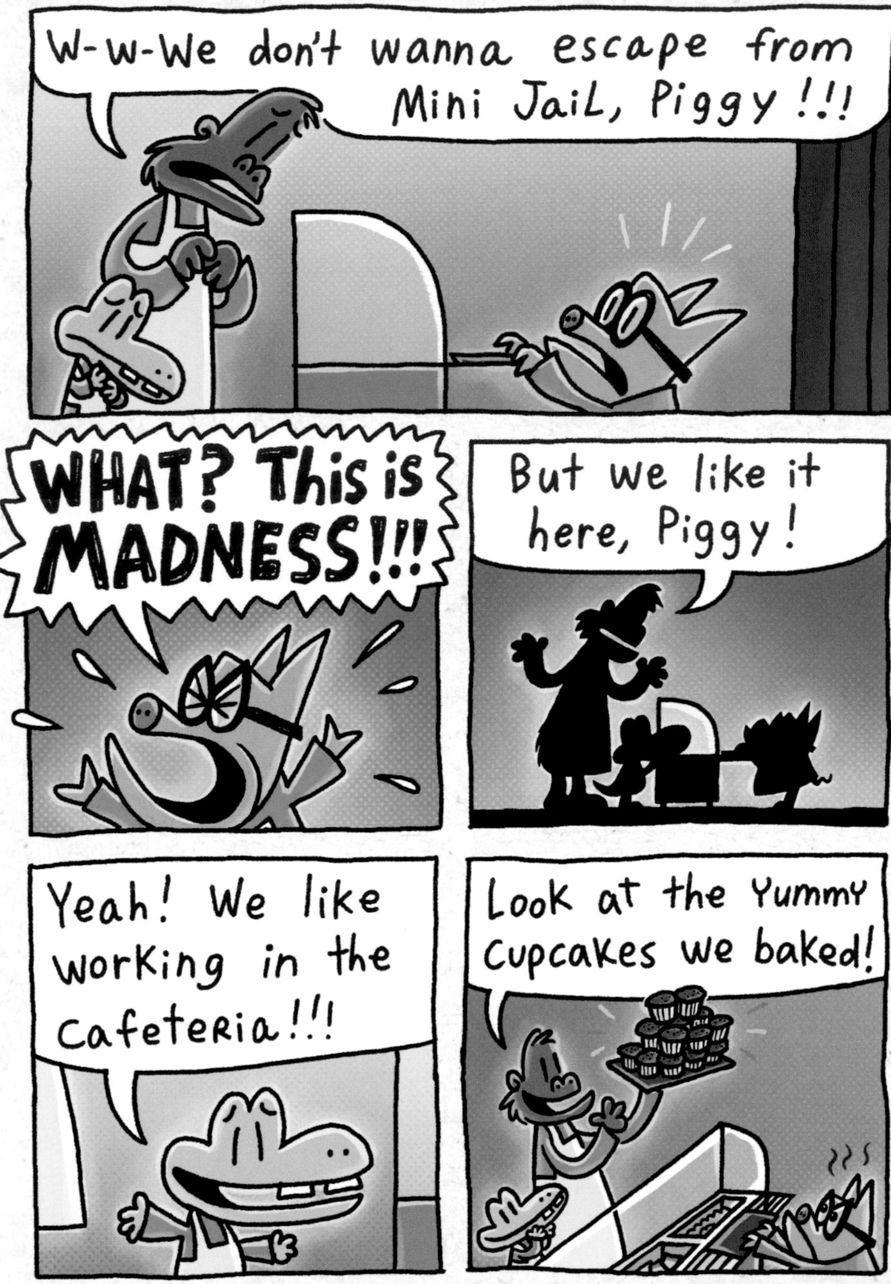
W-W-We don't wanna escape from Mini JaiL, Piggy!!!
WHAT? This is MADNESS!!!
But we like it here, Piggy!
Yeah! We like working in the Cafeteria!!!
Look at the Yummy Cupcakes we baked!

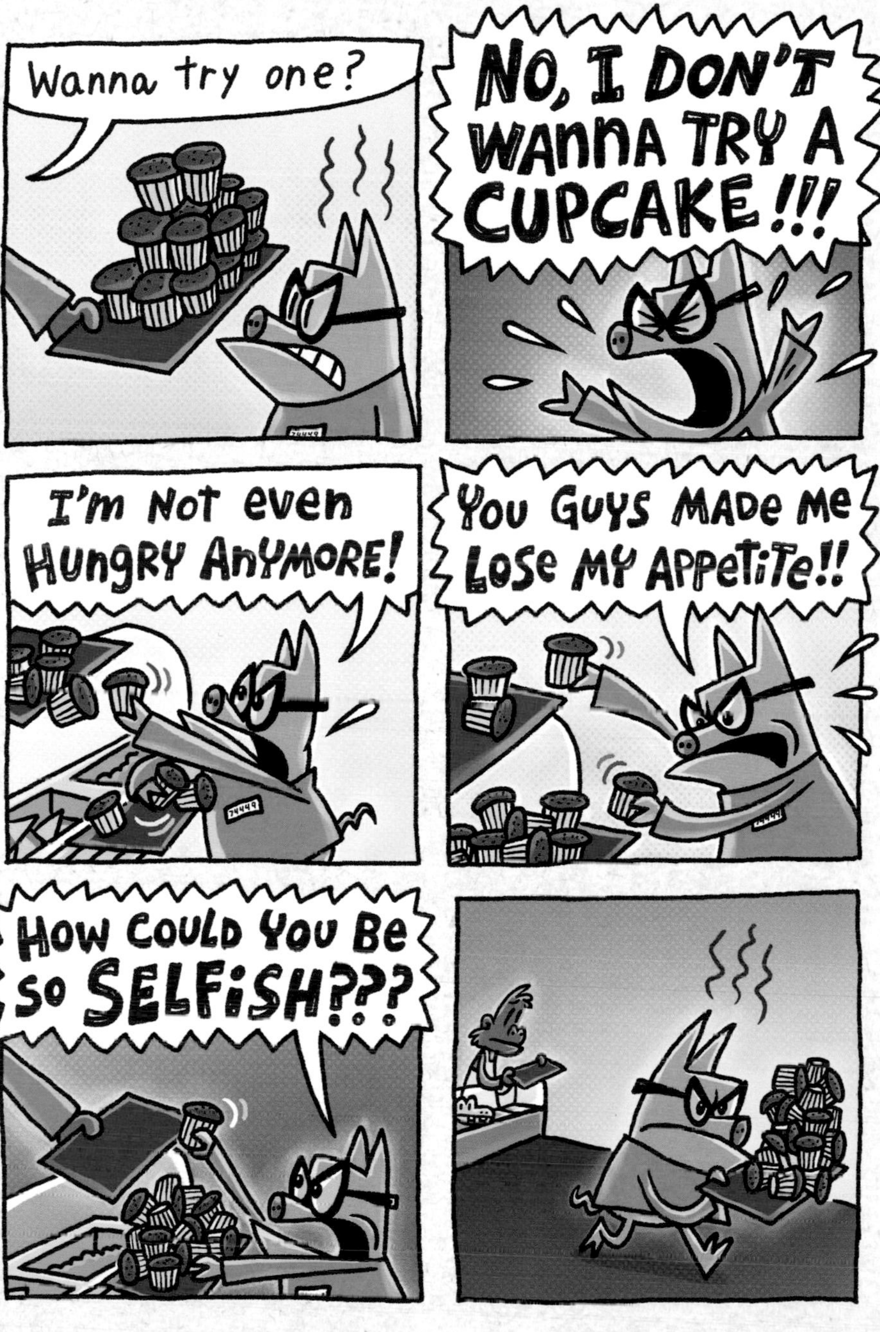
Wanna try one?
NO, I DON'T WANNA TRY A CUPCAKE!!!
I'm Not even HUNGRY ANYMORE!
YOU GUYS MADE ME LOSE MY APPETITE!!
HOW COULD YOU BE SO SELFISH???

39

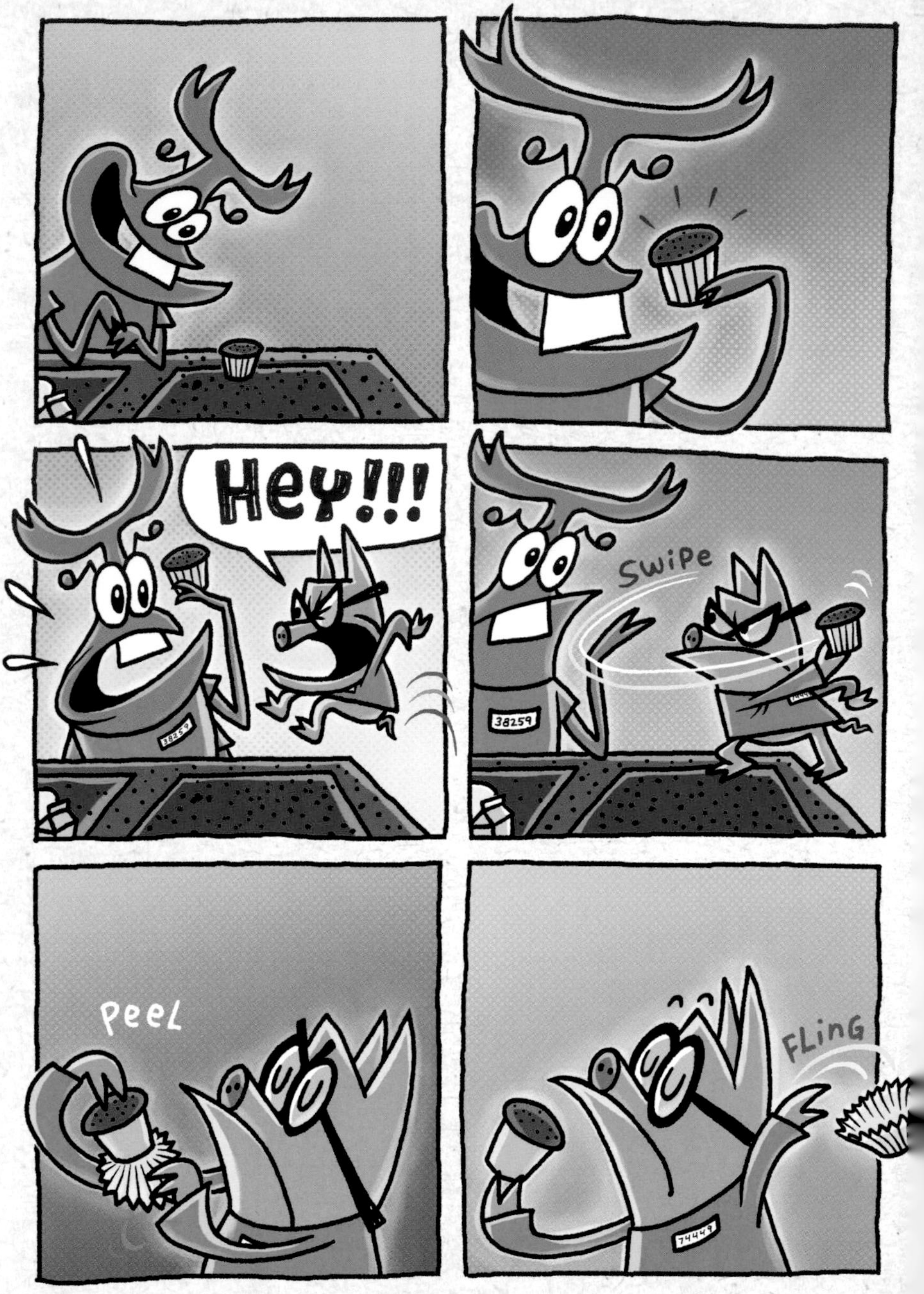
HEY!!!
SWIPE
PEEL
FLING

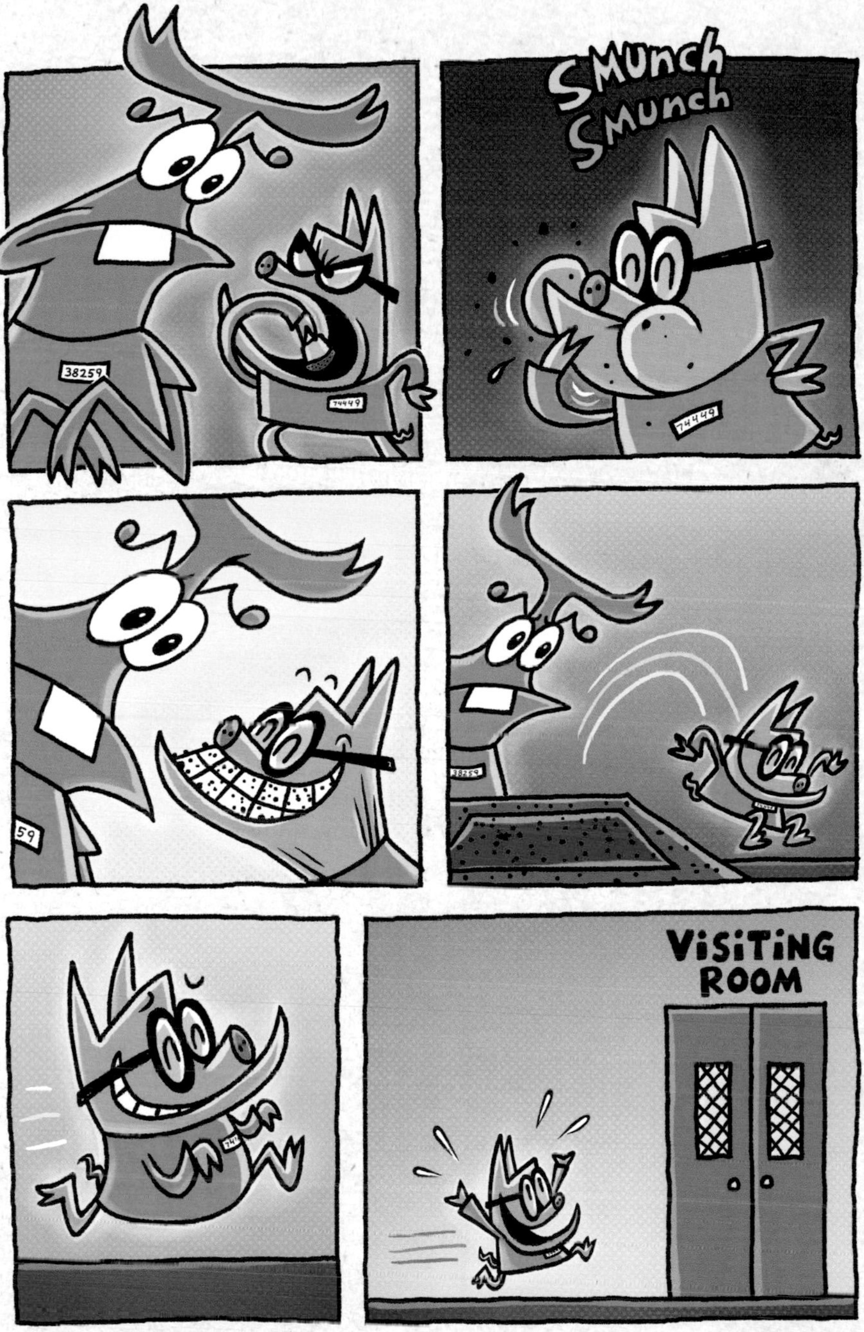
38259
74449
SMUNCH SMUNCH
74449
VISITING ROOM

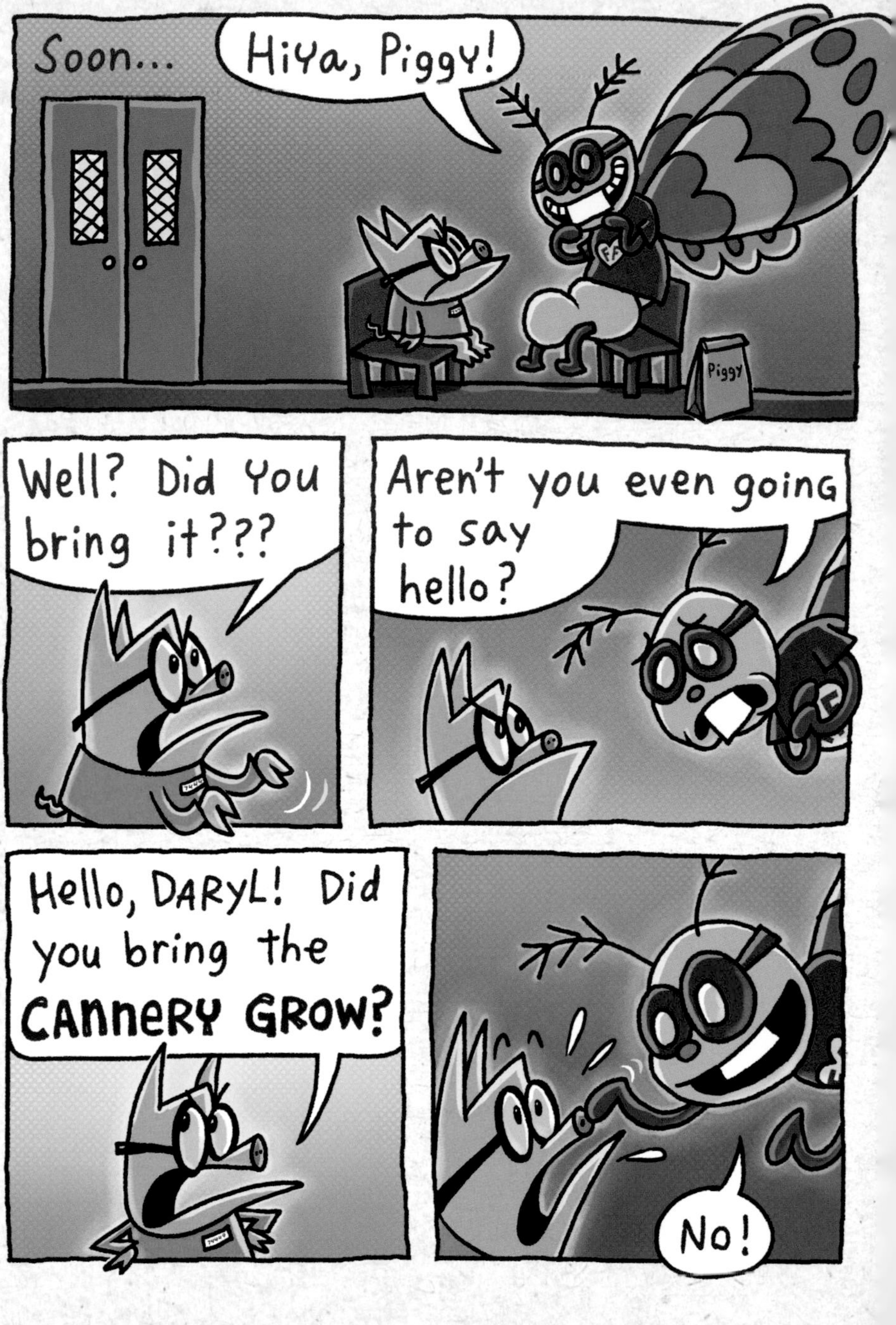
Soon...
Hiya, Piggy!
Piggy
Well? Did you bring it???
Aren't you even going to say hello?
Hello, DARYL! Did you bring the CANNERY GROW?
No!

It's your **COSTUME!!!**

COSTUMe?? What For?

For our **CLuB**, Piggy!!!

Don't you remember the **Friendly Friends?**

SLAp!

I Just recruited **TWO** NEW Members!

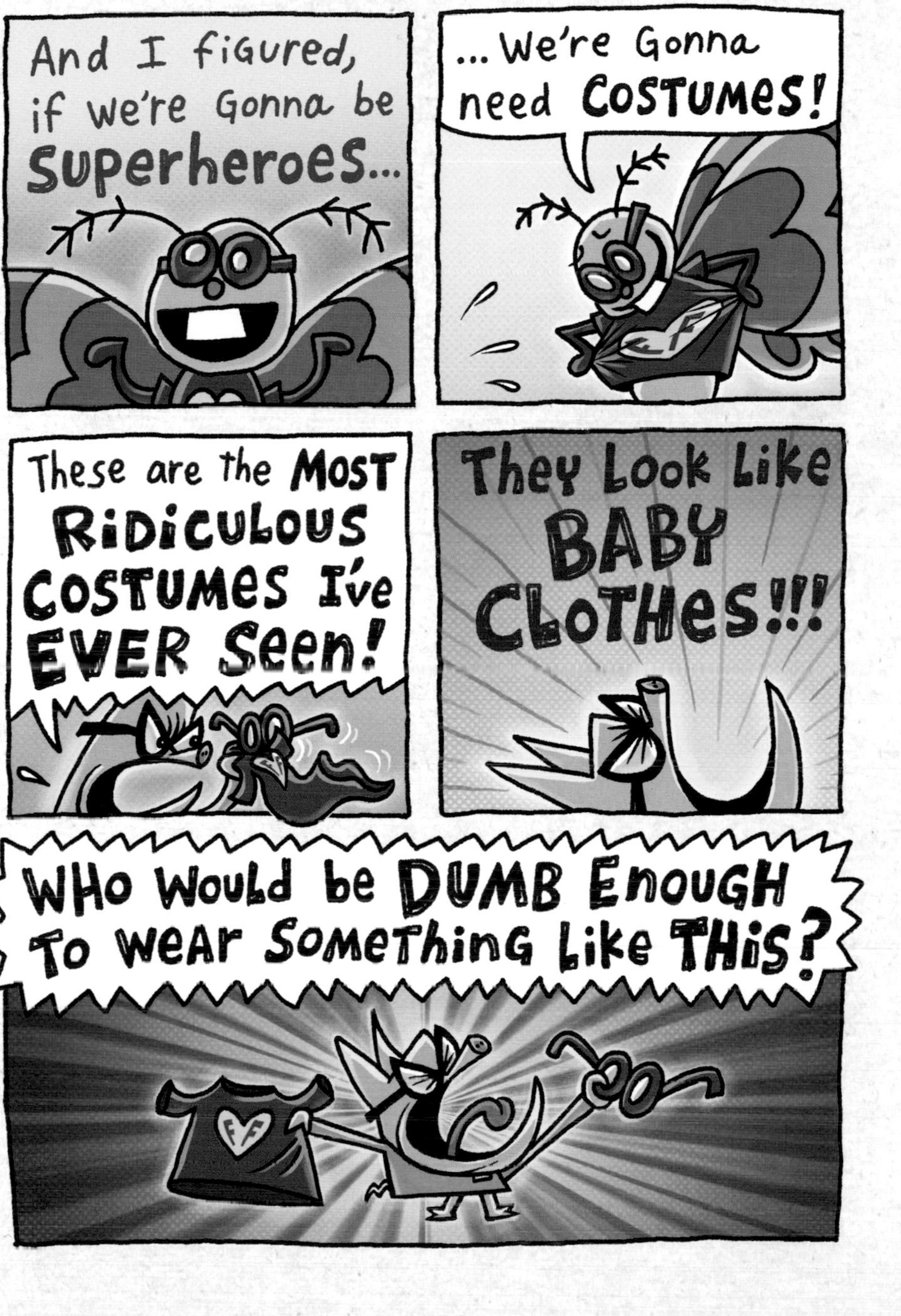
And I figured, if we're gonna be SUPERHEROES...
...we're gonna need COSTUMES!
These are the MOST RIDICULOUS COSTUMES I've EVER seen!
They look like BABY CLOTHES!!!
WHO WOULD BE DUMB ENOUGH TO WEAR SOMETHING LIKE THIS?

CHAPTER 3

Helping Papa

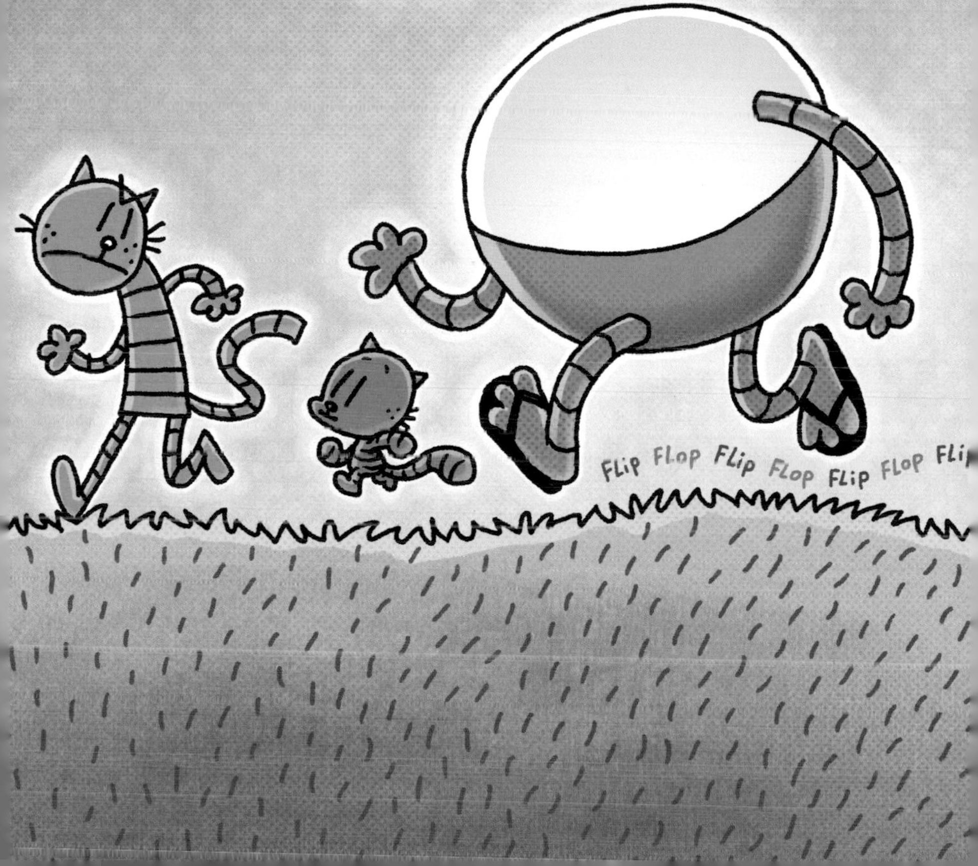
FLip FLop FLip FLop FLip FLop FLi

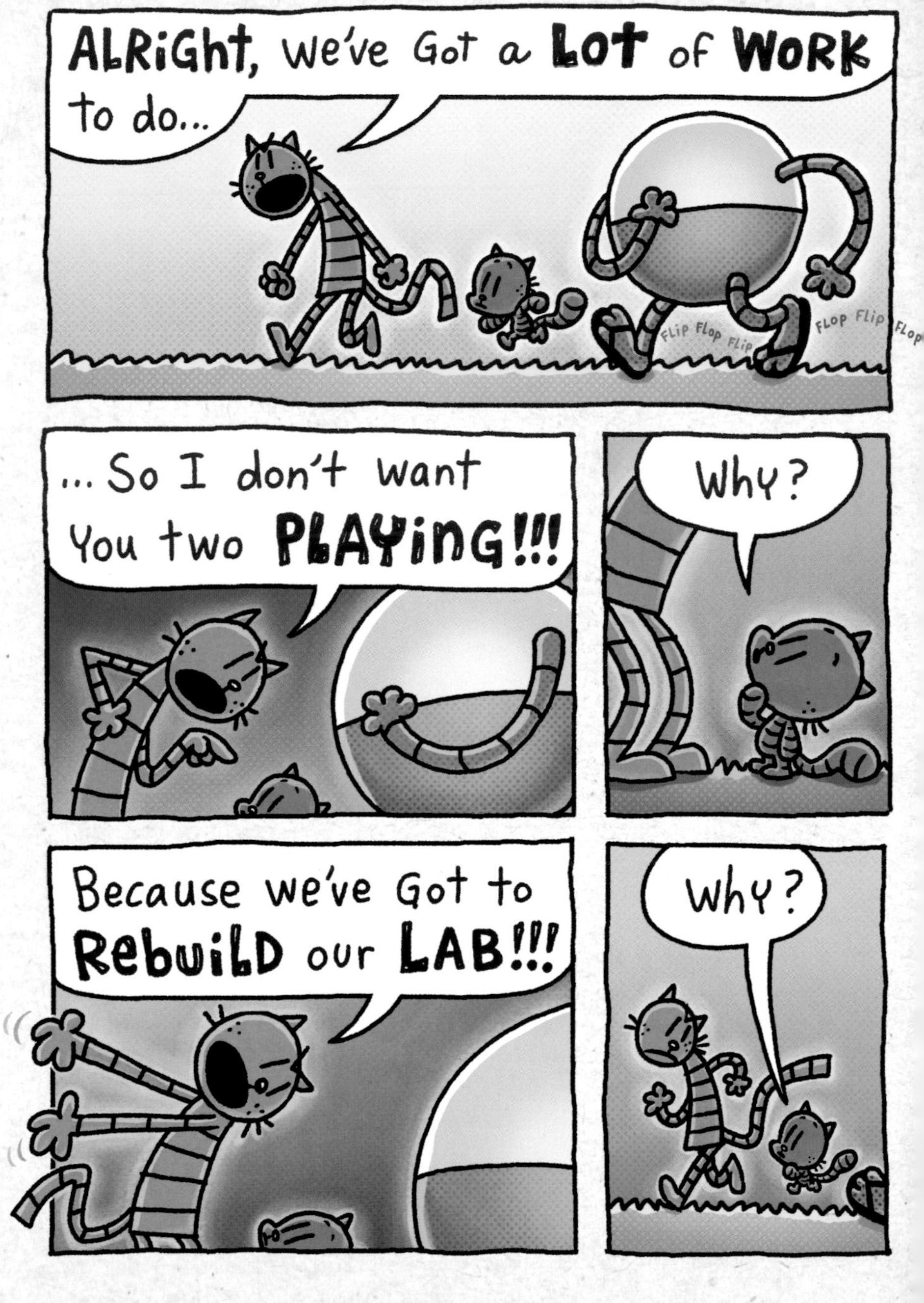

ALRIGHT, we've Got a LOT of WORK to do...
FLIP FLOP FLIP FLOP FLIP FLOP
...So I don't want You two PLAYING!!!
Why?
Because we've Got to REBUILD our LAB!!!
Why?

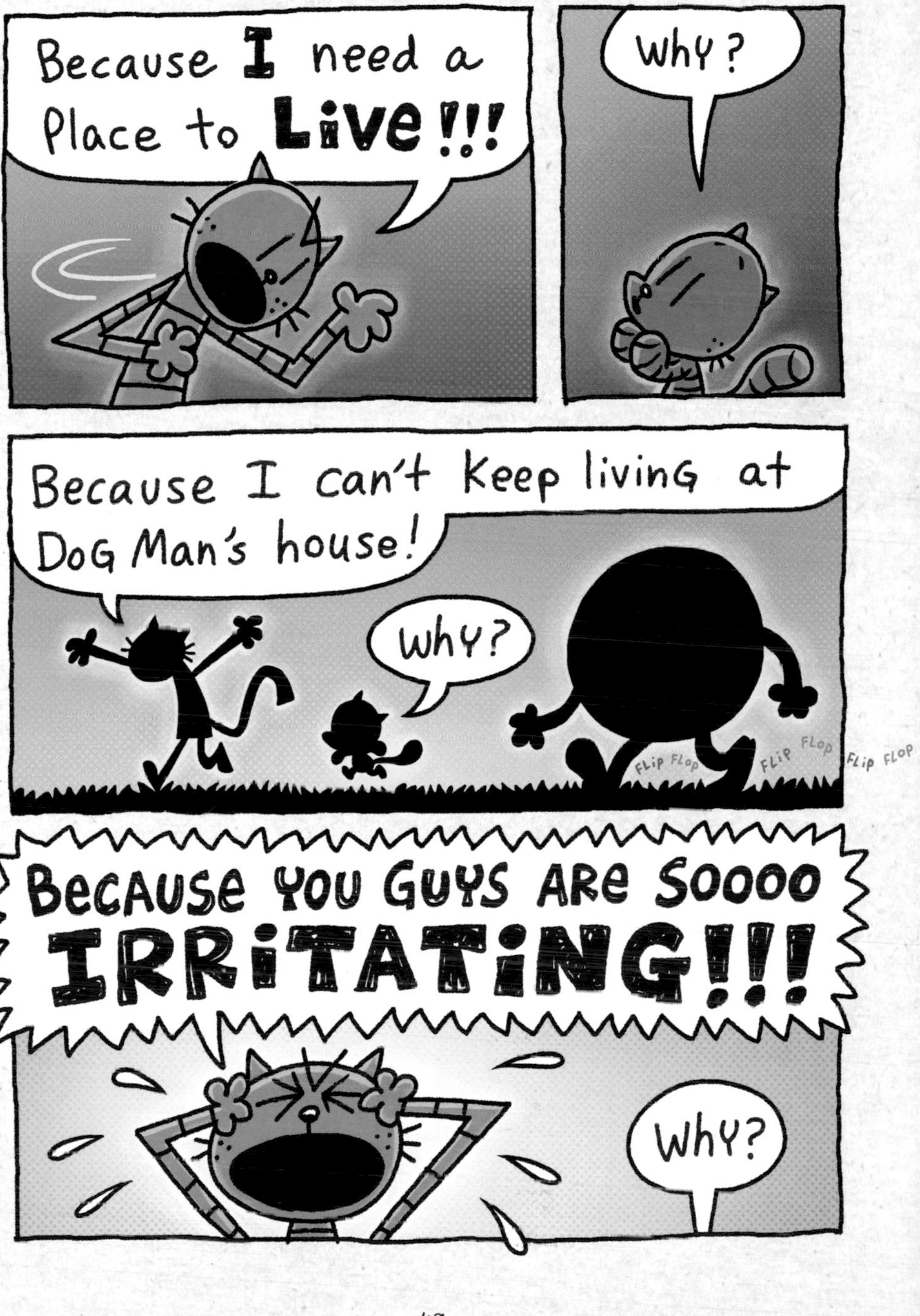
Because I need a Place to LiVe!!!
Why?
Because I can't Keep living at DoG Man's house!
Why?
FLip FLop
FLip FLop
FLip FLop
BeCAUSe YOU GUYS ARe SOOOO IRRiTATiNG!!!
Why?

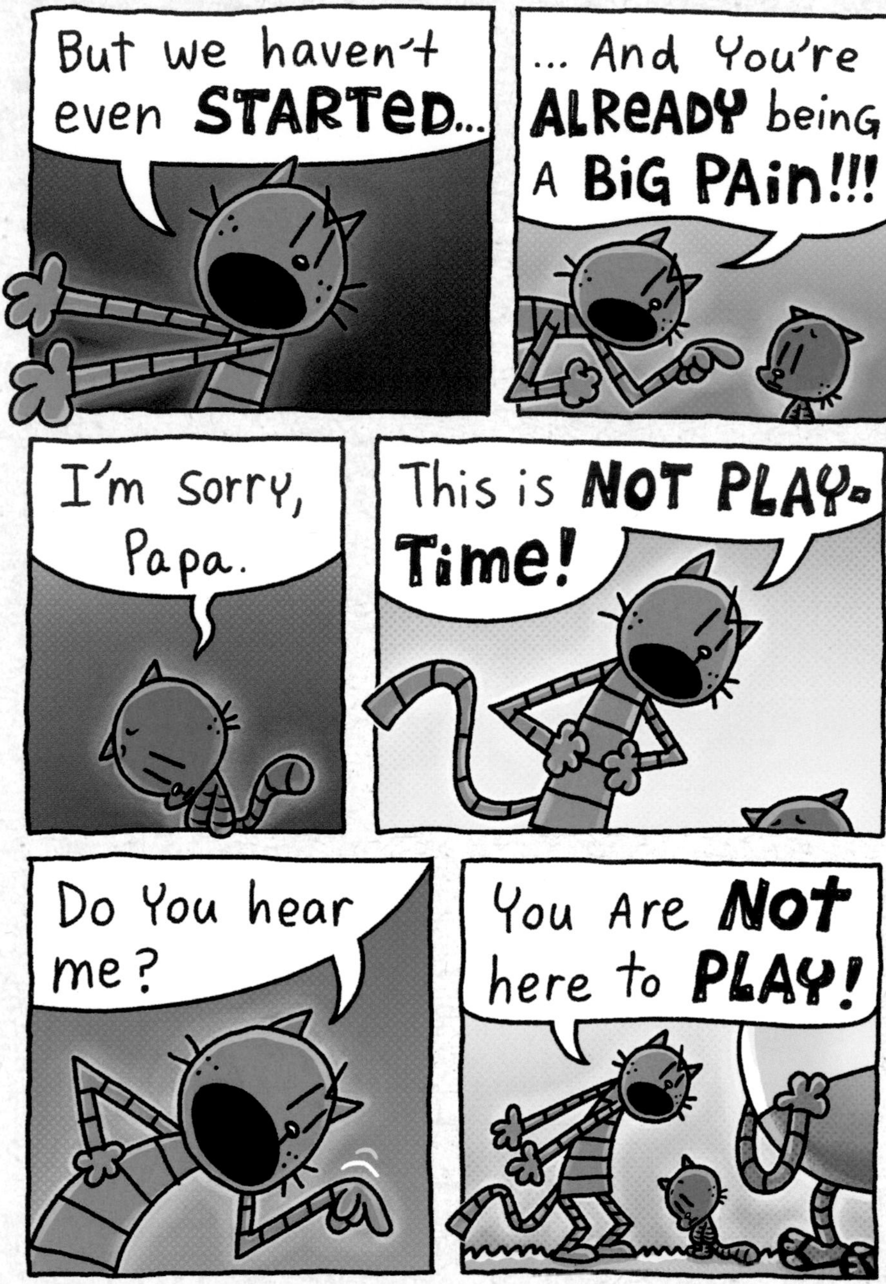

But we haven't even STARTED...
... And You're ALREADY being A BIG PAIN!!!
I'm sorry, Papa.
This is NOT PLAY-Time!
Do You hear me?
You Are NOT here to PLAY!

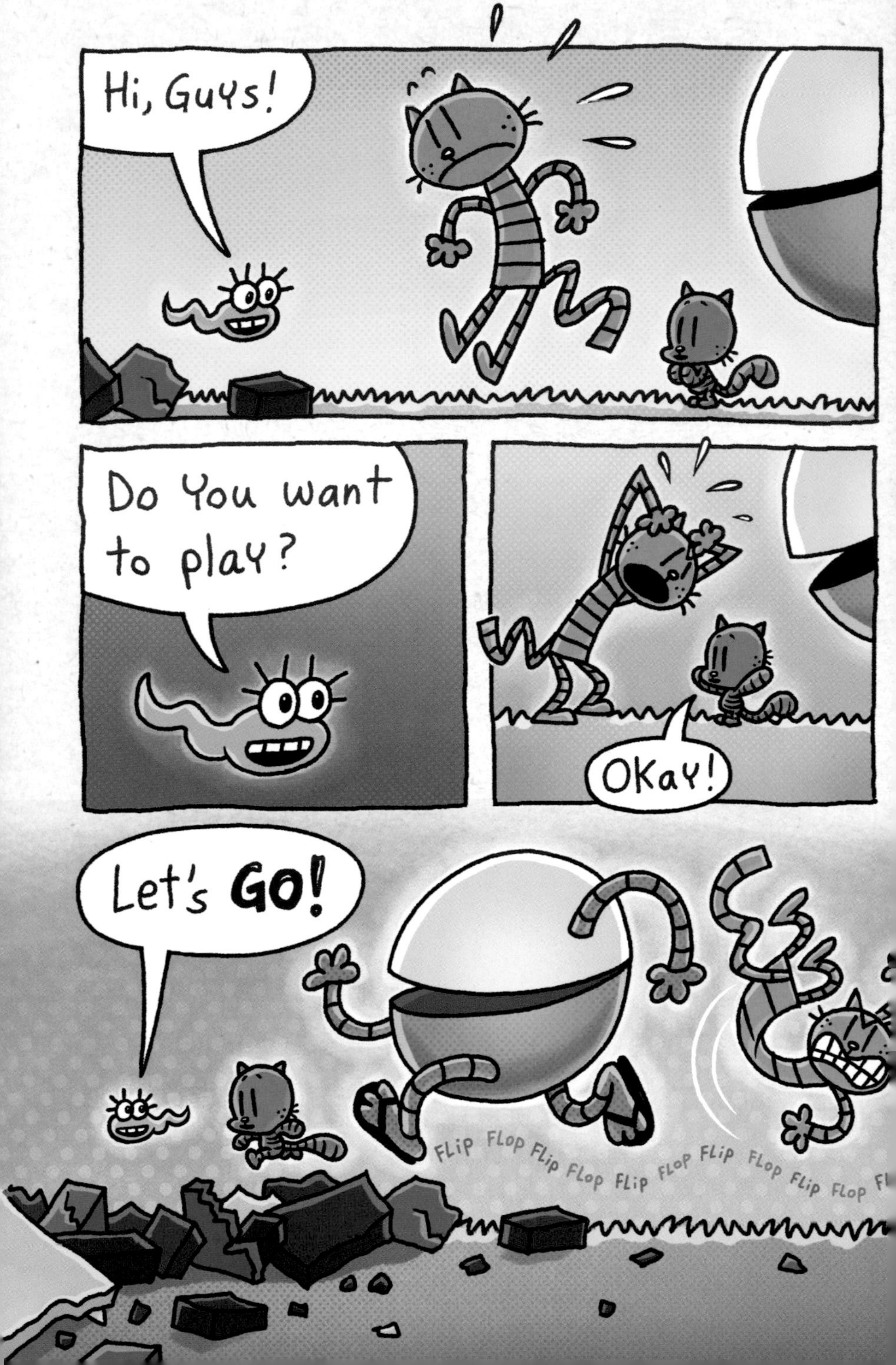
Hi, Guys!
Do You want to play?
OKay!
Let's GO!
FLip FLop FLip FLop FLip FLop FLip FLop FLip FLop

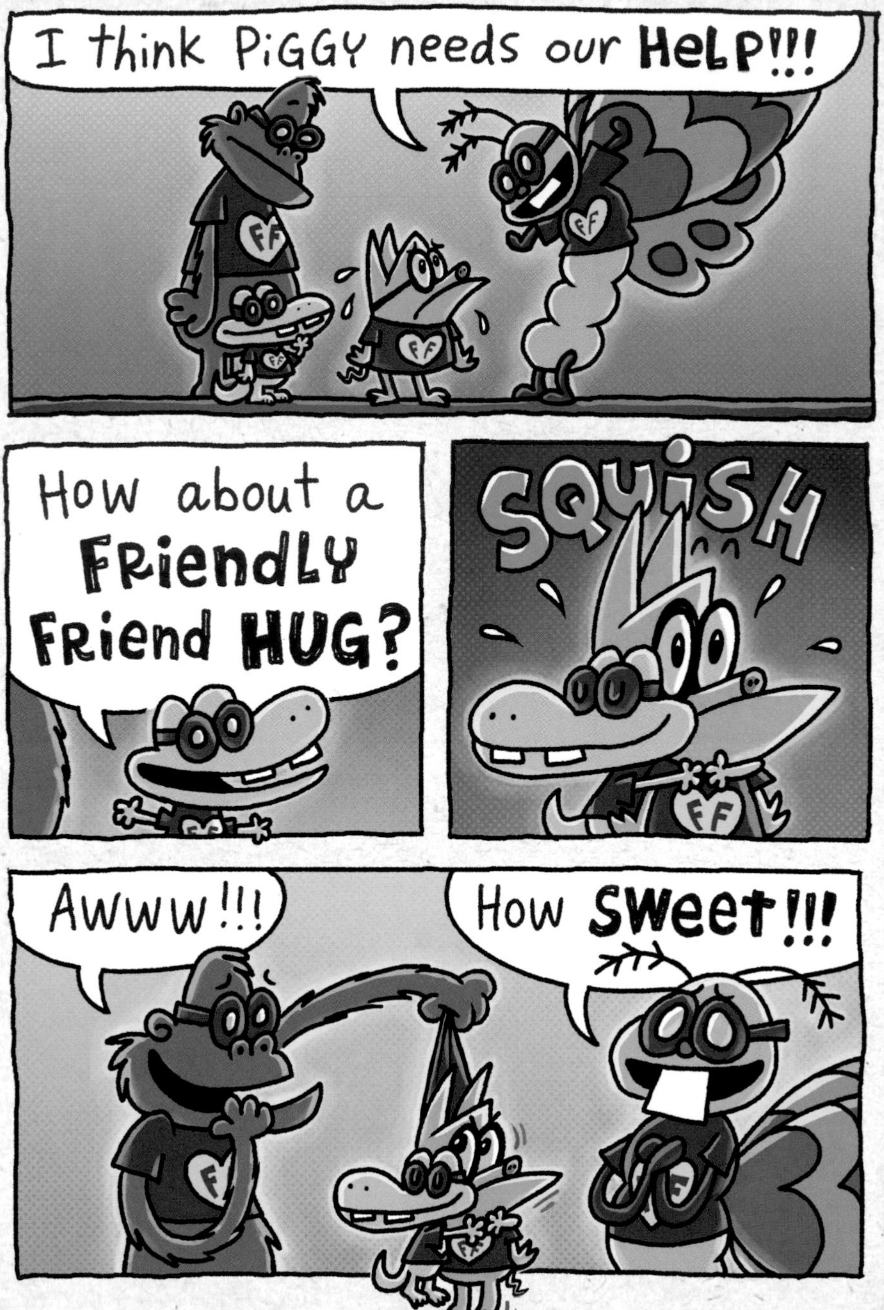
I think PiGGY needs our HELP!!!
How about a FRiendLY FRiend HUG?
SQUiSH
Awww!!!
How SWEET!!!

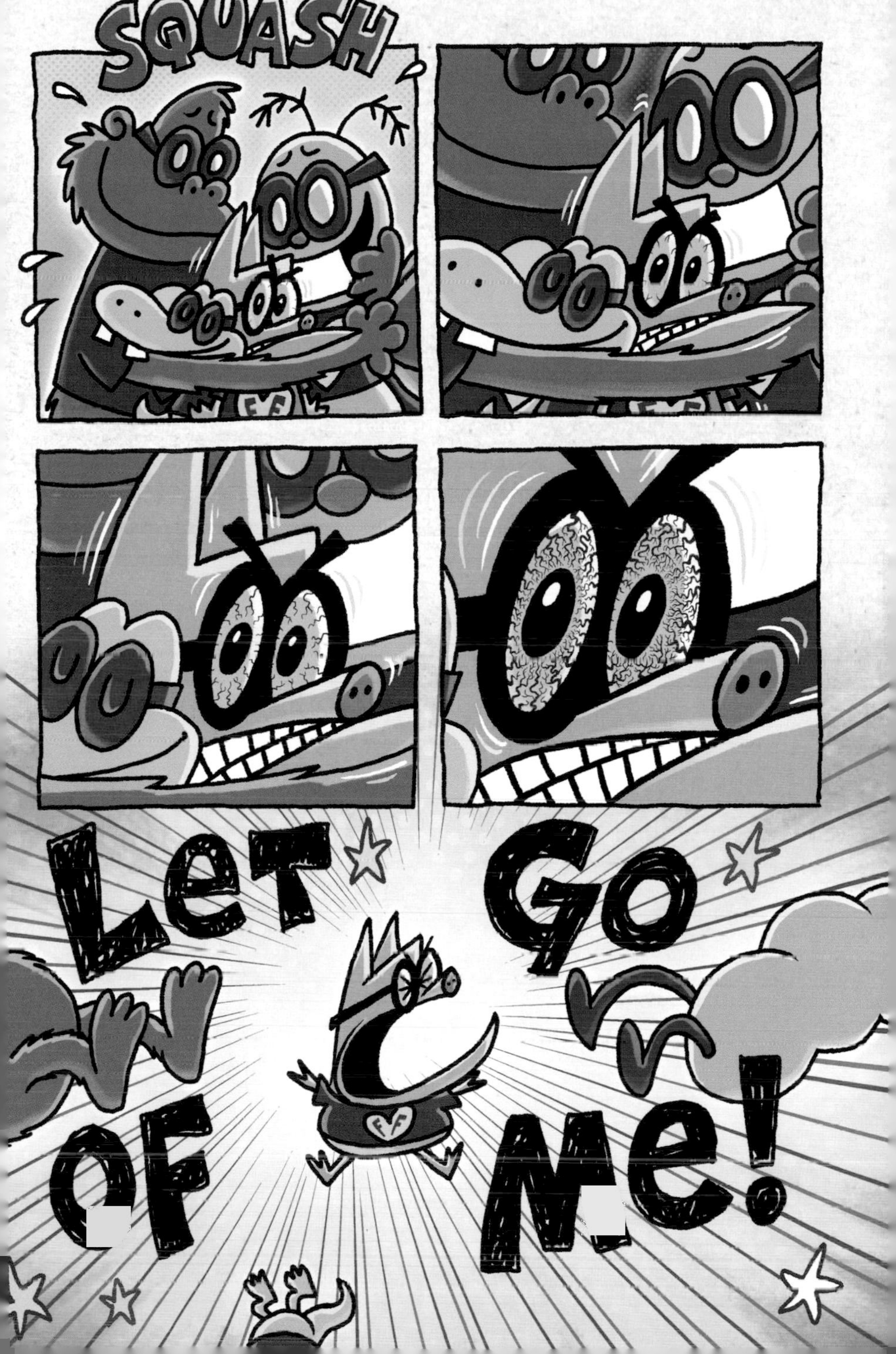
SQUASH
LET GO OF ME!

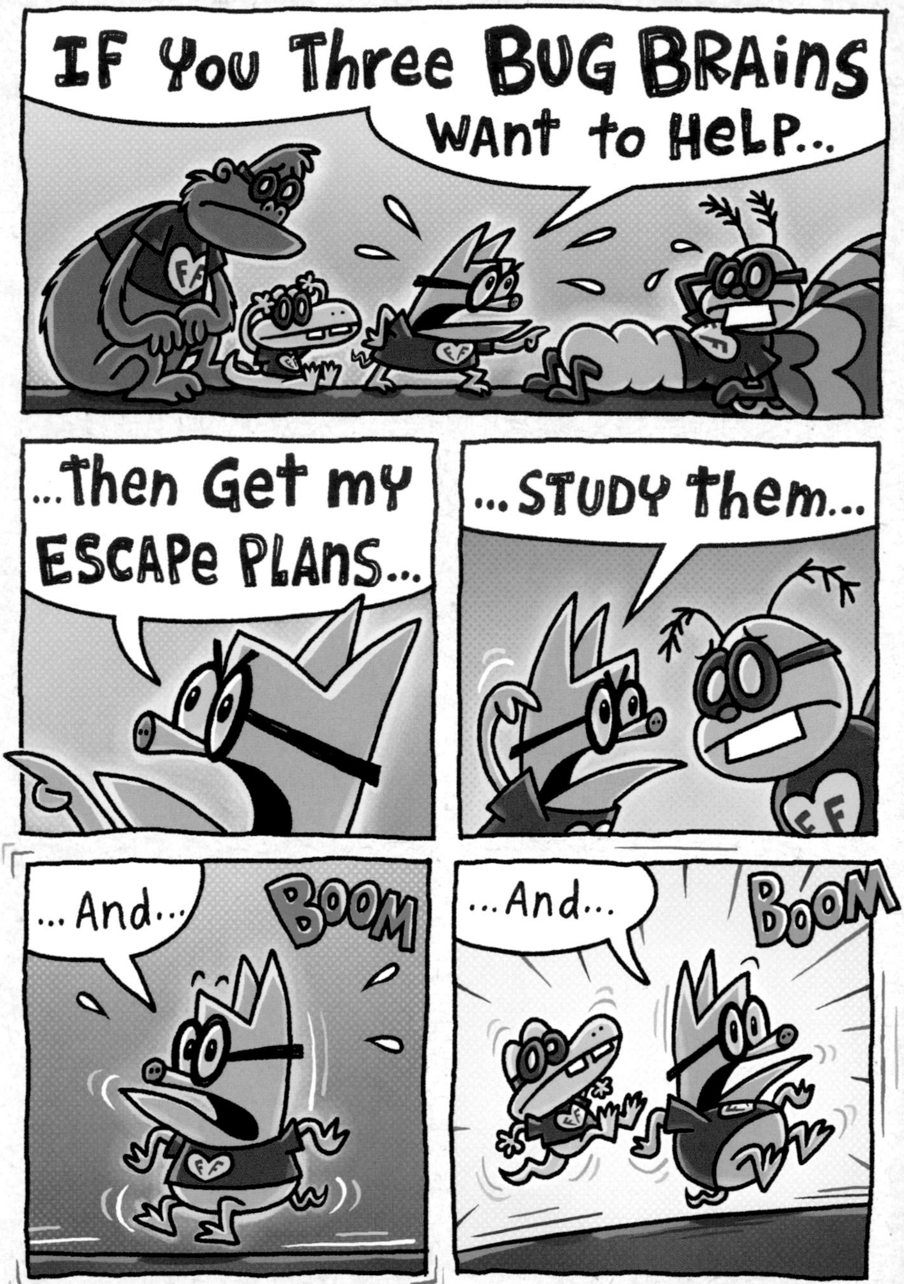
IF You Three BUG BRAINS want to HELP...
...then Get my ESCAPE PLANS...
...STUDY them...
...And...
BOOM
...And...
BOOM

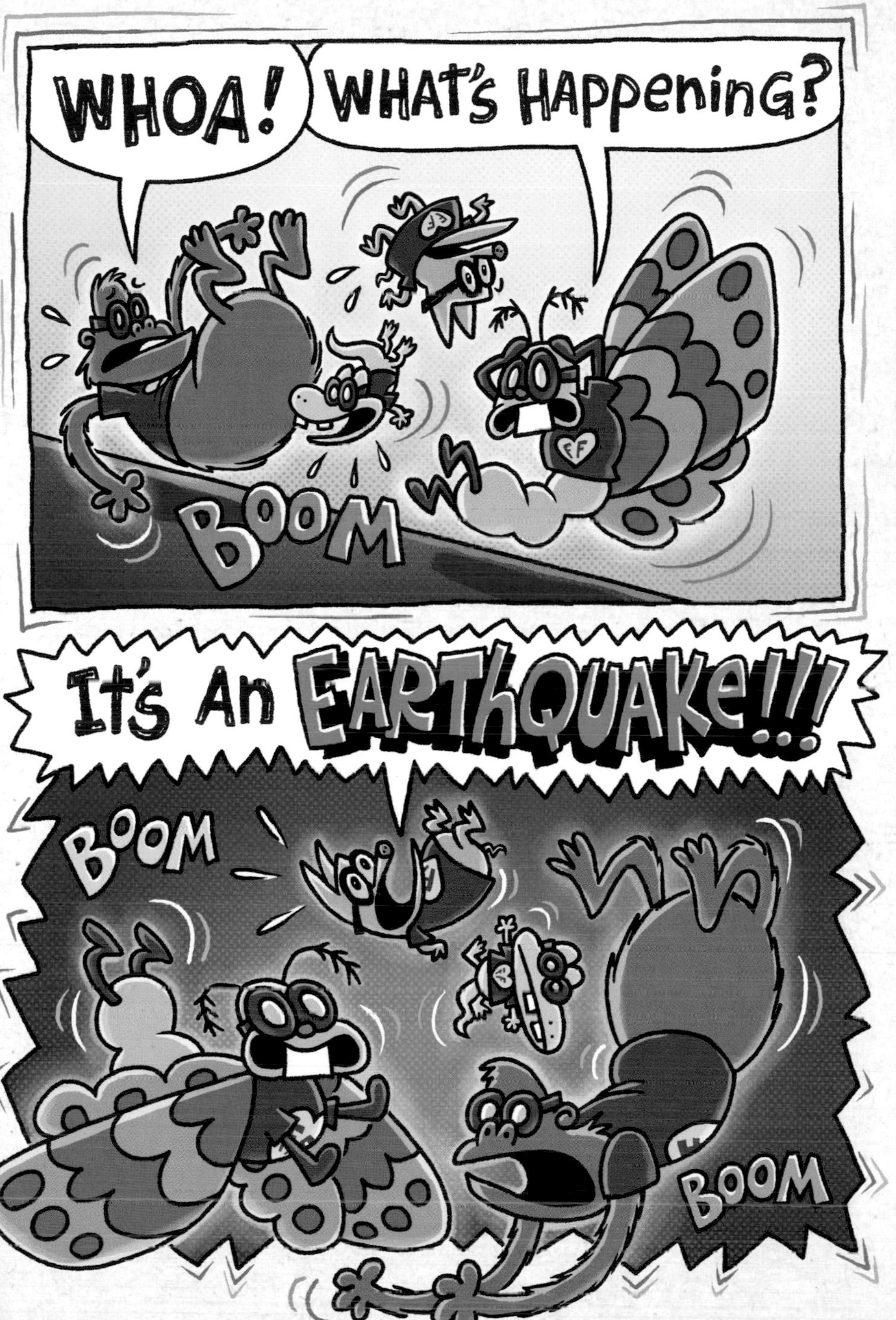
WHOA!
WHAT'S HAPPENING?
BOOM
It's An EARTHQUAKE!!!
BOOM
BOOM

Chapter 4

Bad Mister Stinkles

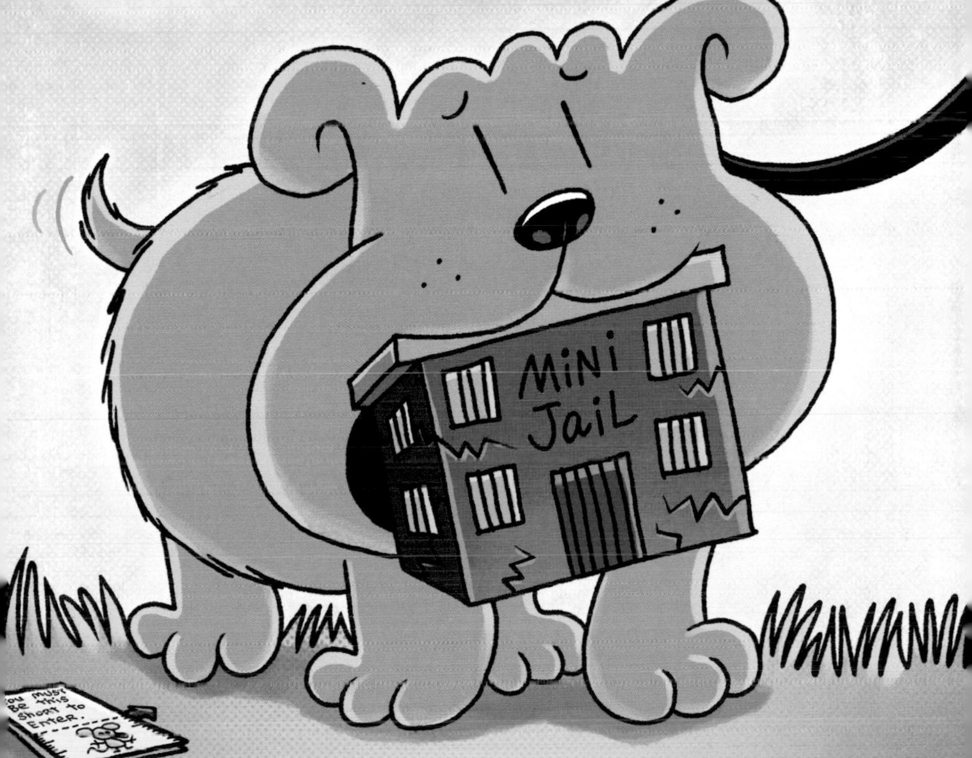
MINI JAIL
ou MUST
BE THIS
SHORT to
ENTER.

Left hand here

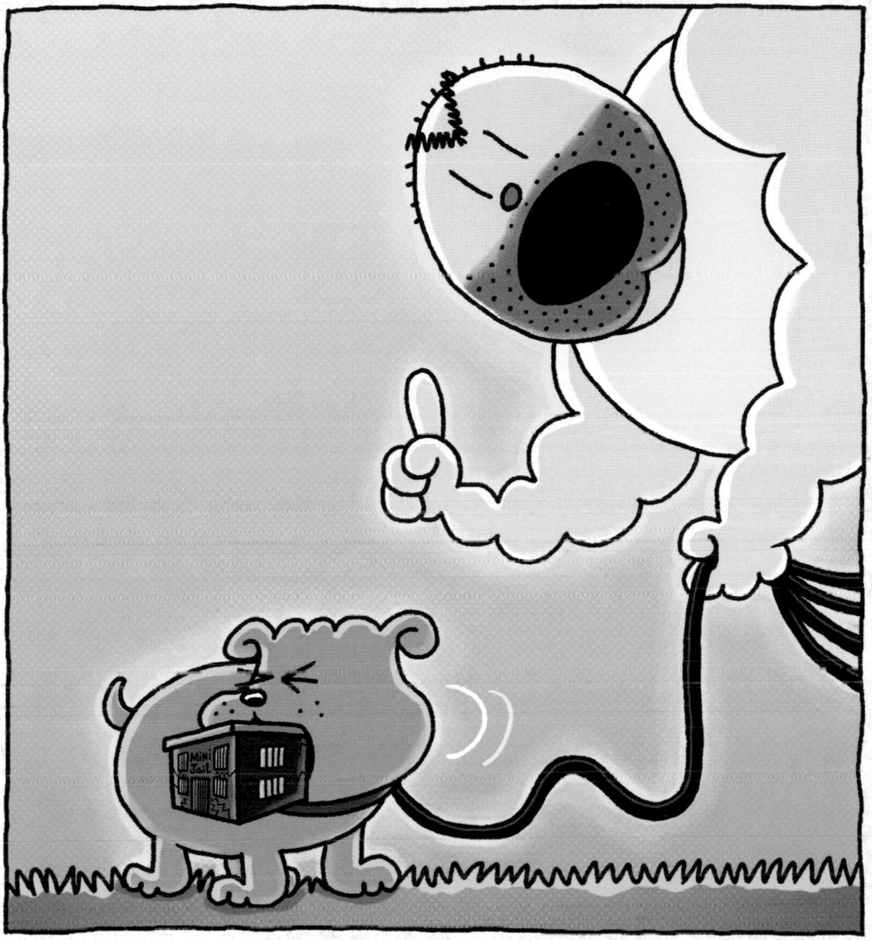
Mini Jail

...YOU DROP THAT MAXIMUM SECURITY CORRECTIONAL FACILITY RIGHT NOW!!!

Right Thumb here.

...YOU Drop that MAXimum Security CORRECTioNAL FACiLity **Right NOW!!!**

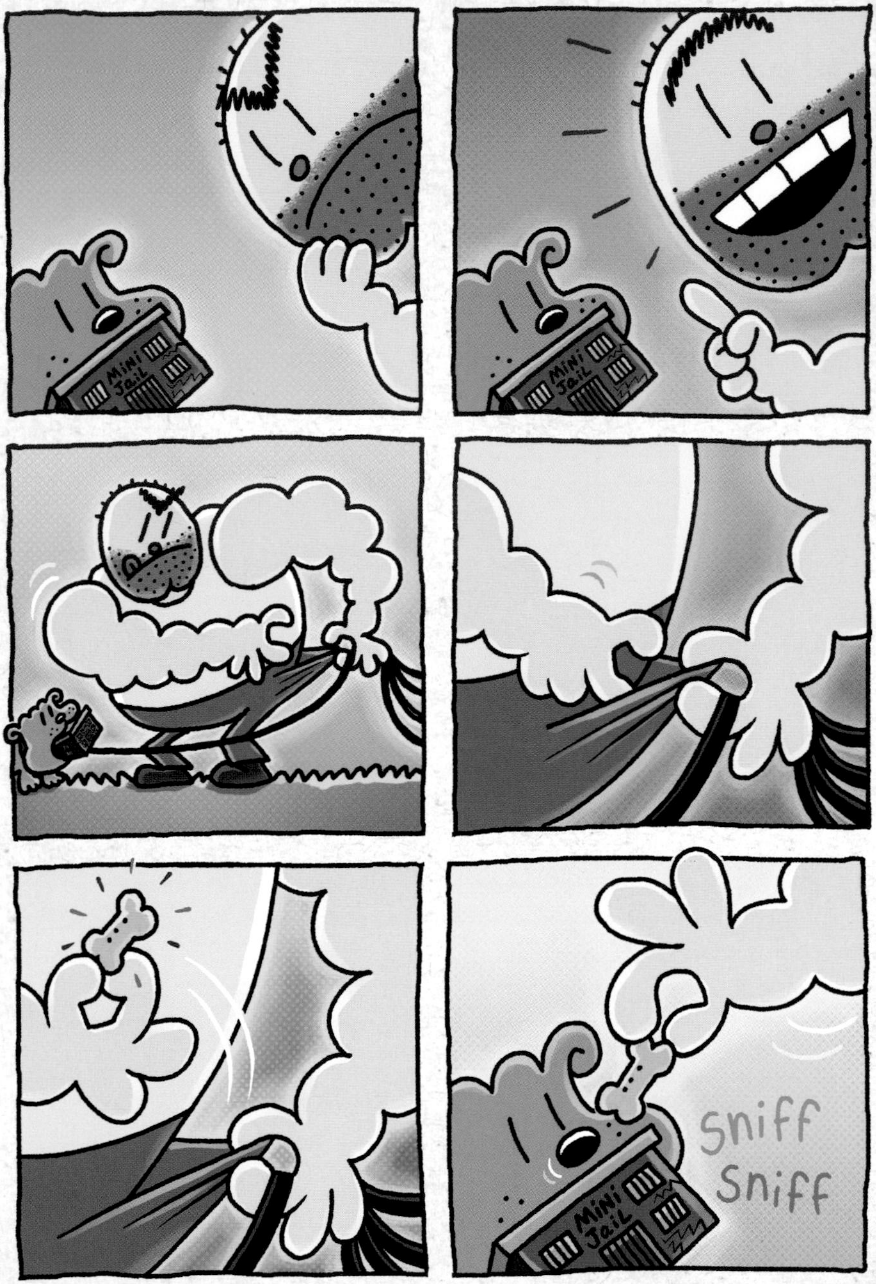
MINI JAIL
MINI JAIL
MINI JAIL
Sniff
Sniff

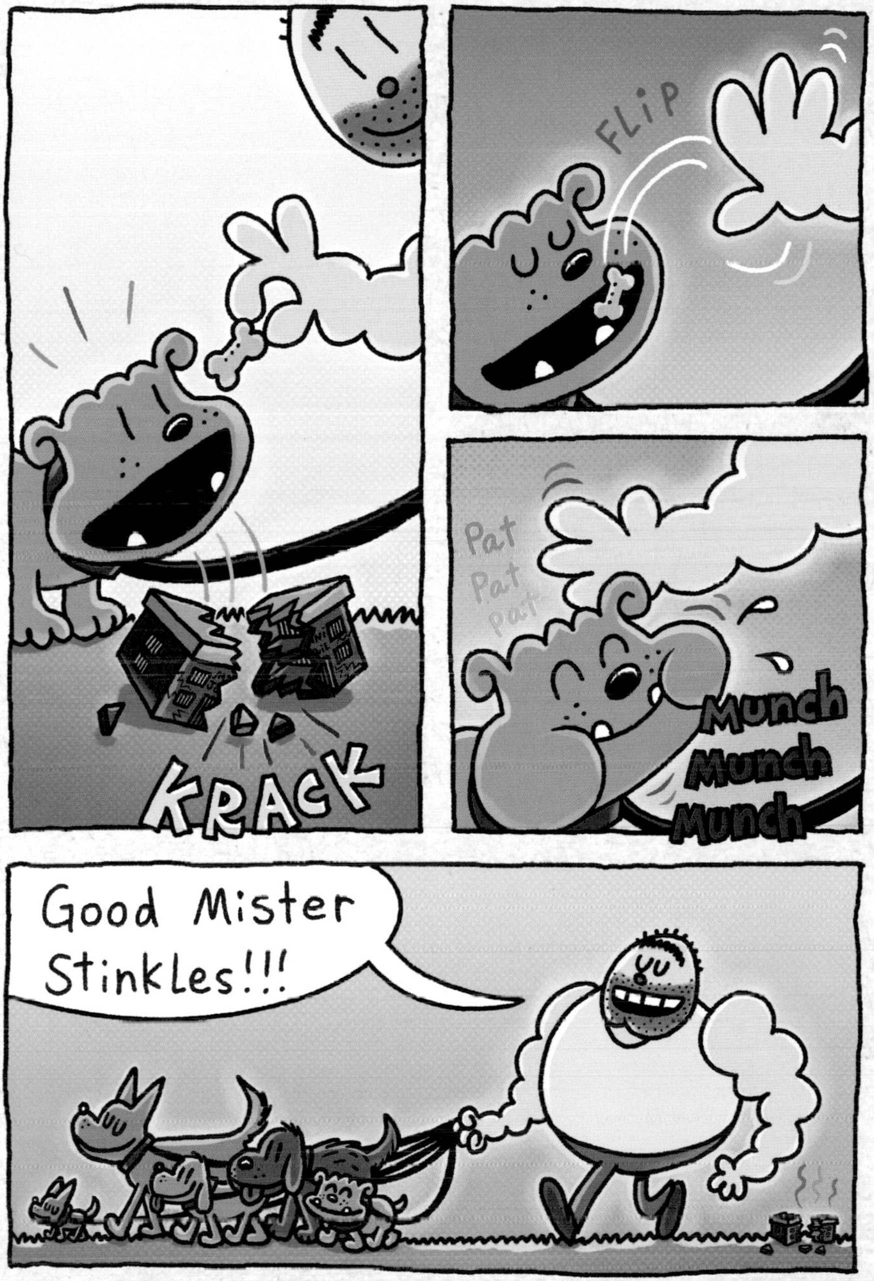
KRACK
FLIP
Pat
Pat
Pat
Munch
Munch
Munch
Good Mister Stinkles!!!

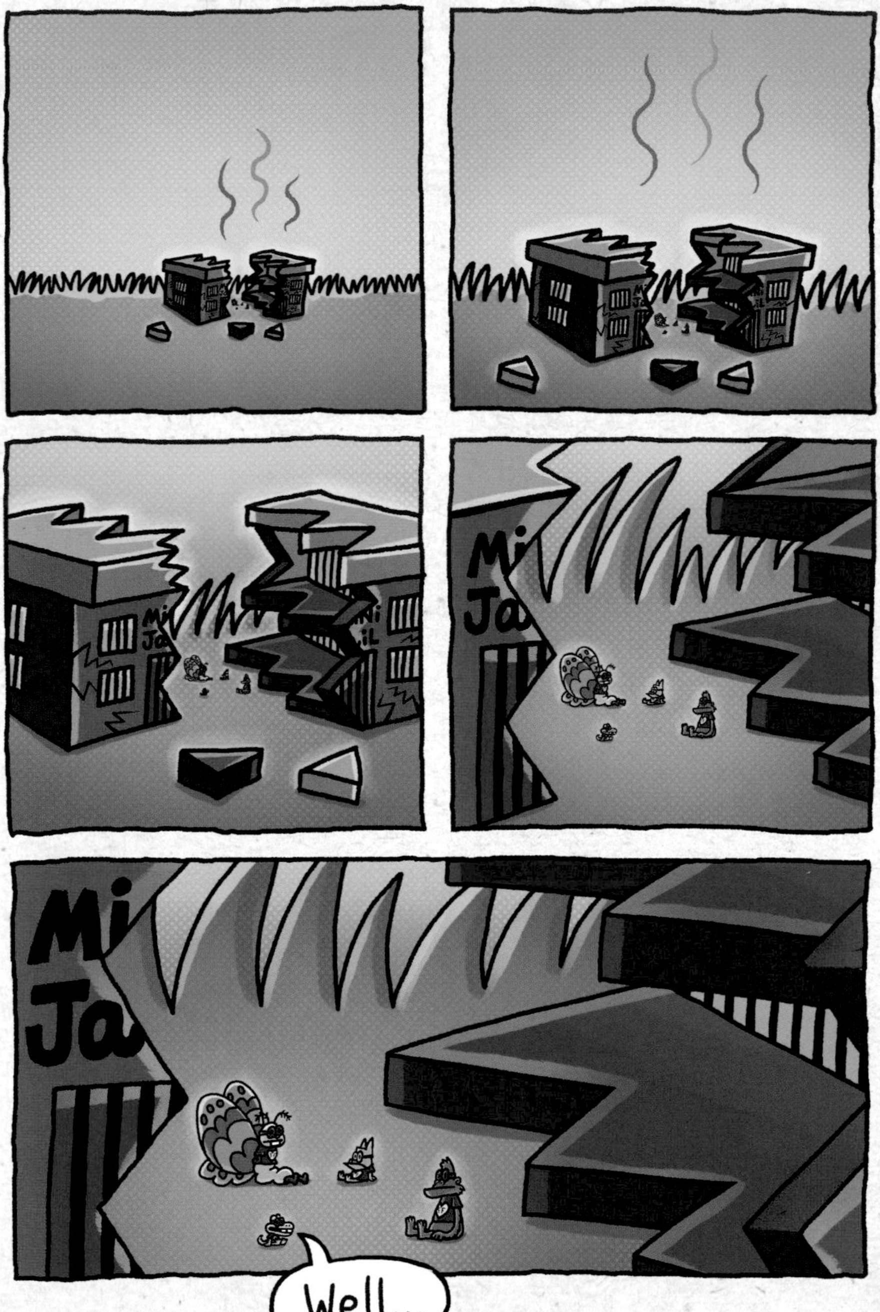
Well...

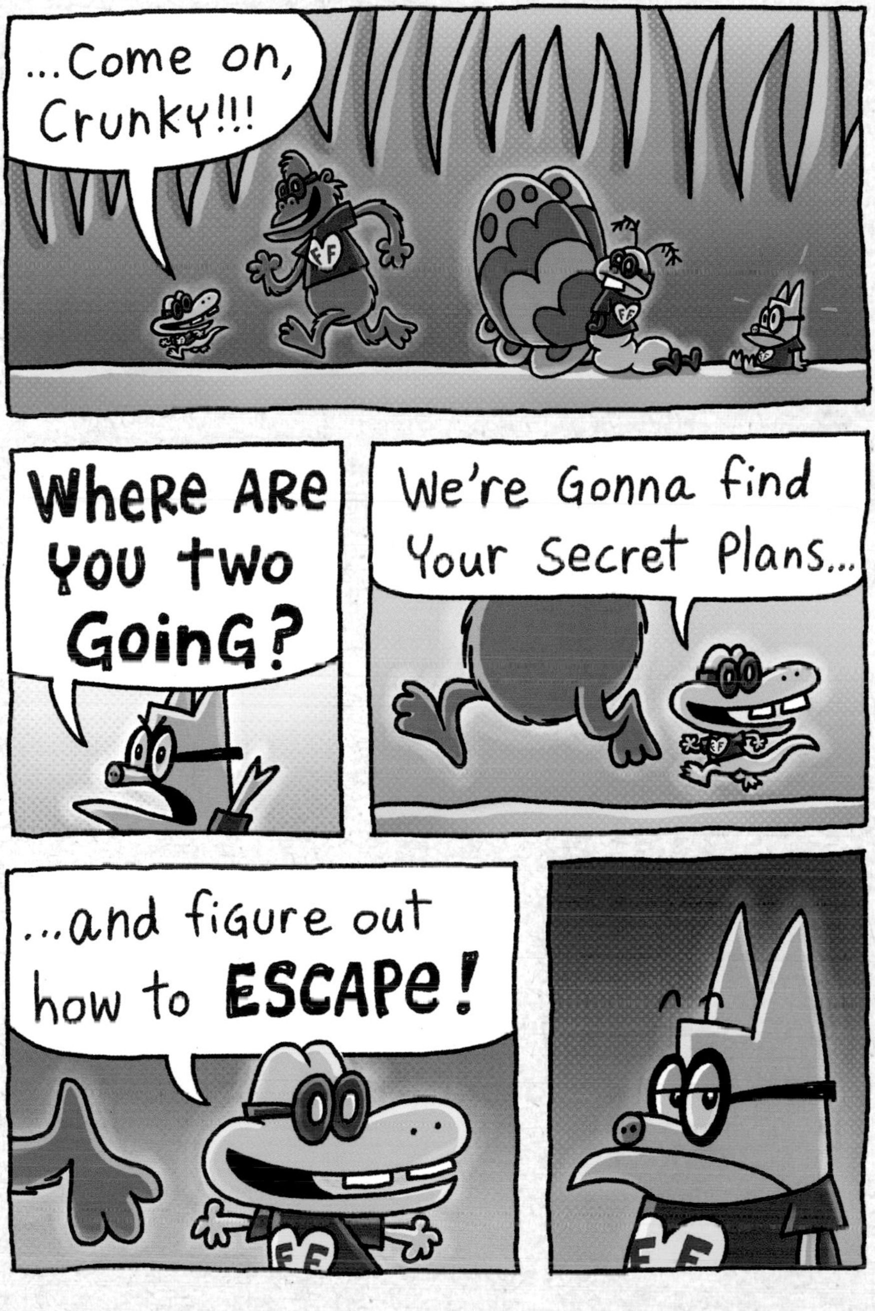
...Come on, Crunky!!!
WHERE ARE YOU two GoinG?
We're Gonna find Your Secret Plans...
...and figure out how to ESCAPE!

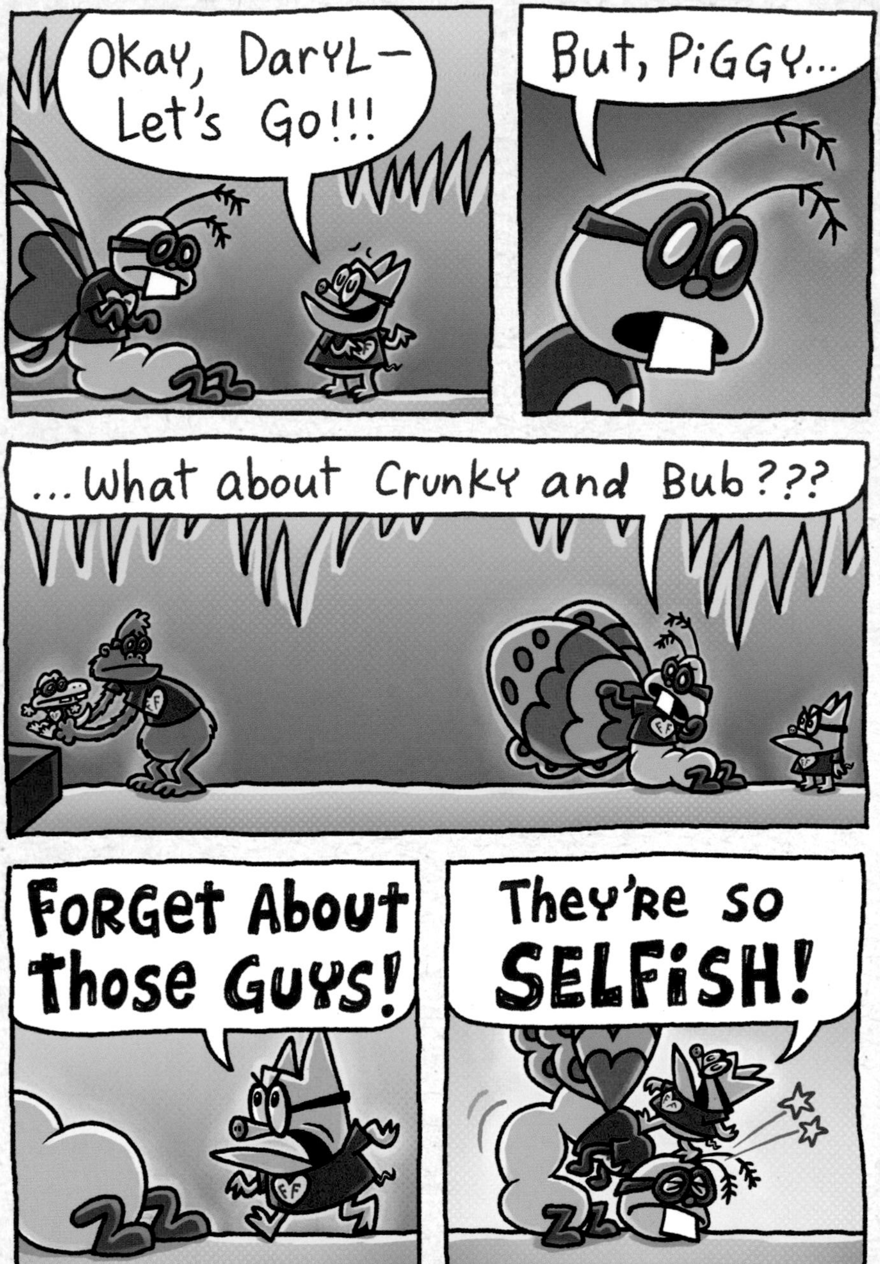

OKAY, DARYL— Let's GO!!!
But, PiGGY...
...What about Crunky and Bub???
FORGET About Those GUYS!
They're so SELFiSH!

CHAPTER 5

A Buncha Stuff That Happened Next

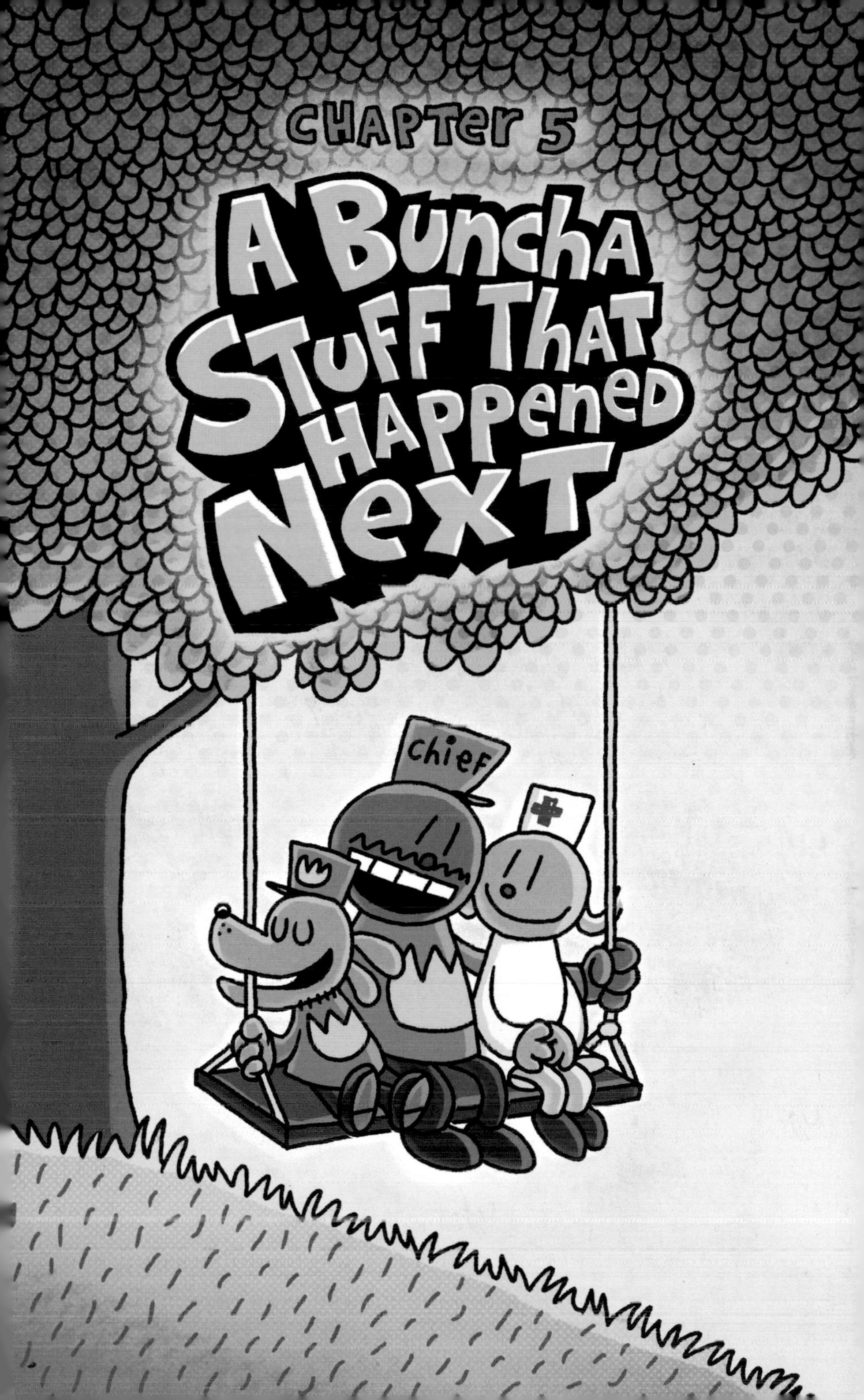
chief

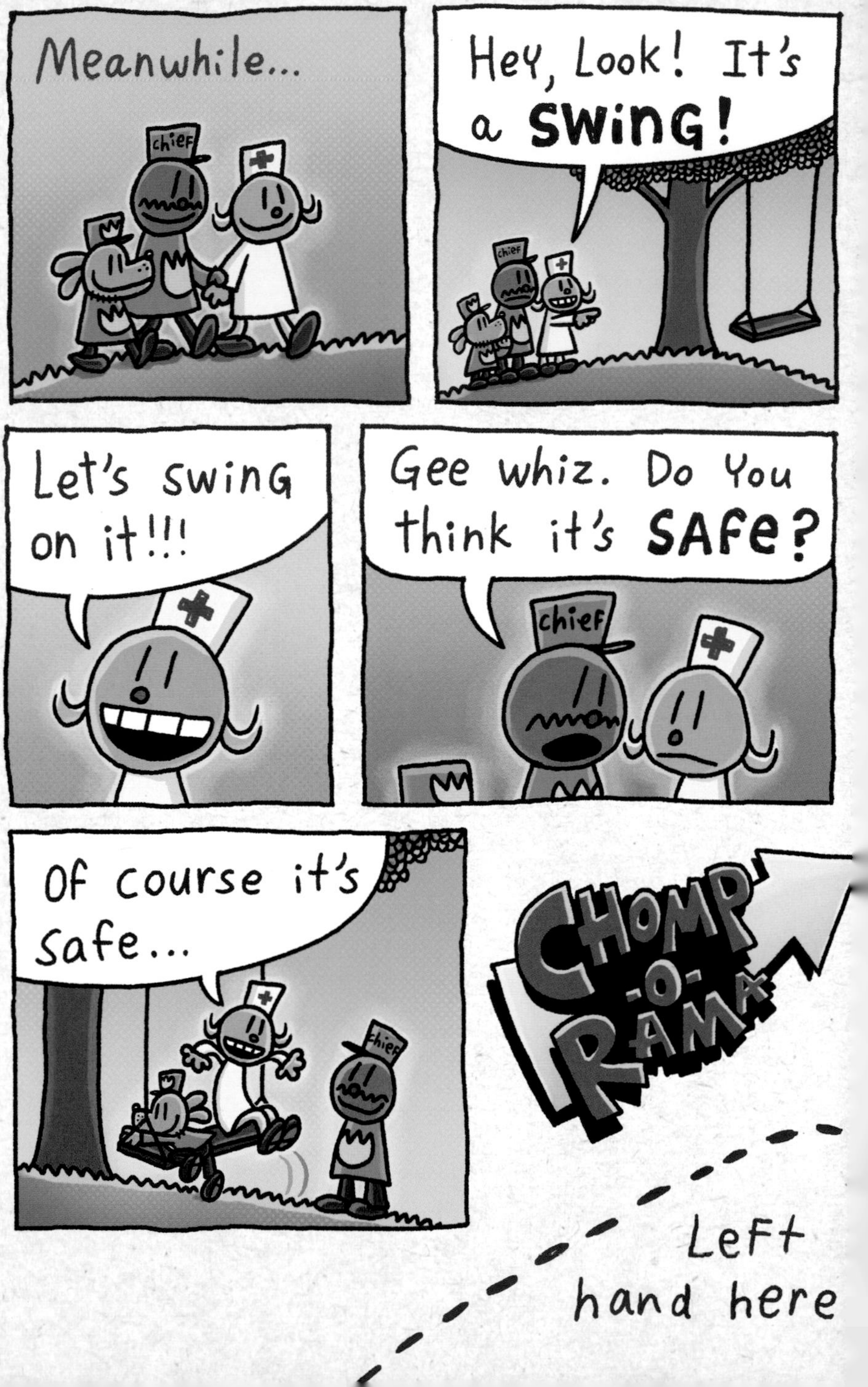
Meanwhile...
Hey, Look! It's a SWING!
Let's swing on it!!!
Gee whiz. Do you think it's SAFE?
Of course it's safe...
CHOMP-O-RAMA
Left hand here

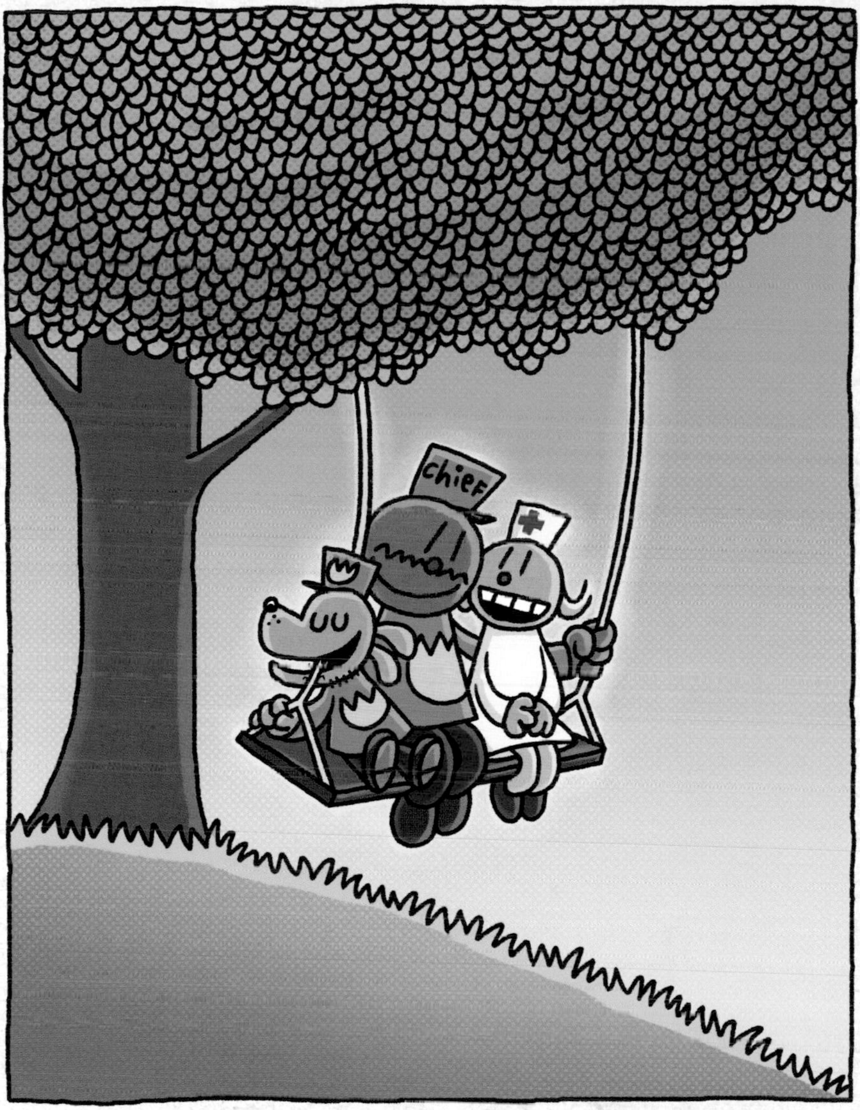
CHIEF

...what could **POSSIBLY** Go **WRONG?**

Right Thumb here.

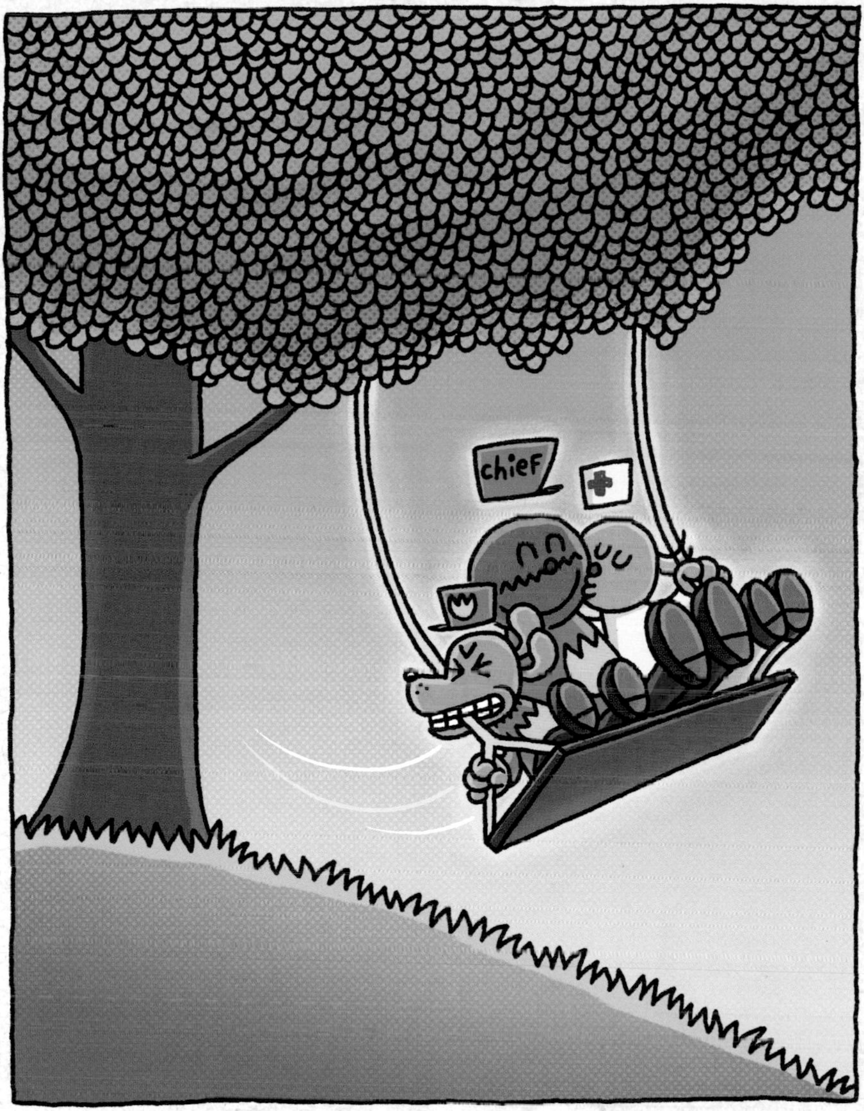
chief

...what could **POSSIBLY** Go **WRONG?**

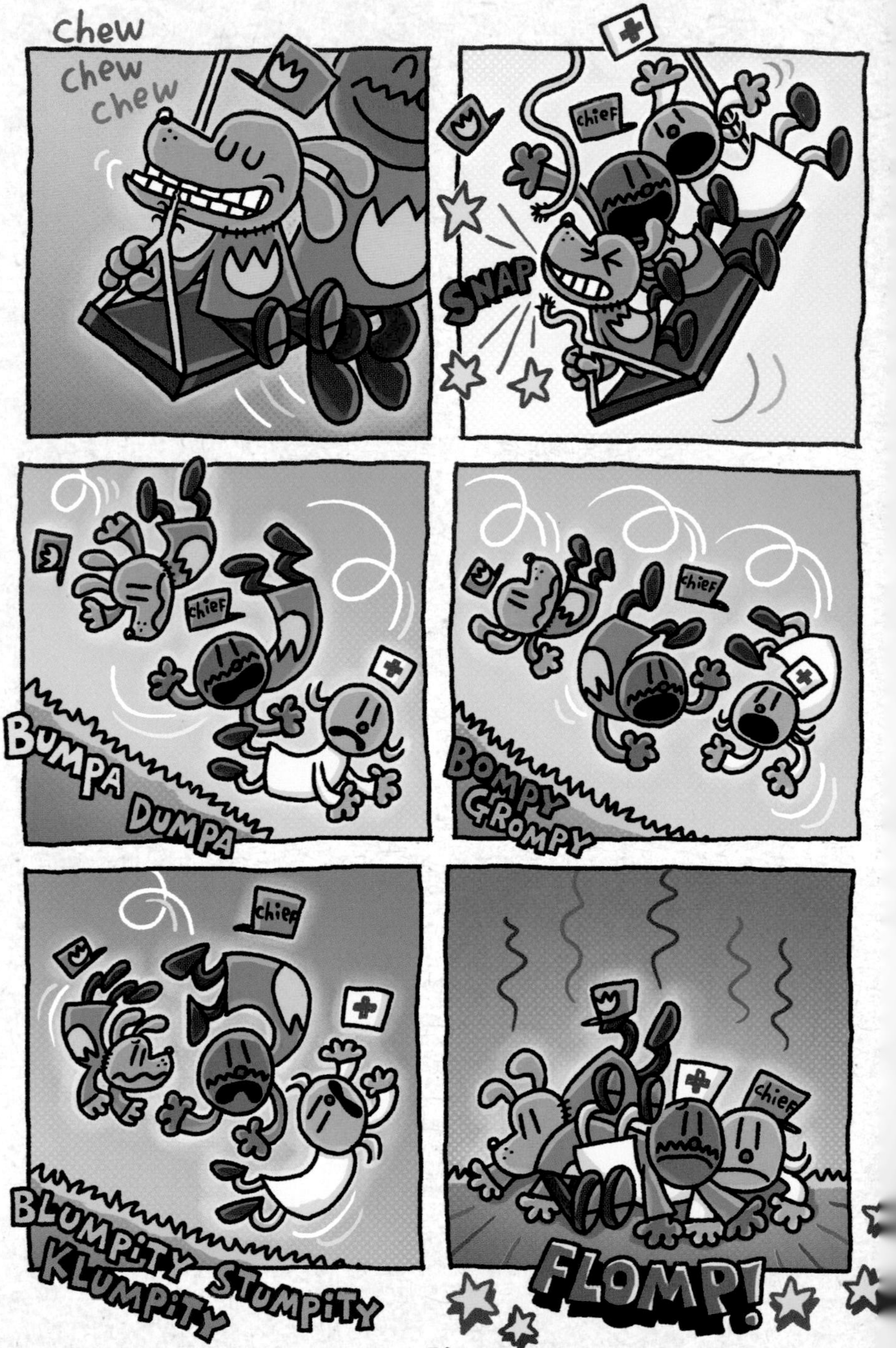
chew
chew
chew
chief
SNAP
chief
BUMPA
DUMPA
chief
BOMPY
GROMPY
chief
BLUMPITY
KLUMPITY
STUMPITY
chief
FLOMP!

I'm — I'm sorry, Nurse Lady.

I'm sorry, too.

Sorry we didn't try that **SOONER!**

LET'S DO it AGAIN!!!

C'mon, fellas!

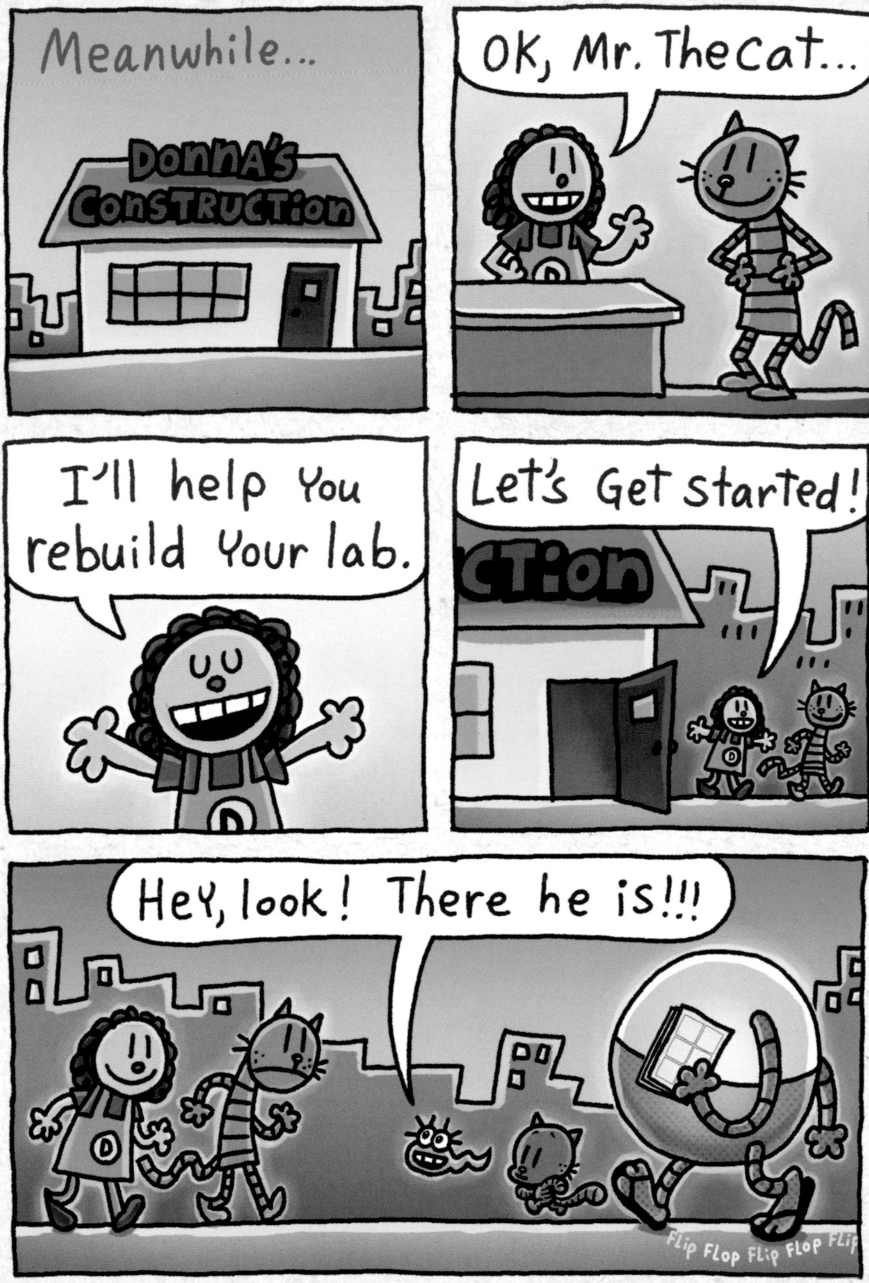
Meanwhile...
DONNA'S CONSTRUCTION
OK, Mr. The Cat...
I'll help You rebuild Your lab.
Let's Get started!
CTion
Hey, look! There he is!!!
FLip FLop FLip FLop FLip

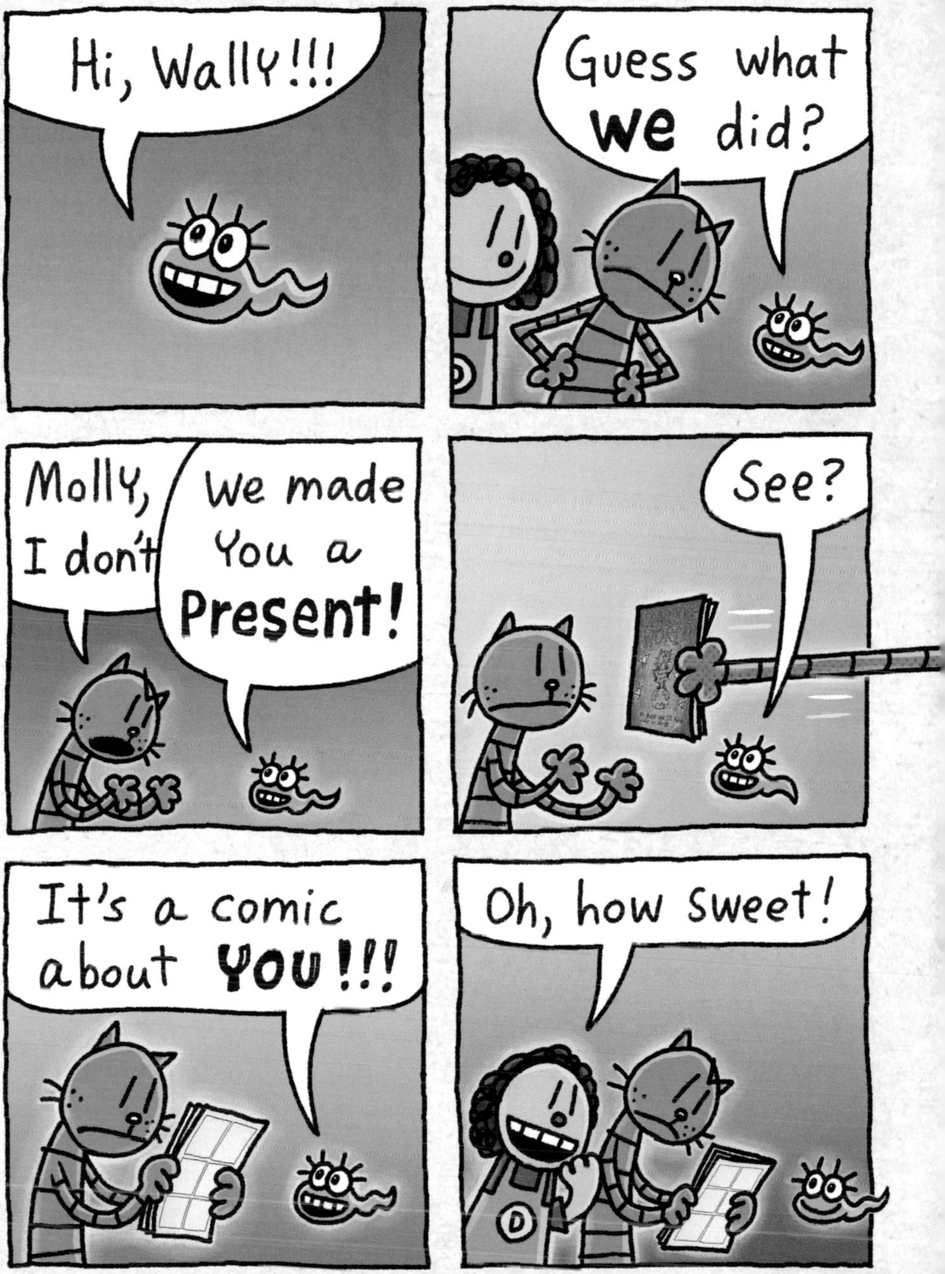
Hi, Wally!!!
Guess what we did?
Molly, I don't
We made you a Present!
See?
It's a comic about YOU!!!
Oh, how sweet!

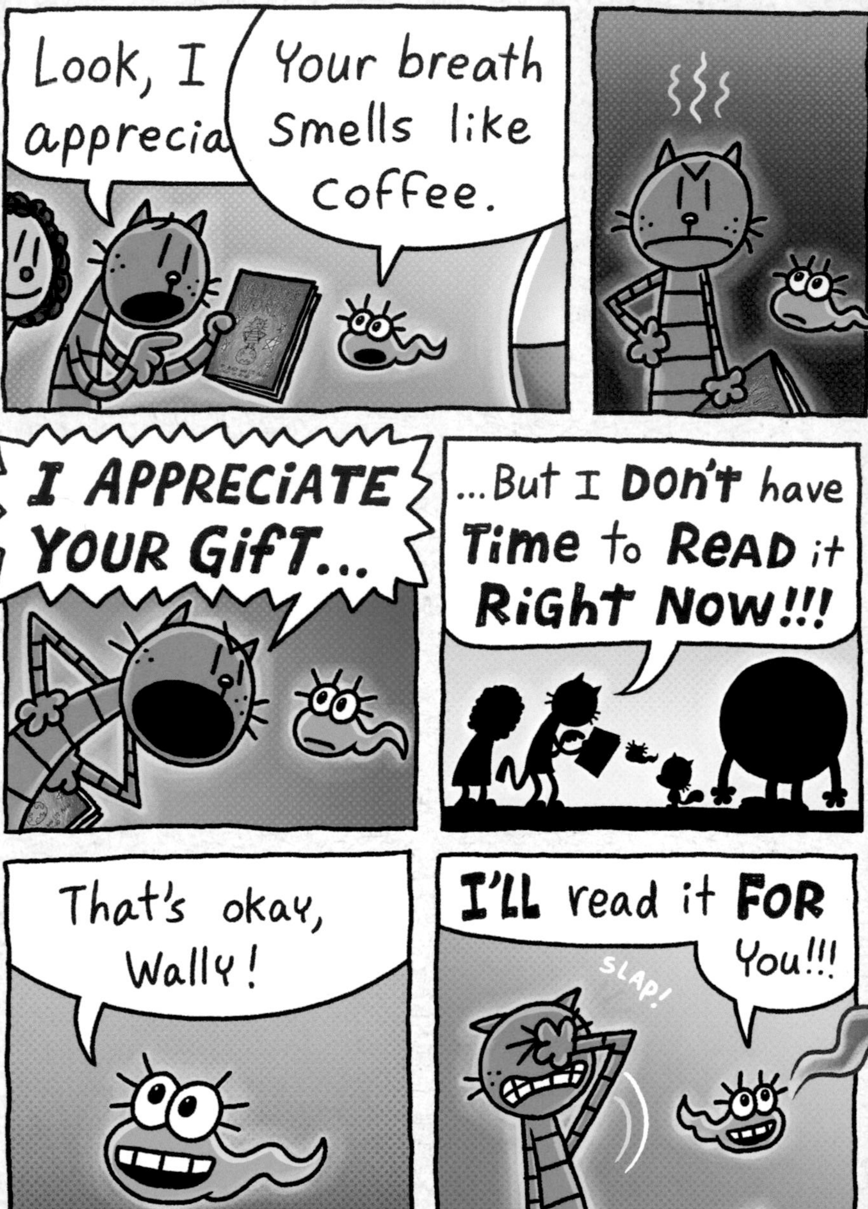
Look, I apprecia
Your breath smells like coffee.
I APPRECIATE YOUR GIFT...
...But I DON'T have Time to READ it RIGHT NOW!!!
That's okay, Wally!
I'LL read it FOR You!!!
SLAP!

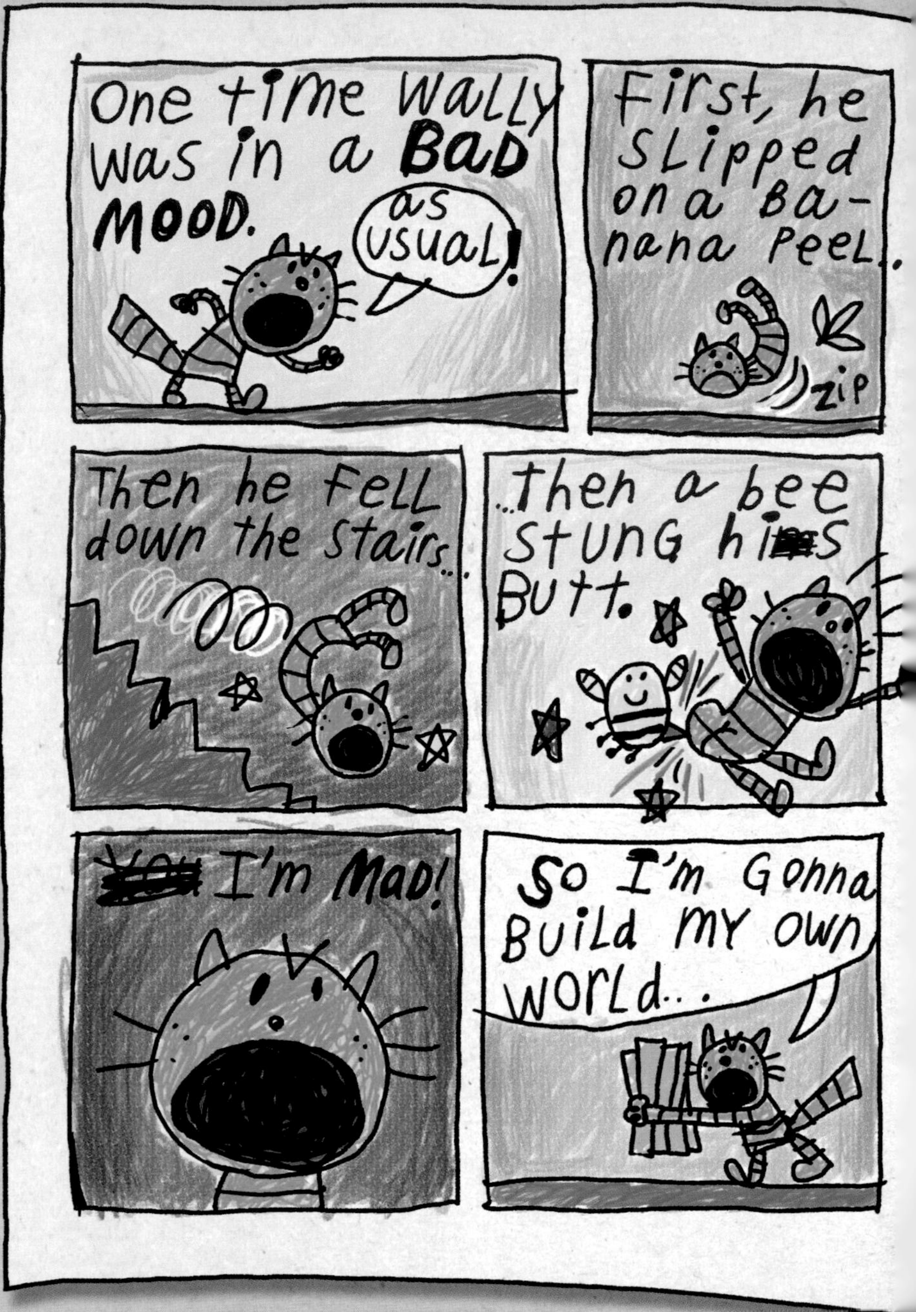
One time Wally was in a BAD MOOD.
as USUAL!
First, he slipped on a Ba-nana peel..
ZIP
Then he fell down the stairs...
...Then a bee stung his Butt.
I'm MAD!
So I'm Gonna Build my own world...

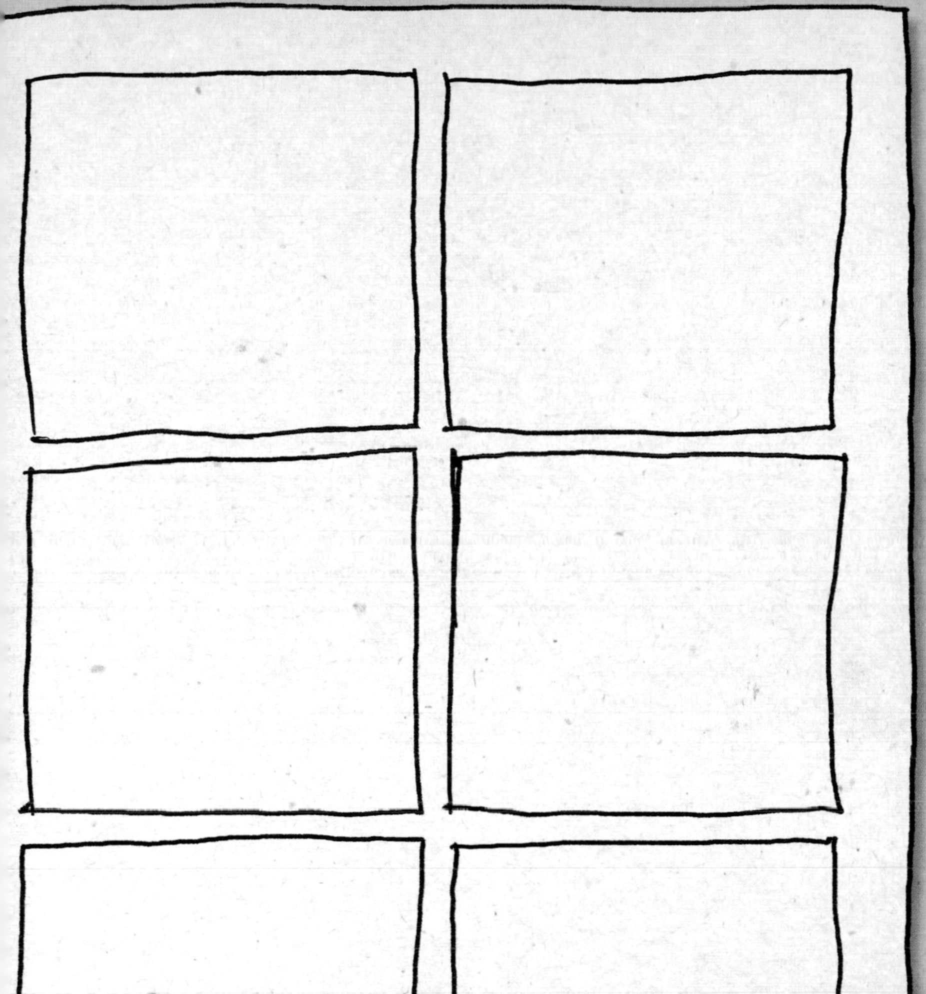

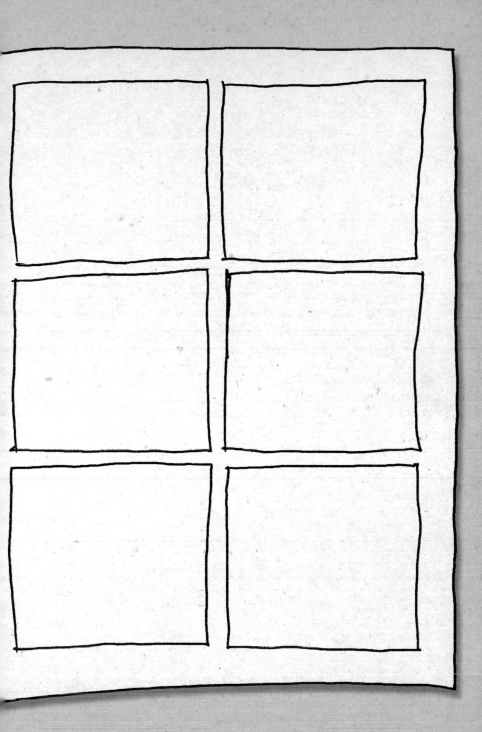

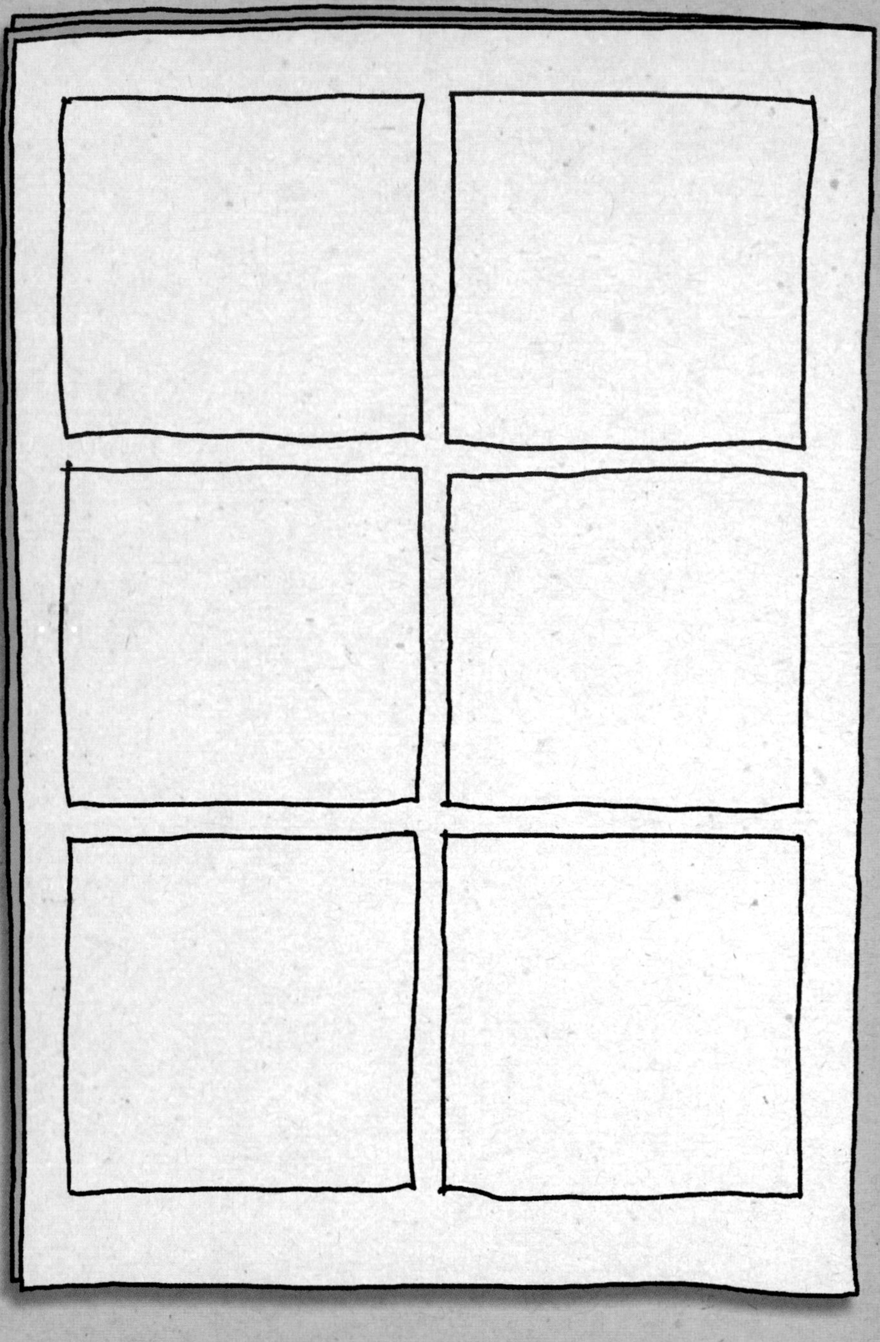

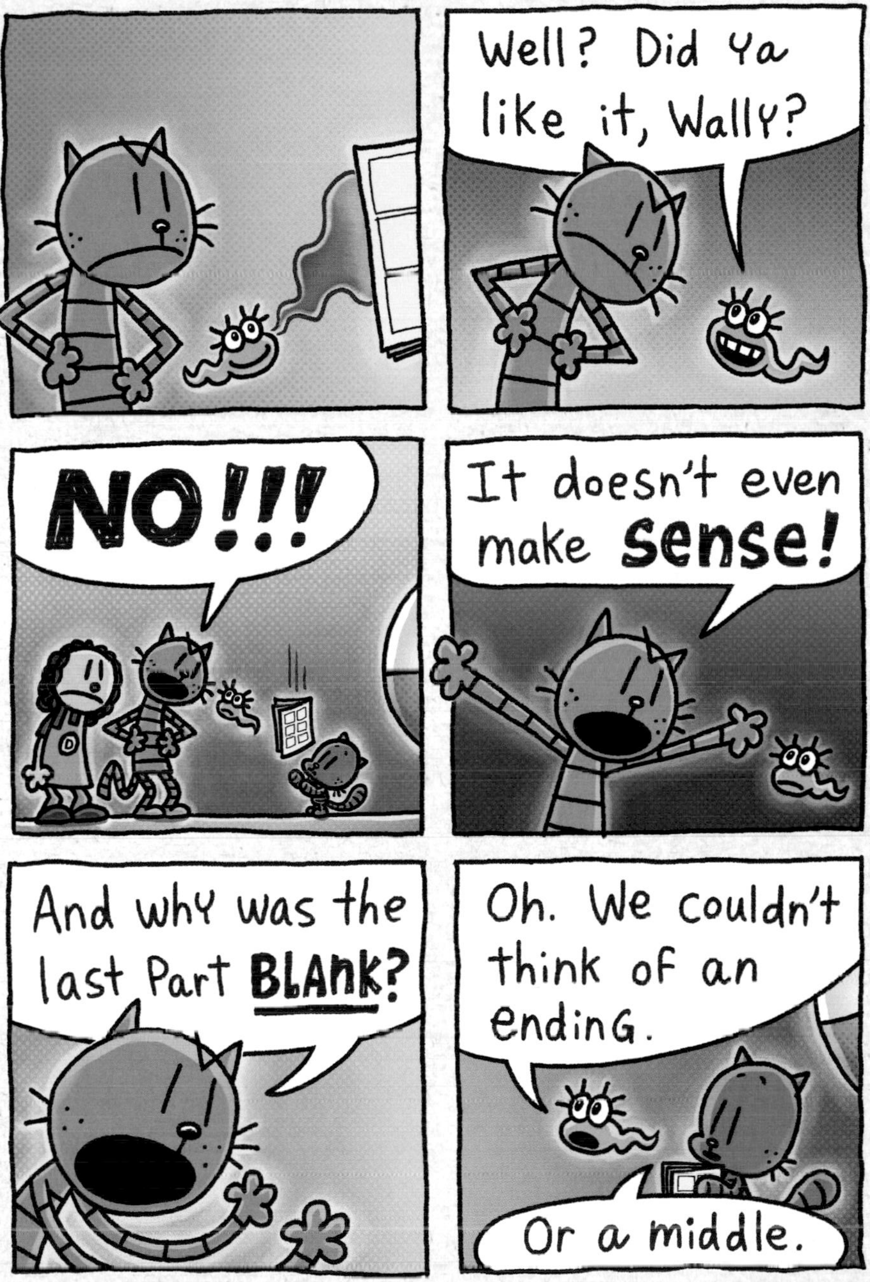
Well? Did ya like it, Wally?
NO!!!
It doesn't even make sense!
And why was the last part BLANK?
Oh. We couldn't think of an ending.
Or a middle.

Is **THiS** what You teach in That **COMiC CLUb** of Yours??? no. no.

IT'S TOO HARD...

...So let's Just **GiVe UP!!!**

Because we're **ALL** A bunch of Little baby...

...QUiTTeRS!

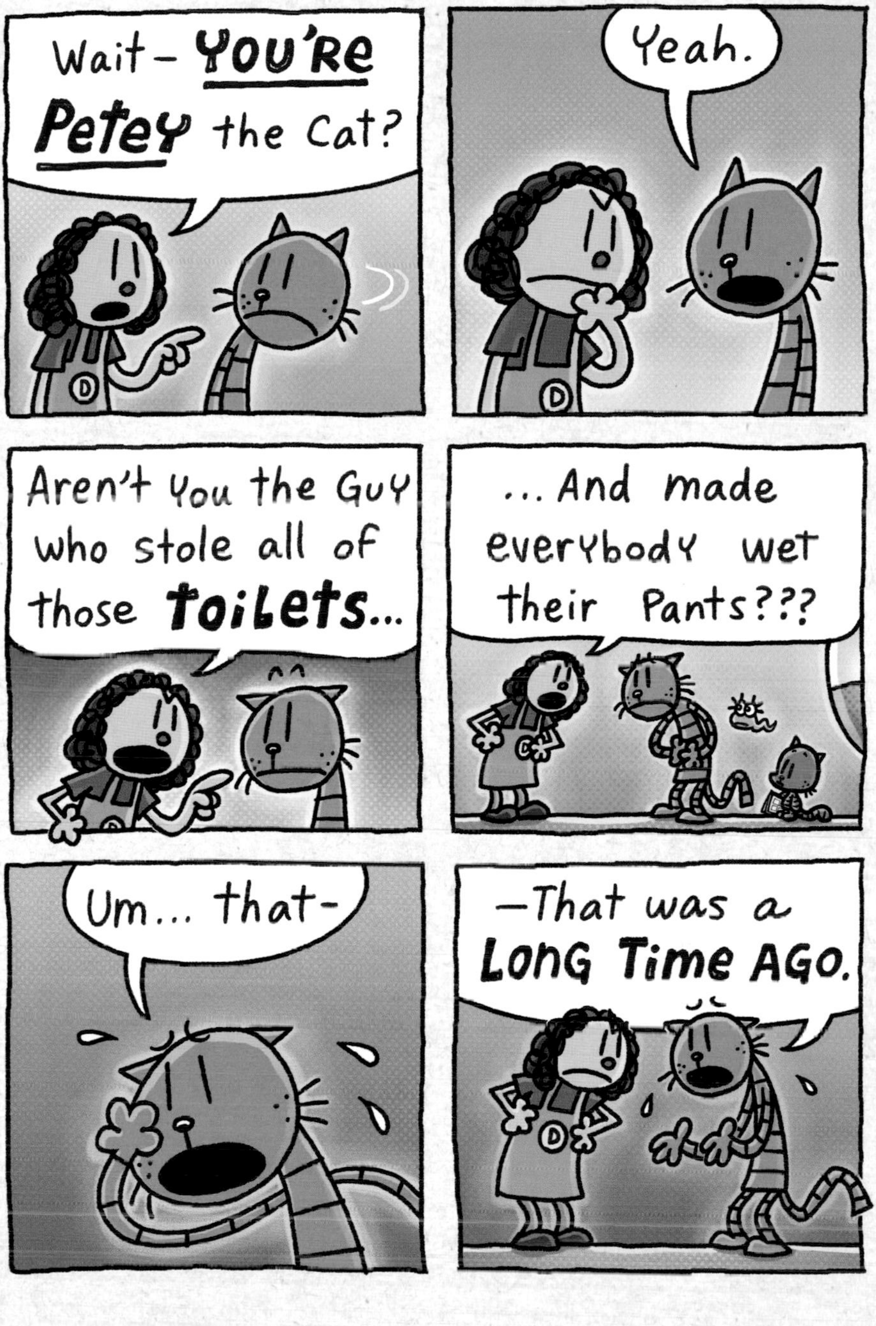
Wait– YOU'RE Petey the Cat?
Yeah.
Aren't you the guy who stole all of those toilets...
...And made everybody wet their pants???
Um... that–
–That was a LONG TIME AGO.

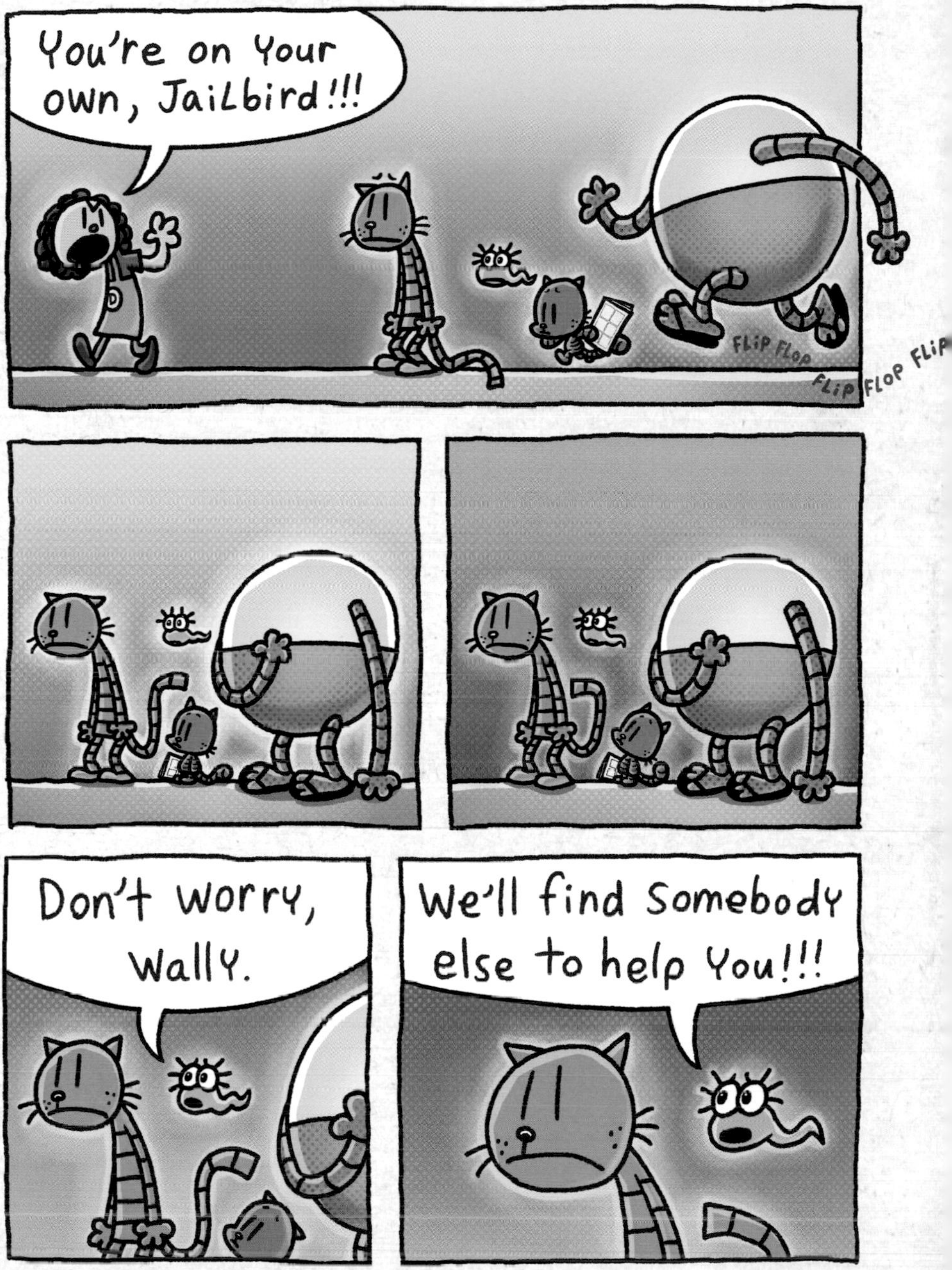
You're on your own, Jailbird!!!
FLIP FLOP
FLIP FLOP FLIP
Don't worry, Wally.
We'll find somebody else to help you!!!

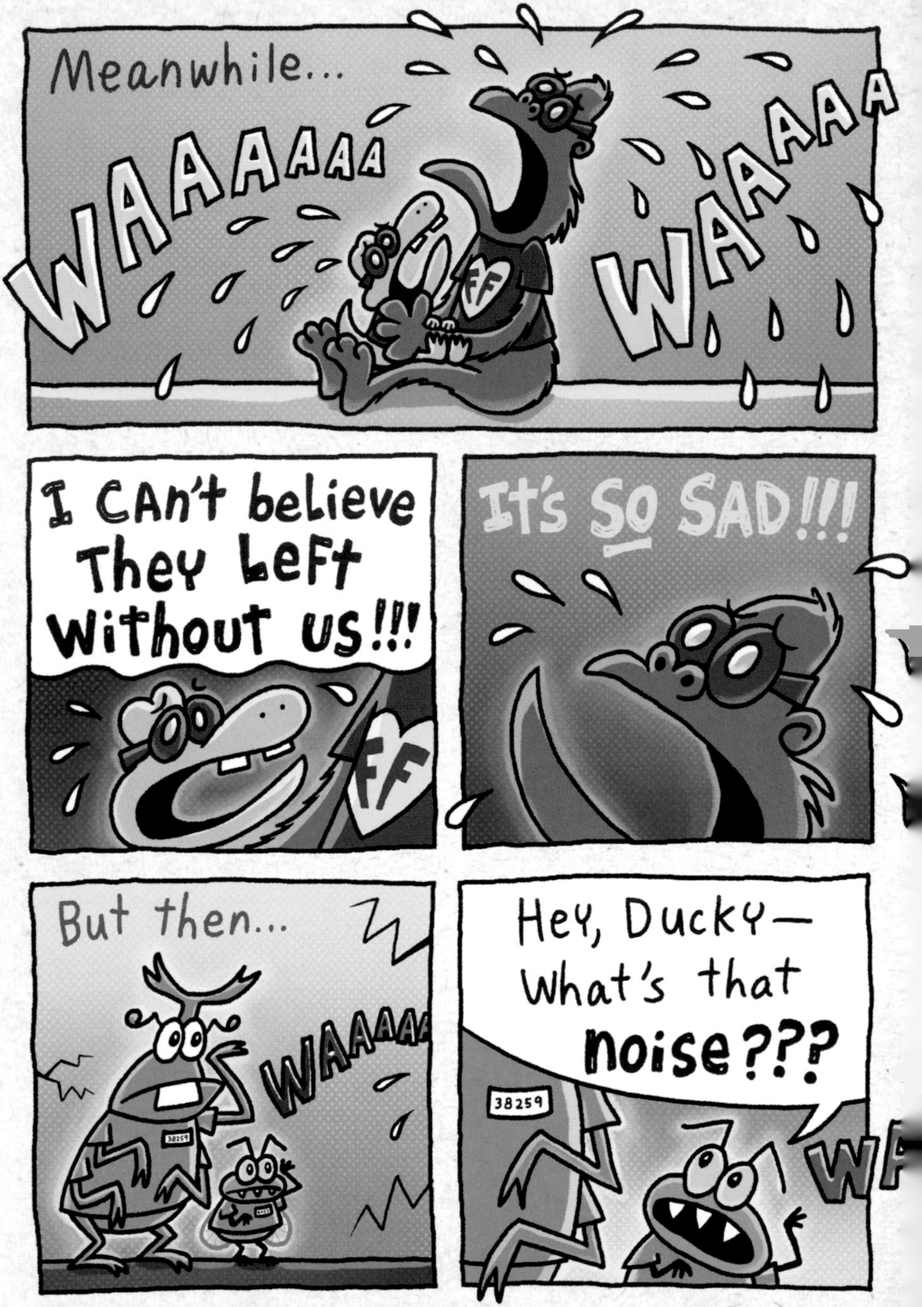

Meanwhile...
WAAAAAAA
WAAAAAAA
I CAN'T believe They LeFt without us!!!
It's SO SAD!!!
But then...
WAAAAA
Hey, Ducky—What's that noise???
38259

CHAPTER 6

Friendly Friends Are GO!

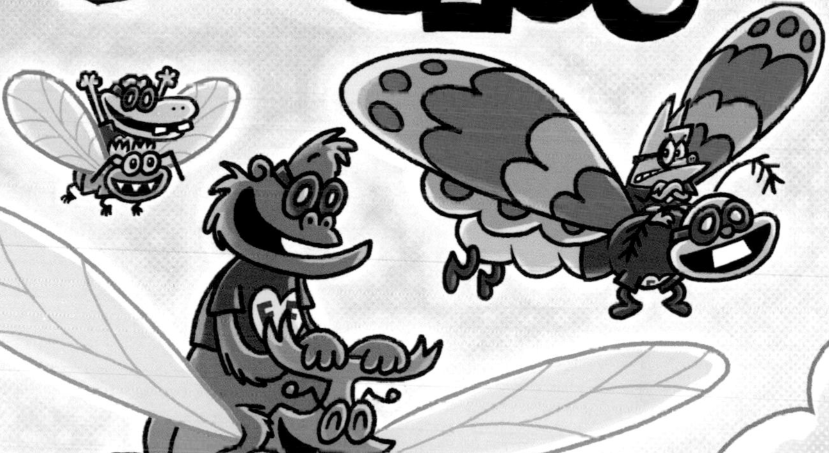

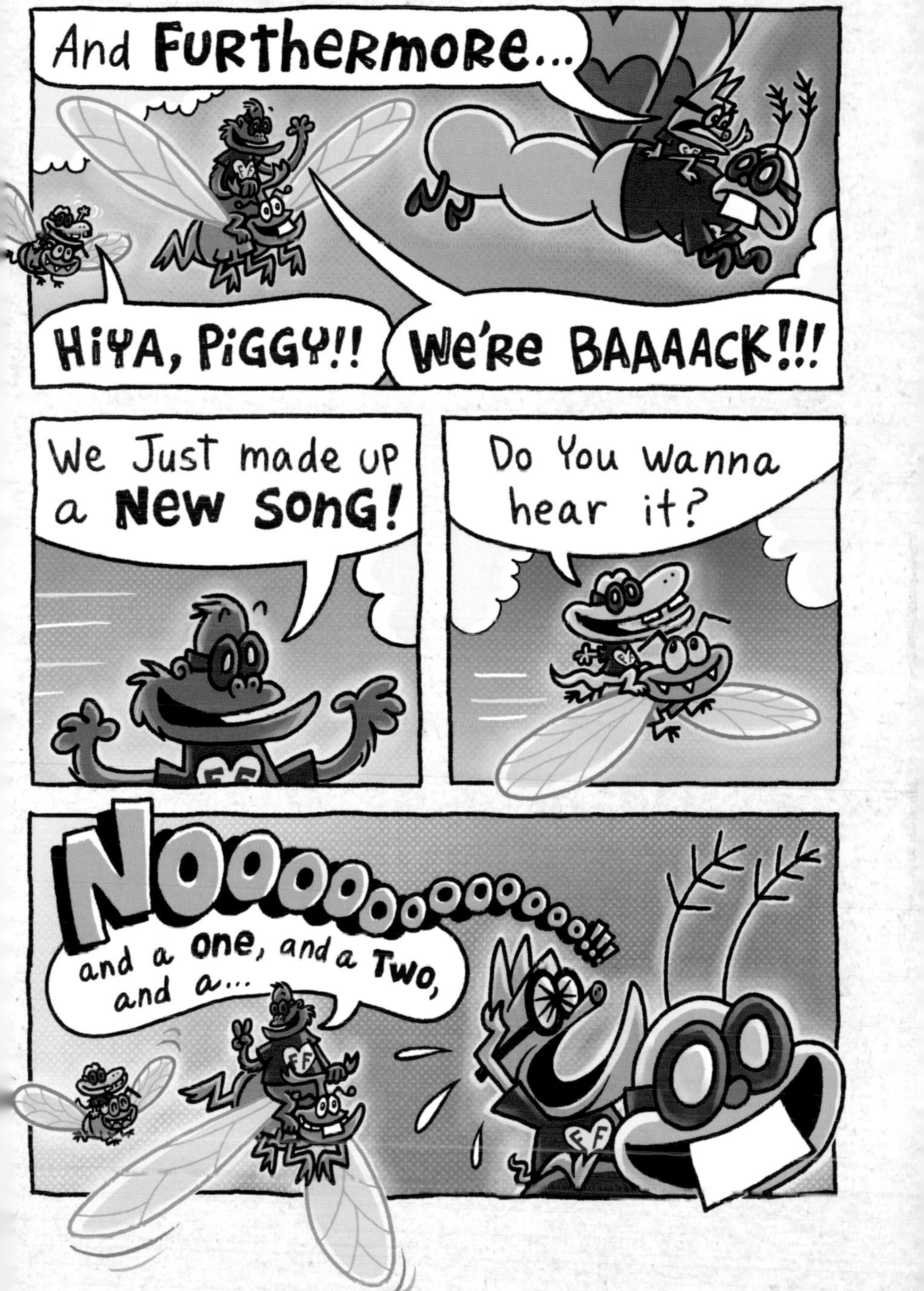

And FURTHERMORE...
HIYA, PIGGY!!
WE'RE BAAAACK!!!
We Just made up a NEW SONG!
Do You wanna hear it?
NOOOOOOOOOOOOOOOO!!!
and a one, and a Two, and a...

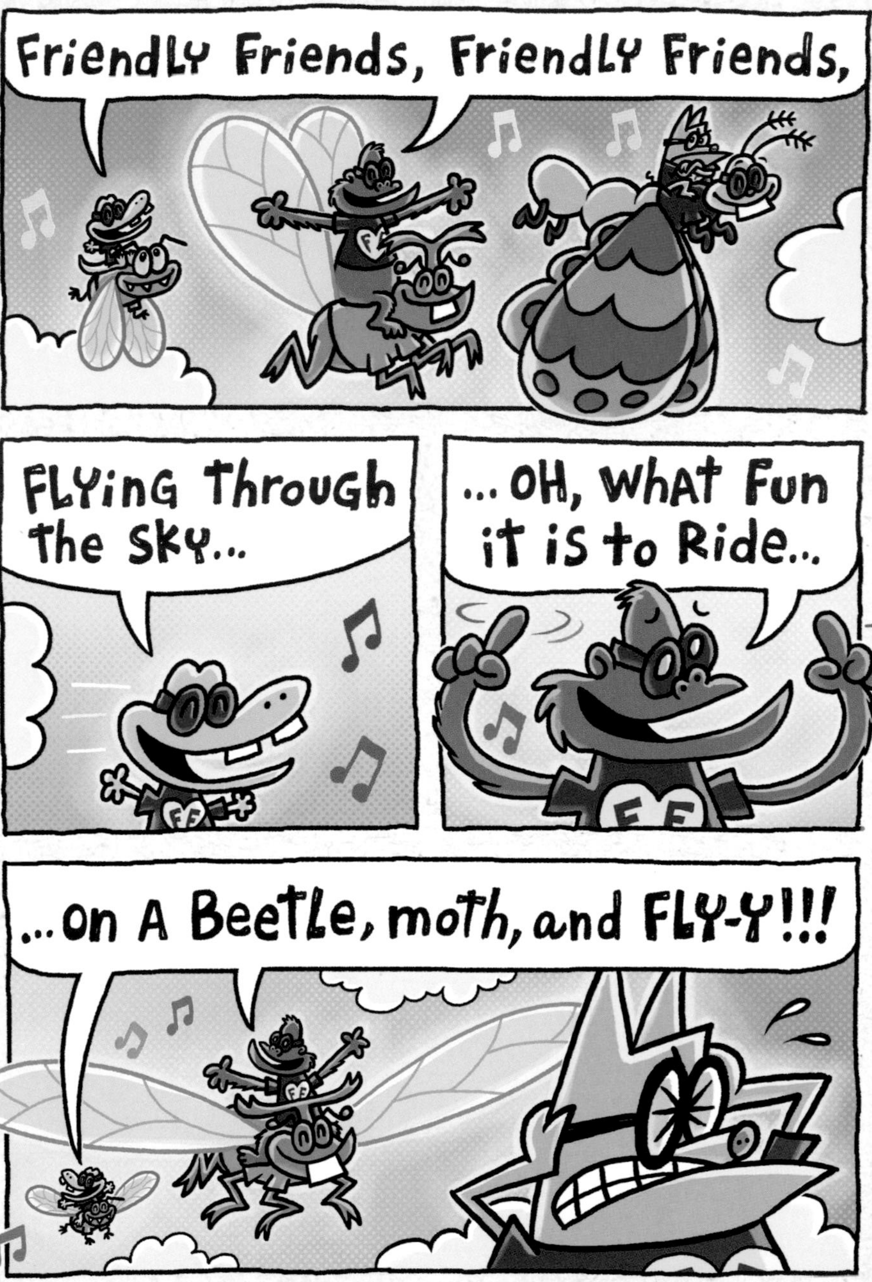
Friendly Friends, Friendly Friends,
FLYing Through the SKY...
...OH, WHAT Fun it is to Ride...
...on A Beetle, moth, and FLY-Y!!!

Note: This song can be sung to the tune of "Jingle Bells."

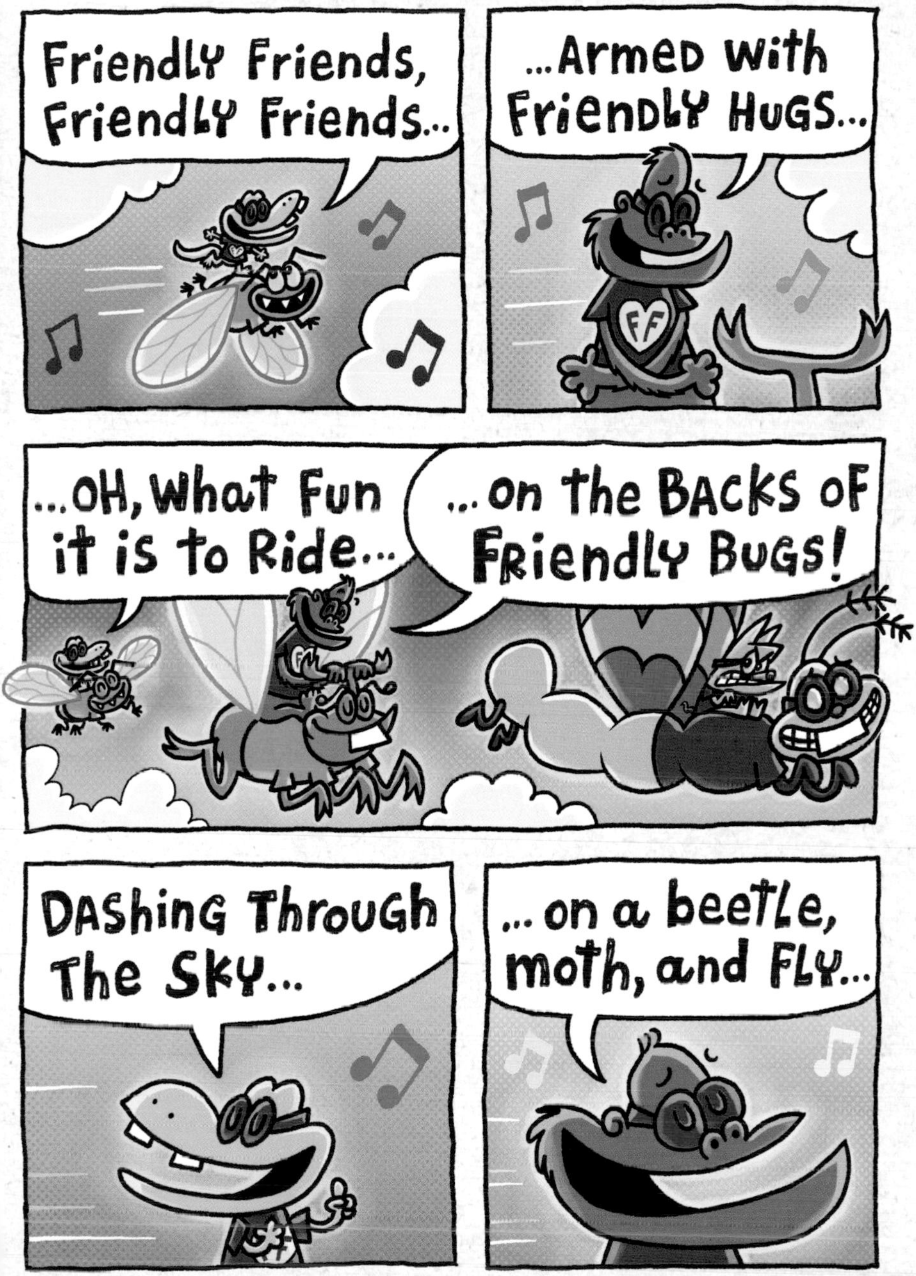
Friendly Friends, Friendly Friends...
...Armed with Friendly HUGS...
...OH, What Fun it is to Ride...
...on the BACKS OF Friendly BUGS!
DASHING Through The SKY...
...on a beetle, moth, and FLY...

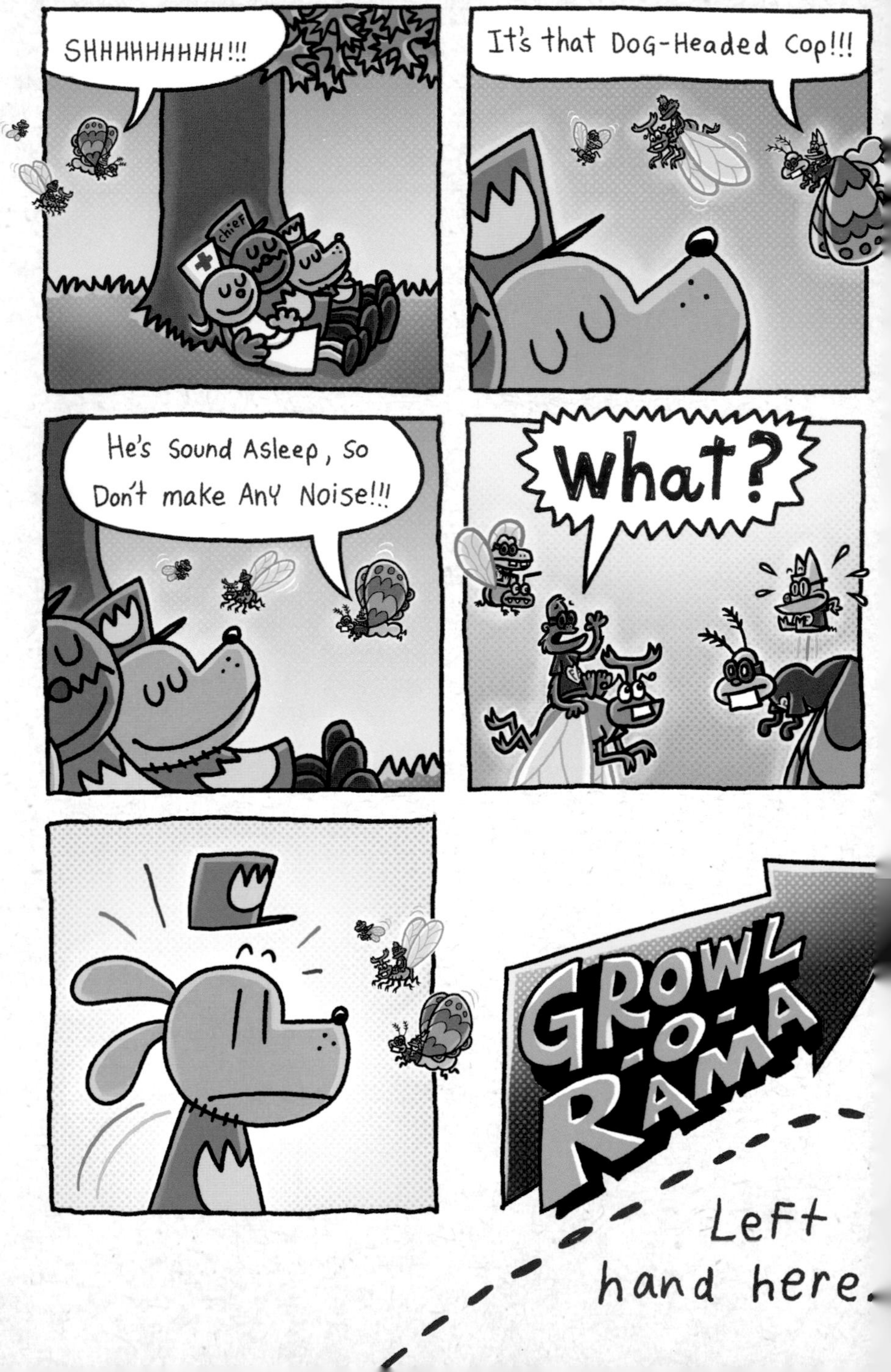
SHHHHHHHHH!!!
It's that DOG-Headed Cop!!!
He's Sound Asleep, So Don't make Any Noise!!!
What?
GROWL-O-RAMA
Left hand here.

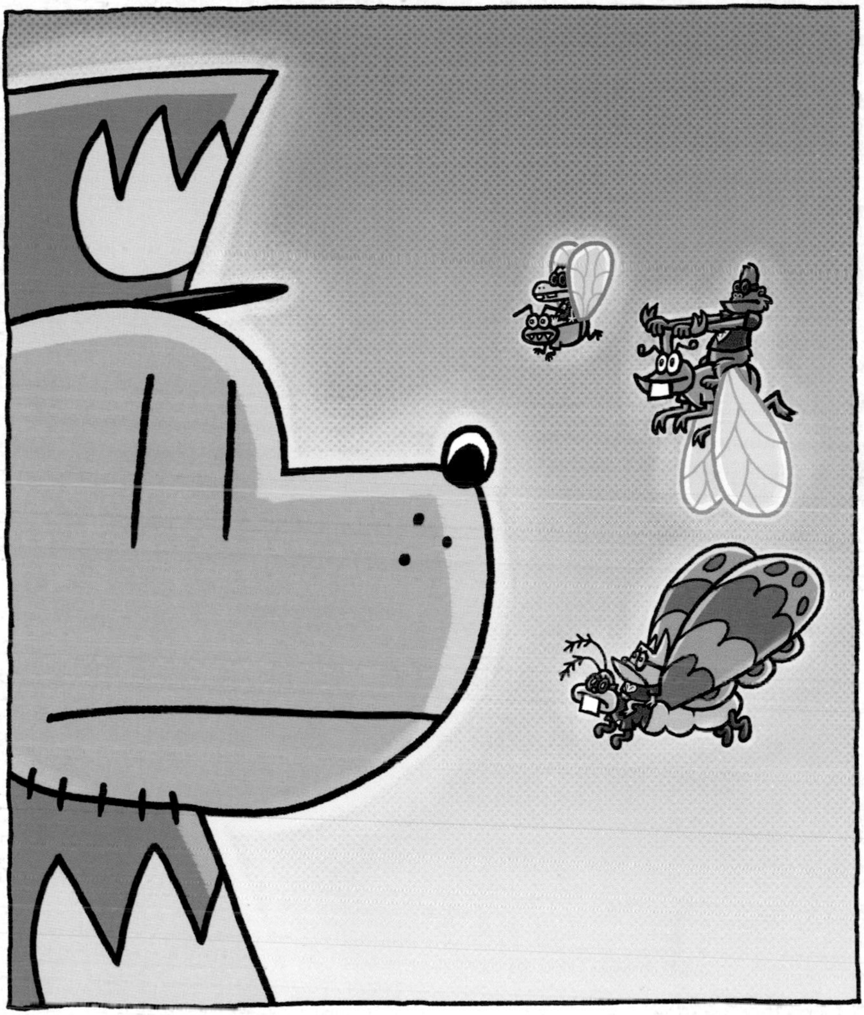

GRR-FACE A GO-GO!

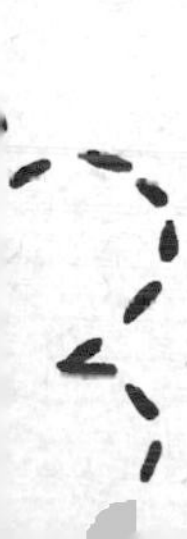

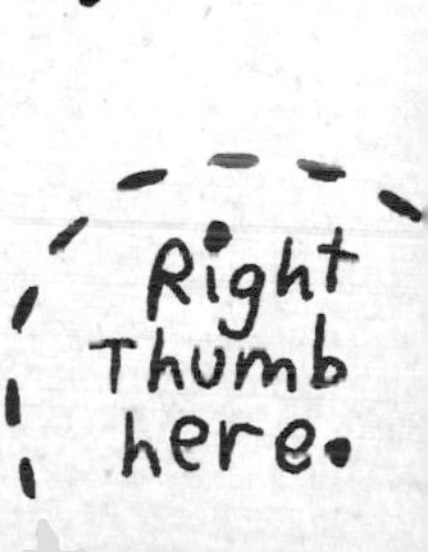
Right
Thumb
here.

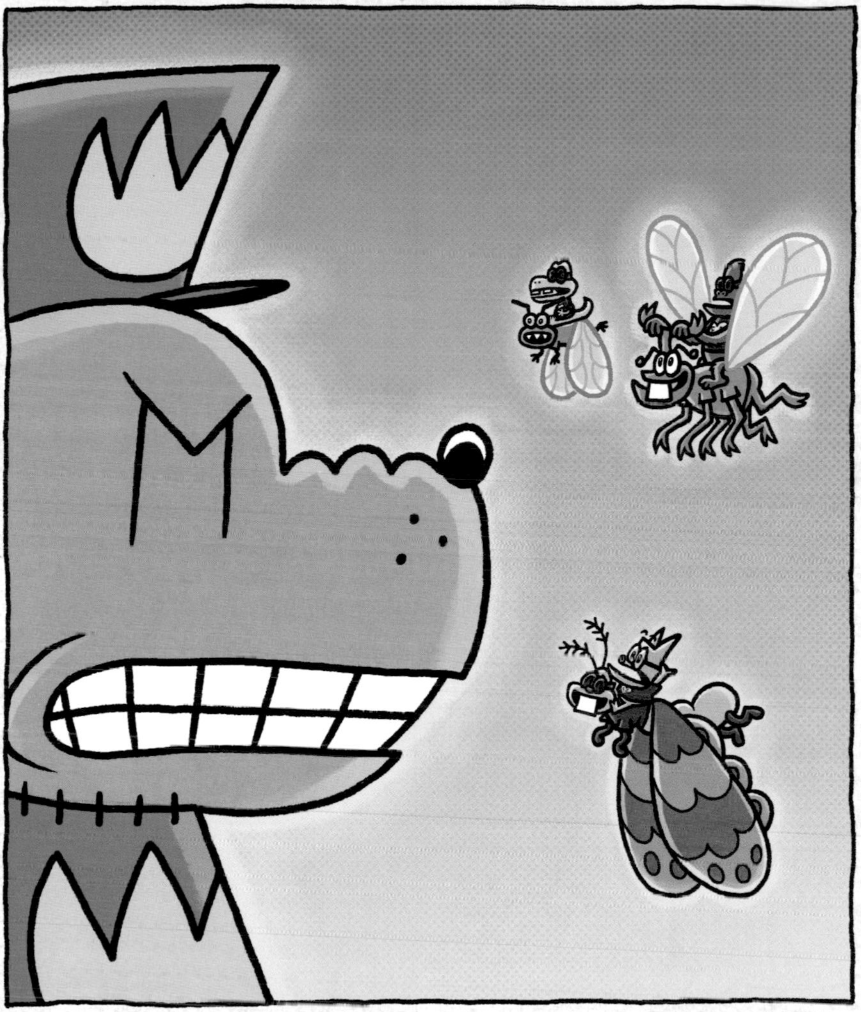

GRR-FACE A GO-GO!

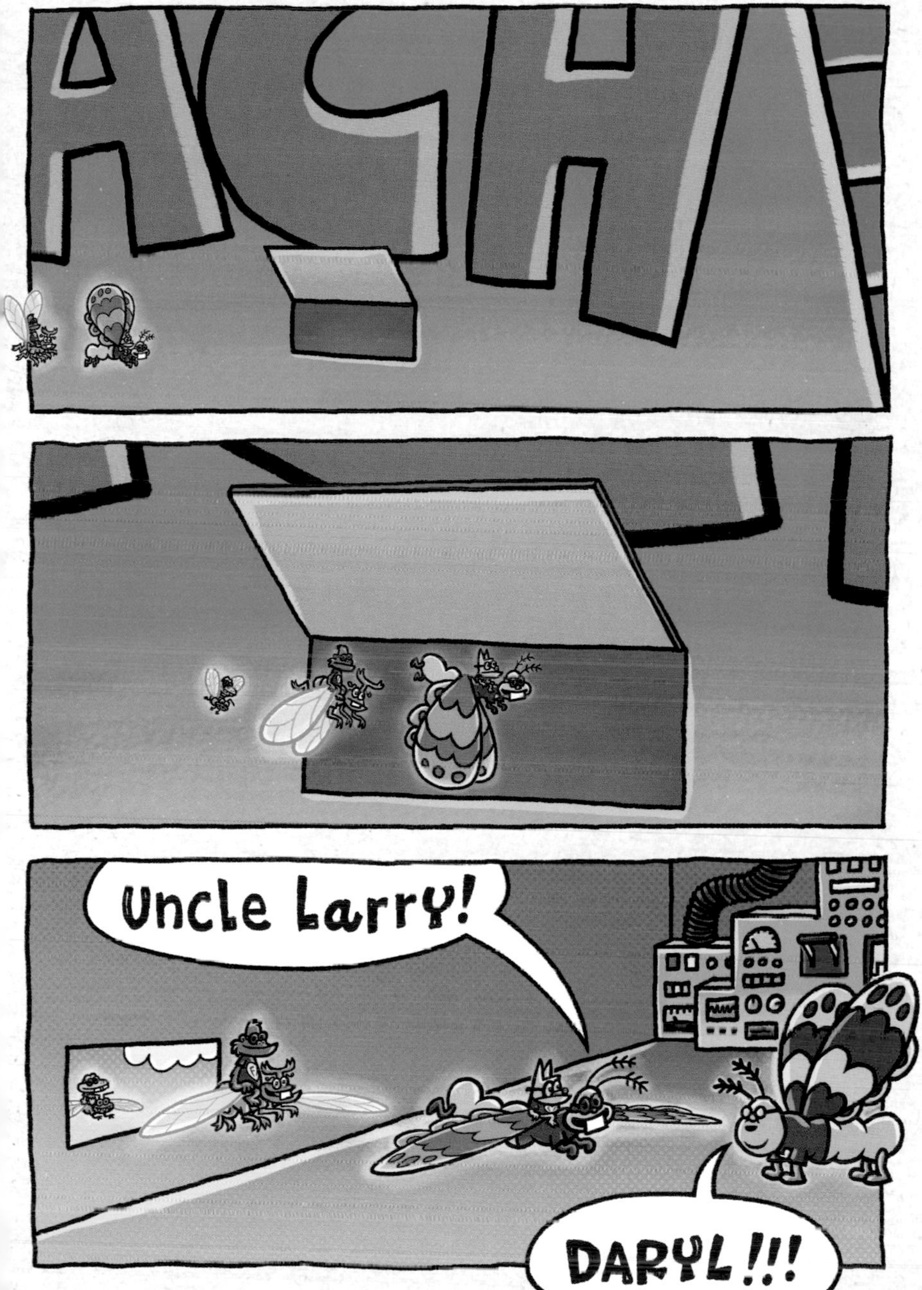
Uncle Larry!
DARYL!!!

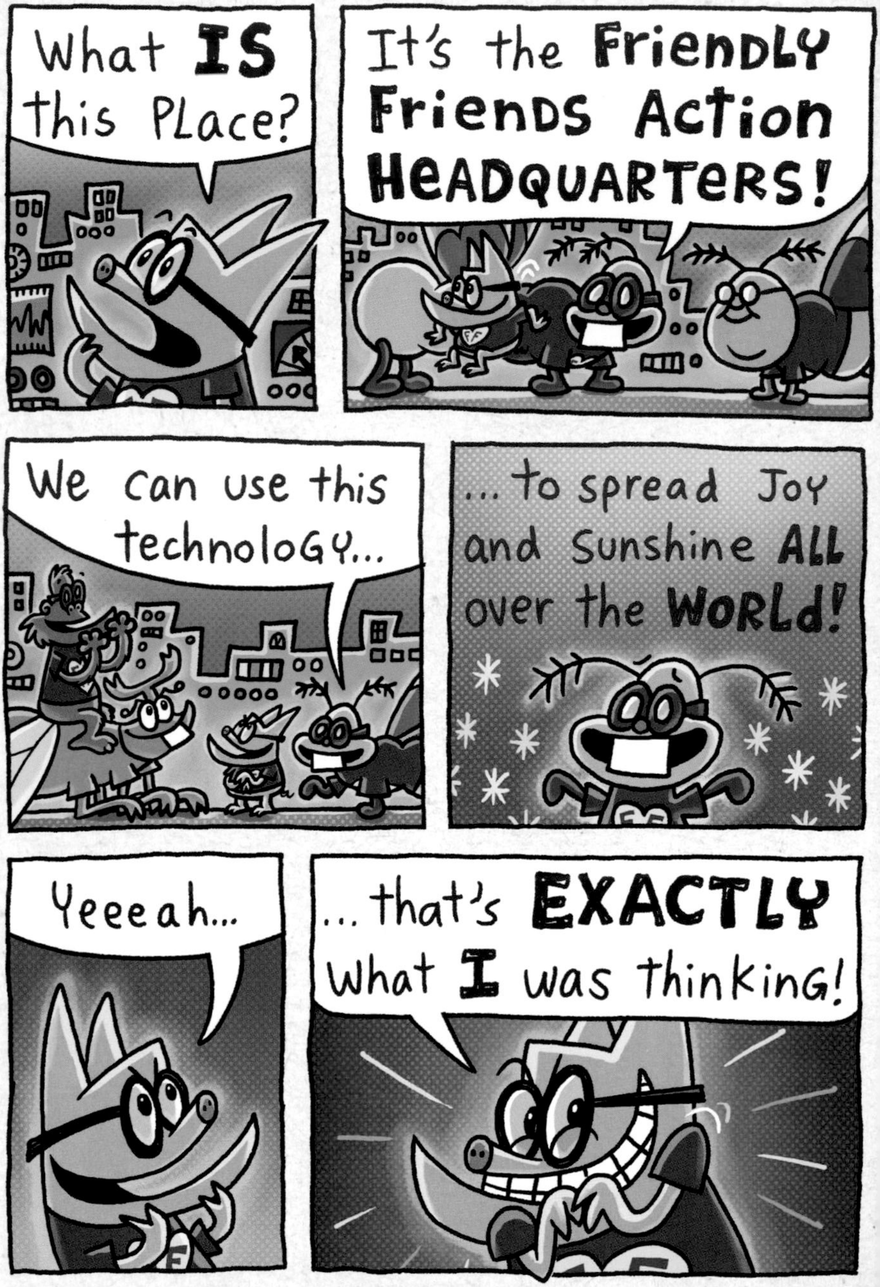
What IS this Place?
It's the FRIENDLY FRIENDS ACTION HEADQUARTERS!
We can use this technology...
... to spread Joy and Sunshine ALL over the WORLD!
Yeeeah...
... that's EXACTLY What I was thinking!

CHAPTER 7

CAT CELL CULTURE

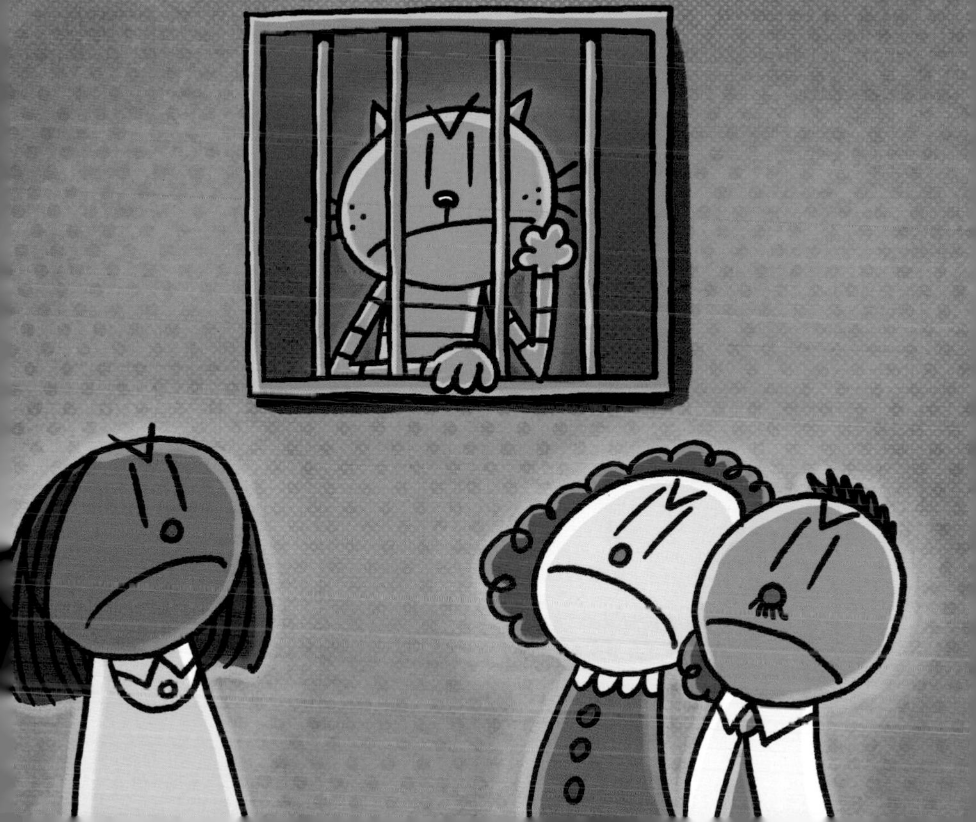

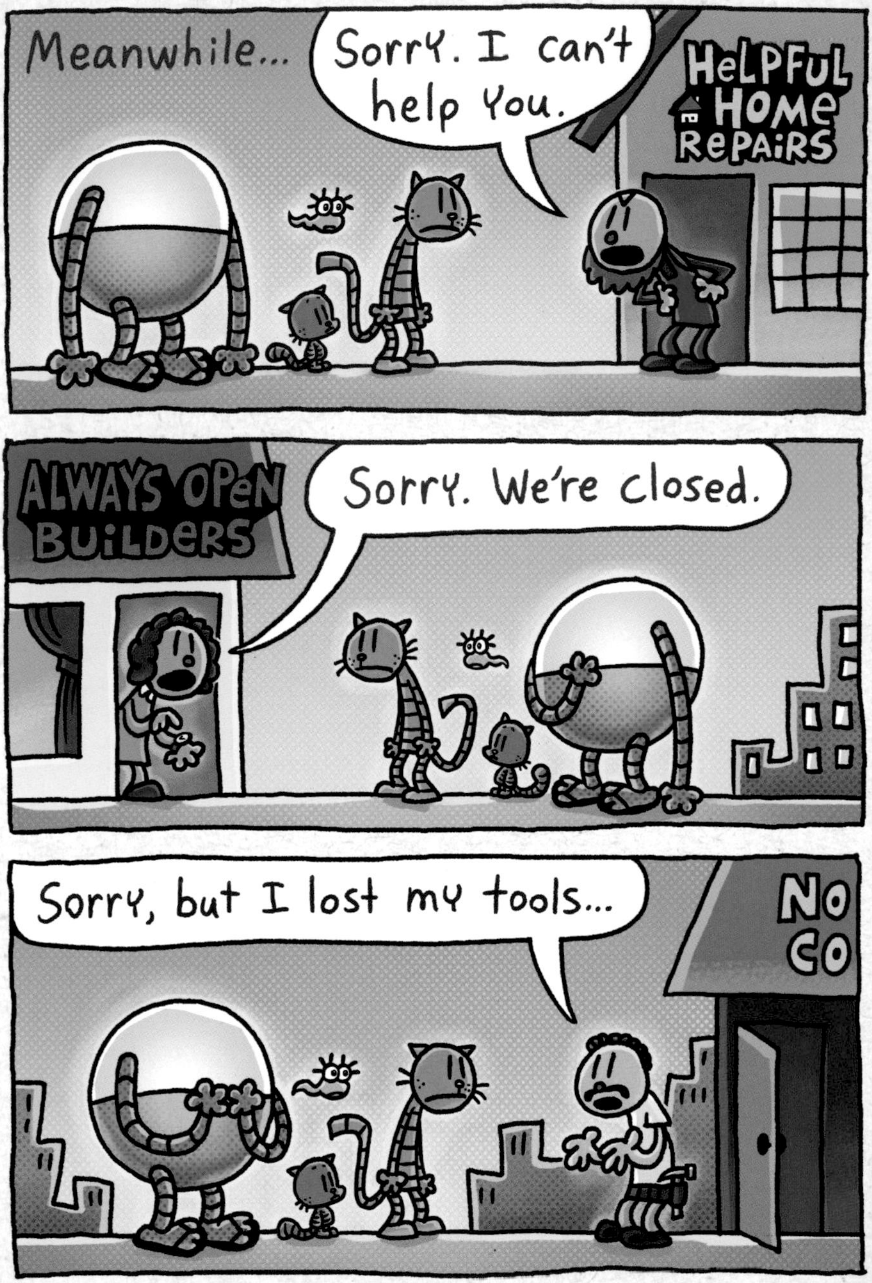
Meanwhile...
Sorry. I can't help you.
HELPFUL HOME REPAIRS
ALWAYS OPEN BUILDERS
Sorry. We're closed.
Sorry, but I lost my tools...
NO
CO

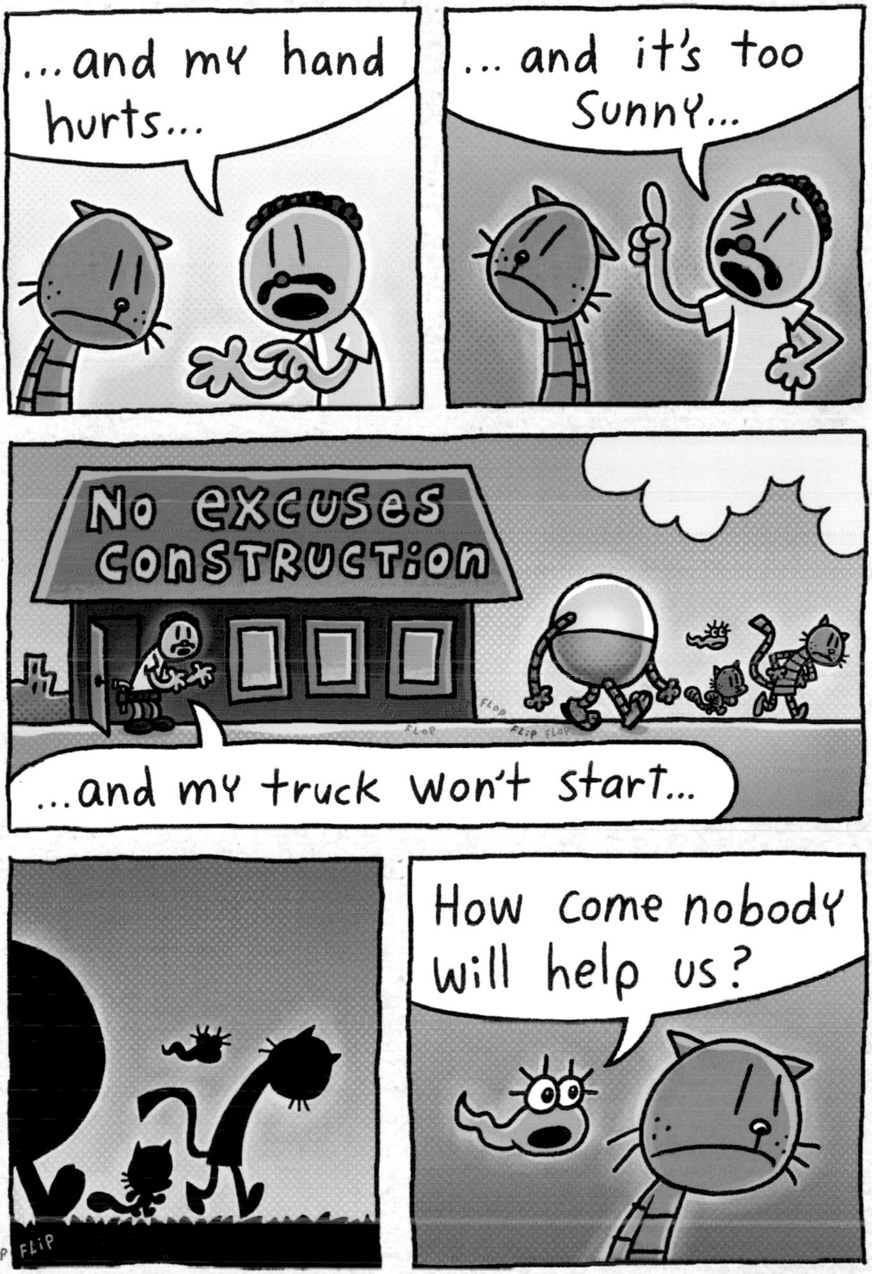
...and my hand hurts...
...and it's too Sunny...
No excuses construction
FLOP
FLIP FLOP
FLOP
...and my truck won't start...
FLIP
How come nobody will help us?

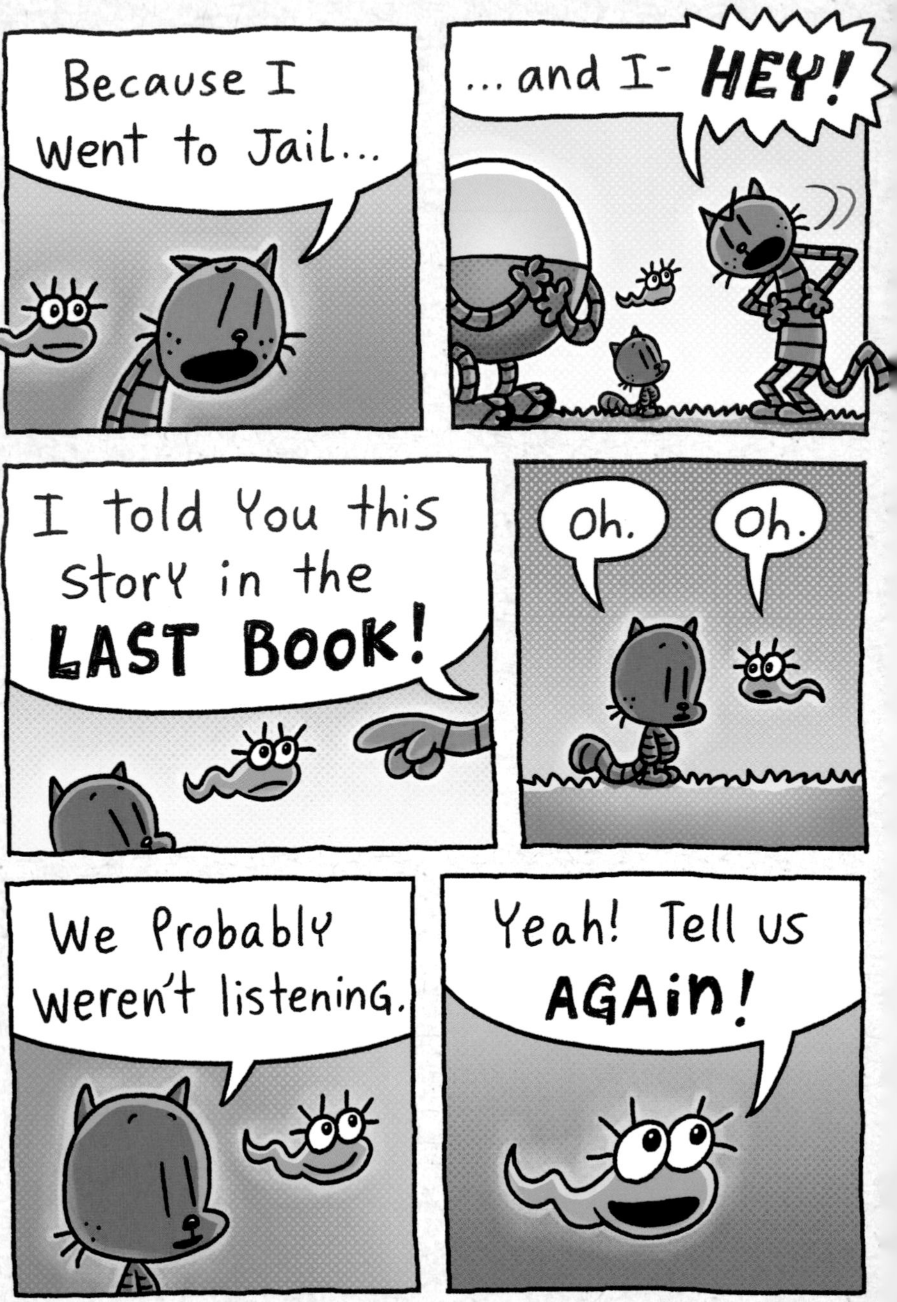
Because I went to Jail...
... and I- HEY!
I told You this story in the LAST BOOK!
Oh.
Oh.
We Probably weren't listening.
Yeah! Tell us AGAIN!

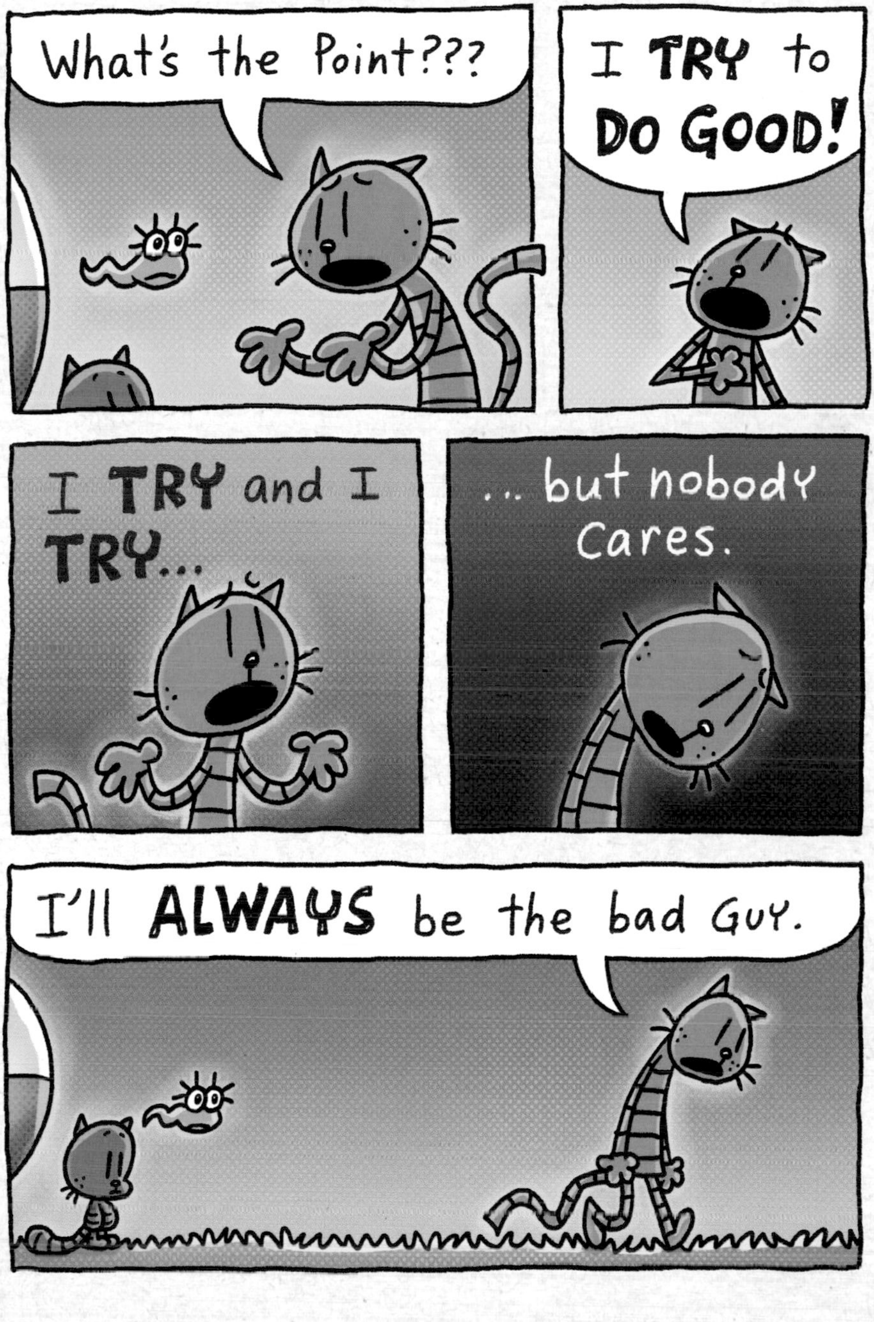
What's the Point???
I TRY to DO GOOD!
I TRY and I TRY...
... but nobody Cares.
I'll ALWAYS be the bad Guy.

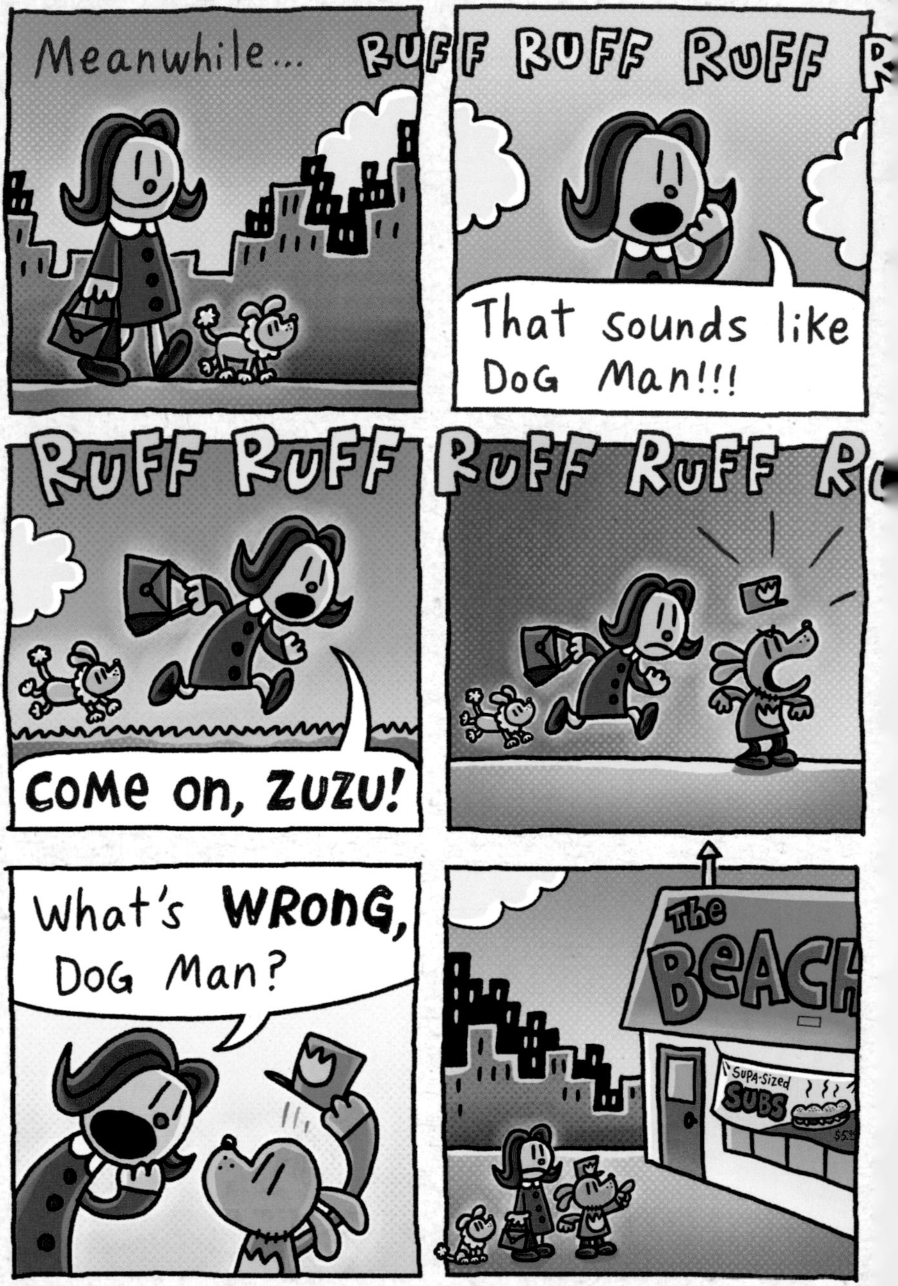
Meanwhile...
RUFF RUFF RUFF
That sounds like DOG Man!!!
RUFF RUFF RUFF RUFF
COME on, ZUZU!
What's WRONG, DOG Man?
The BEACH
SUPA-Sized SUBS

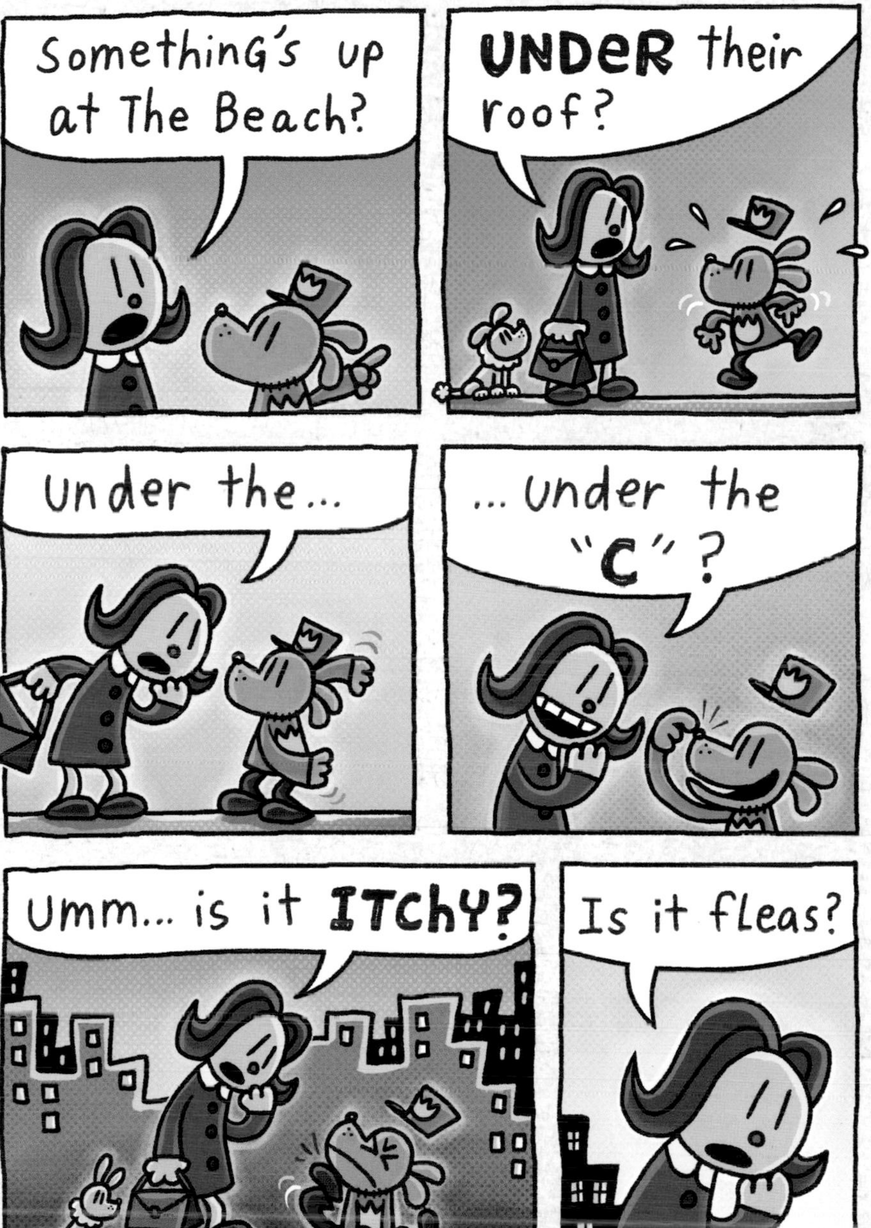
Something's up at The Beach?
UNDER their roof?
Under the...
...Under the "C"?
Umm... is it ITCHY?
Is it fleas?

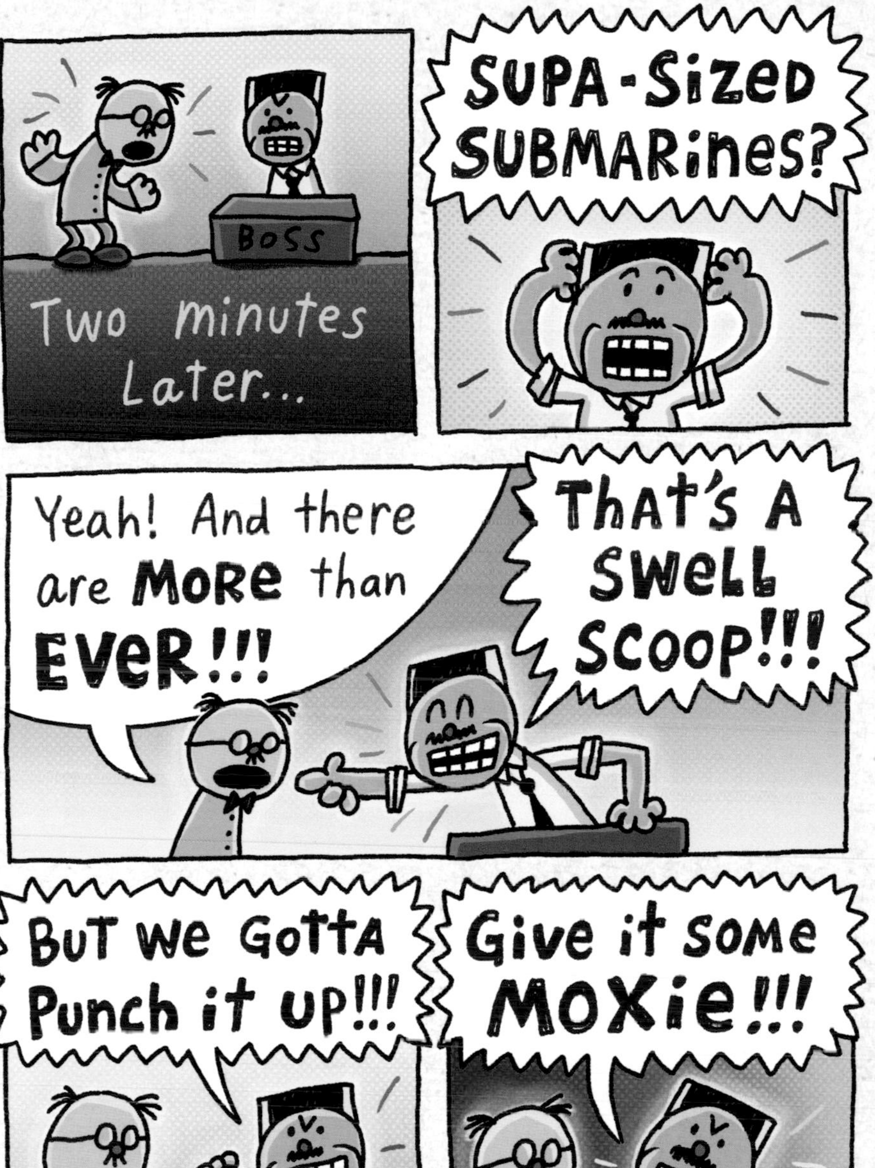
Two minutes Later...
SUPA-Sized SUBMARines?
Yeah! And there are MORE than EVER!!!
That's A SWELL SCOOP!!!
BUT WE GOTTA Punch it UP!!!
Give it SOME MOXie!!!

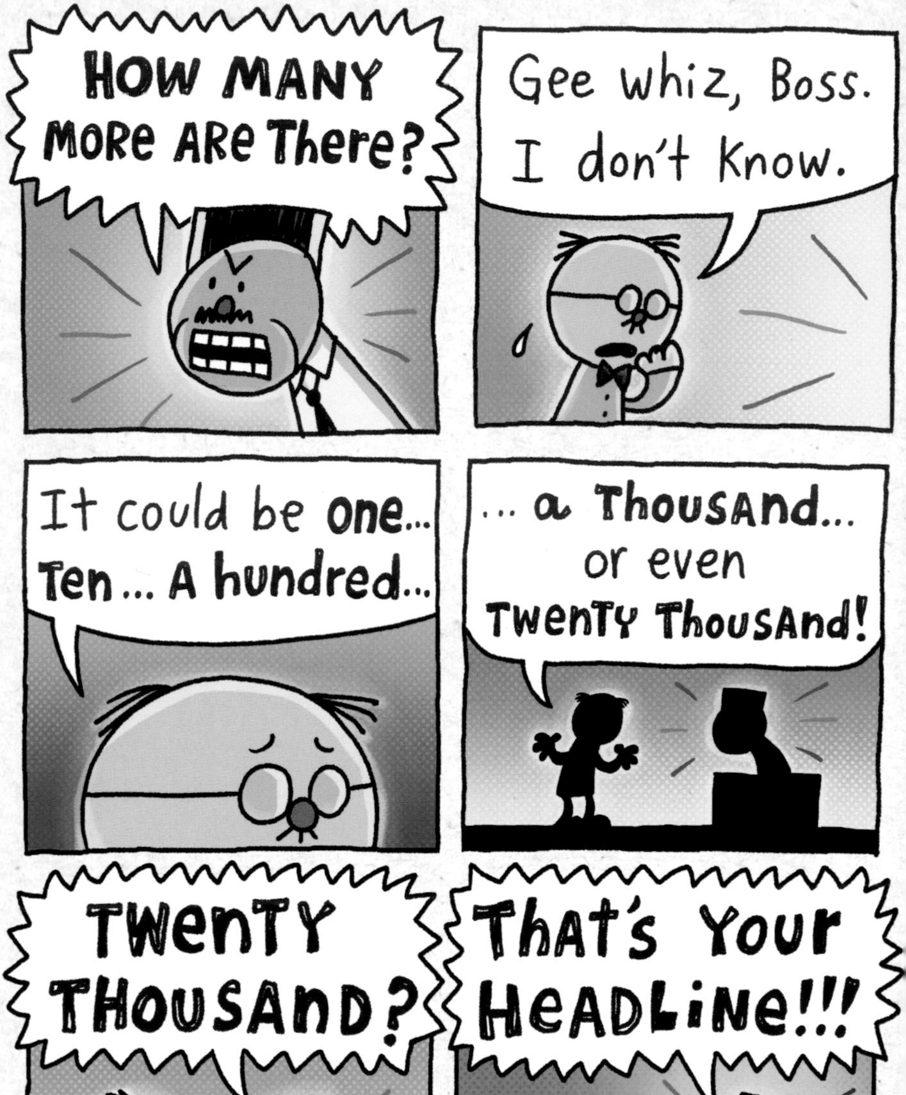

124

TWENTY THOUSAND FLEAS UNDER THE SEA!!!

NOW GO WRITE ME A STORY I CAN SINK MY CHOPPERS INTO!!!

BAM

OKay, but...

...those **NUMBERS** miGht not be true.

BOSS

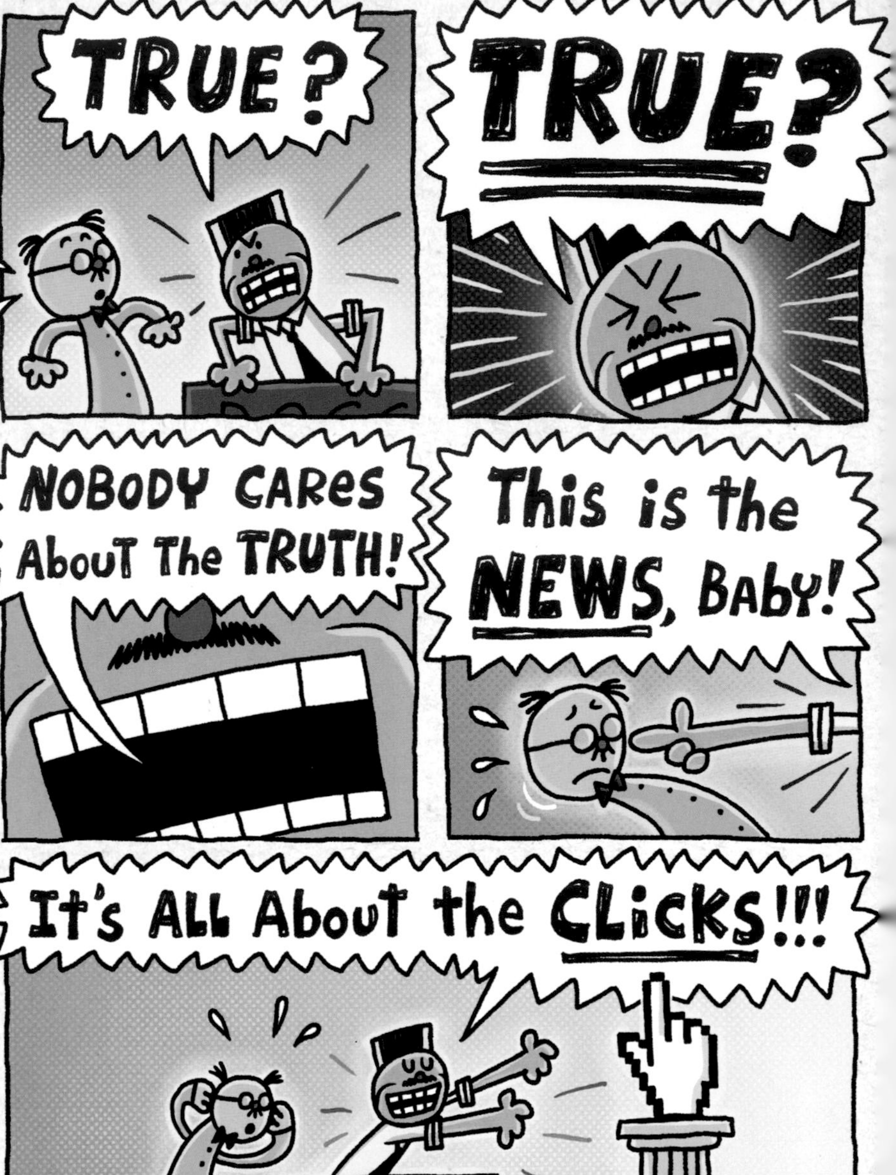

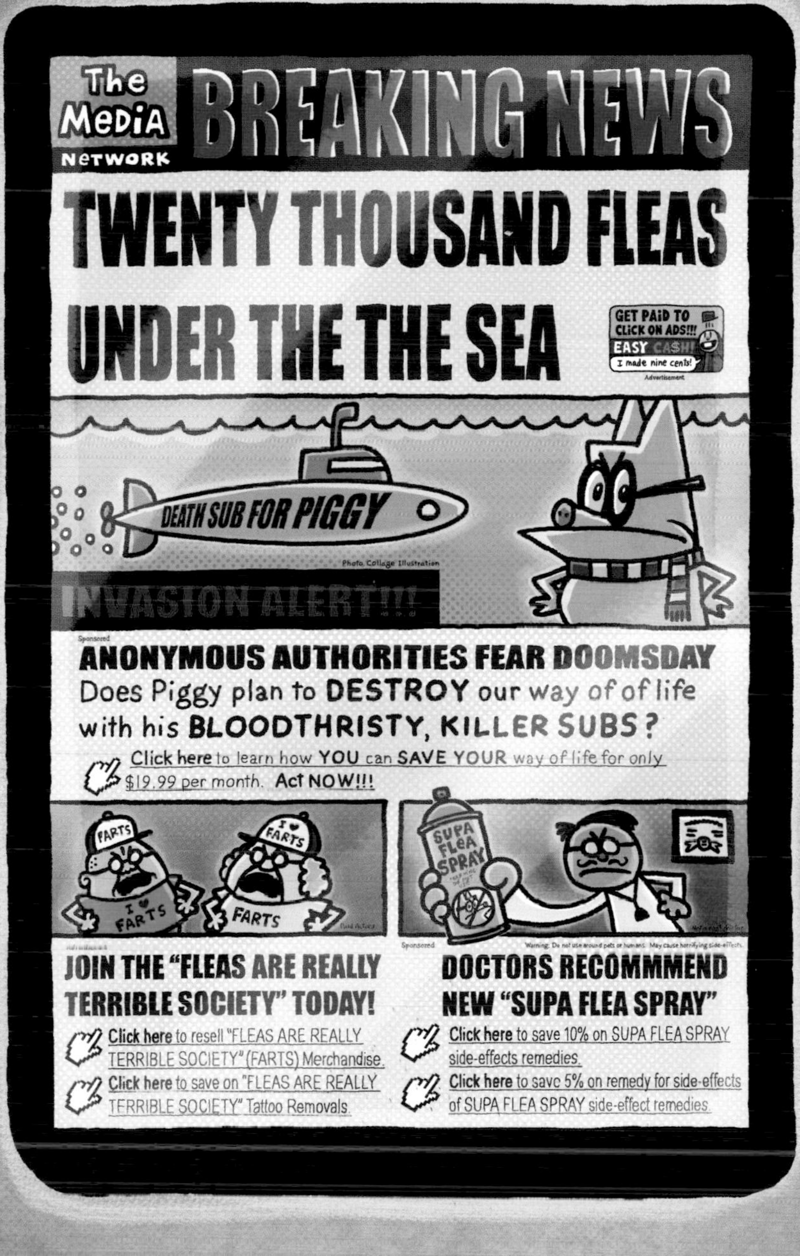

ChaPTeR 8

The MeDiA NeTwork — BREAKING NEWS

TWENTY THOUSAND FLEAS
UNDER THE THE SEA

DEATH SUB FOR PIGGY

Photo Collage Illustration

INVASION ALERT!!!

ANONYMOUS AUTHORITIES FEAR DOOMSDAY

Does Piggy plan to **DESTROY** our way of of life with his **BLOODTHRISTY, KILLER SUBS?**

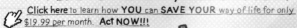 **Click here** to learn how **YOU** can **SAVE YOUR** way of life for only $19.99 per month. **Act NOW!!!**

JOIN THE "FLEAS ARE REALLY TERRIBLE SOCIETY" TODAY!

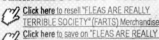 **Click here** to resell "FLEAS ARE REALLY TERRIBLE SOCIETY" (FARTS) Merchandise.

Click here to save on "FLEAS ARE REALLY TERRIBLE SOCIETY" Tattoo Removals.

DOCTORS RECOMMEND NEW "SUPA FLEA SPRAY"

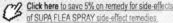 **Click here** to save 10% on SUPA FLEA SPRAY side-effects remedies.

Click here to save 5% on remedy for side-effects of SUPA FLEA SPRAY side-effect remedies.

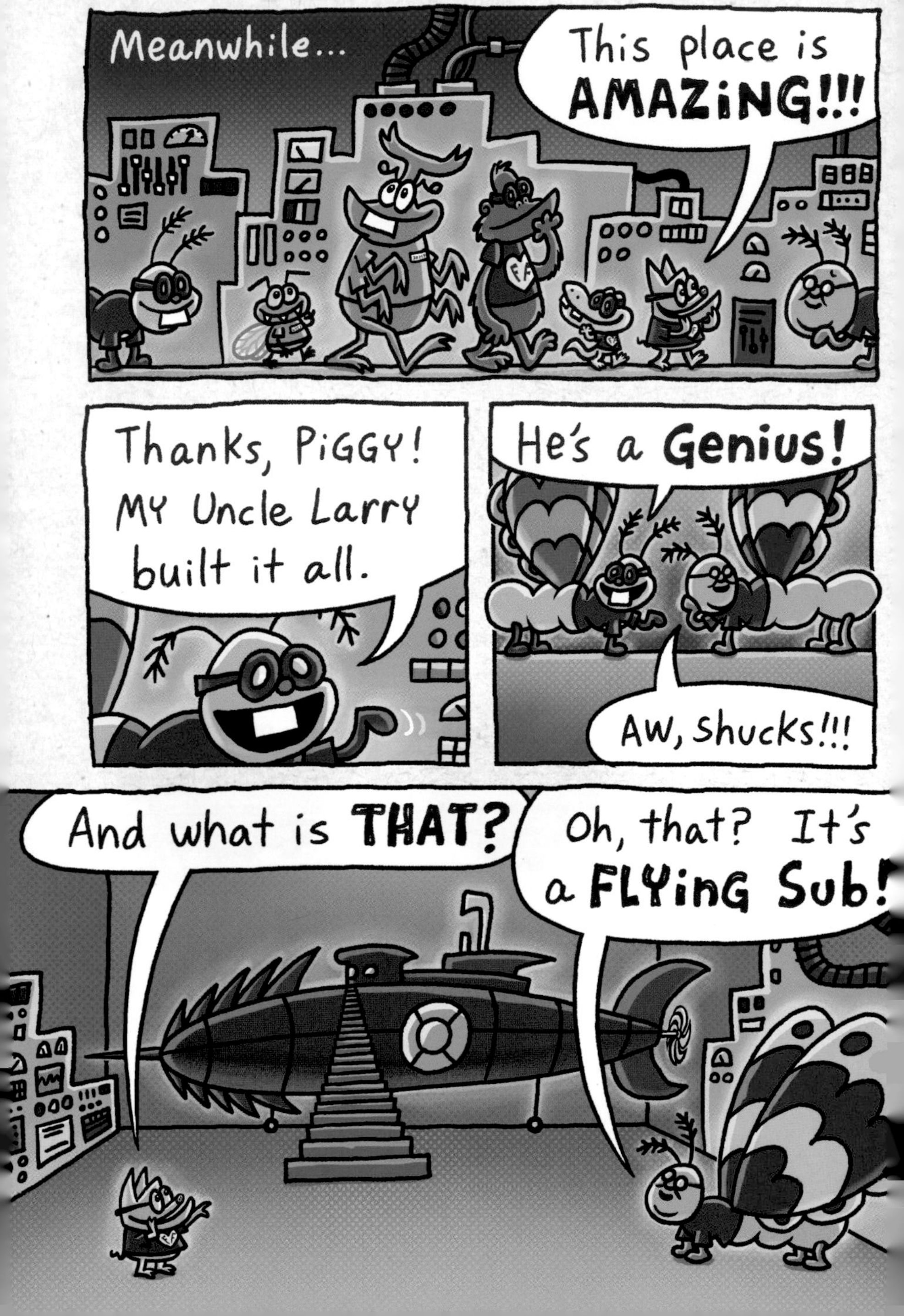
Meanwhile...
This place is AMAZiNG!!!
Thanks, PiGGY! MY Uncle Larry built it all.
He's a Genius!
AW, Shucks!!!
And what is THAT?
Oh, that? It's a FLYinG Sub!

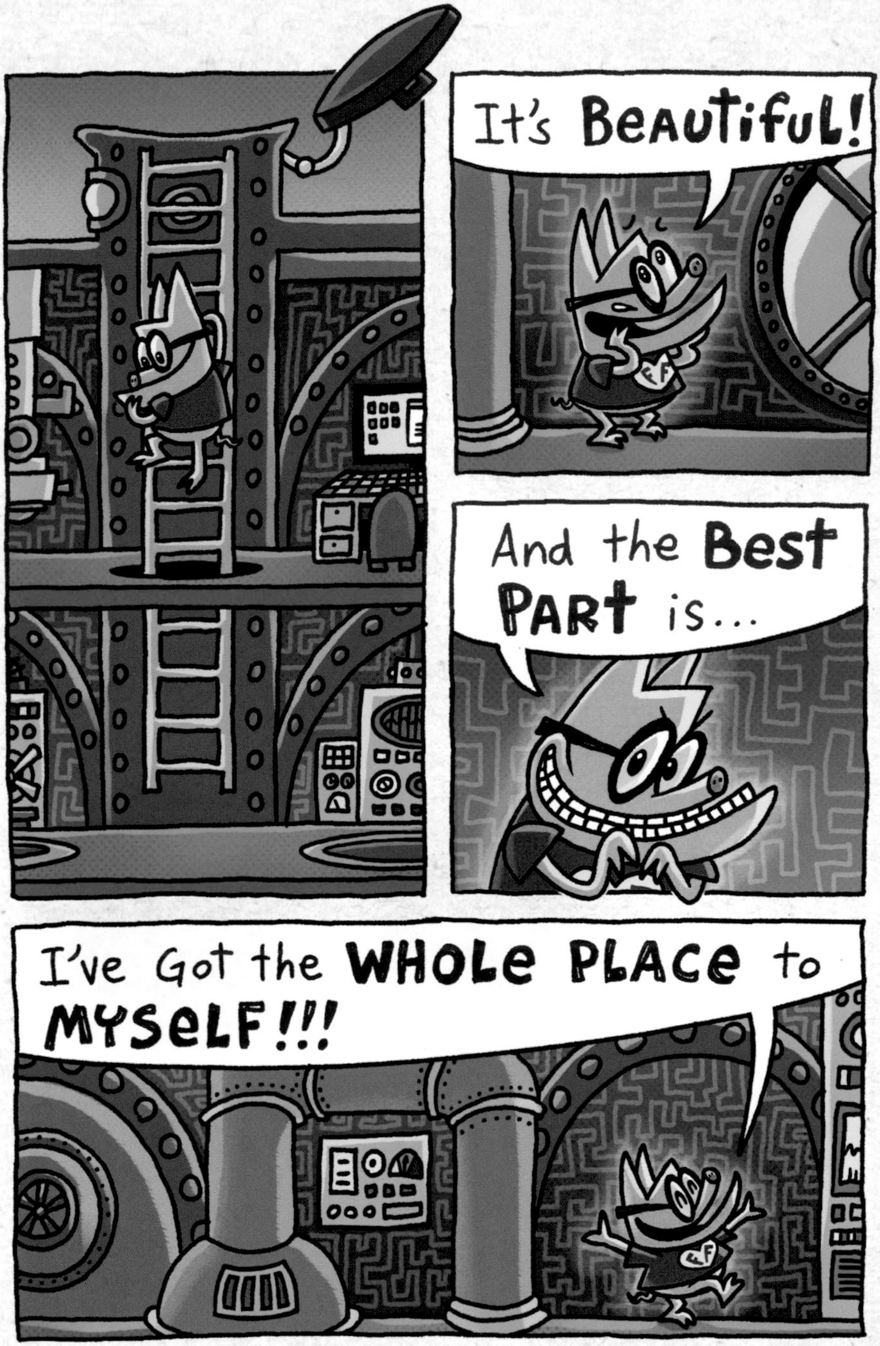
It's BEAUTIFUL!
And the Best PART is...
I've Got the WHOLE PLACE to MYSELF!!!

Don't worry, PiGGY...

...Watch **this!!!**

Our built-in **Size-O-Tron** can make this sub **SHRiNK!!!**

K·A·KLUNK

SUB WILL SHRINK IN FIVE SECONDS...

...FOUR...

...THREE...

... TWO ...

... ONE ...

SHRINKING NOW

And so...

SUPA-Sized SUBS
$5.99

Nice Job, Uncle Larry!!!

Aw, shucks!

Now can You make us Grow **SUPA BiG?**

I Sure can!!!

Size -O- TRON

SUPA DOOPA BiG
SUPA BiG
BiG
NORMAL
SMALL
SMALL

KA KLUNK

SUB WILL GROW IN FIVE SECONDS...

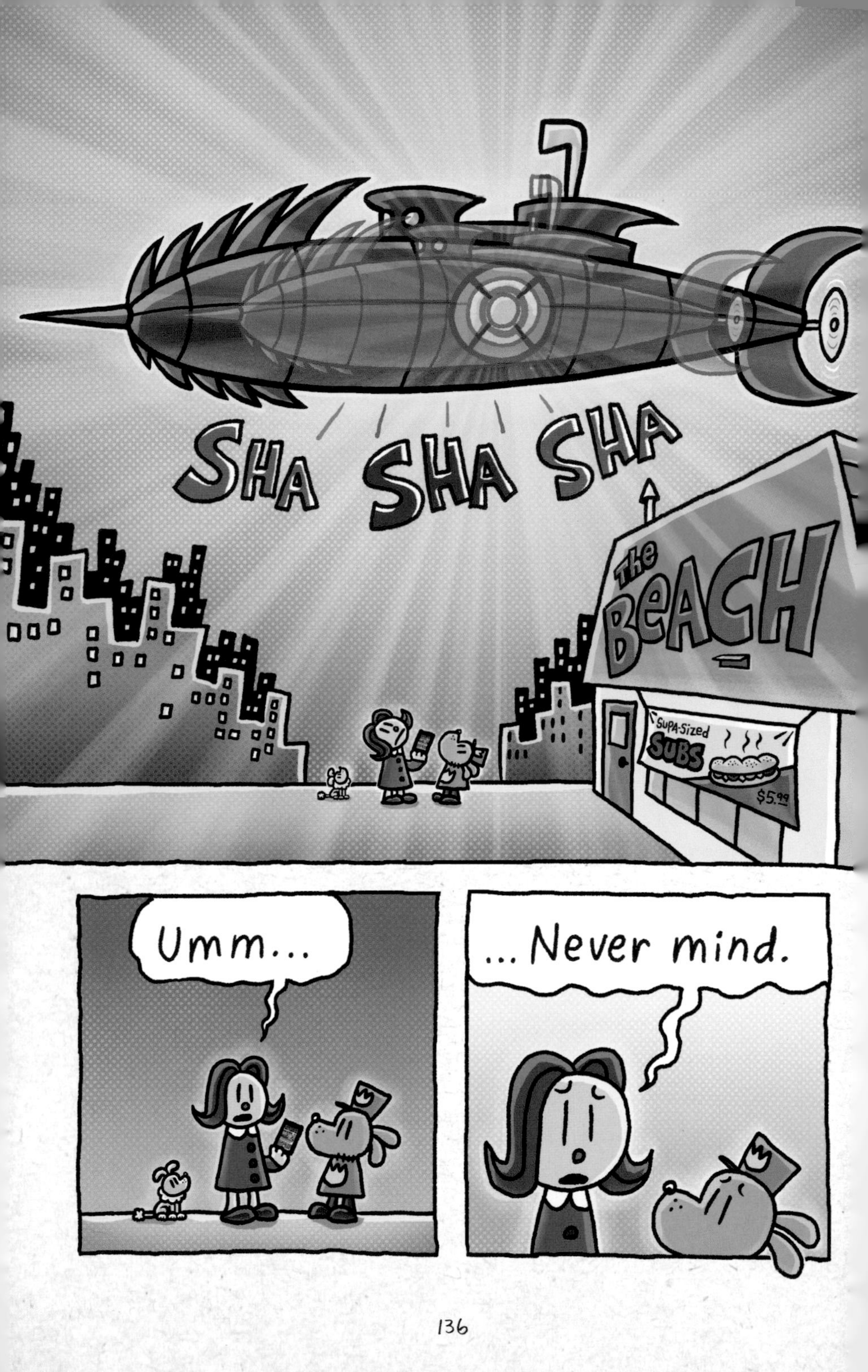
SHA SHA SHA
The BEACH
SUPA-Sized SUBS
$5.99
Umm...
...Never mind.

CHAPTER 9

FOLLOW THAT SUB

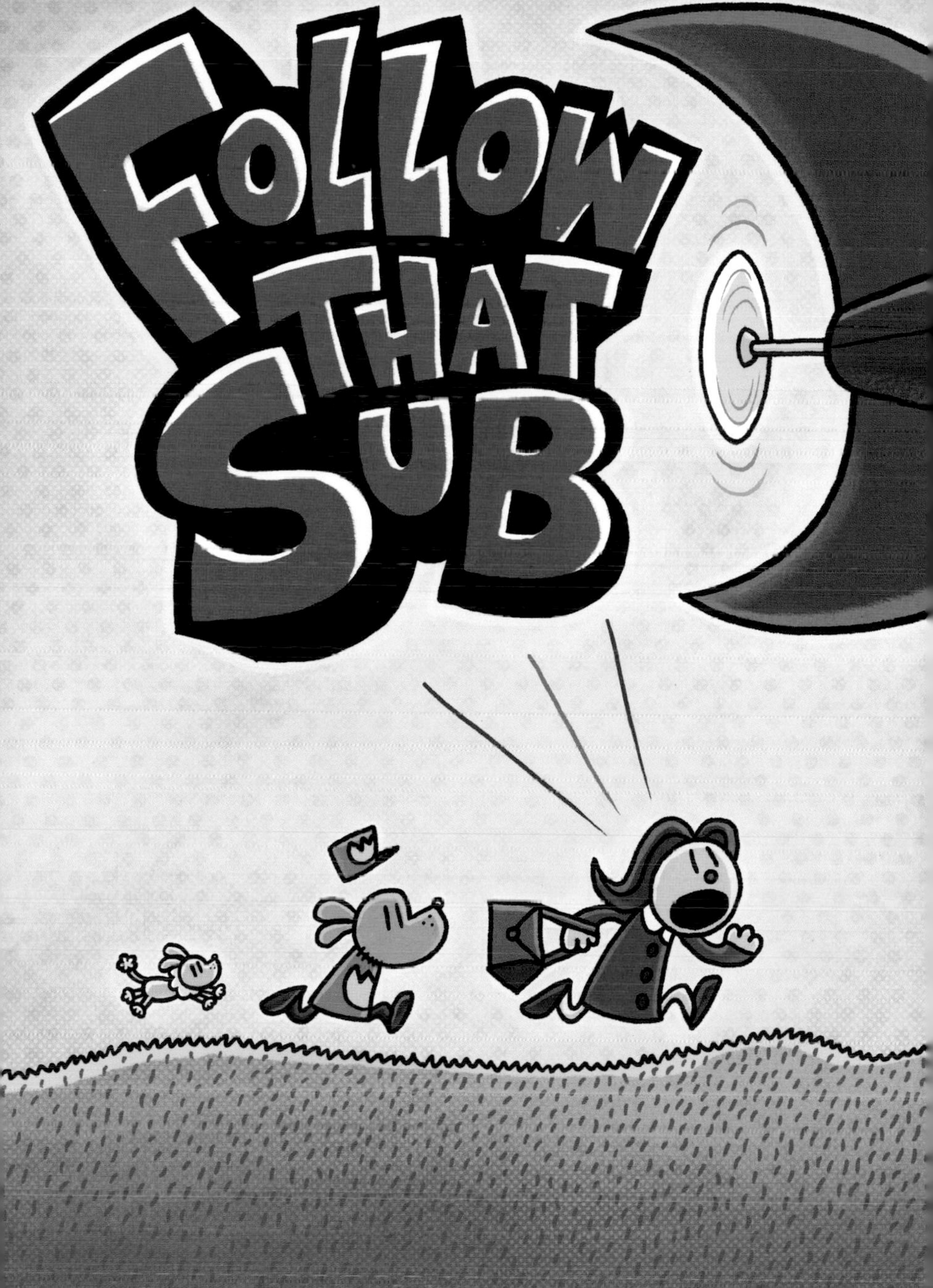

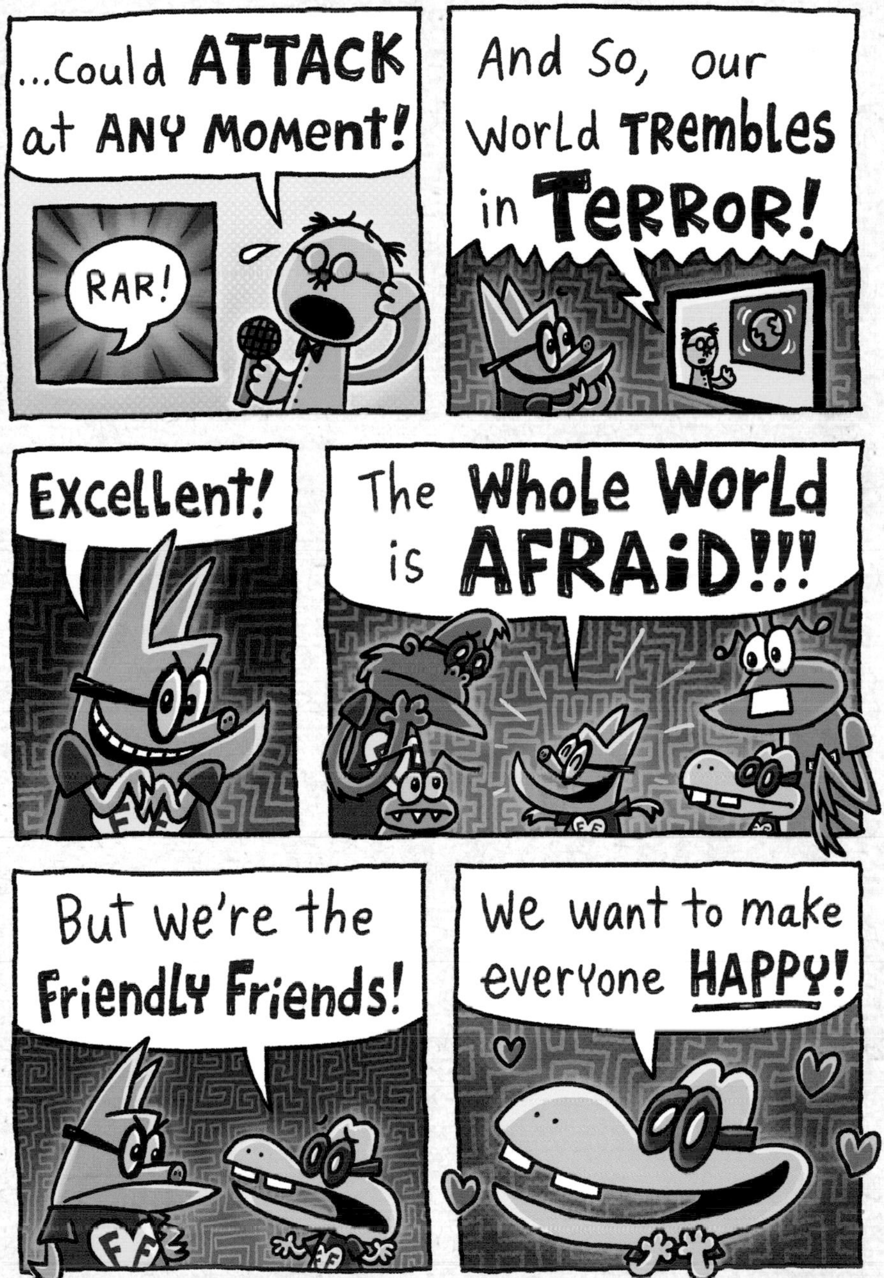
...Could ATTACK at ANY MOMENT!
RAR!
And So, our World TREMBLES in TERROR!
Excellent!
The Whole World is AFRAID!!!
But we're the Friendly Friends!
We want to make everyone HAPPY!

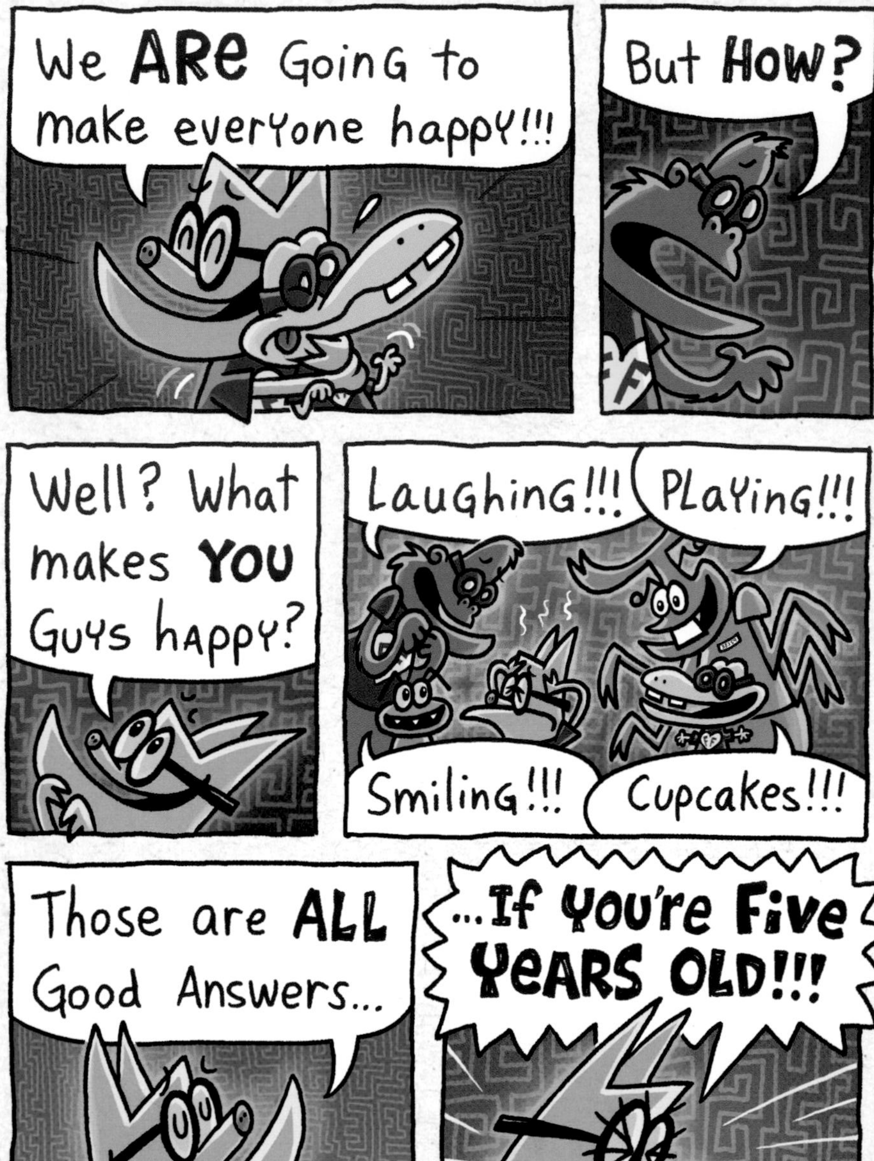

We **ARE** Going to make everyone happy!!!
But **HOW?**
Well? What makes **YOU** Guys happy?
Laughing!!!
Playing!!!
Smiling!!!
Cupcakes!!!
Those are **ALL** Good Answers...
...If You're Five Years OLD!!!

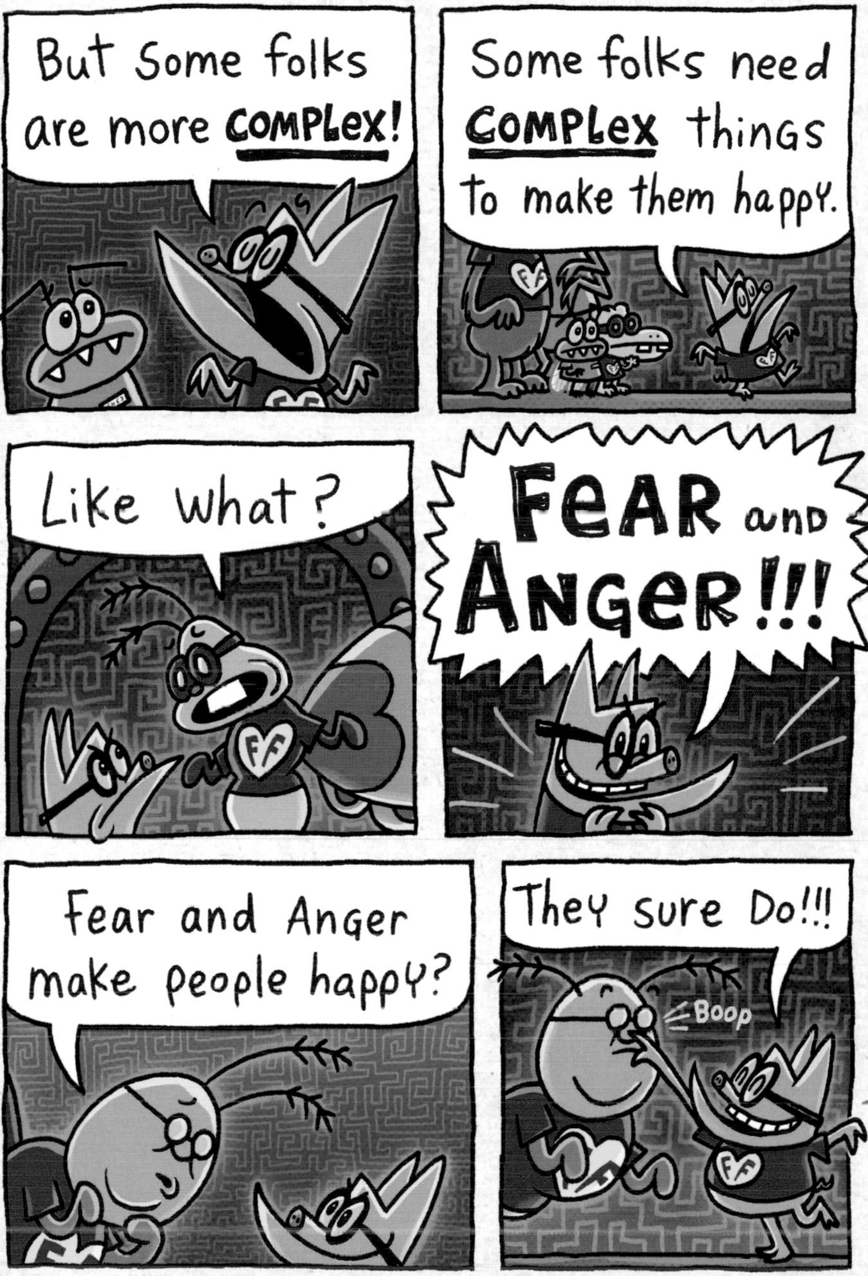
But some folks are more COMPLEX!
Some folks need COMPLEX things to make them happy.
Like what?
FEAR and ANGER!!!
Fear and Anger make people happy?
They sure Do!!!
Boop

FEAR and ANGER trigger DOPAMINE Receptors in the BRAIN...

...And **THAT** makes People **HAPPY!**

We've **ALREADY SCARED** them...

Now we need to make them **MAD!**

But **HOW?**

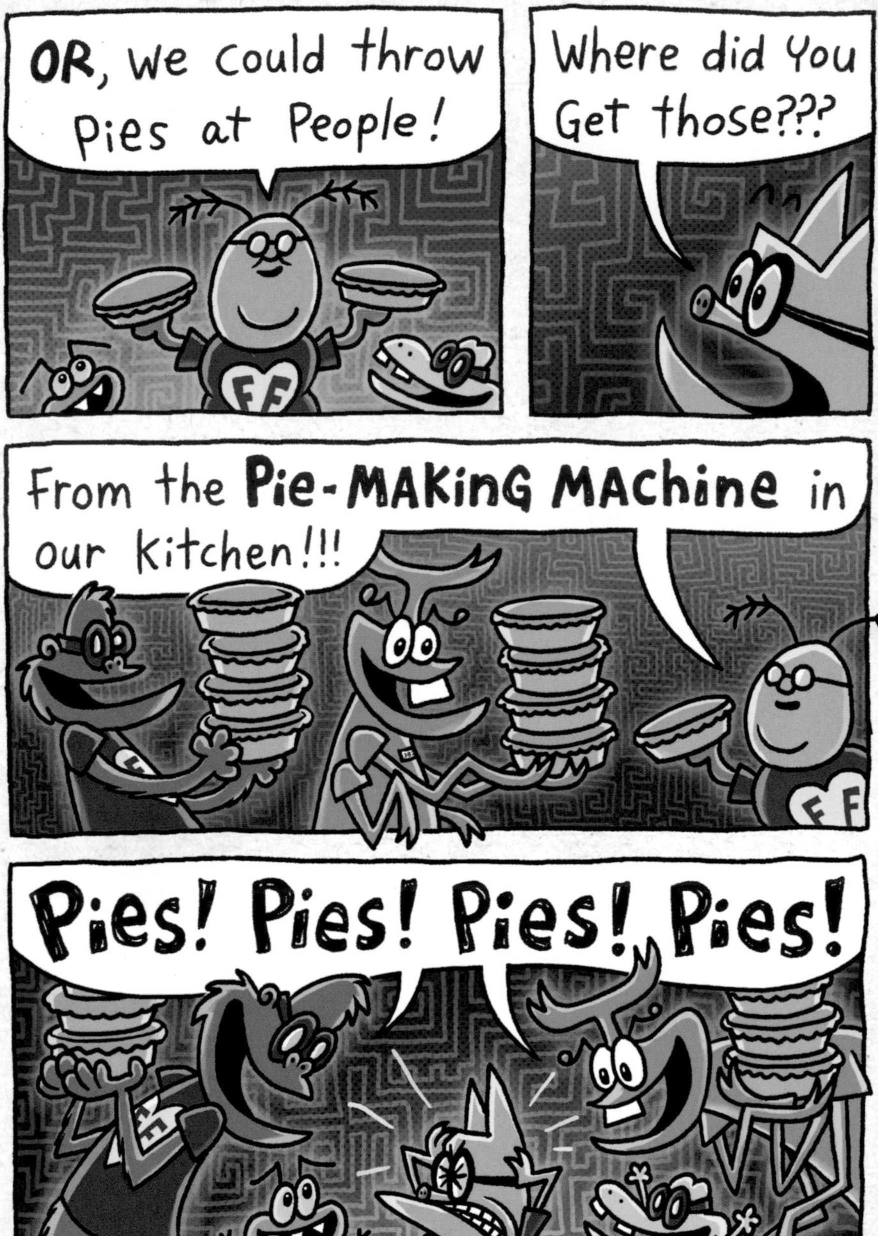
OR, we could throw pies at people!
Where did you get those???
From the Pie-MAKING MACHINE in our kitchen!!!
Pies! Pies! Pies! Pies!

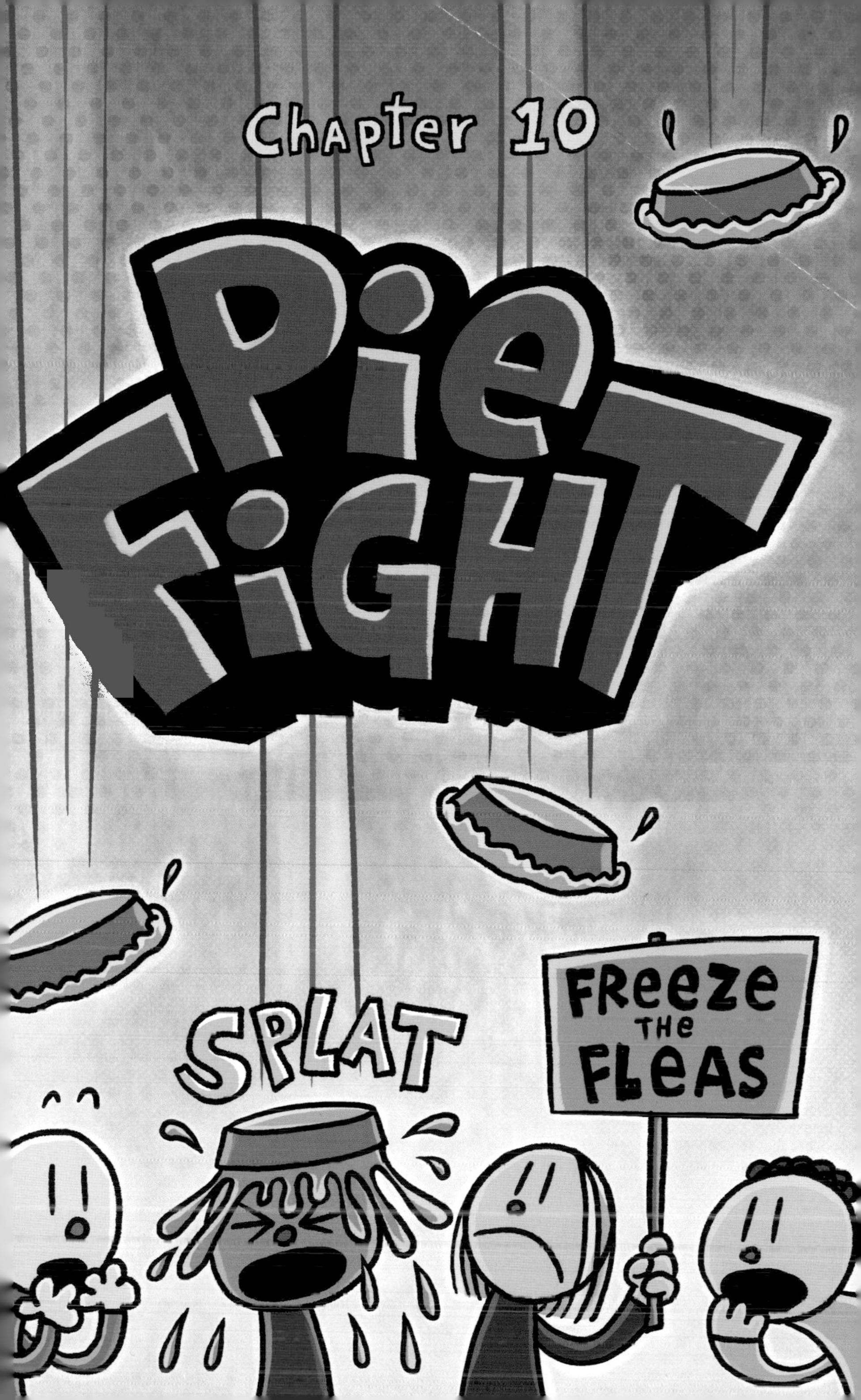
Chapter 10
Pie Fight
SPLAT
Freeze the FLEAS

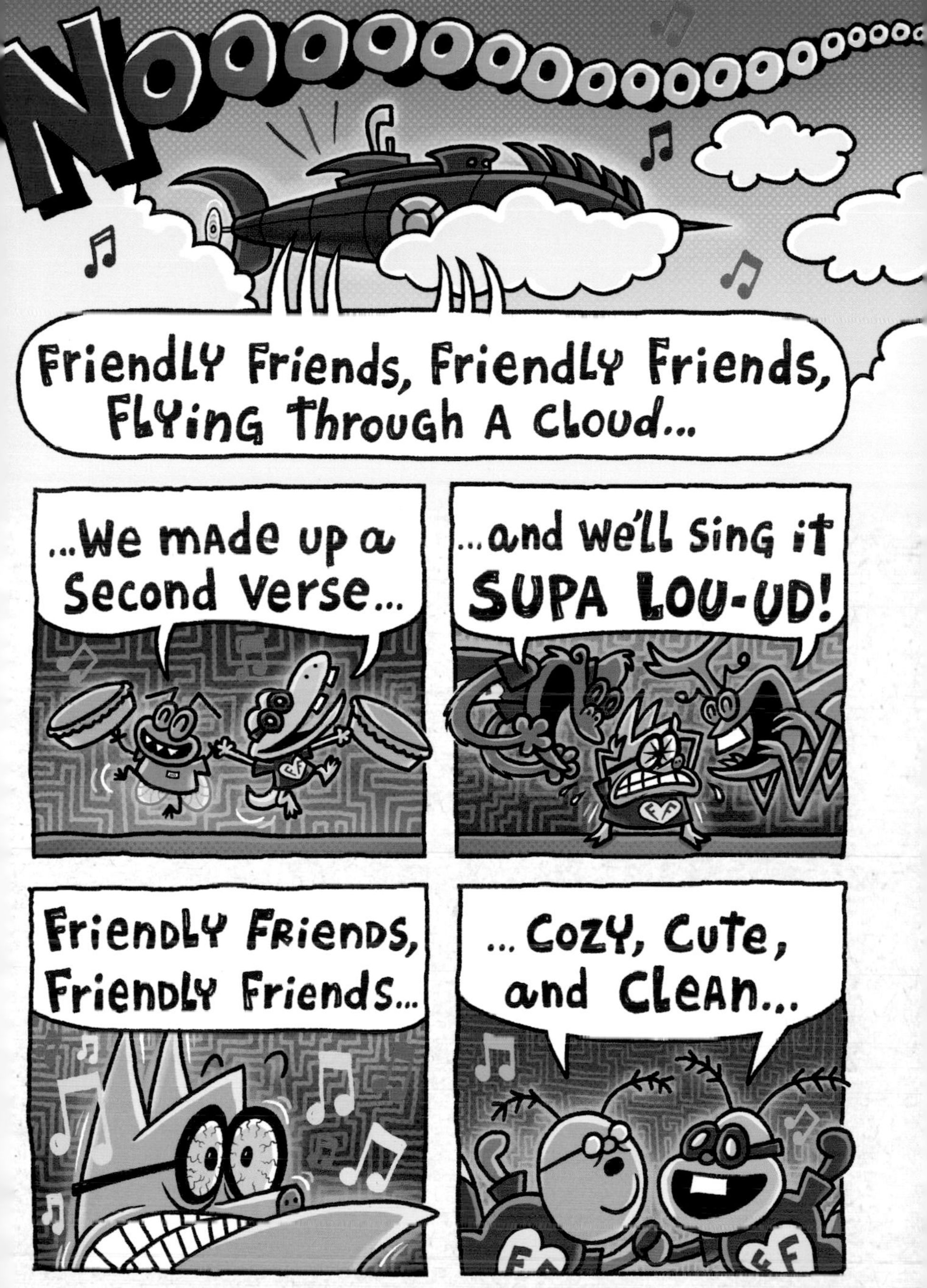
NOOOOOOOOOOOOOOOOOOOOOOO
Friendly Friends, Friendly Friends, Flying through a cloud...
...We made up a second verse...
...and we'll sing it SUPA LOU-UD!
Friendly Friends, Friendly Friends...
...Cozy, Cute, and Clean...

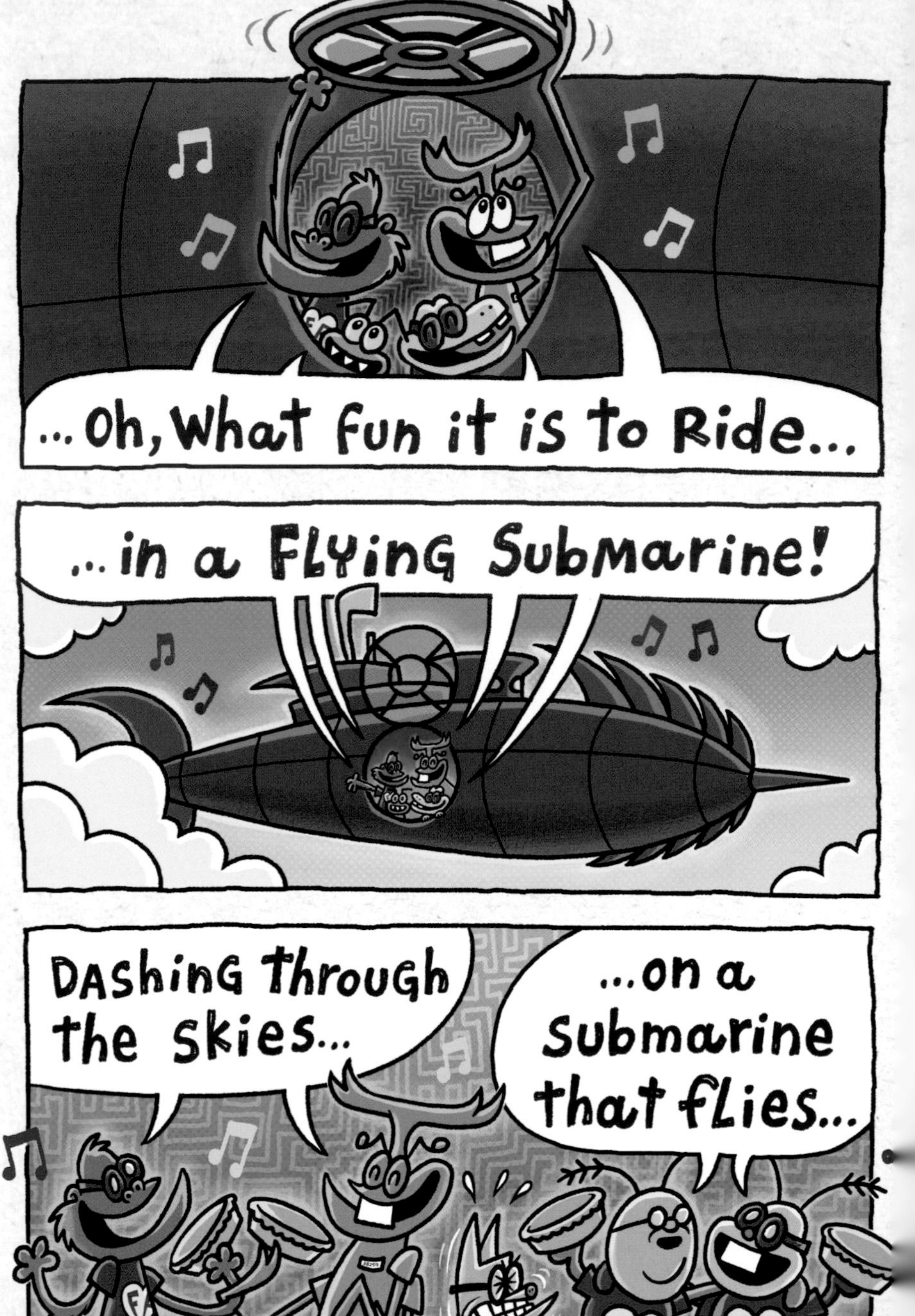
...Oh, What fun it is to Ride...
...in a FLYING Submarine!
DASHING Through the Skies...
...on a Submarine that fLies...

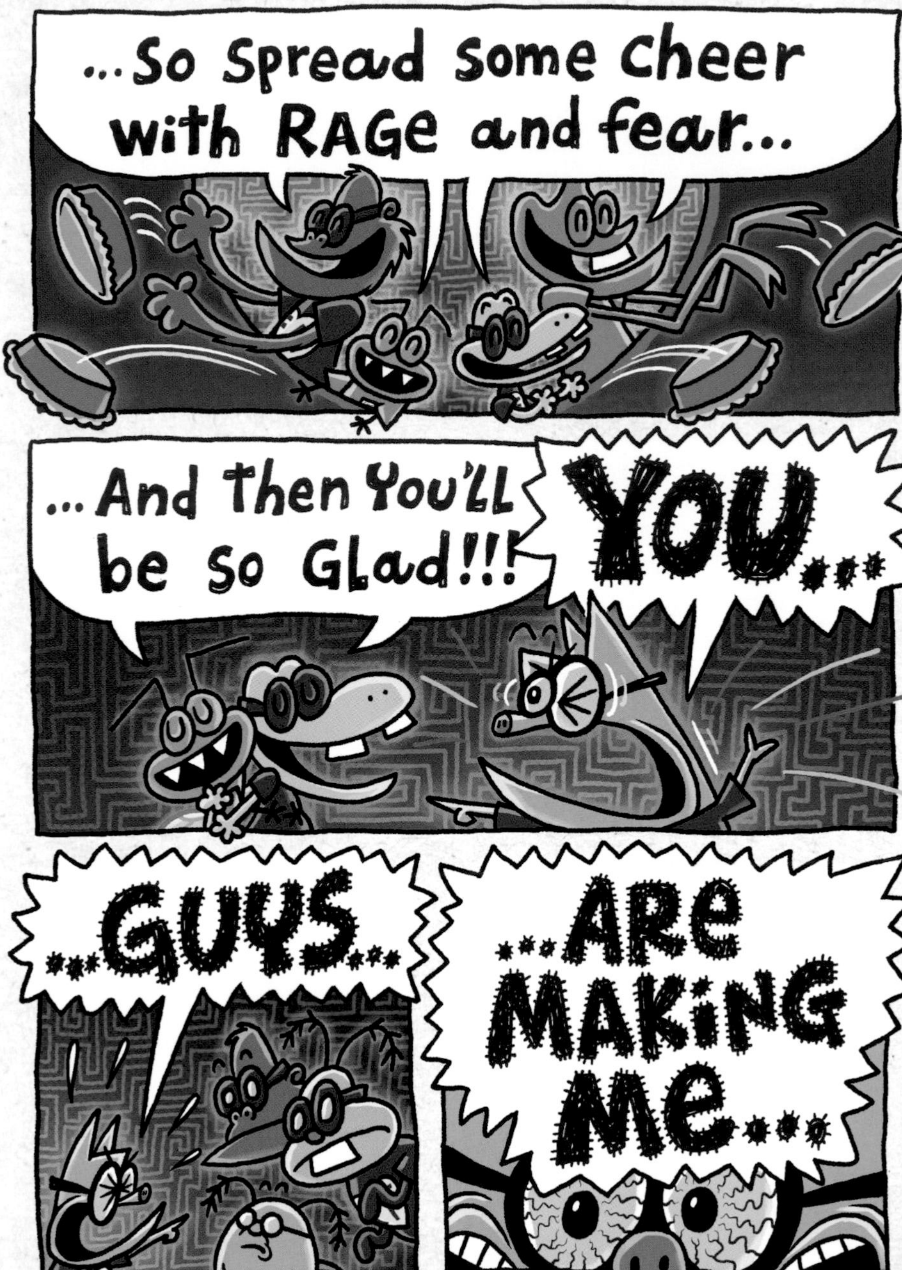
...So Spread some cheer with RAGE and fear...
...And Then You'll be so Glad!!!
YOU...
...GUYS...
...ARE MAKING ME...

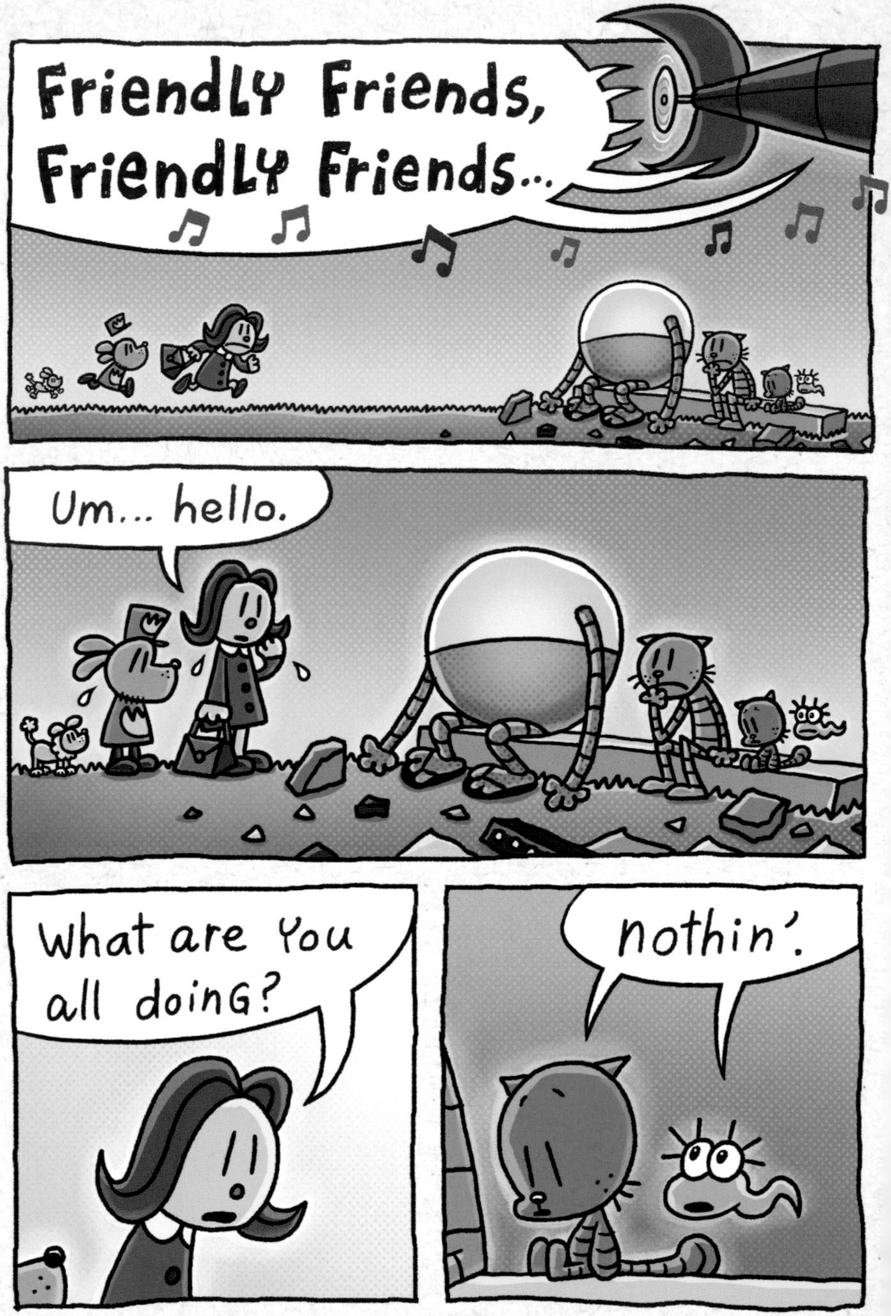

Friendly Friends, Friendly Friends...
Um... hello.
What are you all doing?
nothin'.

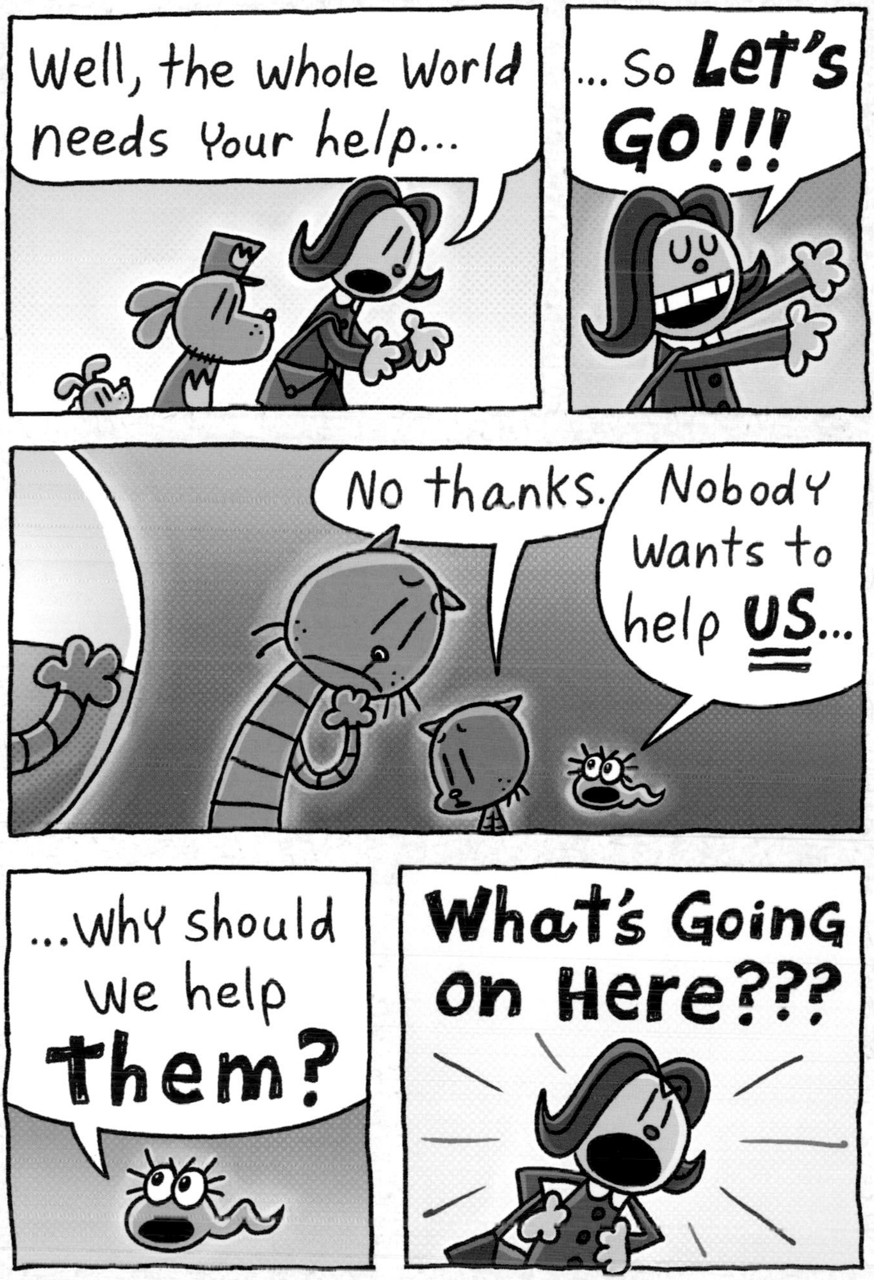
Well, the whole world needs your help...
...So Let's GO!!!
No thanks.
Nobody wants to help US...
...Why should we help them?
What's Going on Here???

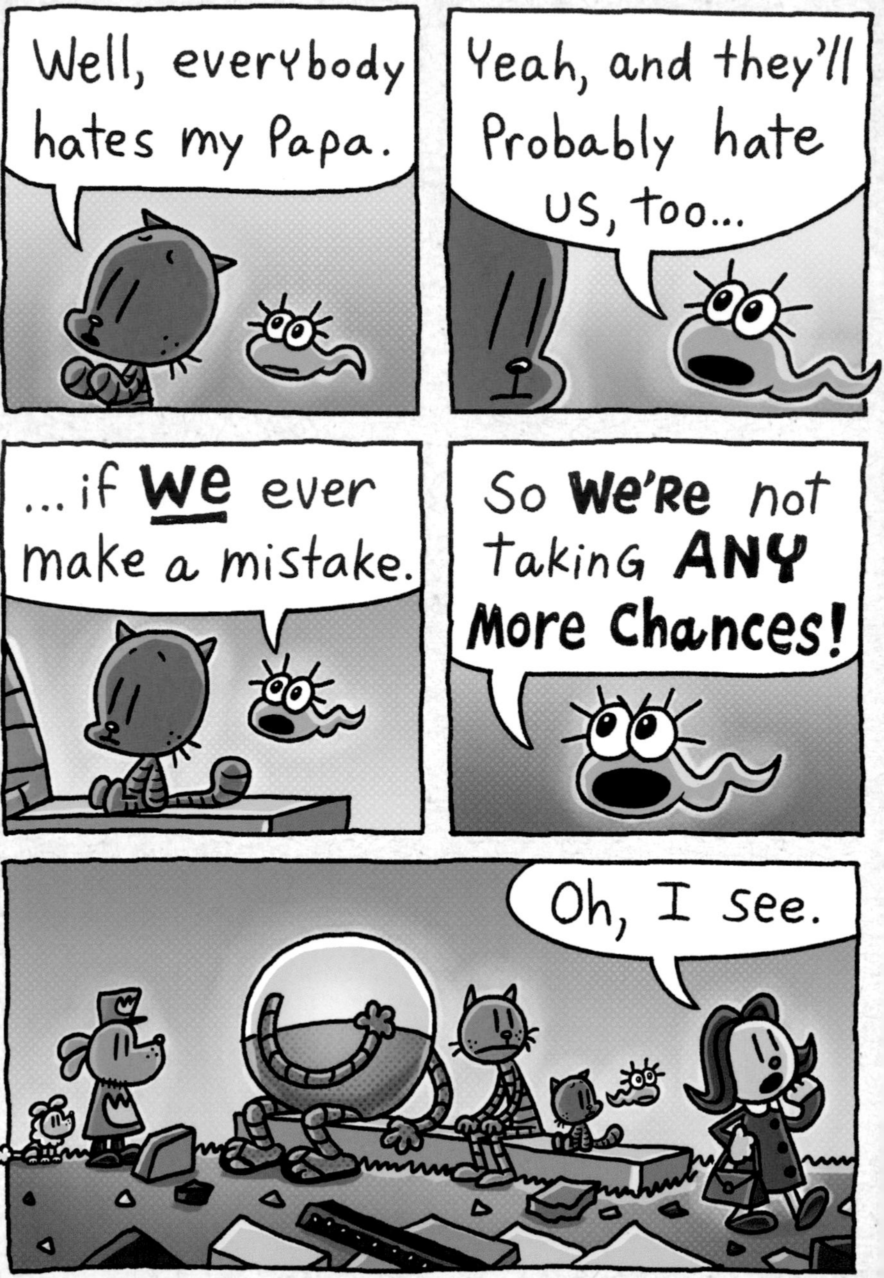
Well, everybody hates my Papa.
Yeah, and they'll Probably hate us, too...
...if we ever make a mistake.
So we're not taking ANY More Chances!
Oh, I see.

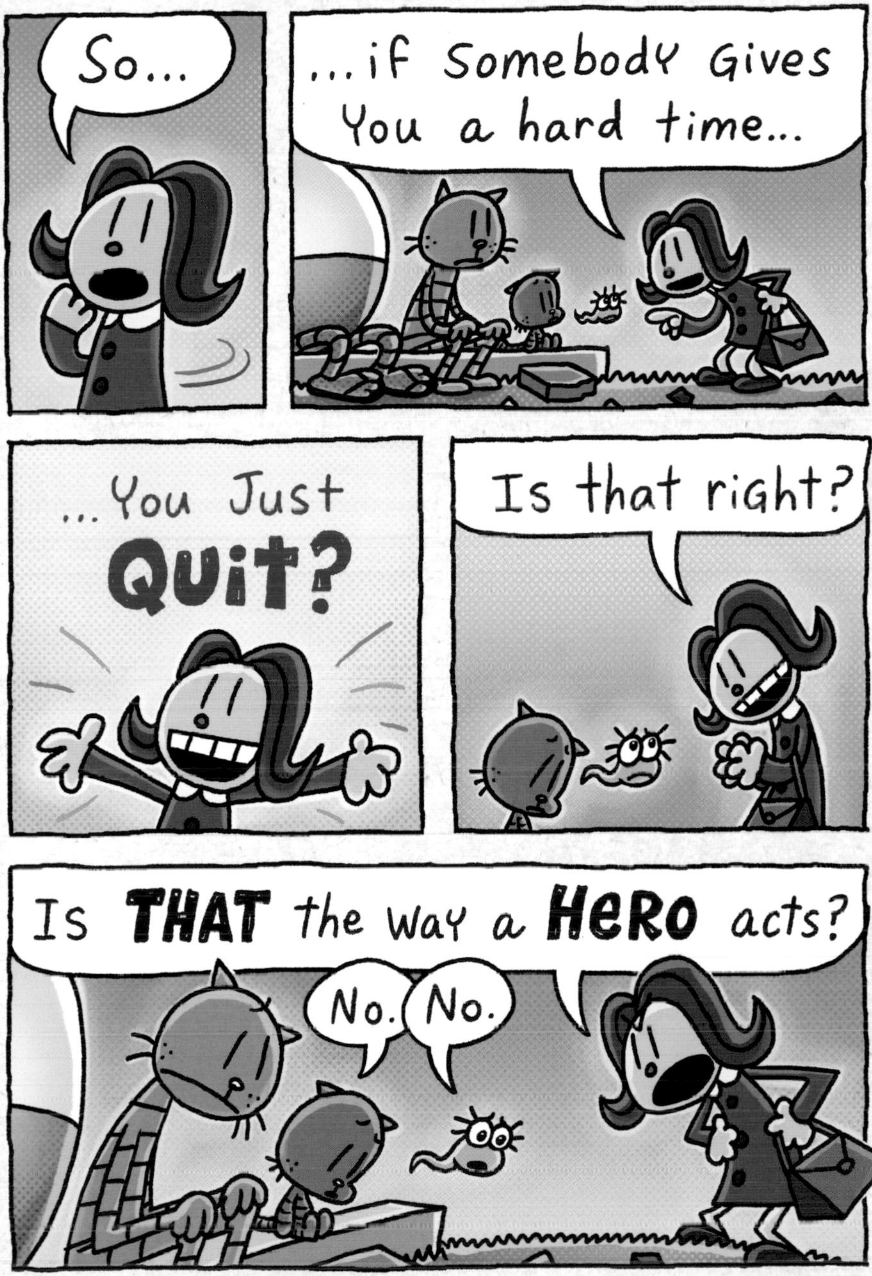
So...
...if Somebody Gives You a hard time...
...You Just QUIT?
Is that right?
Is THAT the way a HERO acts?
No.
No.

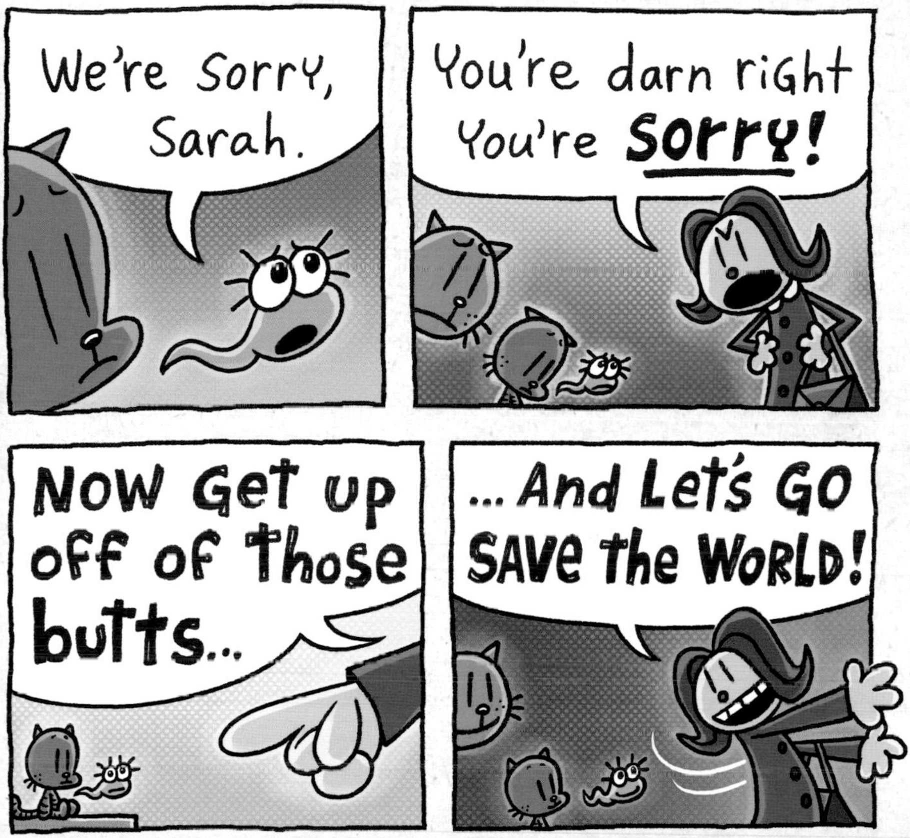
We're sorry, Sarah.
You're darn right you're **sorry**!
NOW get up off of those butts...
...And let's GO SAVE the WORLD!

And so...

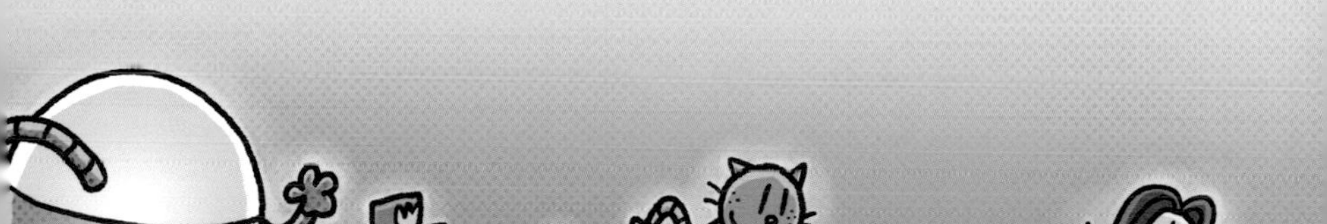
FLOP FLIP FLOP FLIP

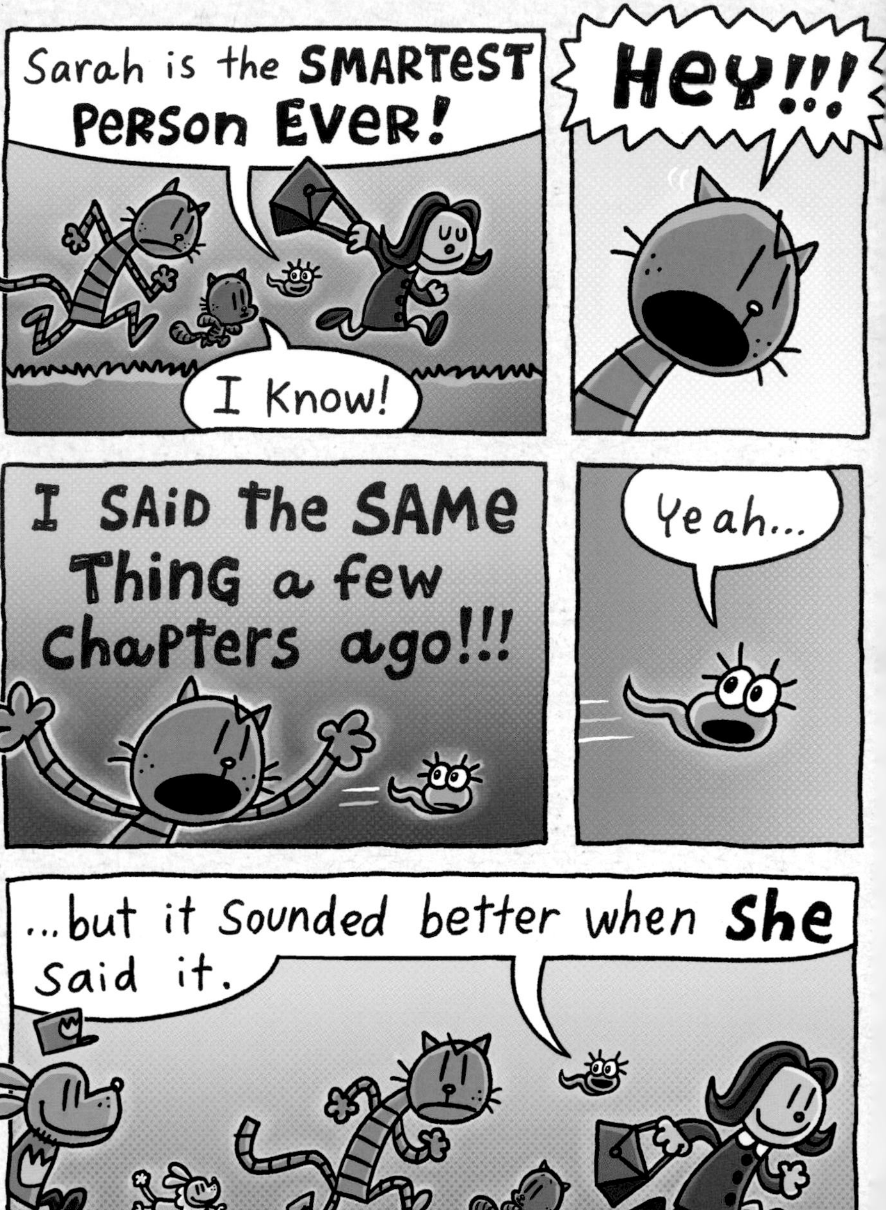
Sarah is the SMARTEST PERSON EVER!
I Know!
HEY!!!
I SAID the SAME Thing a few Chapters ago!!!
Yeah...
...but it Sounded better when She said it.

CHAPTER 11

PIGGY MAKES HIS MOVE

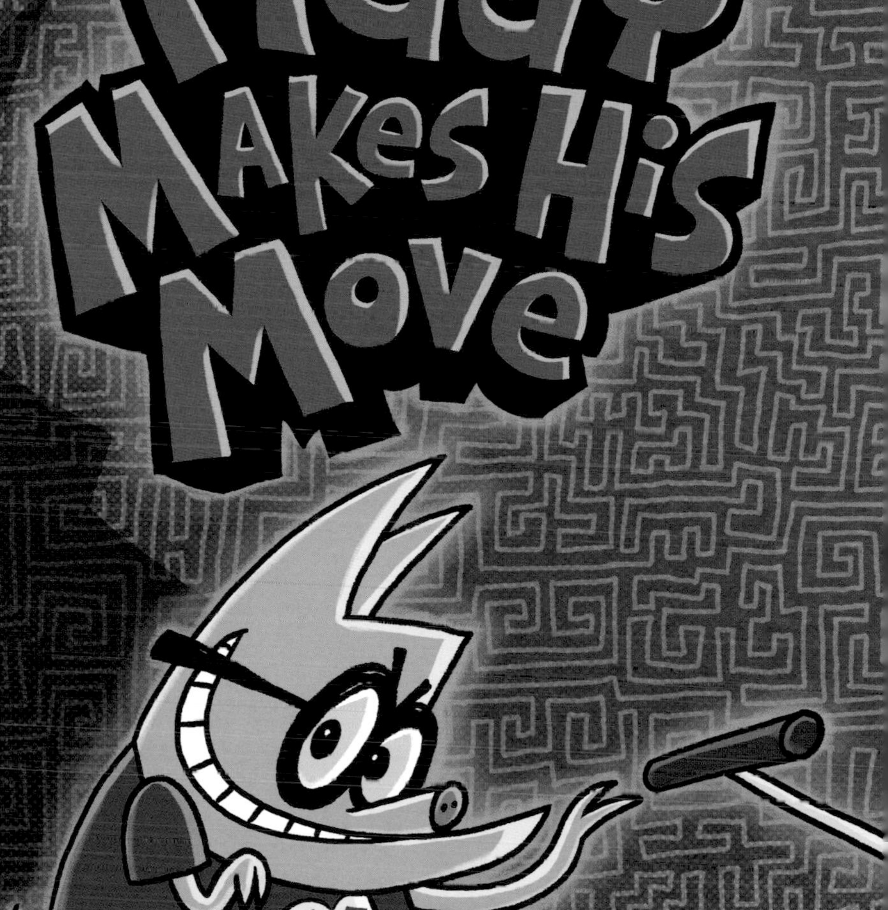

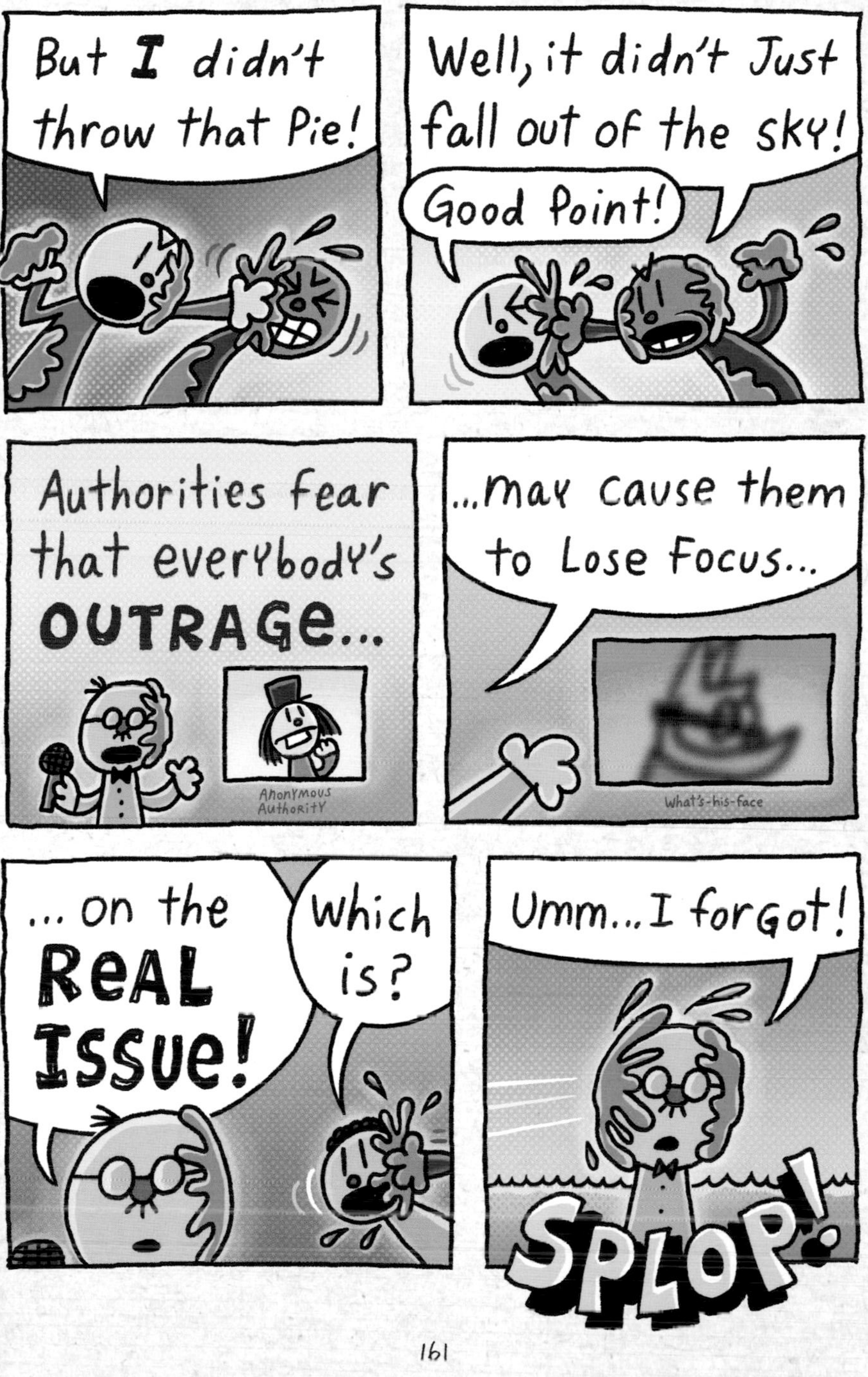

But I didn't throw that Pie!
Well, it didn't Just fall out of the SKY!
Good Point!
Authorities fear that everybody's OUTRAGE...
Anonymous Authority
...may cause them to Lose Focus...
What's-his-face
... on the REAL ISSUE!
Which is?
Umm... I forGot!
SPLOP!

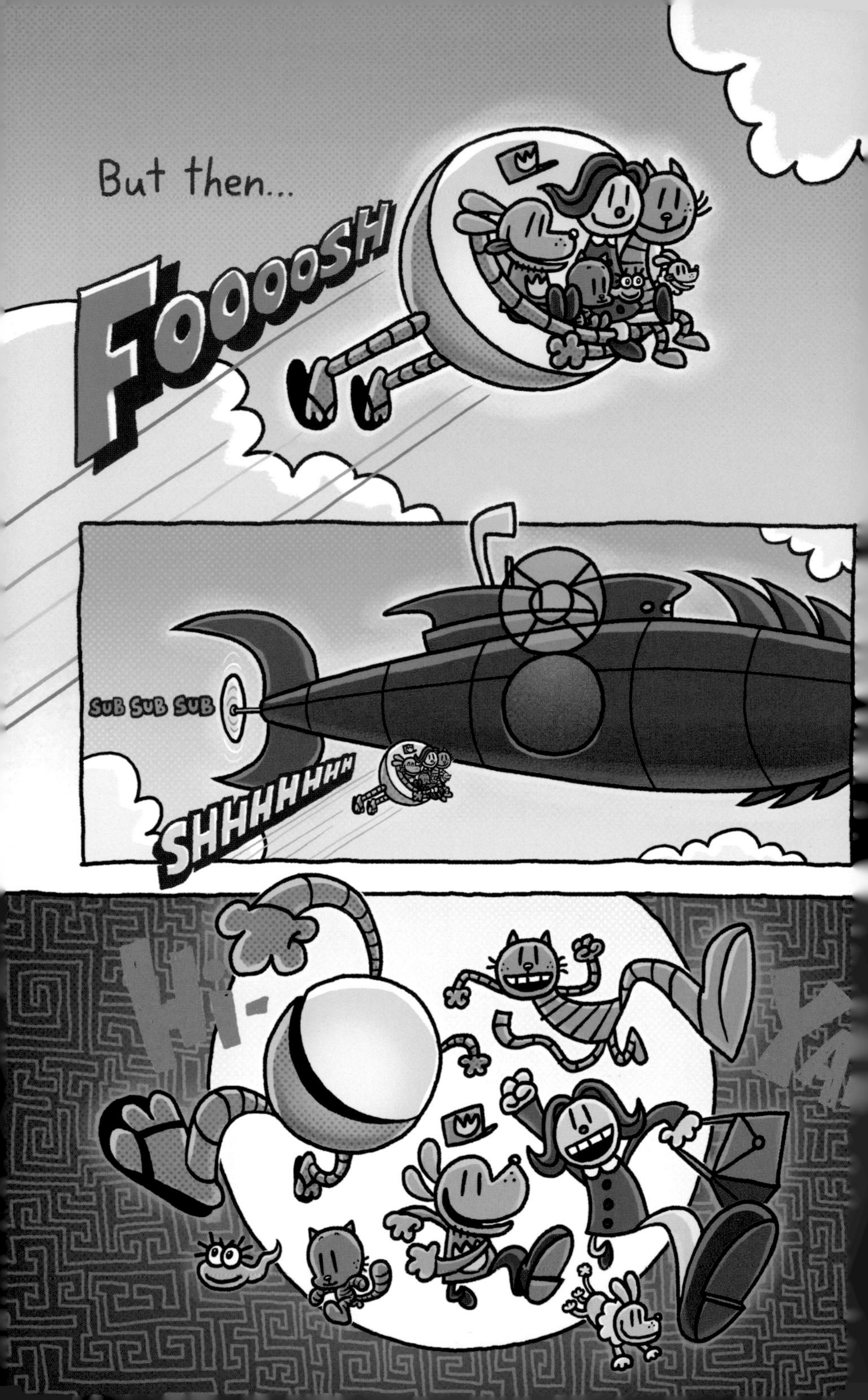

But then...
FOOOOSH
SUB SUB SUB
SHHHHHHH
HI-
YA

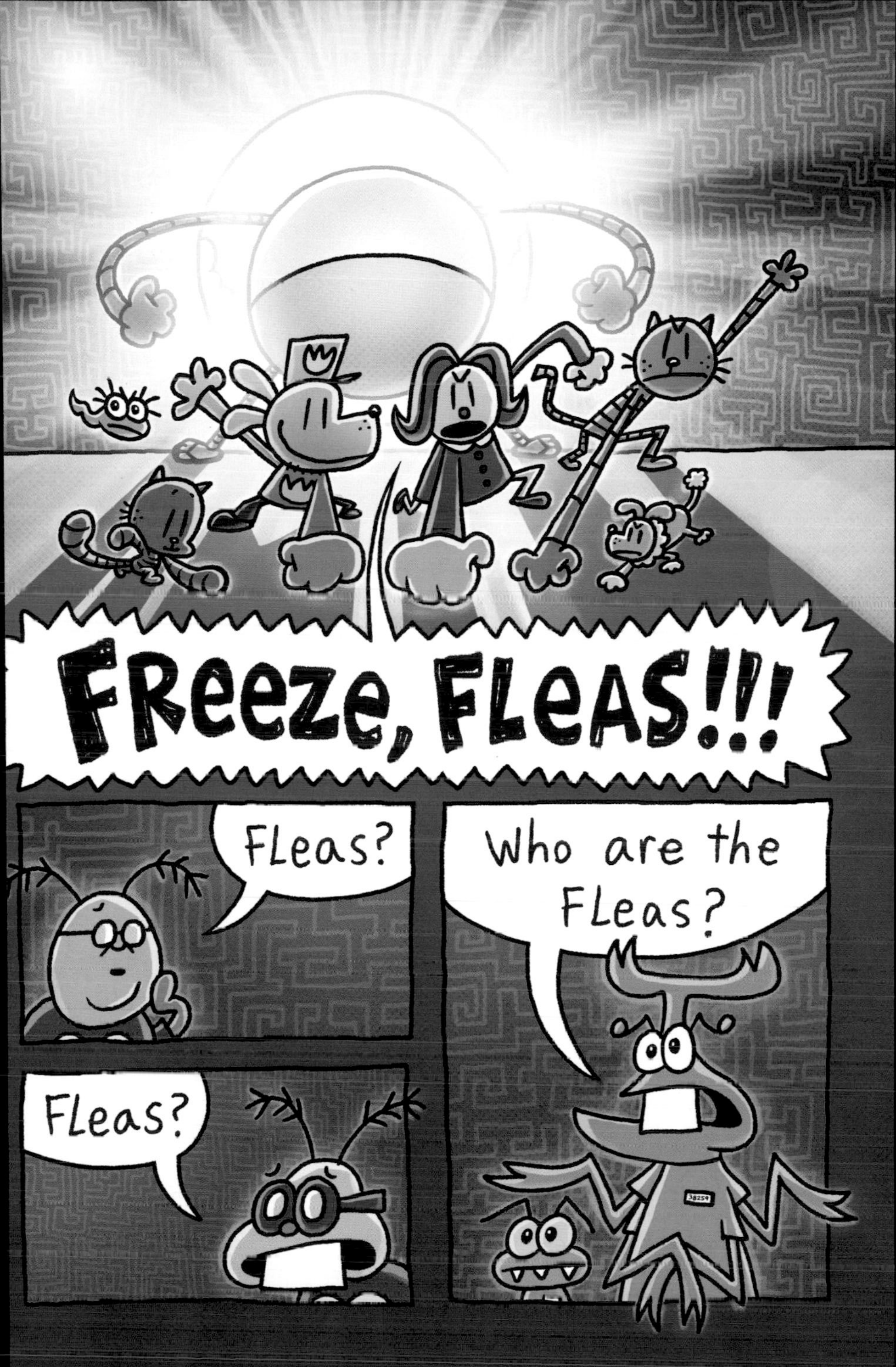
FREEZE, FLEAS!!!
Fleas?
Who are the Fleas?
Fleas?
38259

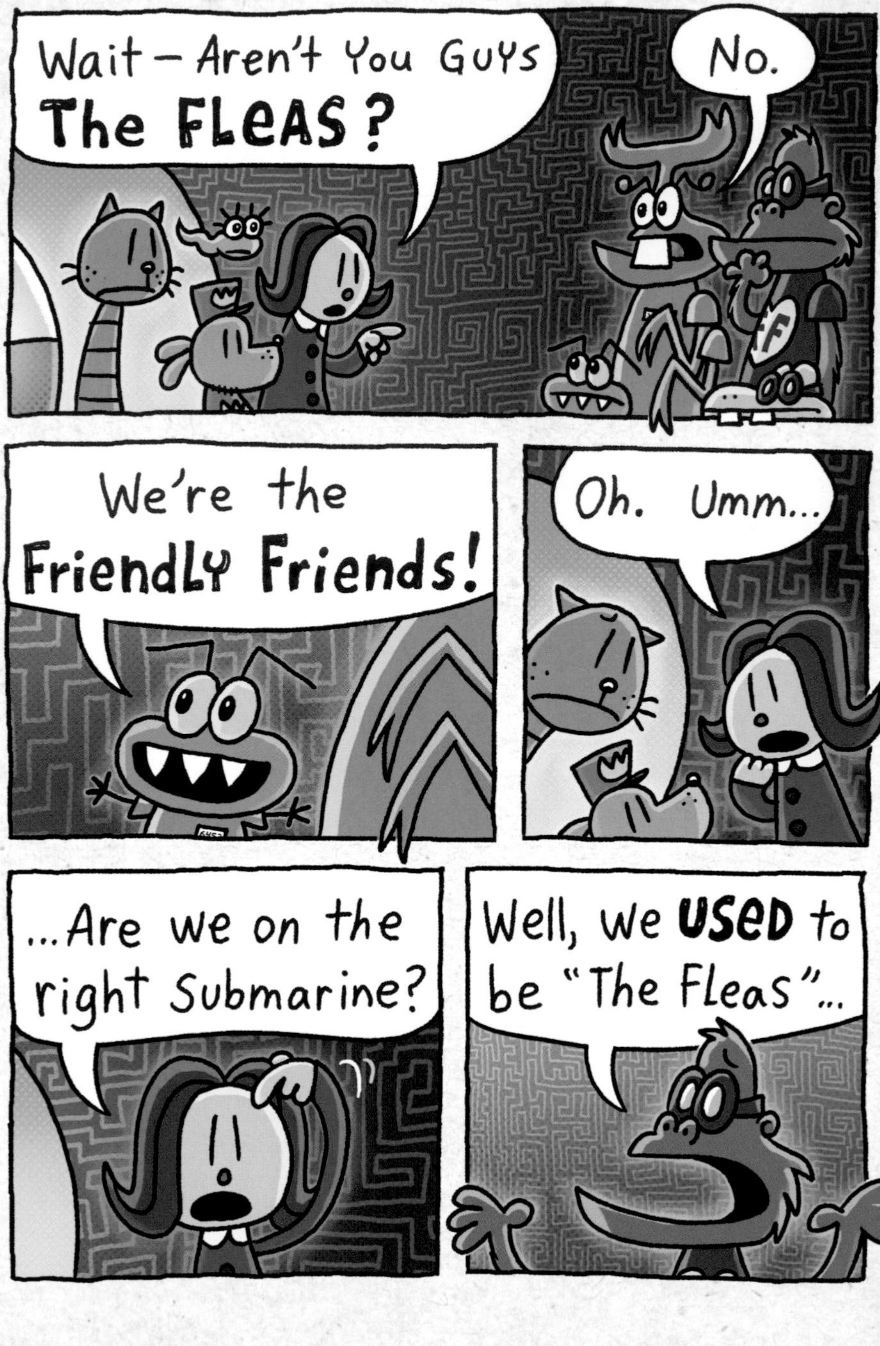
Wait—Aren't You Guys The FLEAS?
No.
We're the Friendly Friends!
Oh. Umm...
...Are we on the right Submarine?
Well, we USED to be "The Fleas"...

...but then we char

I DON'T believe MY **LUCK**!!!

EVERYBODY I **CAN'T STAND**...

...is **TOGETHER** in **ONE PLACE**!

NOW'S MY **Chance**...

...To **DESTROY THEM ALL**!!!

KA-
KLUNK

SUB WILL SHRINK IN FIVE SECONDS...

SNAP

...FOUR...

...THREE...

...TWO...

All of my Problems...

...are Getting smaller and smaller!!!

Bye-bye, **Losers!**

I think I'll send them all off...

...with a STANDING OVATION!

SLAP-O-RAMA

Let's Get PiGGY With it!

Left hand here.

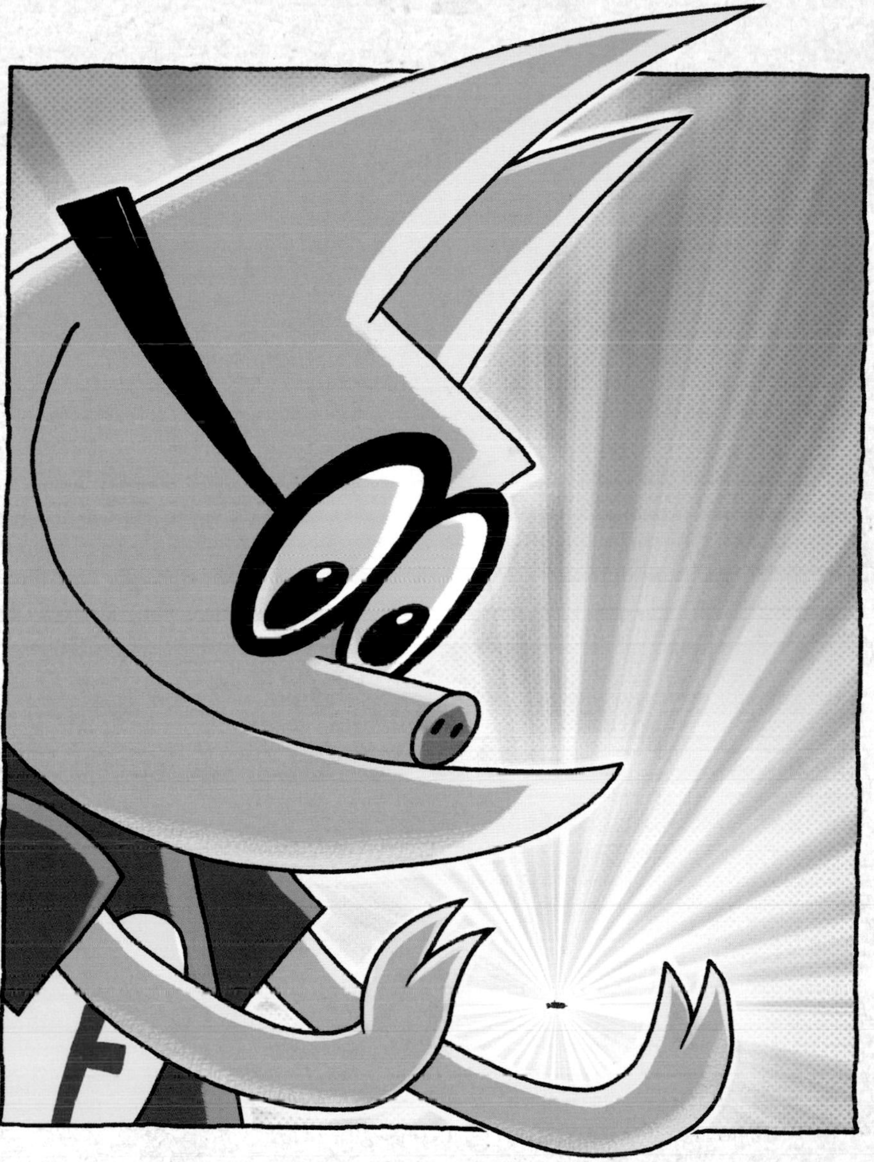

C'mon, Get SLAPPY!

Right Thumb here.

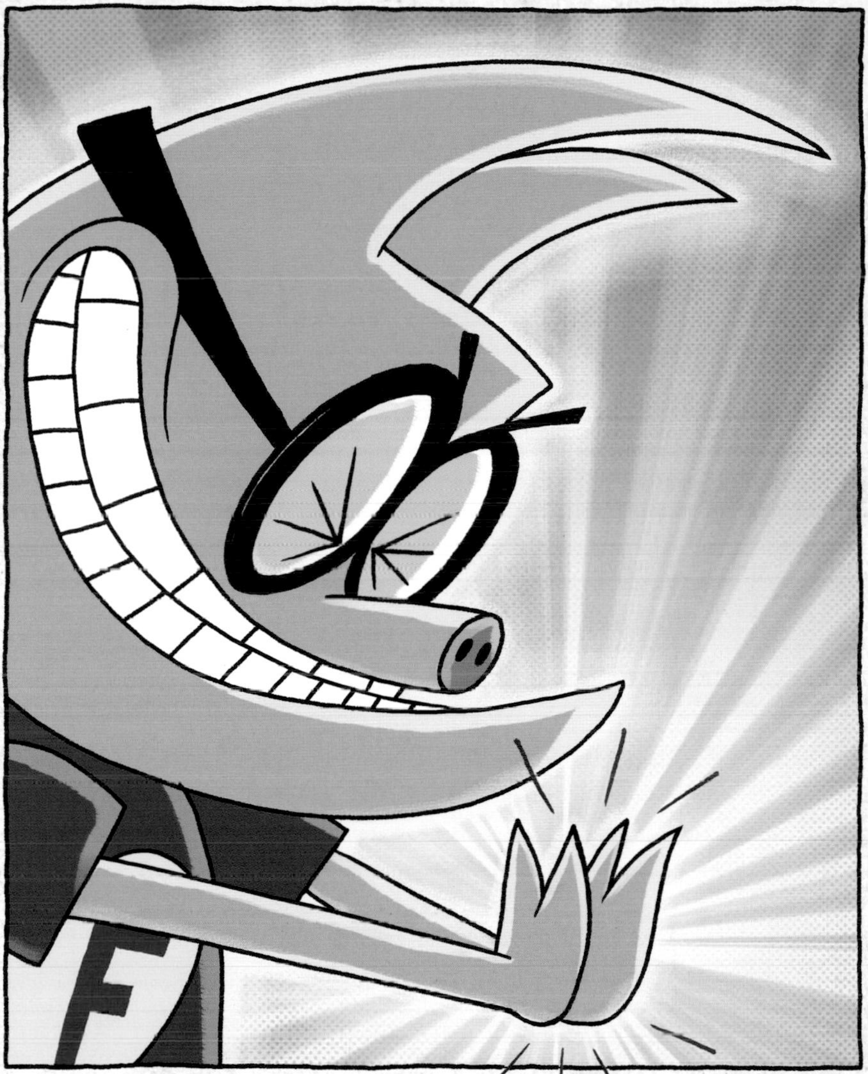

C'mon, Get SLAPPY!

Chapter 12

ZOOM IN

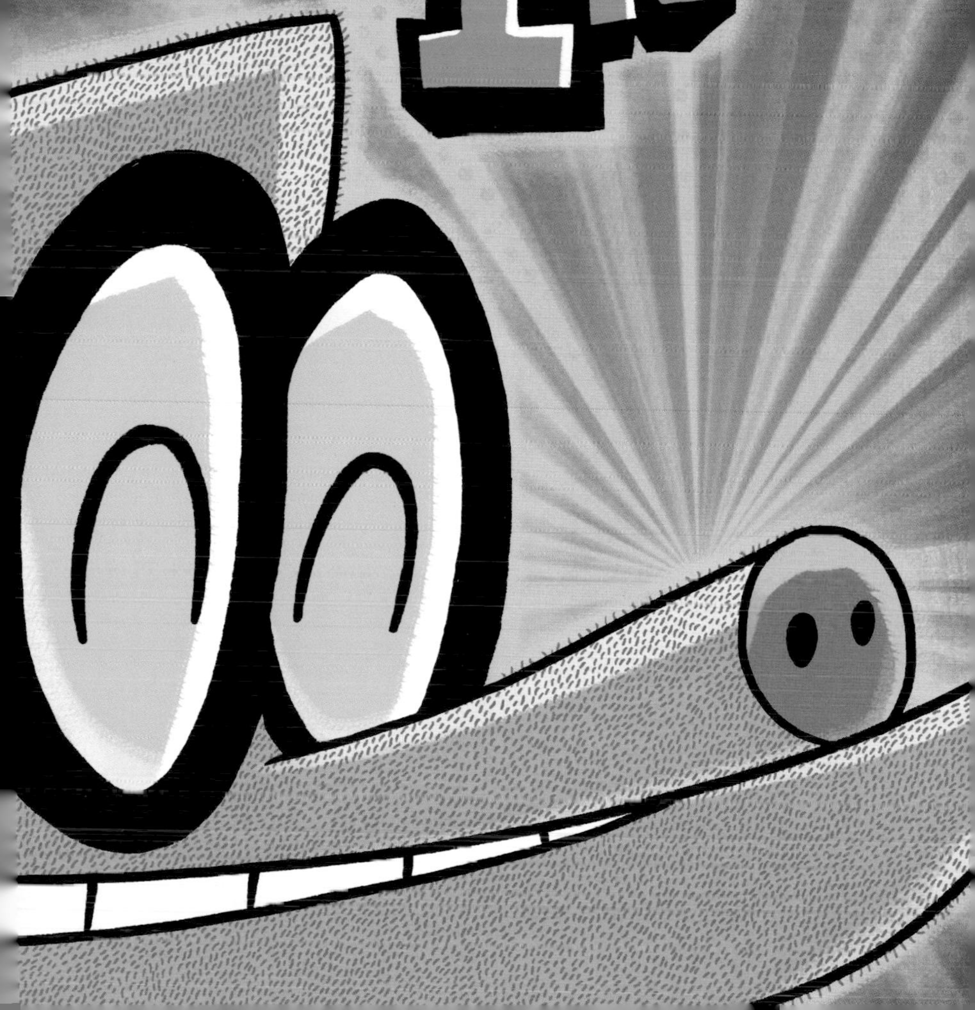

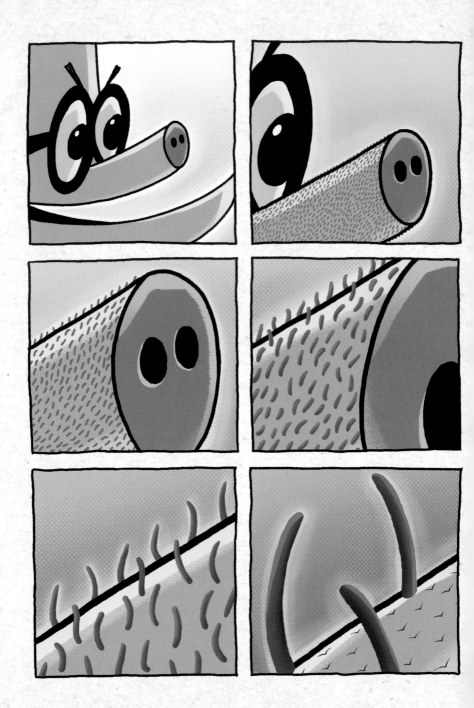

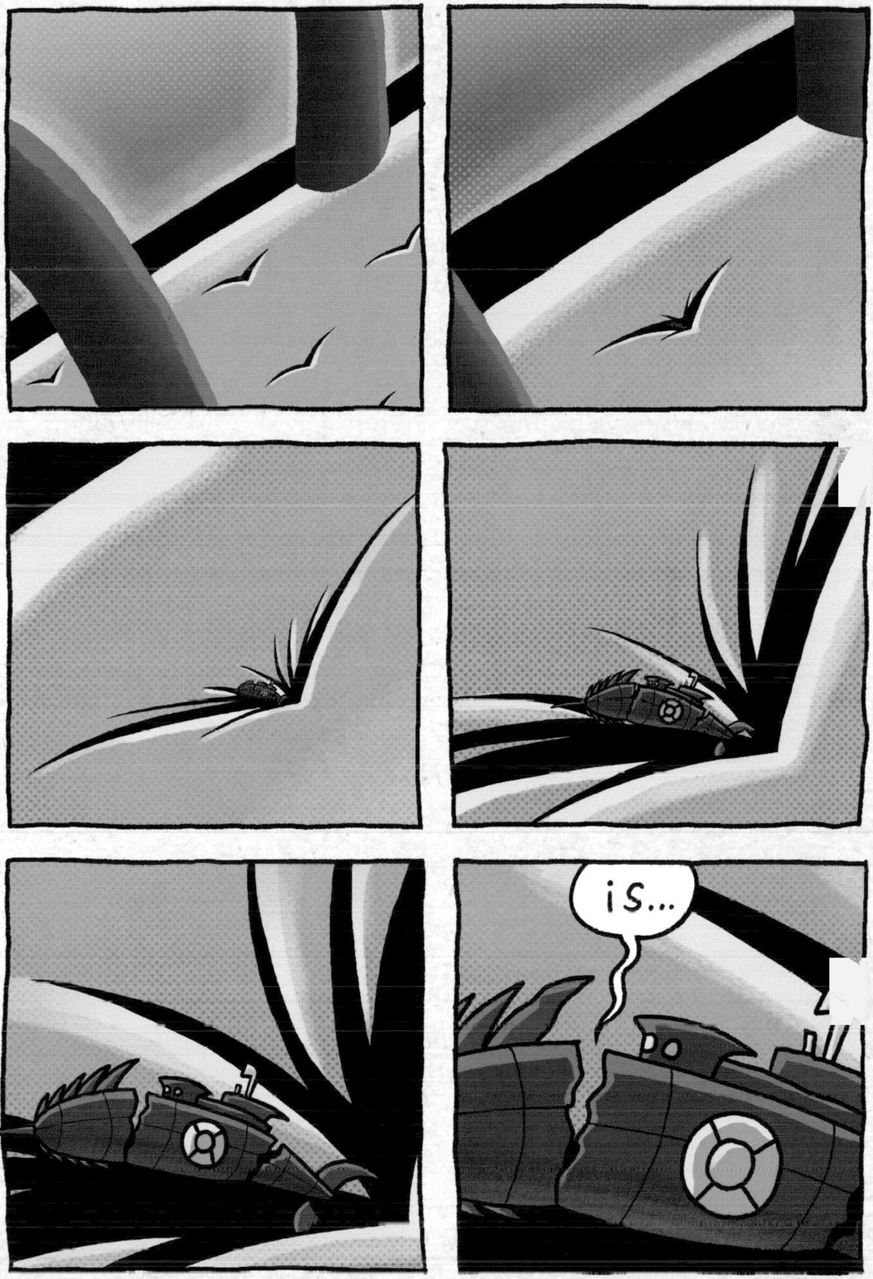
is...

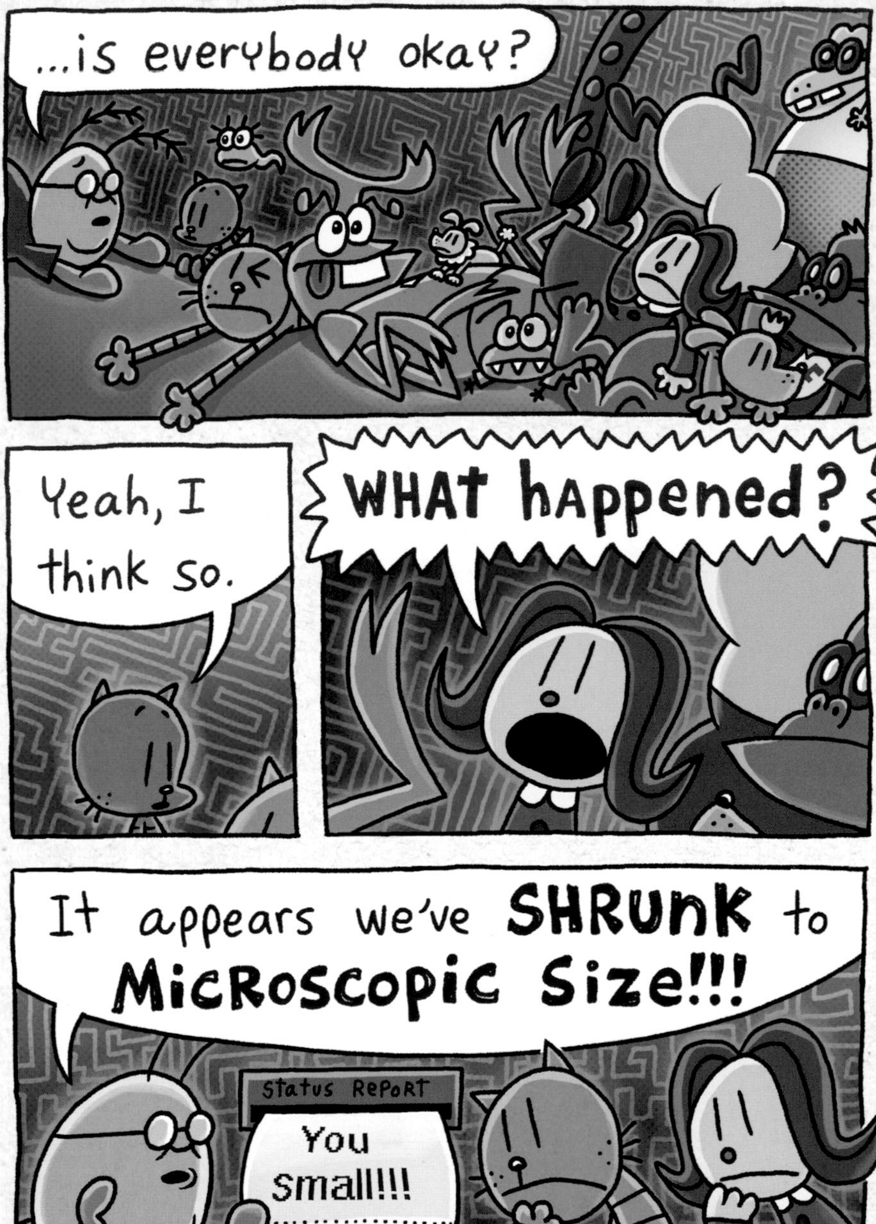
...is everybody okay?
Yeah, I think so.
WHAT happened?
It appears we've SHRUNK to MICROSCOPIC Size!!!
STATUS REPORT
You small!!!

LET'S JUST GROW BIG AGAIN!!!

WE CAN'T!

OUR SIZE-O-TRON IS BUSTED!!!

Well, Goodbye, Bub!

So Long, Crunky!

YAAAAAAAAAAAAAAAAAAAaaaaaaan

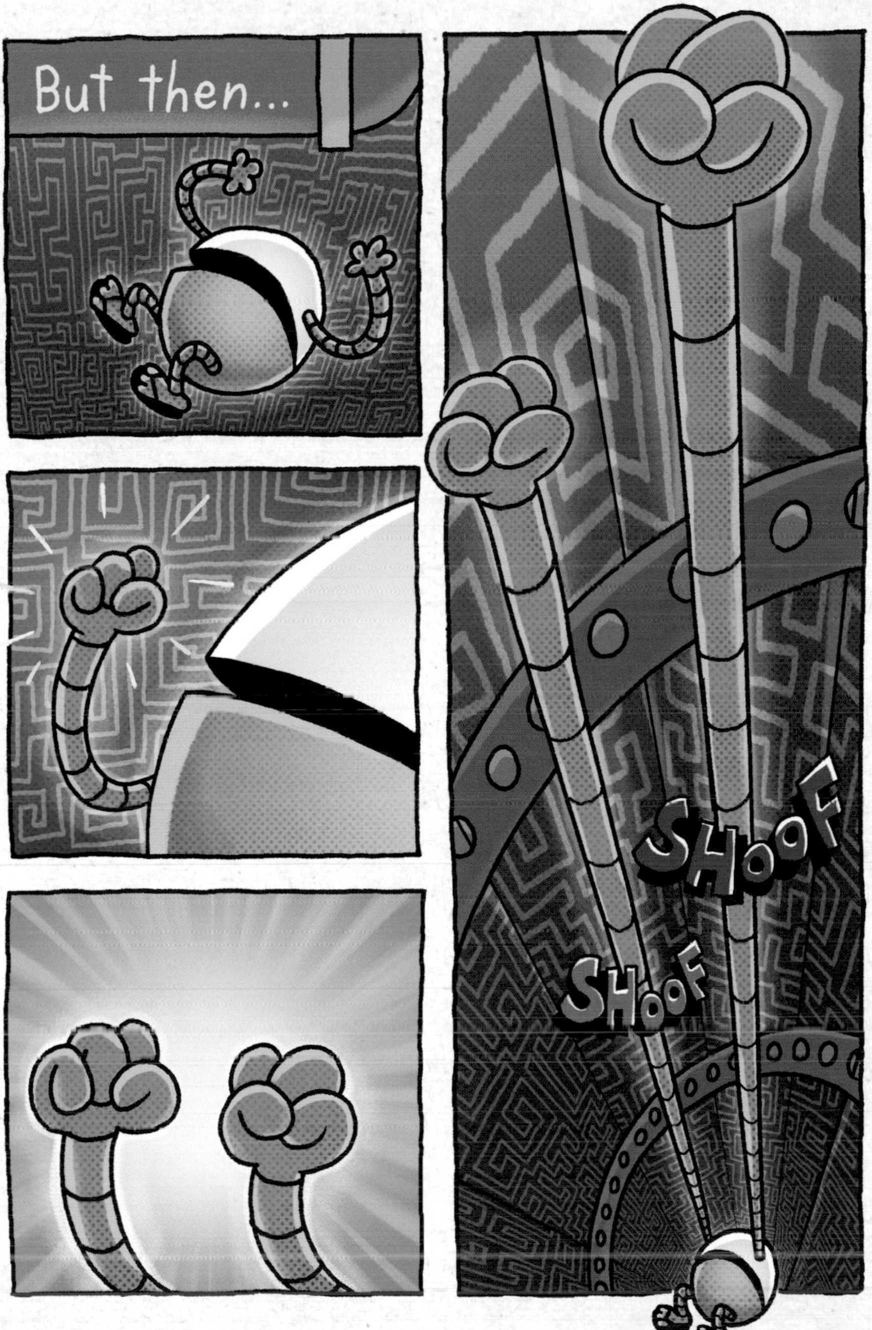
But then...
SHOOF
SHOOF

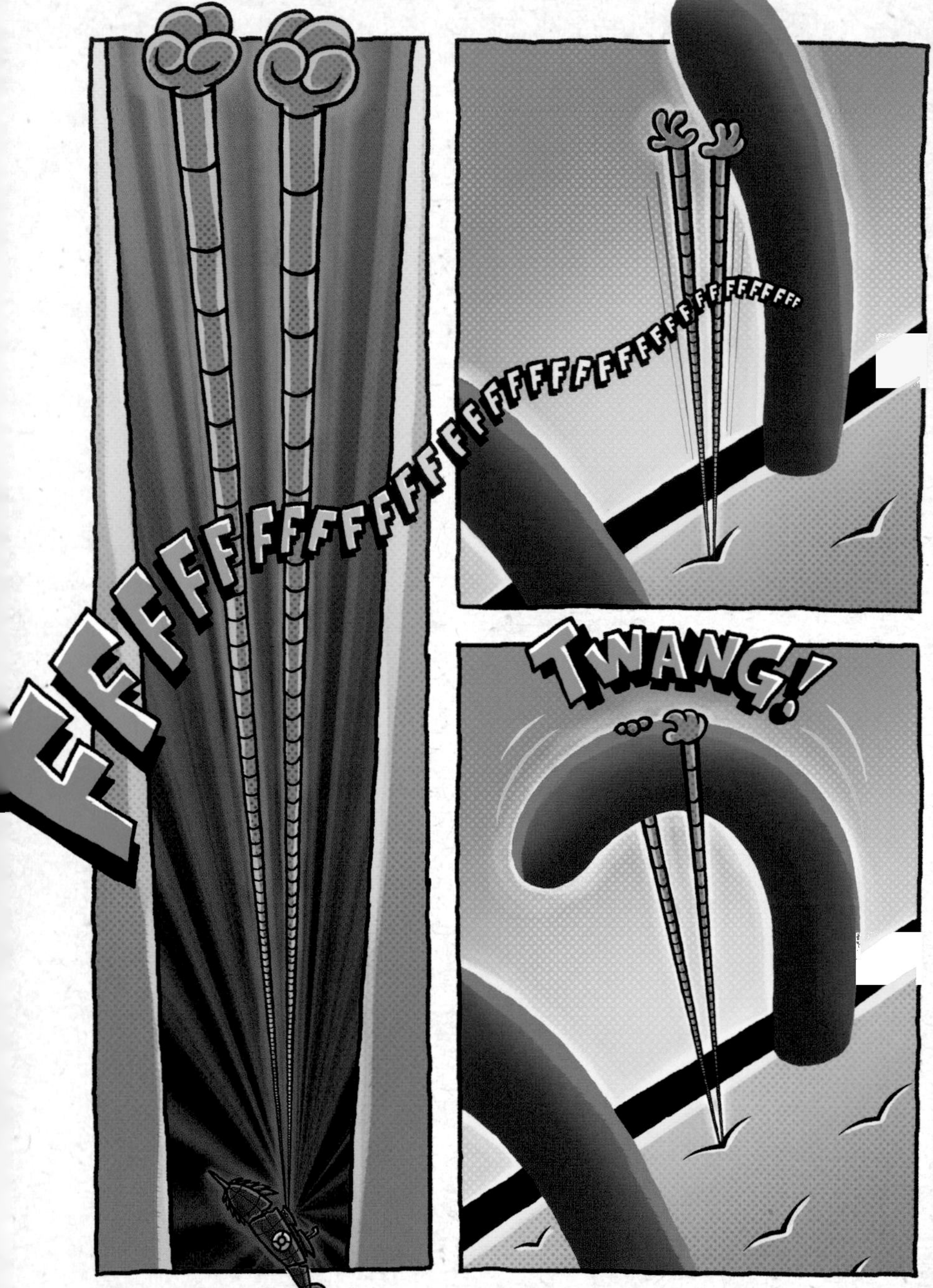
FFFFFFFFFFFFFFFFFFFFFFFFFFFFFFFFFFFFFFFF
TWANG!

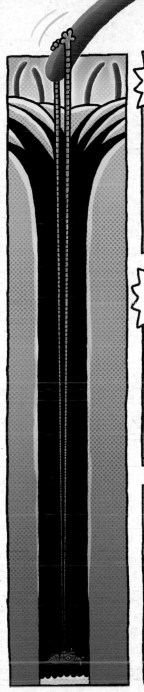

80-HD SAVED US!!!

HOORAY for 80-HD!

We're not out of this Yet...

YOU in BIG trouble, brah. ....

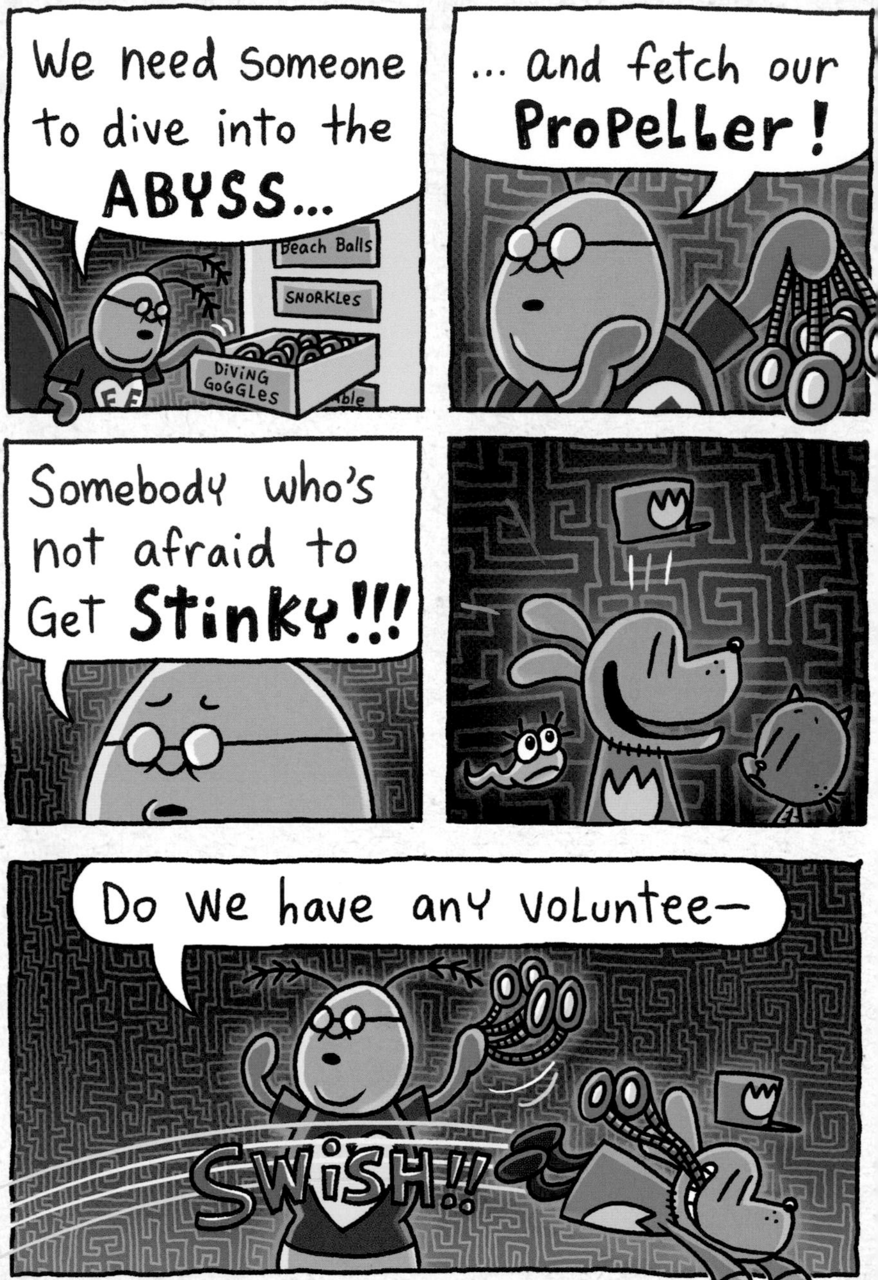
We need Someone to dive into the ABYSS...
Beach Balls
SNORKLES
DIVING GOGGLES
... and fetch our PROPELLER!
Somebody who's not afraid to Get STINKY!!!
Do we have any voluntee—
SWISH!!

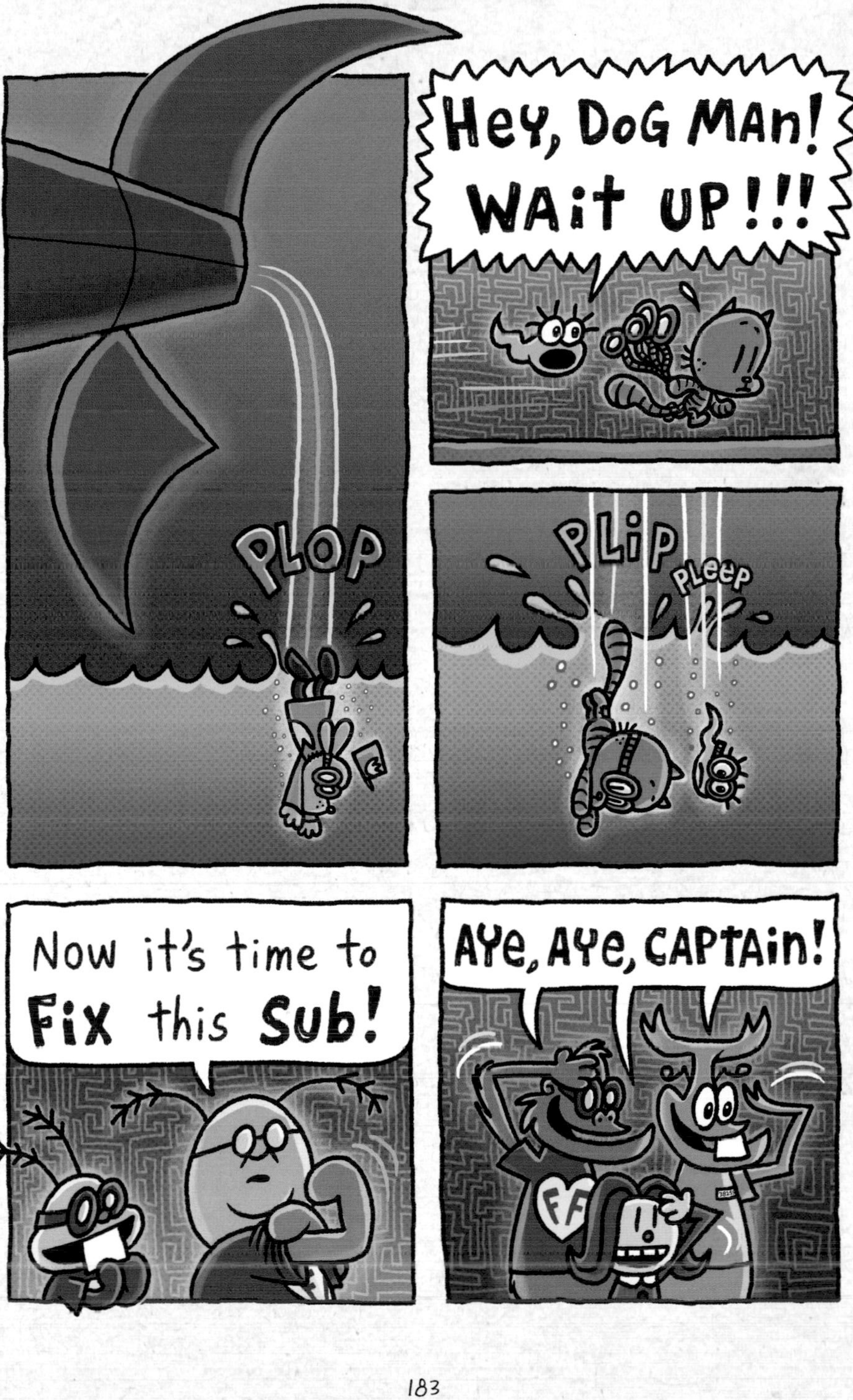
PLOP
Hey, DoG MAn! WAit UP!!!
PLiP
PLeep
Now it's time to Fix this Sub!
AYe, AYe, CAPTAin!

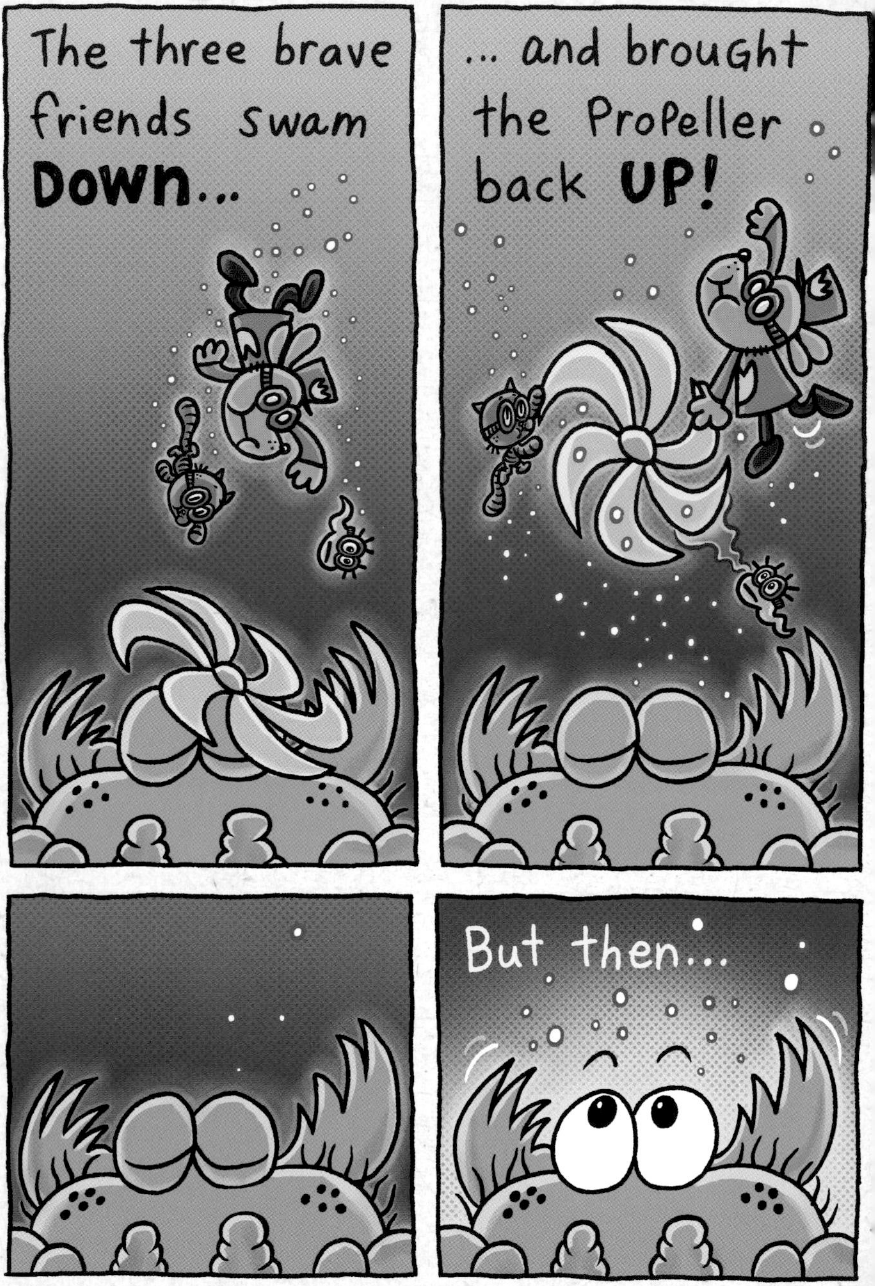
The three brave friends swam **DOWN**...
... and brought the propeller back **UP!**
But then...

CHAPTER 13

THIS MITE BE A PROBLEM

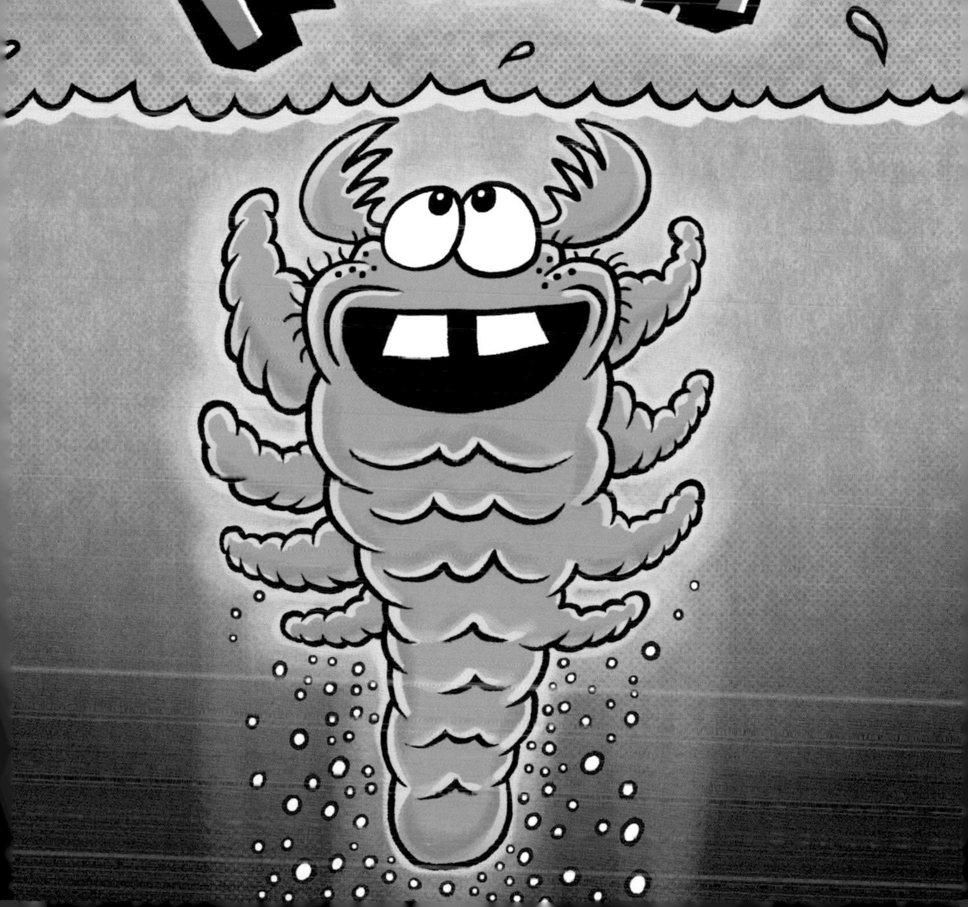

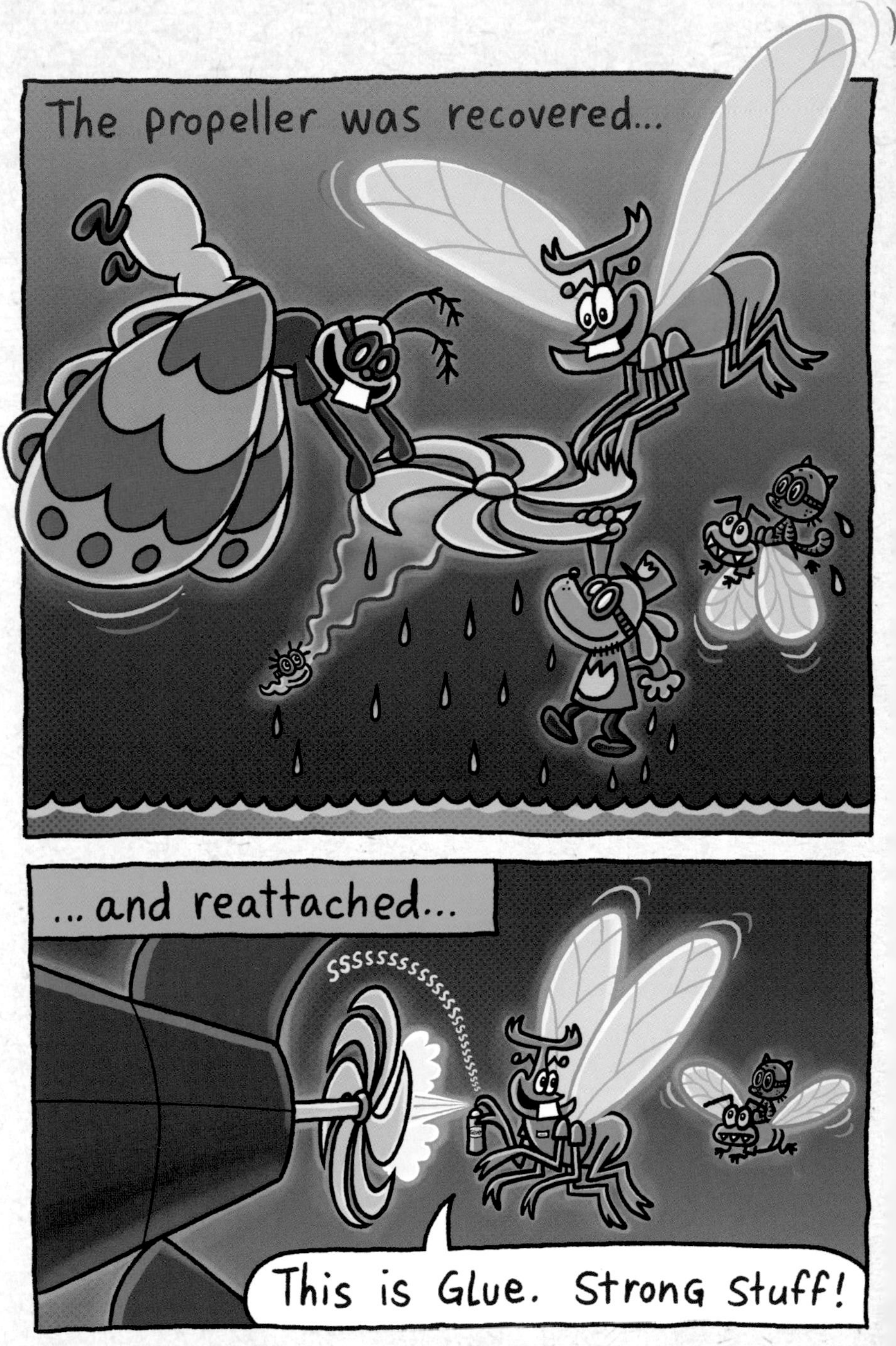
The propeller was recovered...
... and reattached...
This is Glue. Strong Stuff!

...and soon the damaged Sub...

This is tape. Strong Stuff!

...was set to soar again!!!

This is acrylic latex caulk. Strong Stuff!

I think we're ready to go!!!

What could possibly go wrong???

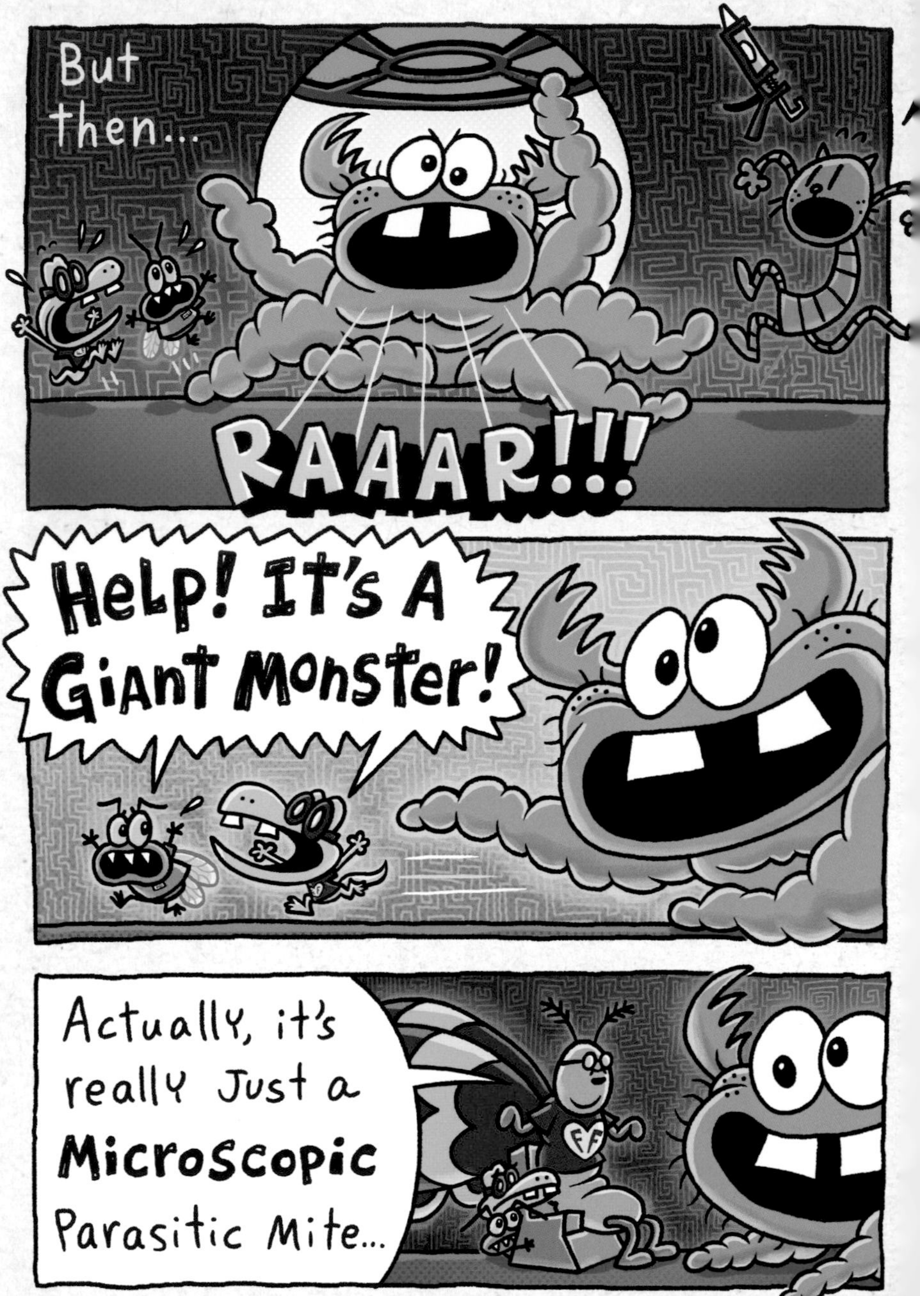
But then...
RAAAR!!!
Help! It's A Giant Monster!
Actually, it's really Just a Microscopic Parasitic Mite...

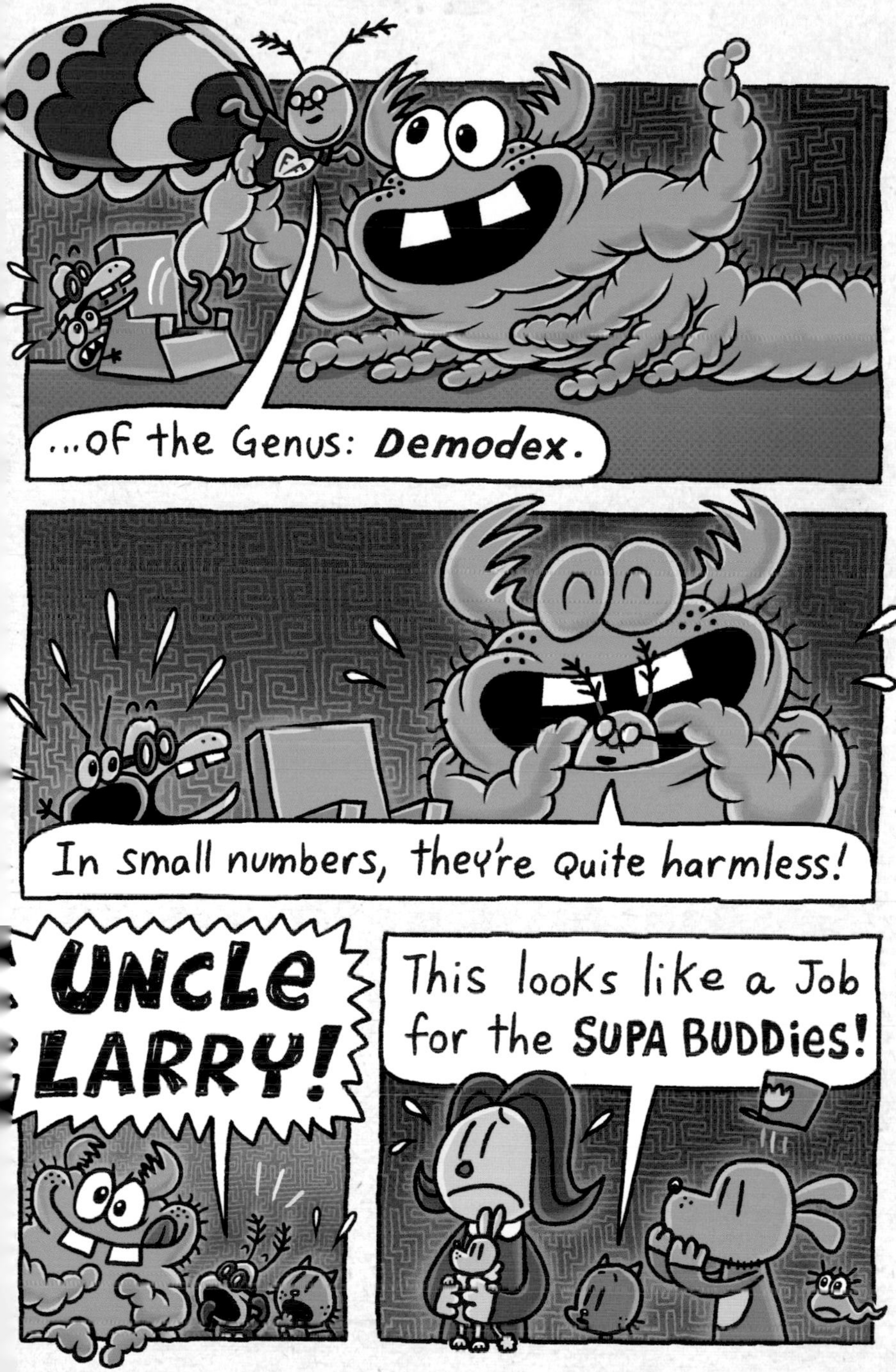
...of the Genus: Demodex.
In small numbers, they're quite harmless!
UNCLE LARRY!
This looks like a Job for the SUPA BUDDies!

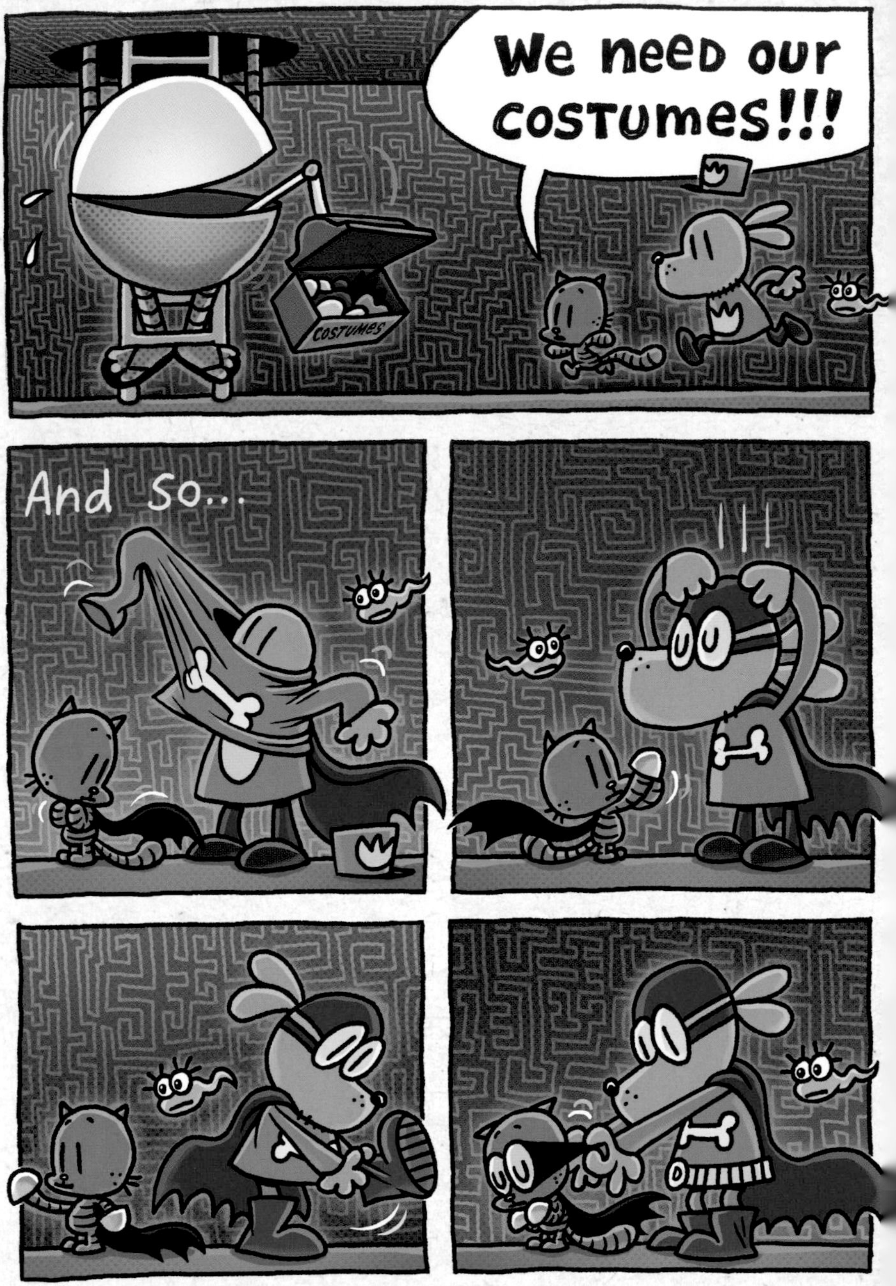
We need our COSTUMES!!!
COSTUMES
And so...

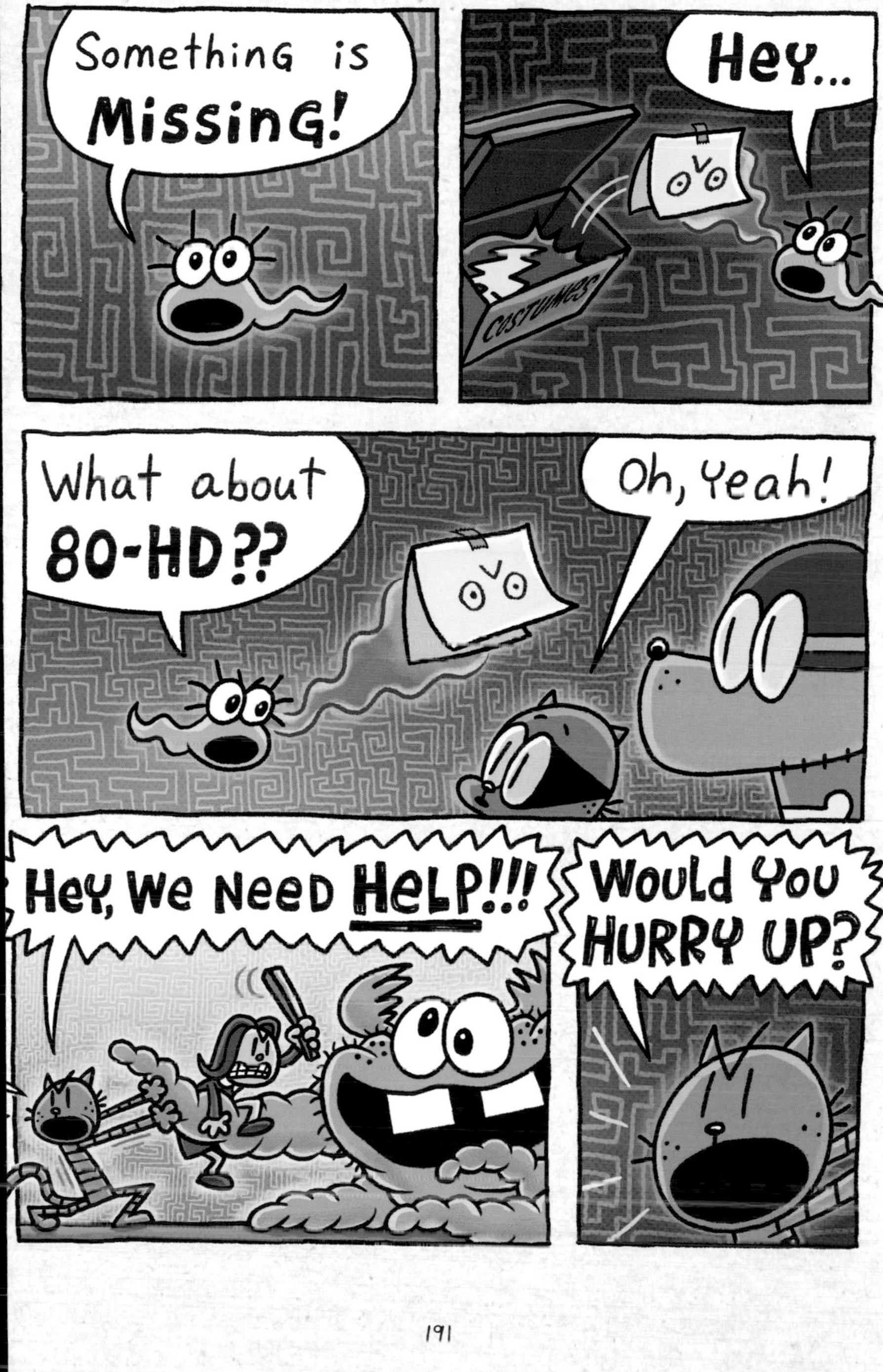
Something is MISSING!
Hey...
COSTUMES
What about 80-HD??
Oh, Yeah!
Hey, We Need HELP!!!
Would You HURRY UP?

WE ARE HURRY UPPING!

You guys can't be the **SUPA Buddies**...

...if you don't Got **80-HD!!!**

She's right! 80-HD's hands are **FULL!**

Maybe I can take his place.

But you don't have a costume!

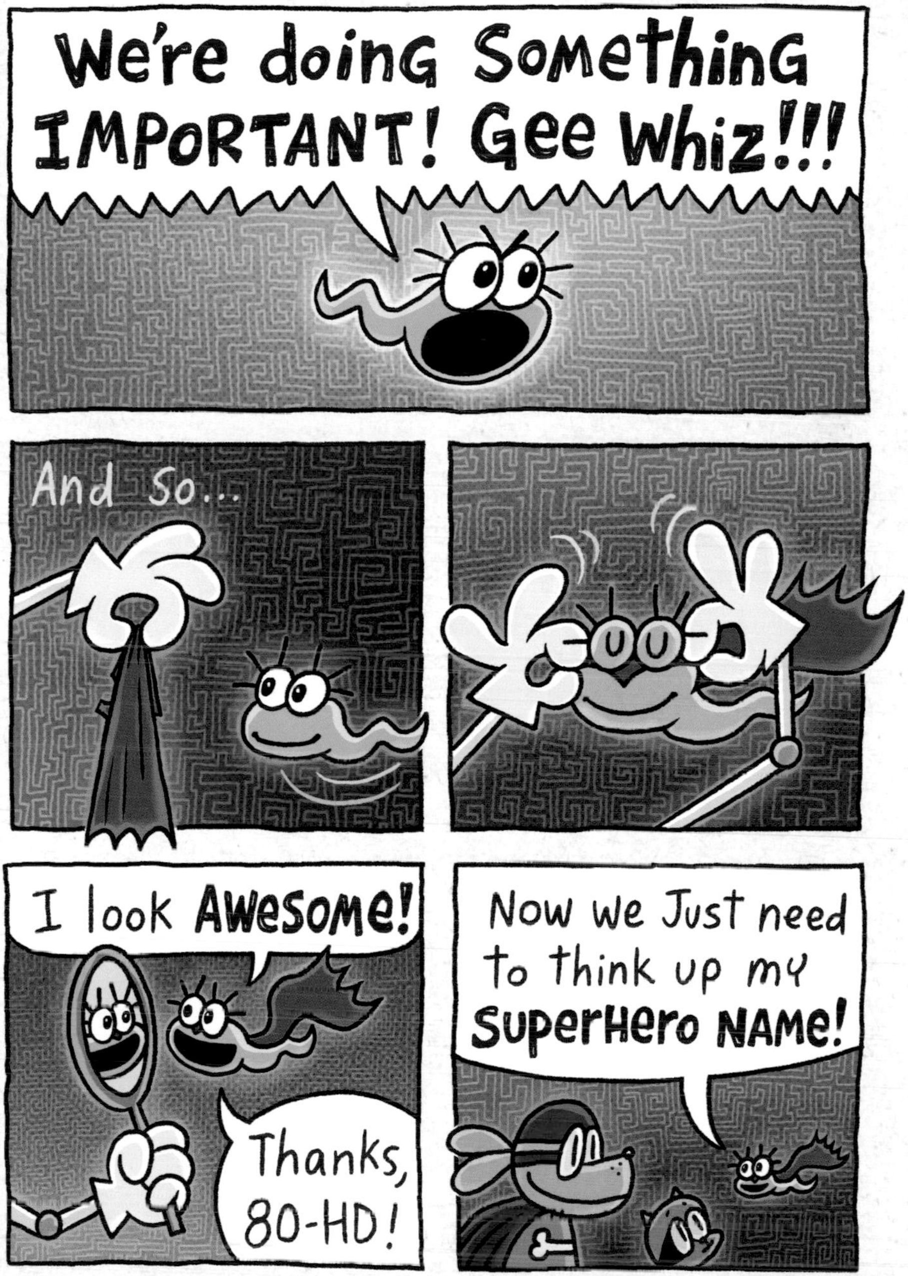
We're doing Something IMPORTANT! Gee Whiz!!!
And so...
I look AWESOME!
Thanks, 80-HD!
Now we Just need to think up my SuperHero NAME!

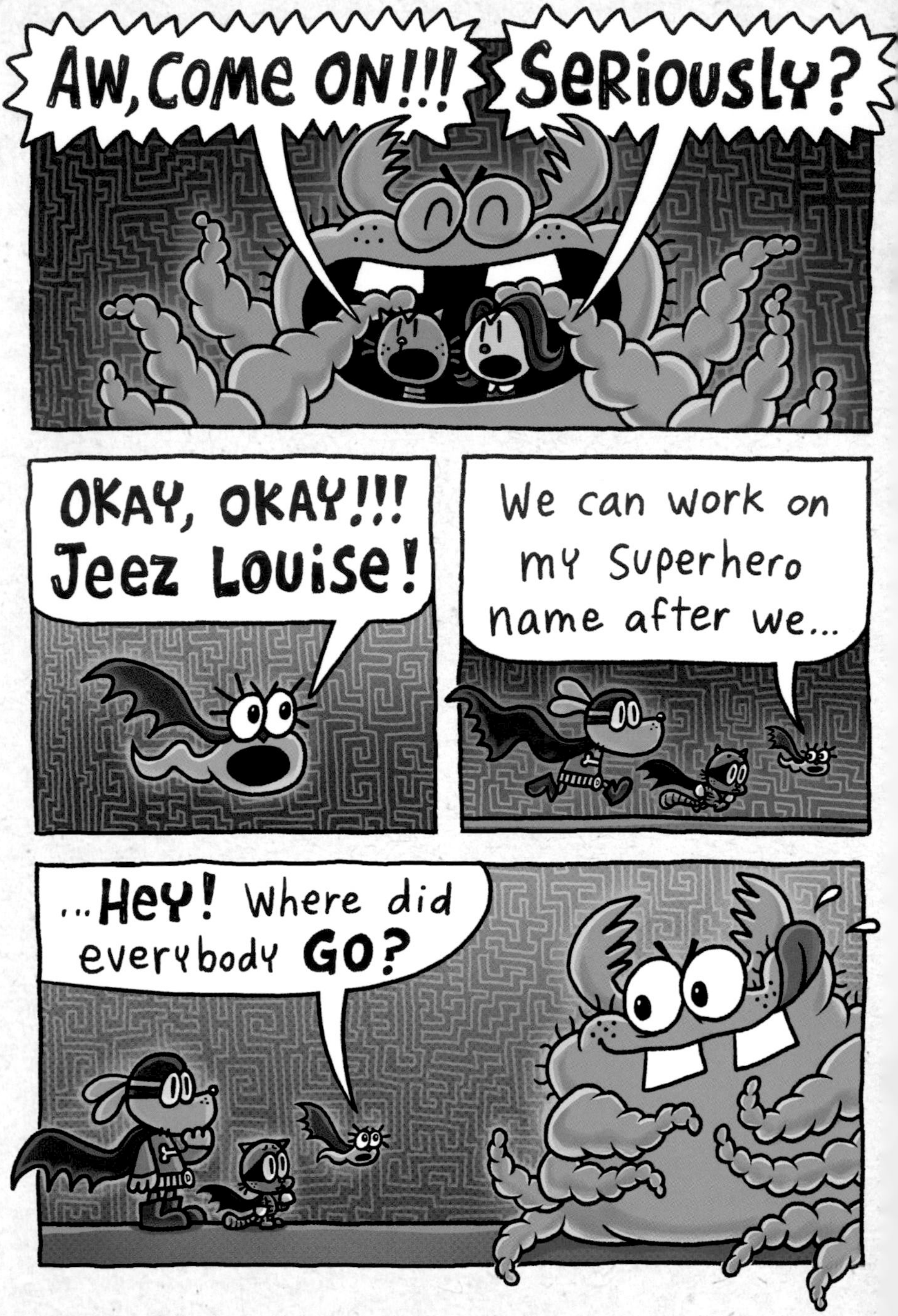
AW, COME ON!!!
SERIOUSLY?
OKAY, OKAY!!! Jeez Louise!
We can work on my superhero name after we...
...HEY! Where did everybody GO?

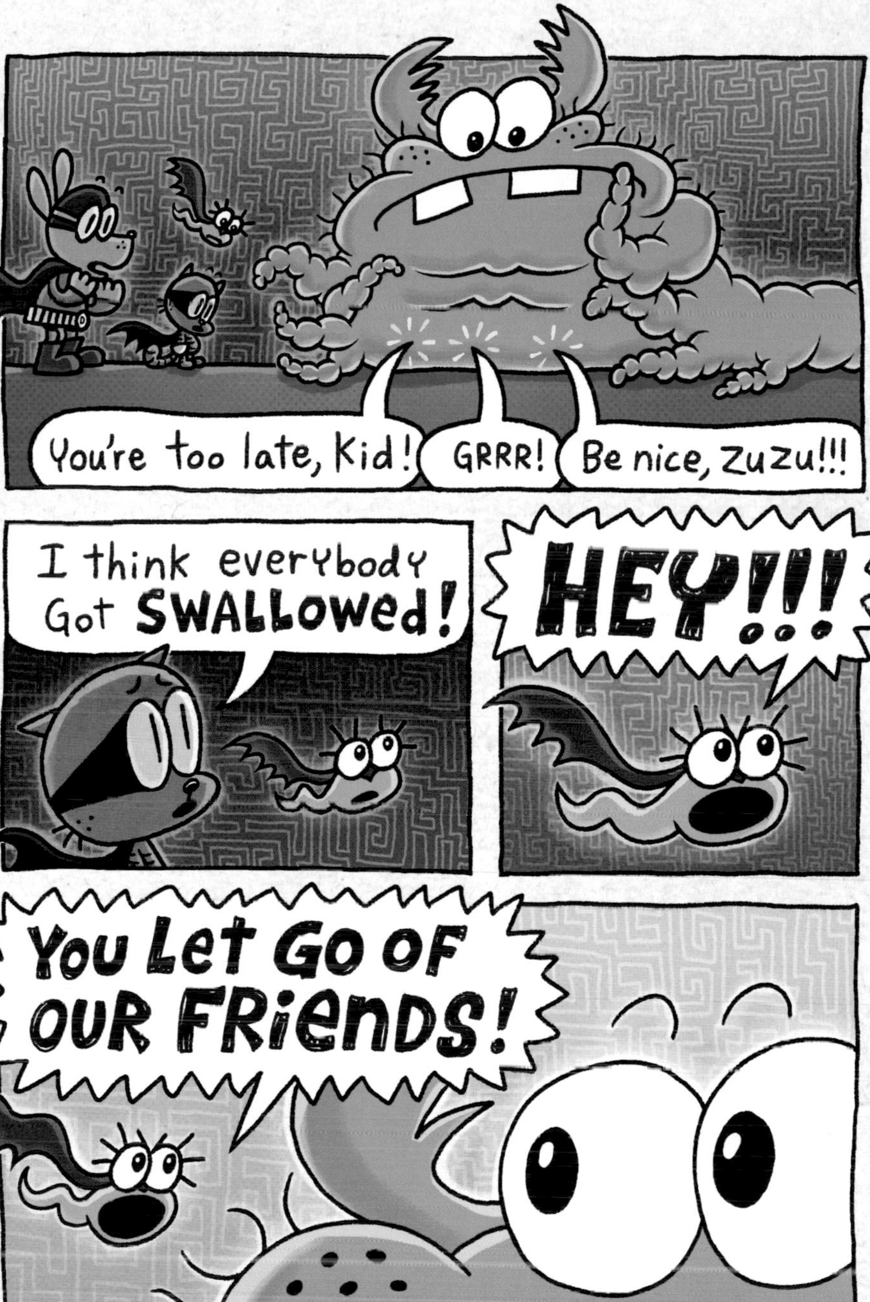
You're too late, Kid!
GRRR!
Be nice, Zuzu!!!
I think everybody Got SWALLOWED!
HEY!!!
You Let GO OF OUR FRIENDS!

Mitey Fighty

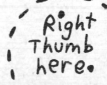

Right
Thumb
here.

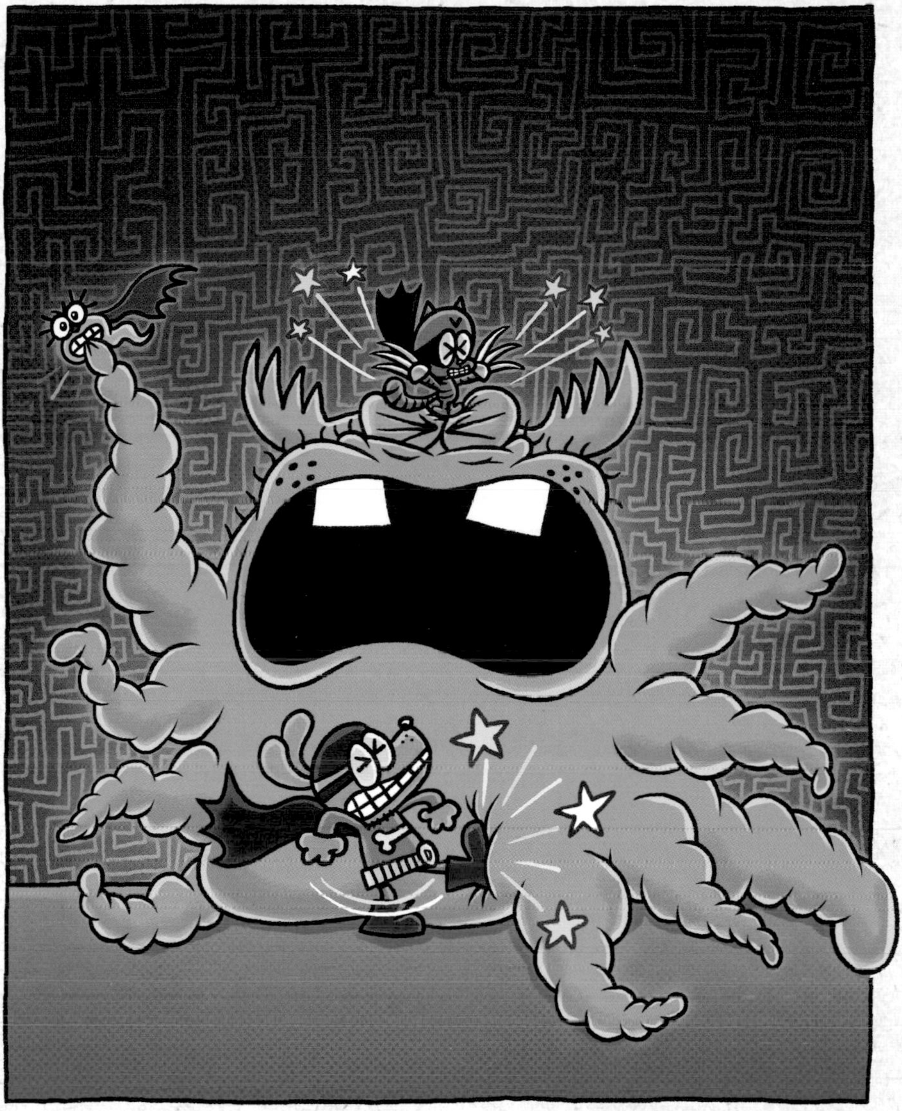

Mitey Fighty

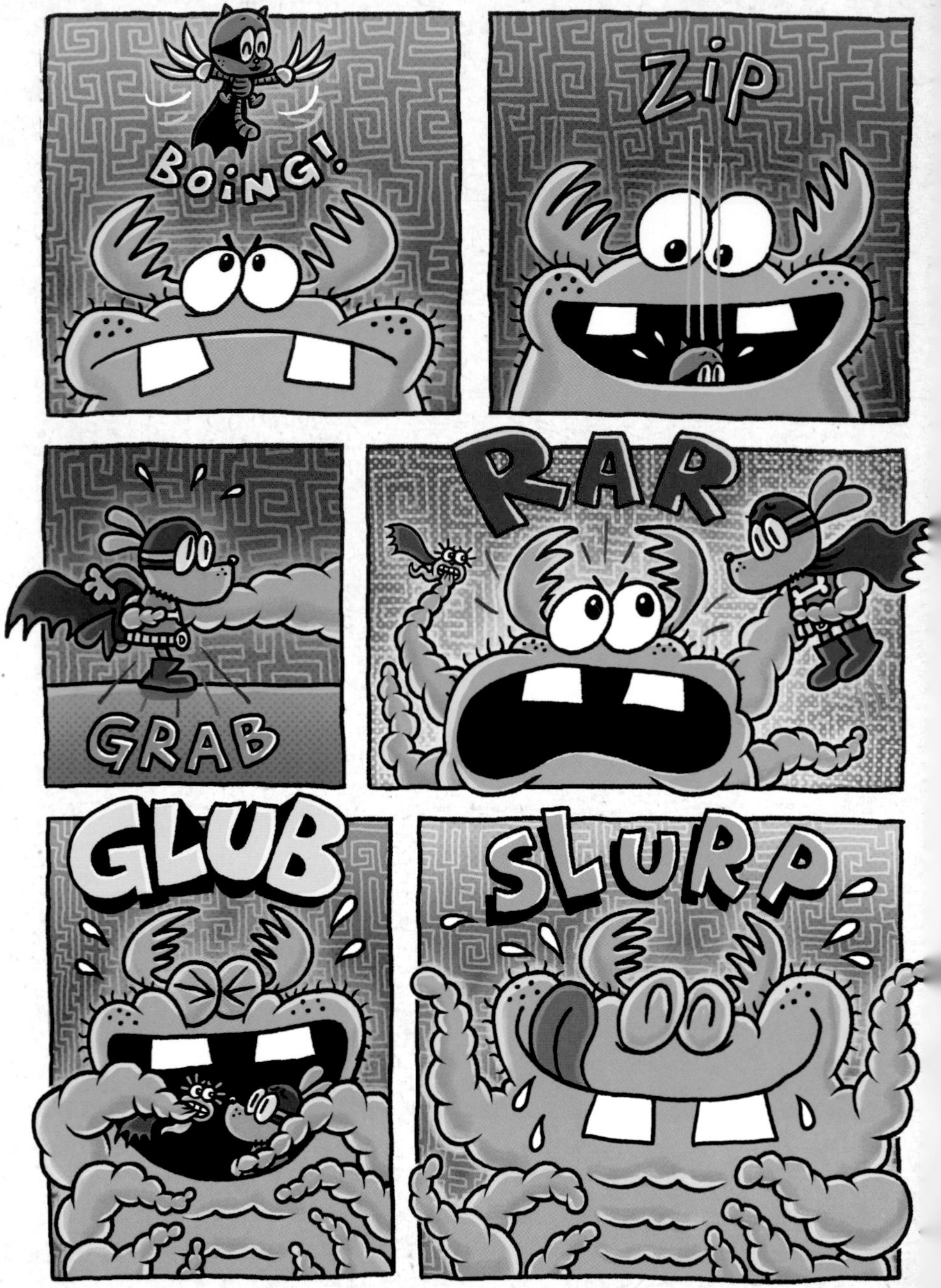
BOING!
ZIP
GRAB
RAR
GLUB
SLURP

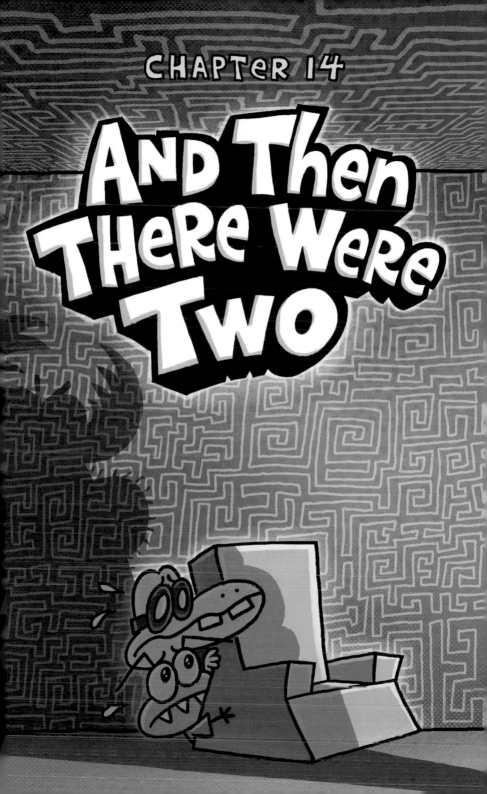

CHAPTER 14

AND THEN THERE WERE TWO

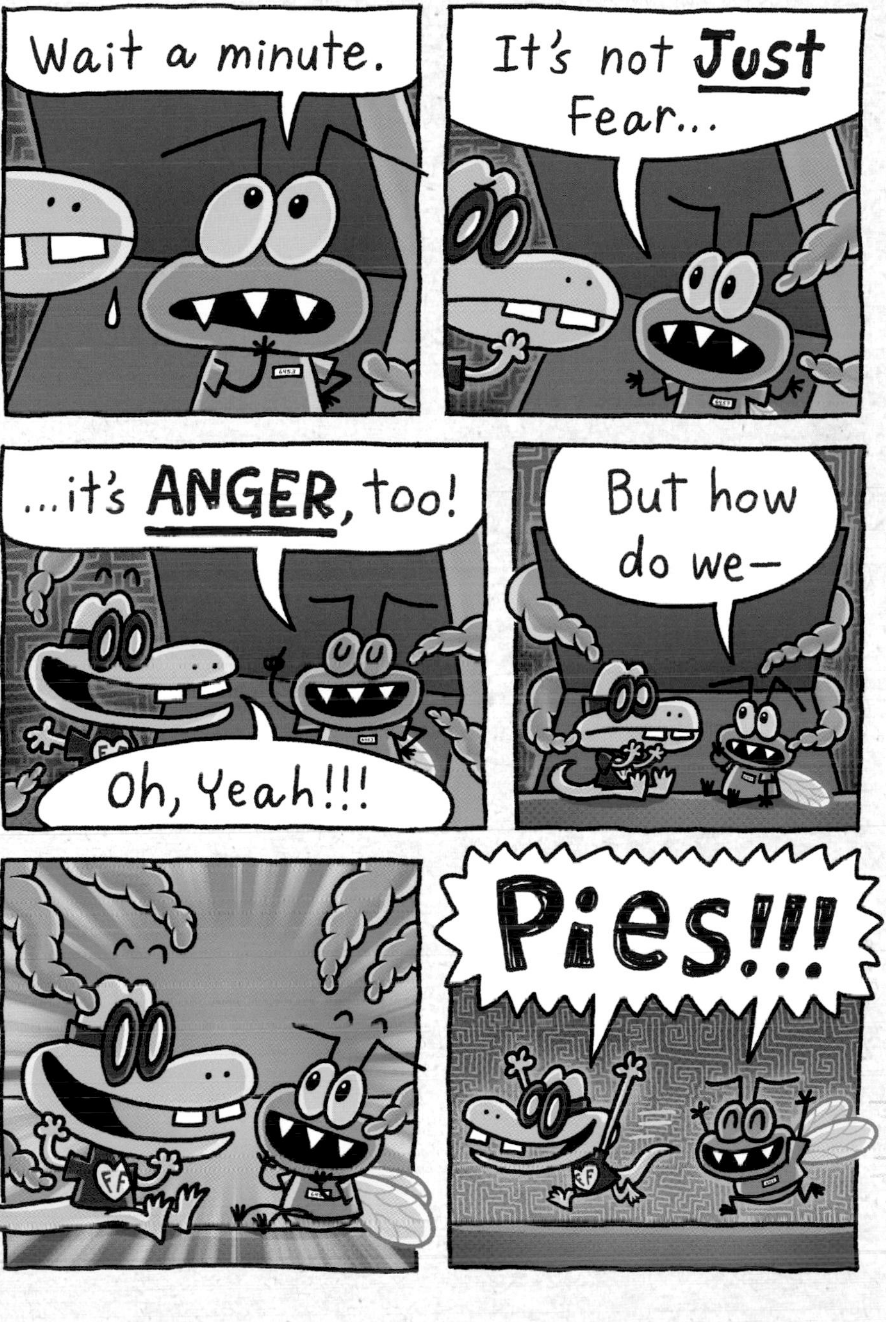
Wait a minute.
It's not JUST Fear...
...it's ANGER, too!
Oh, Yeah!!!
But how do we—
Pies!!!

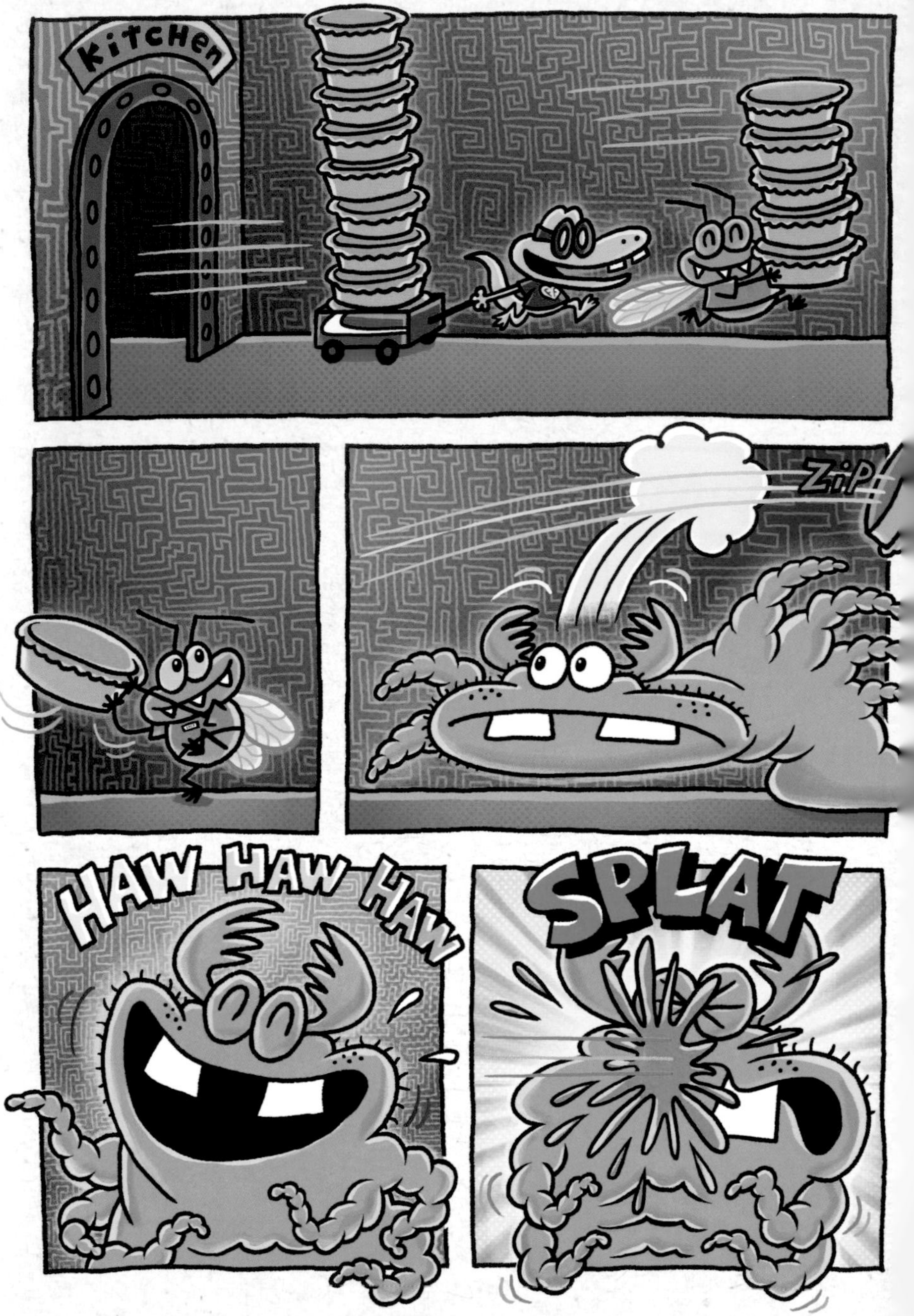
KiTCHeN
ZiP
HAW HAW HAW HAW
SPLAT

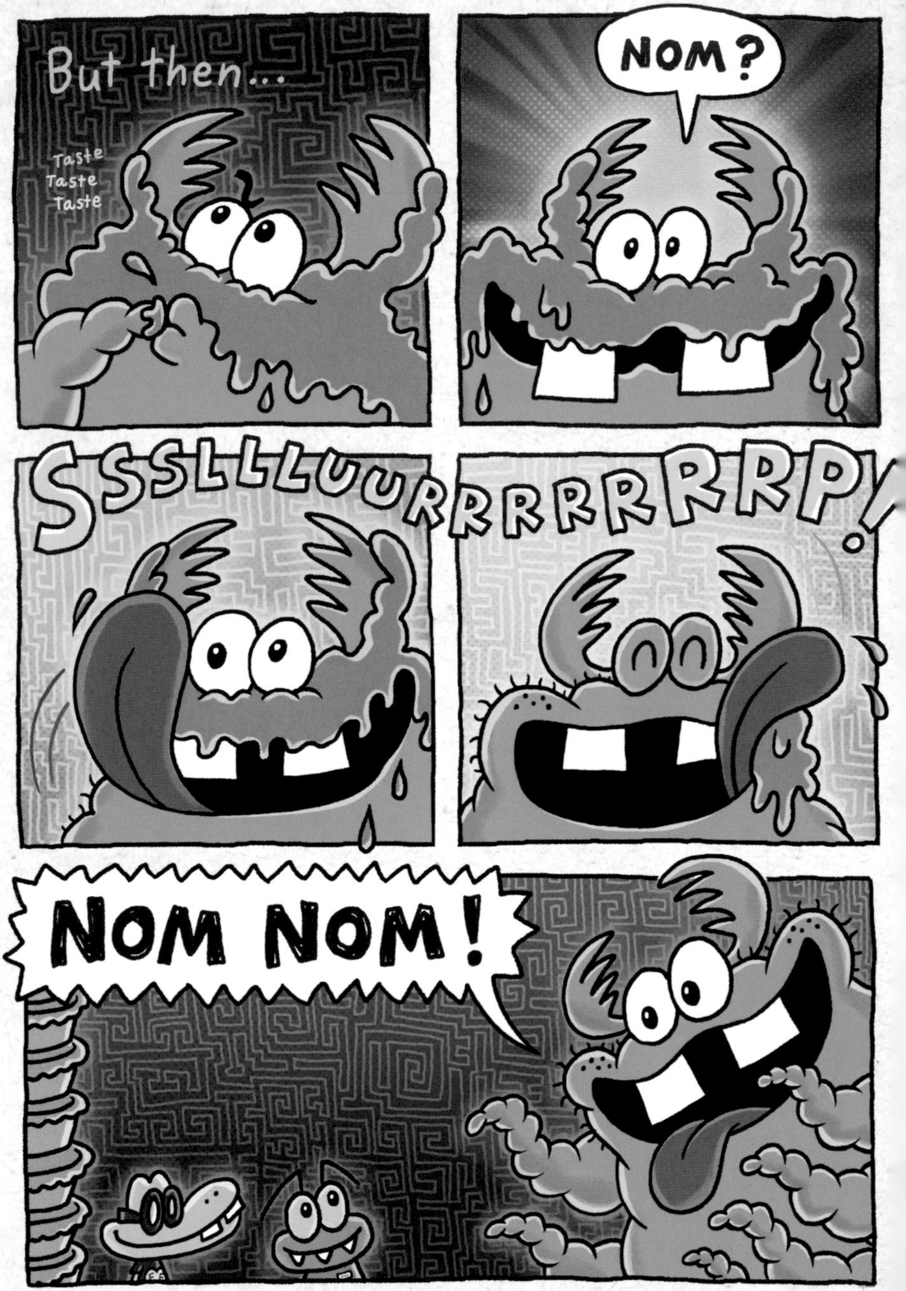
But then...
Taste
Taste
Taste
NOM?
SSSLLLUURRRRRRRP!
NOM NOM!

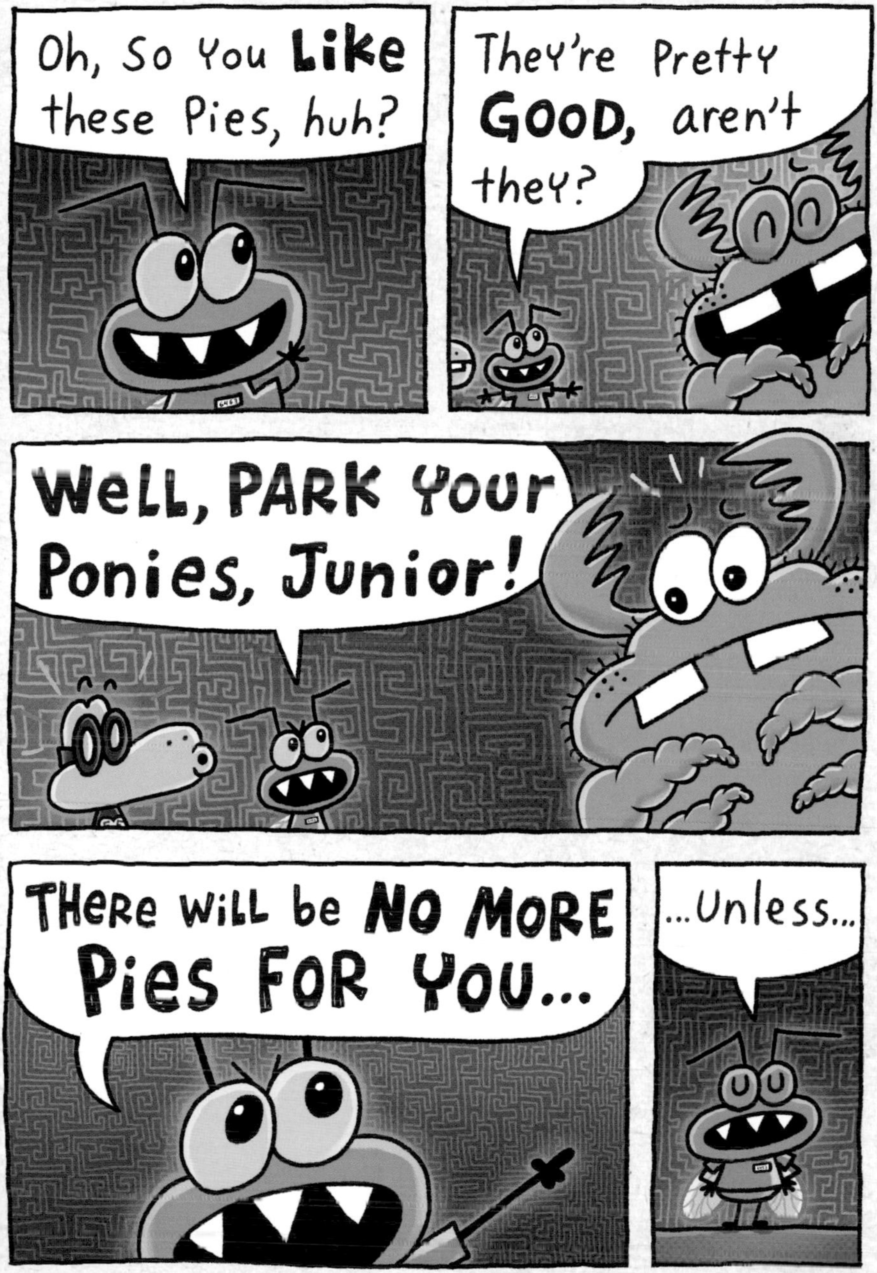
Oh, So You LIKE these Pies, huh?
They're Pretty GOOD, aren't they?
WELL, PARK YOUR Ponies, Junior!
THERE WILL be NO MORE Pies FOR YOU...
...Unless...

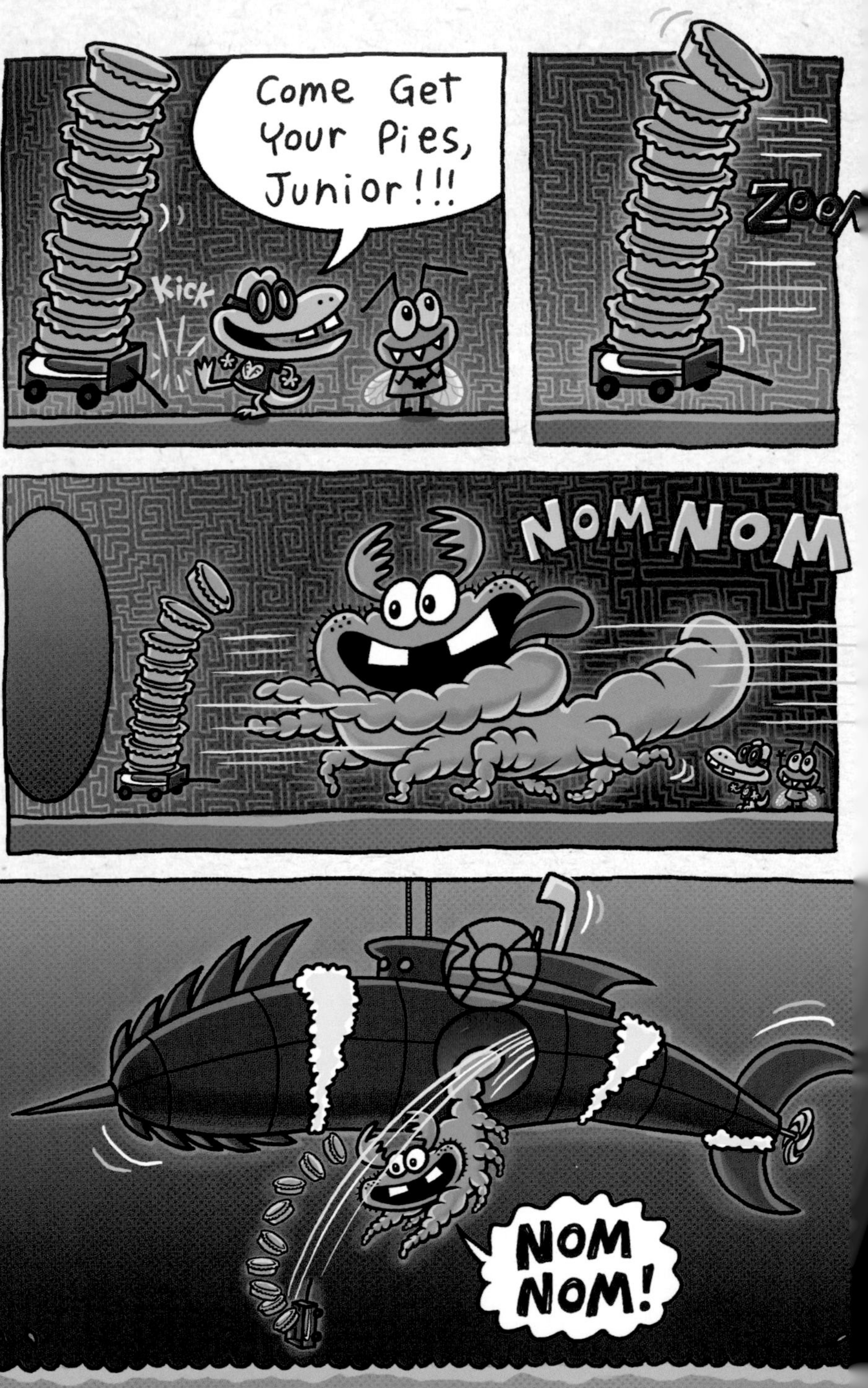
Come Get Your Pies, Junior!!!
KICK
NOM NOM
NOM NOM!

Hey, Uncle Larry? Yes?

Can we Grow **SUPA DOOPA BiG**?

Gosh! We've never Tried **THAT** before!

Size -O- TRON

Let's do it!!!

KAT-KLUNK

Size -O- TRON

SUPA DOOPA BIG
SUPA BIG
BIG
NORMAL
SMALL
SUPA SMALL

SUB WILL GROW IN FIVE SECONDS...

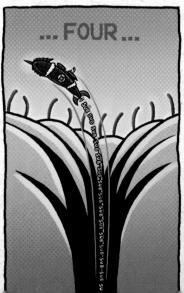

...FOUR...

CHAPTER 15

EXACTLY ONE HUNDRED AND NINE SECONDS EARLIER

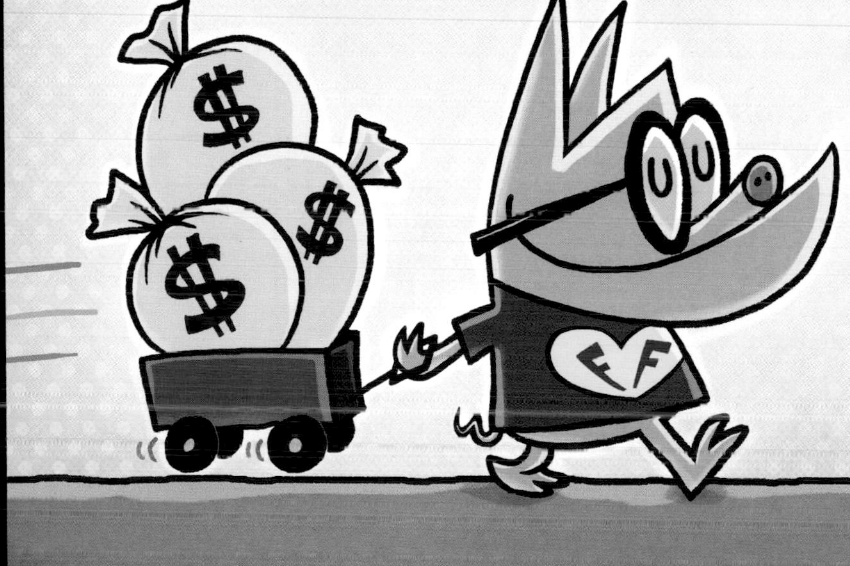

$
$
$
FF

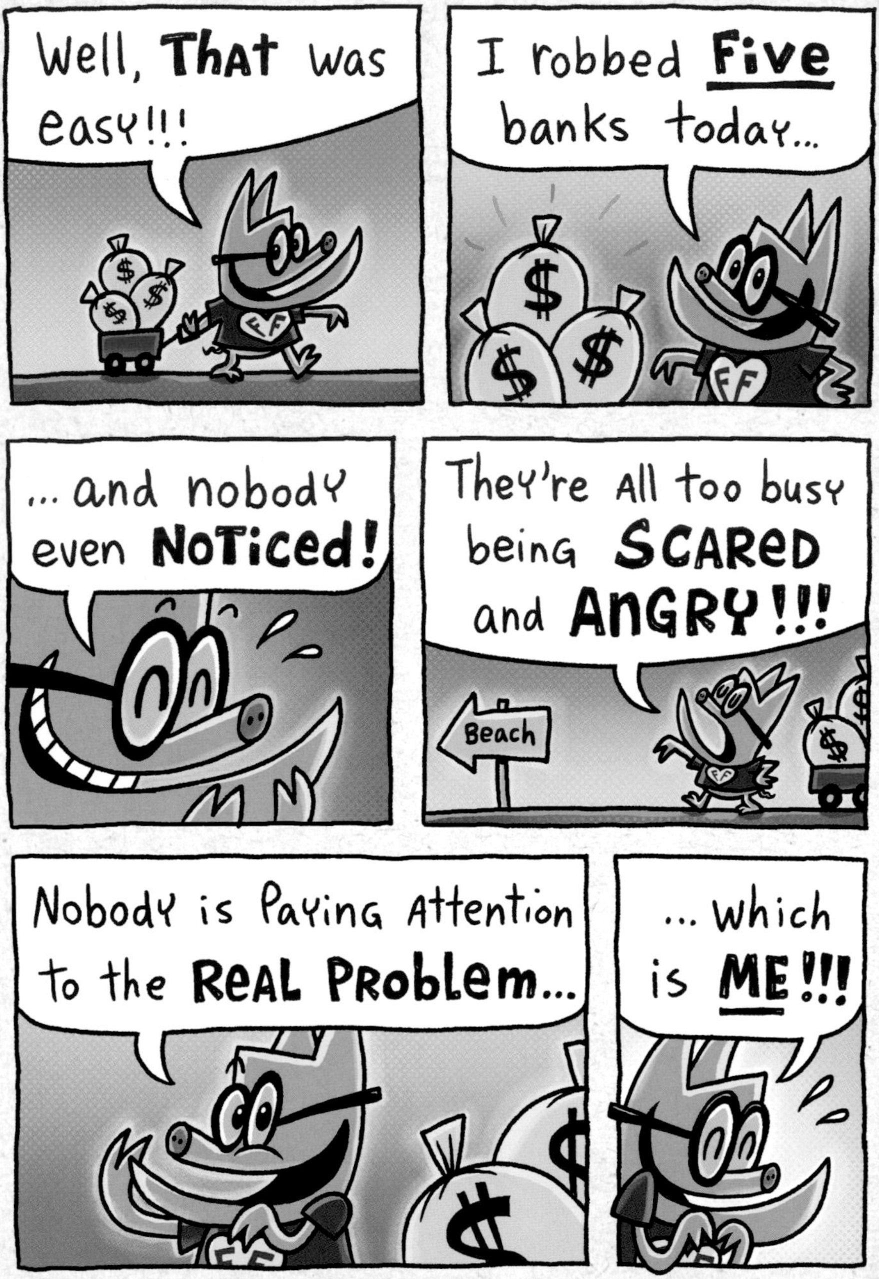
Well, THAT was easy!!!
I robbed FIVE banks today...
... and nobody even NOTICED!
They're all too busy being SCARED and ANGRY!!!
Beach
Nobody is paying attention to the REAL PROBLEM...
... which is ME!!!

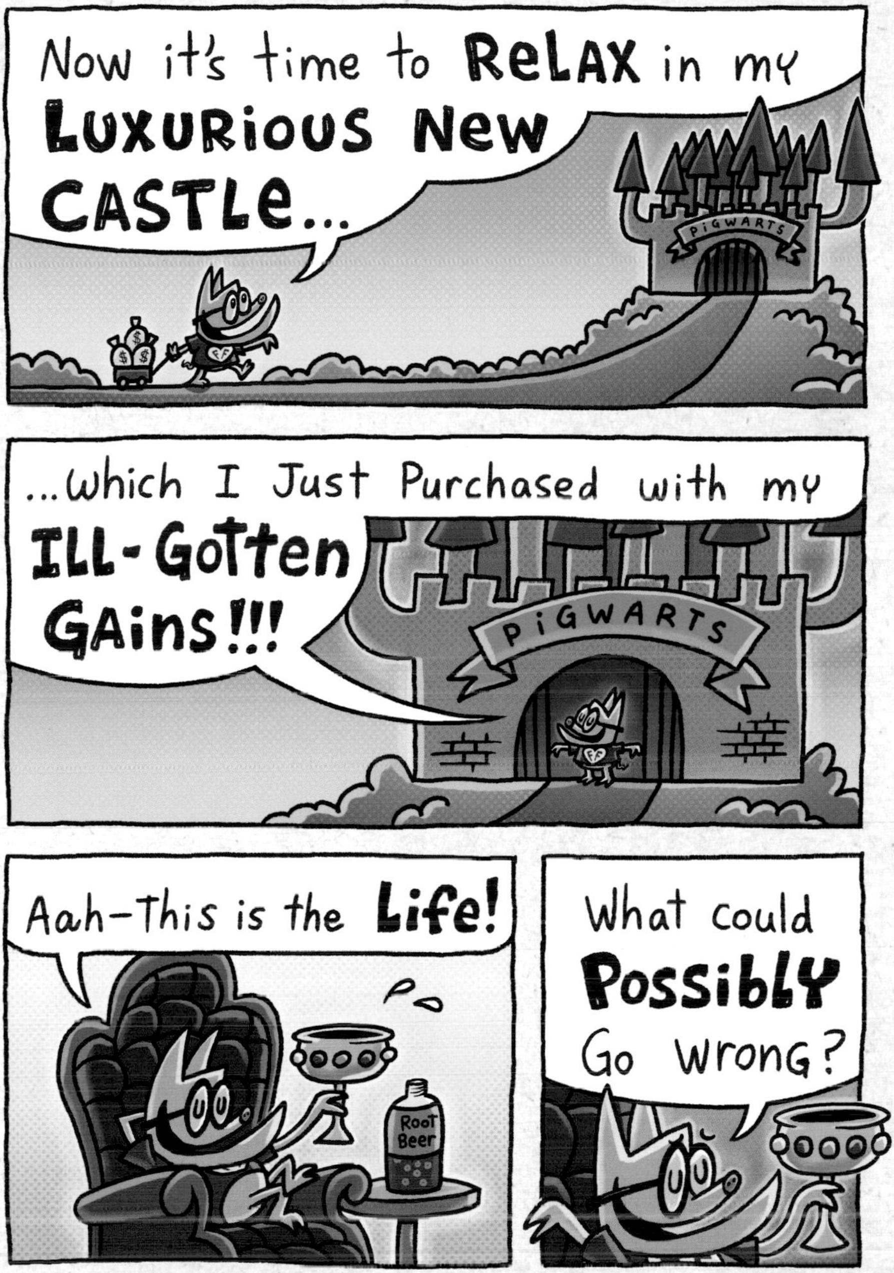
Now it's time to RELAX in my LUXURIOUS NEW CASTLE...
PIGWARTS
...Which I Just Purchased with my ILL-GOTTEN GAINS!!!
PIGWARTS
Aah—This is the Life!
Root Beer
What could Possibly Go Wrong?

But then...

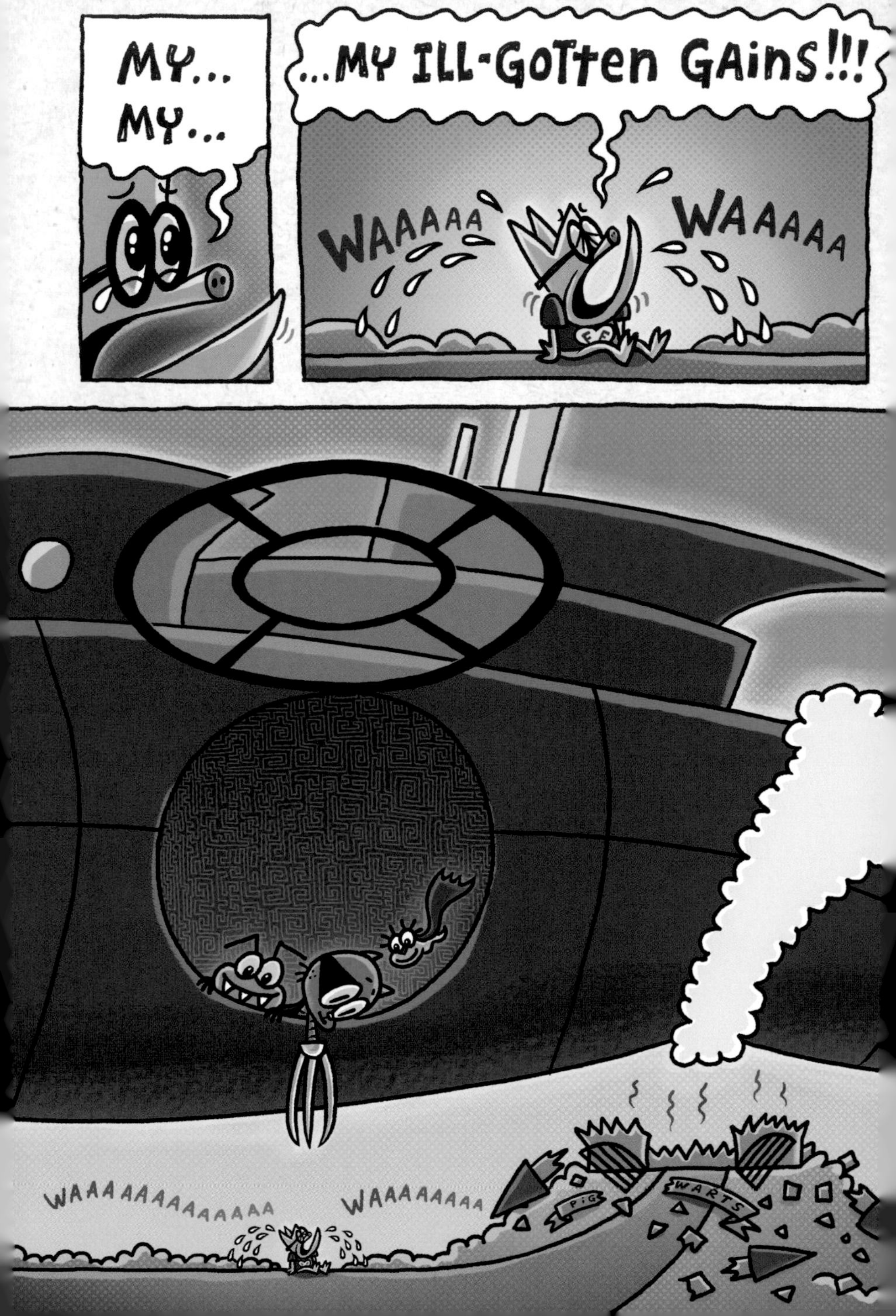
MY...
MY...
...MY ILL-GOTTEN GAINS!!!
WAAAAA
WAAAAAA
WAAAAAAAAAAAAA
WAAAAAAAA
PIG
WARTS

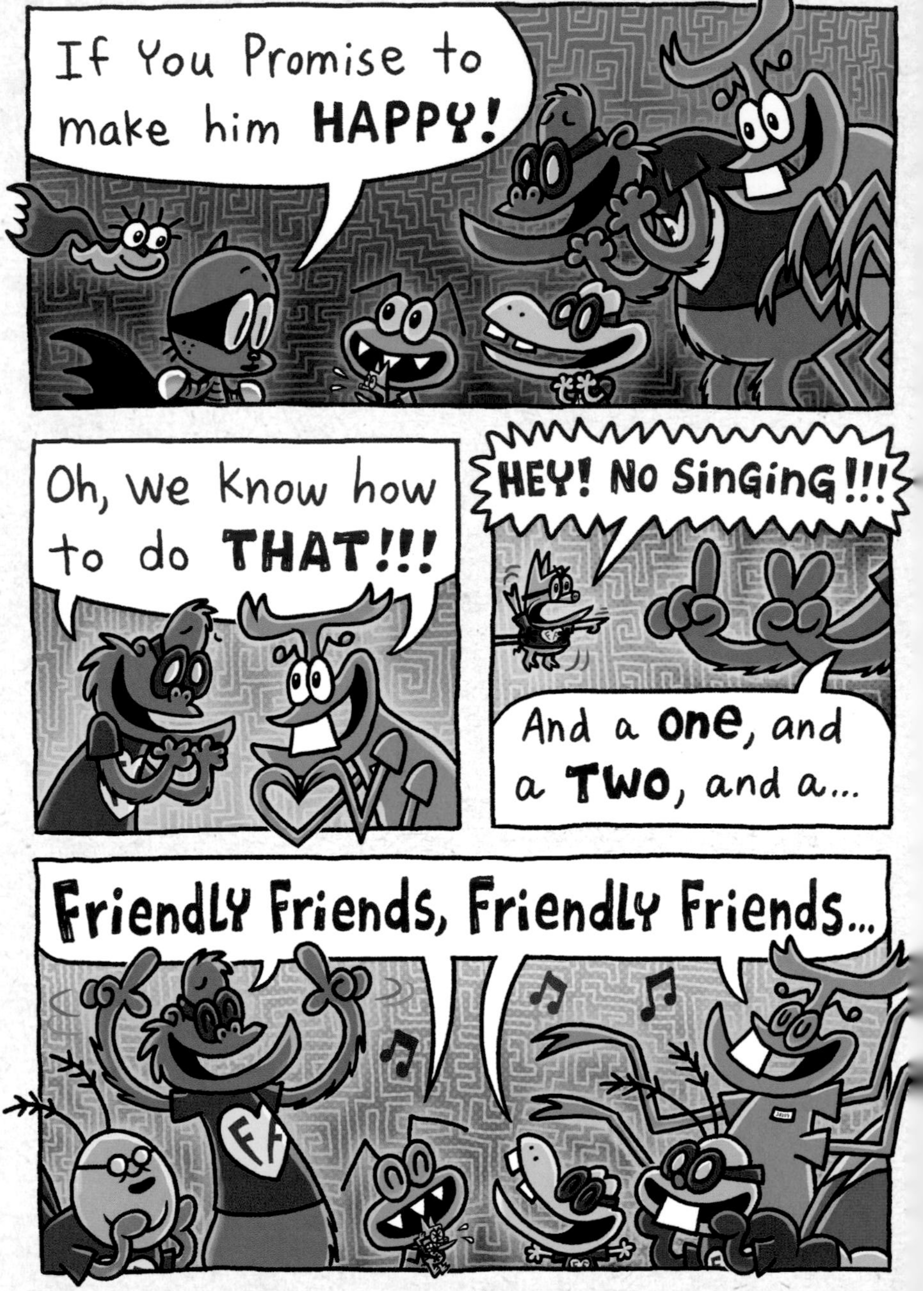
If You Promise to make him HAPPY!
Oh, we know how to do THAT!!!
HEY! No SinGinG!!!
And a one, and a TWO, and a...
FriendLY Friends, FriendLY Friends...

Friendly Friends, Friendly Friends...

...watch him eat his meal...

...OH, what fun...

...to see him run...

...on a Friendly hamster wheel!!!

WAAAAAAAAA

Chapter 16

In Search of the Depth

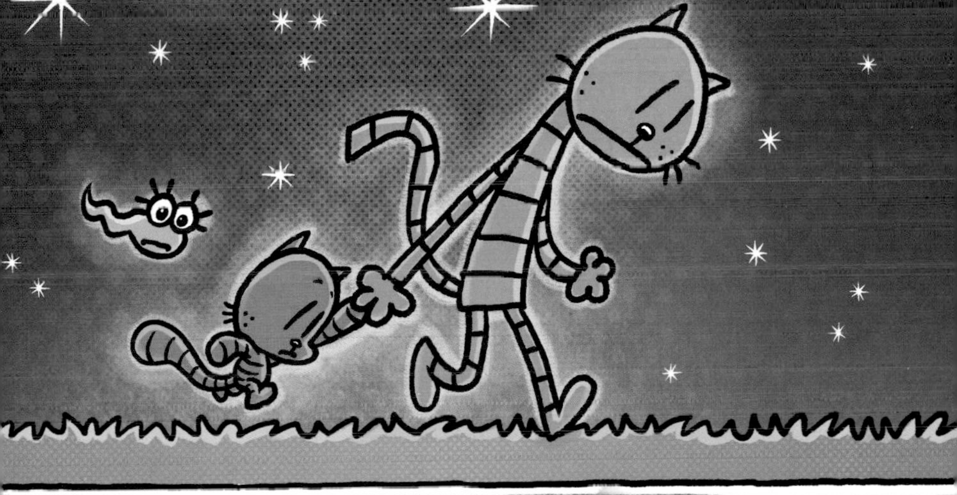

...and friends we sort of forgot about ten chapters ago...

...all worked together...

...to help Petey rebuild his Lab.

Soon, it was time to stop for the day.

Let's all Go to Dog Man's house!

We can eat Supper together!

HOORAY!!!

And So...

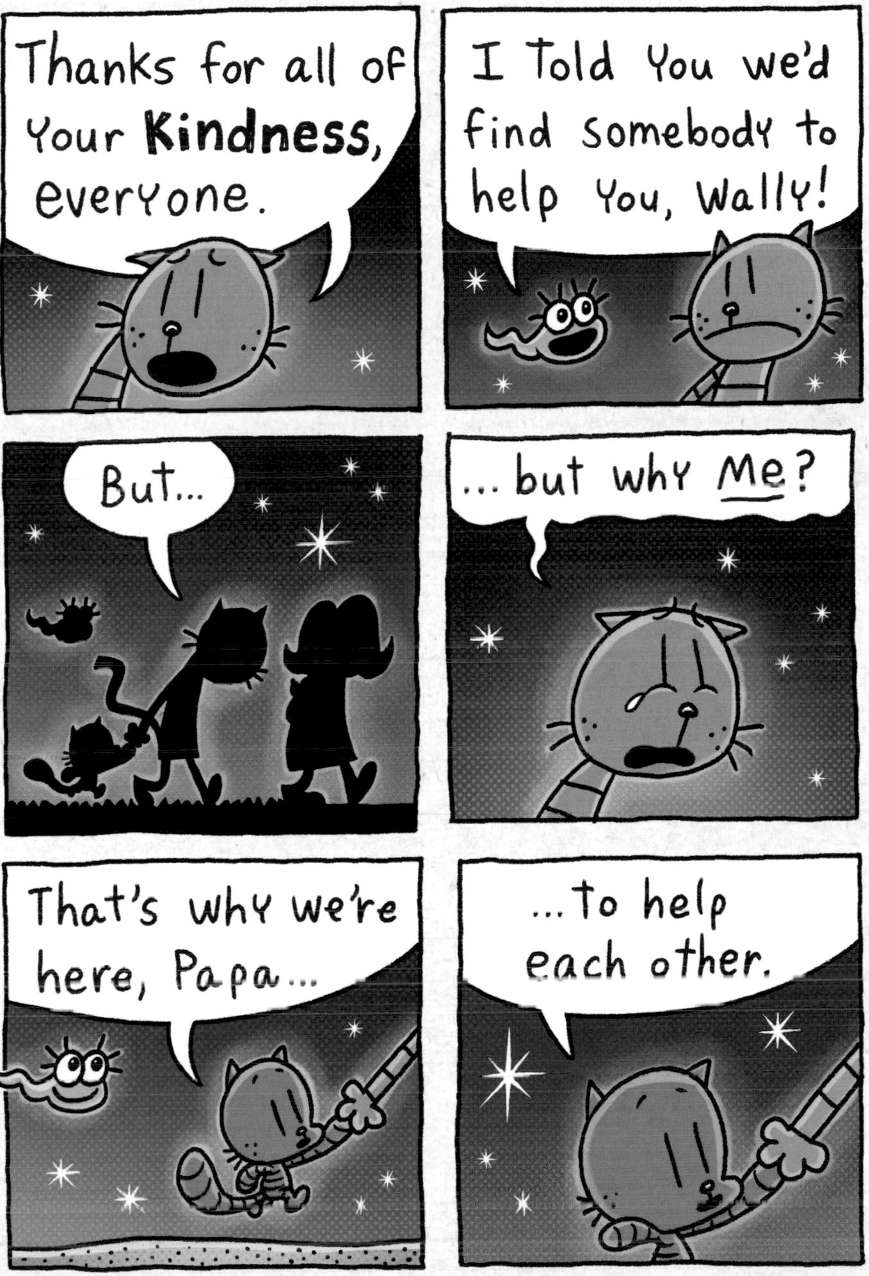
Thanks for all of your **Kindness**, everyone.
I told you we'd find somebody to help you, Wally!
But...
... but why Me?
That's why we're here, Papa...
... to help each other.

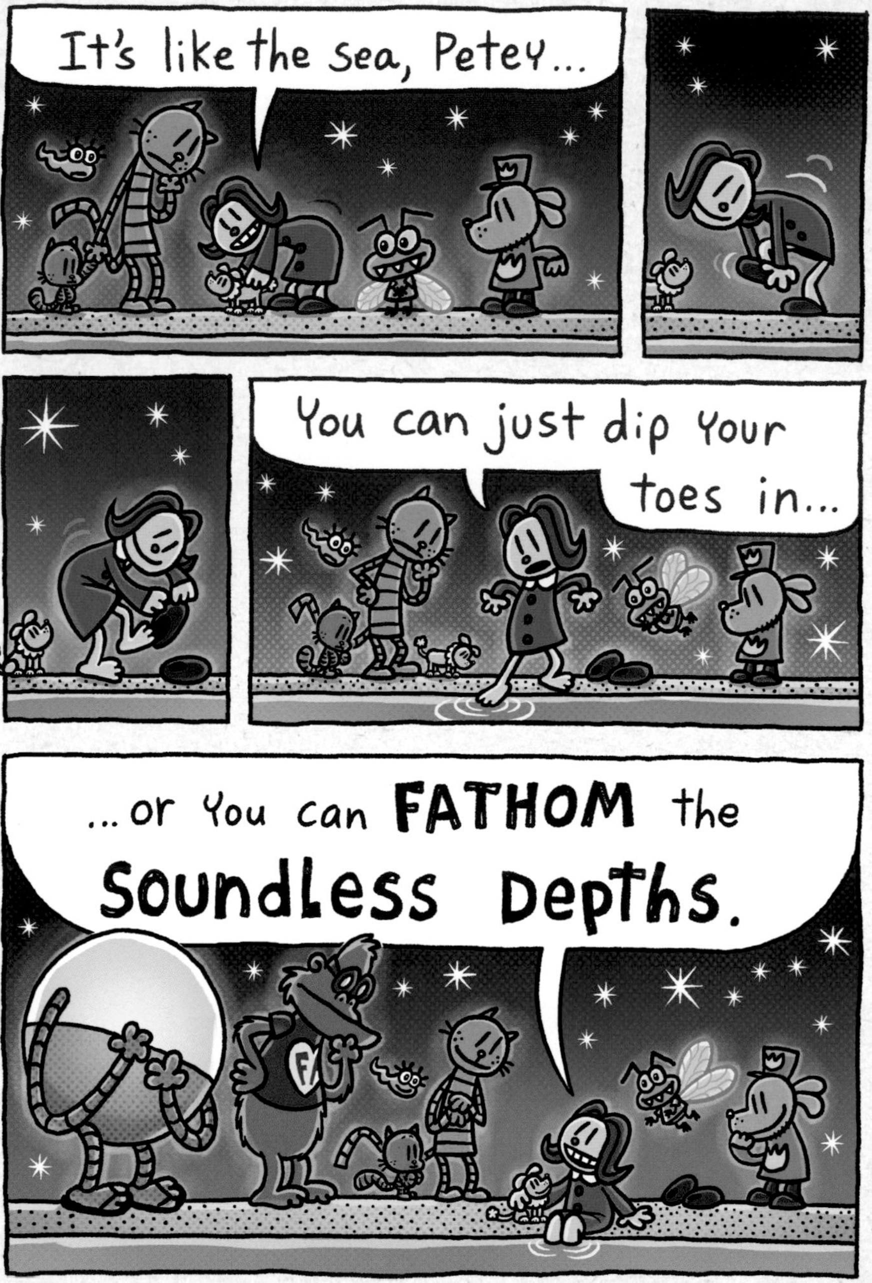
It's like the sea, Petey...
You can just dip your toes in...
...or you can FATHOM the Soundless Depths.

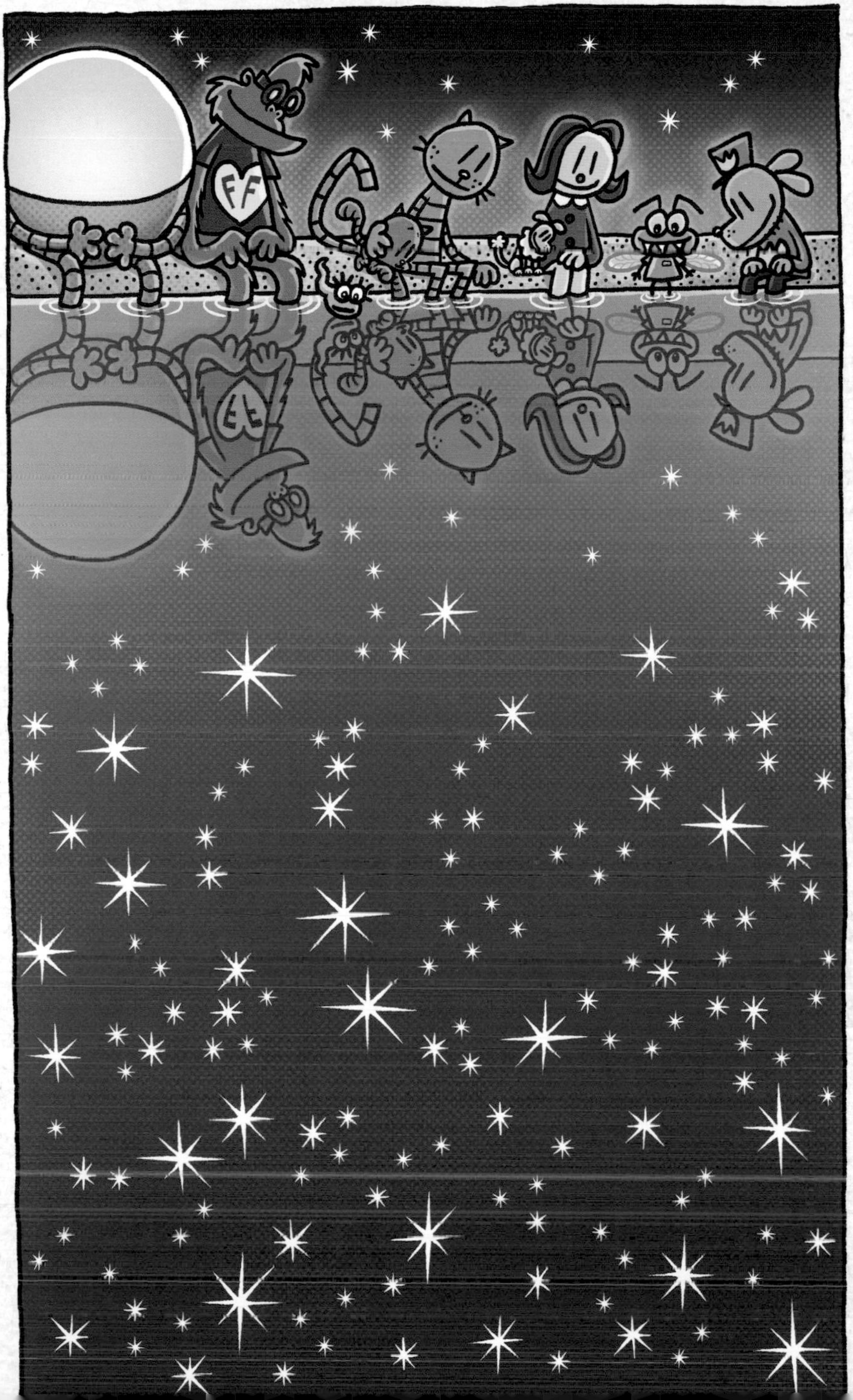

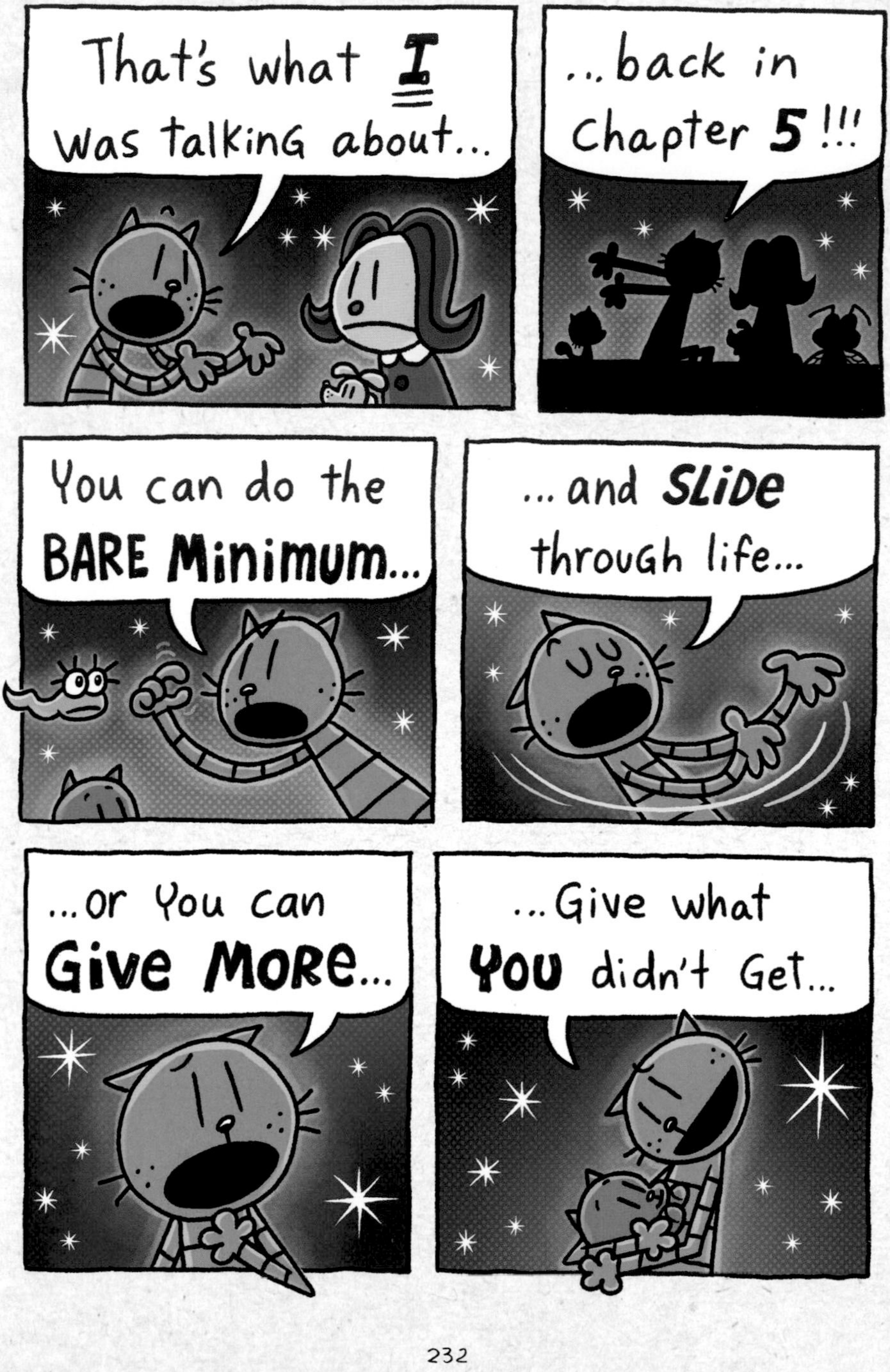
That's what I was talking about...
...back in Chapter 5!!!
You can do the BARE Minimum...
...and SLIDE through life...
...or You can Give MORE...
...Give what YOU didn't Get...

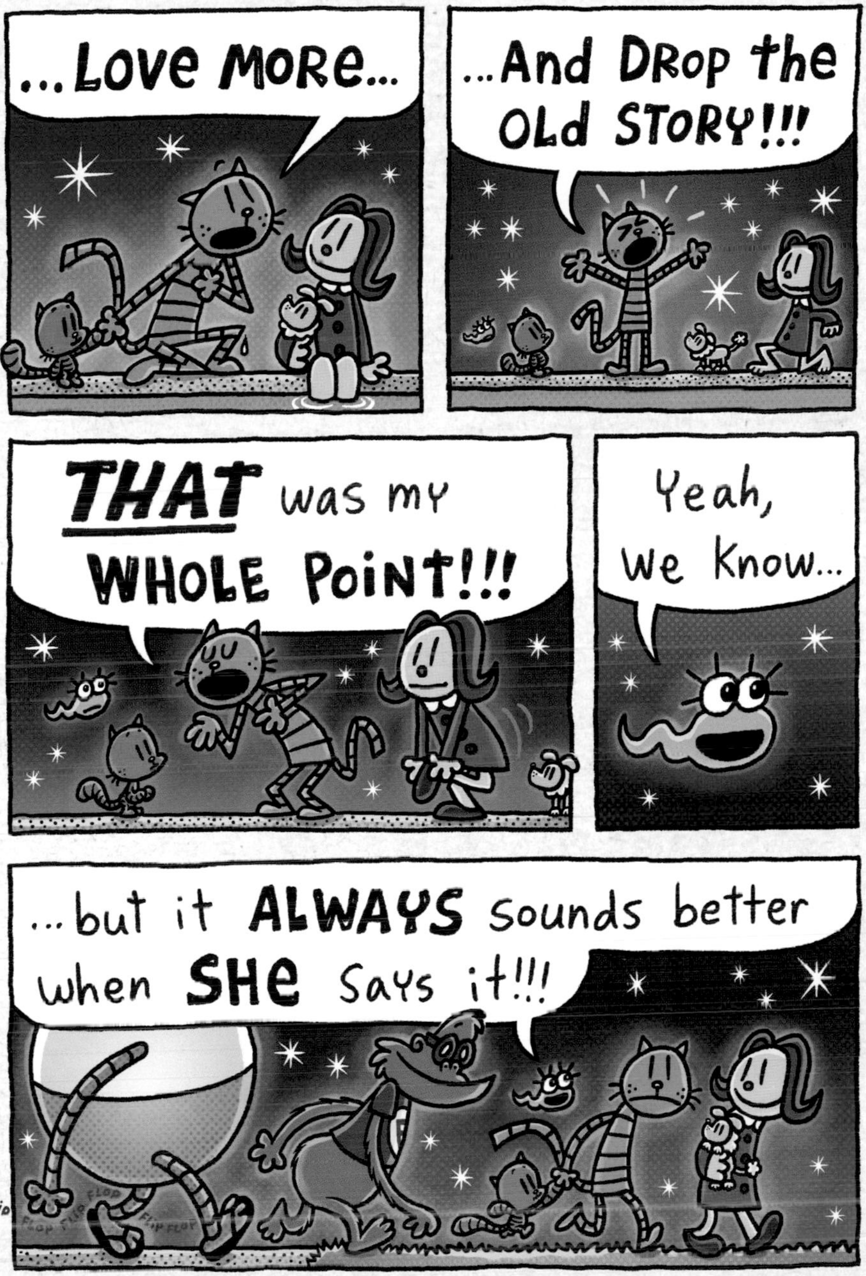
...Love MORE...
...And DRop the OLd STORY!!!
THAT was my WHOLE POINT!!!
Yeah, we Know...
...but it ALWAYS sounds better when SHE says it!!!

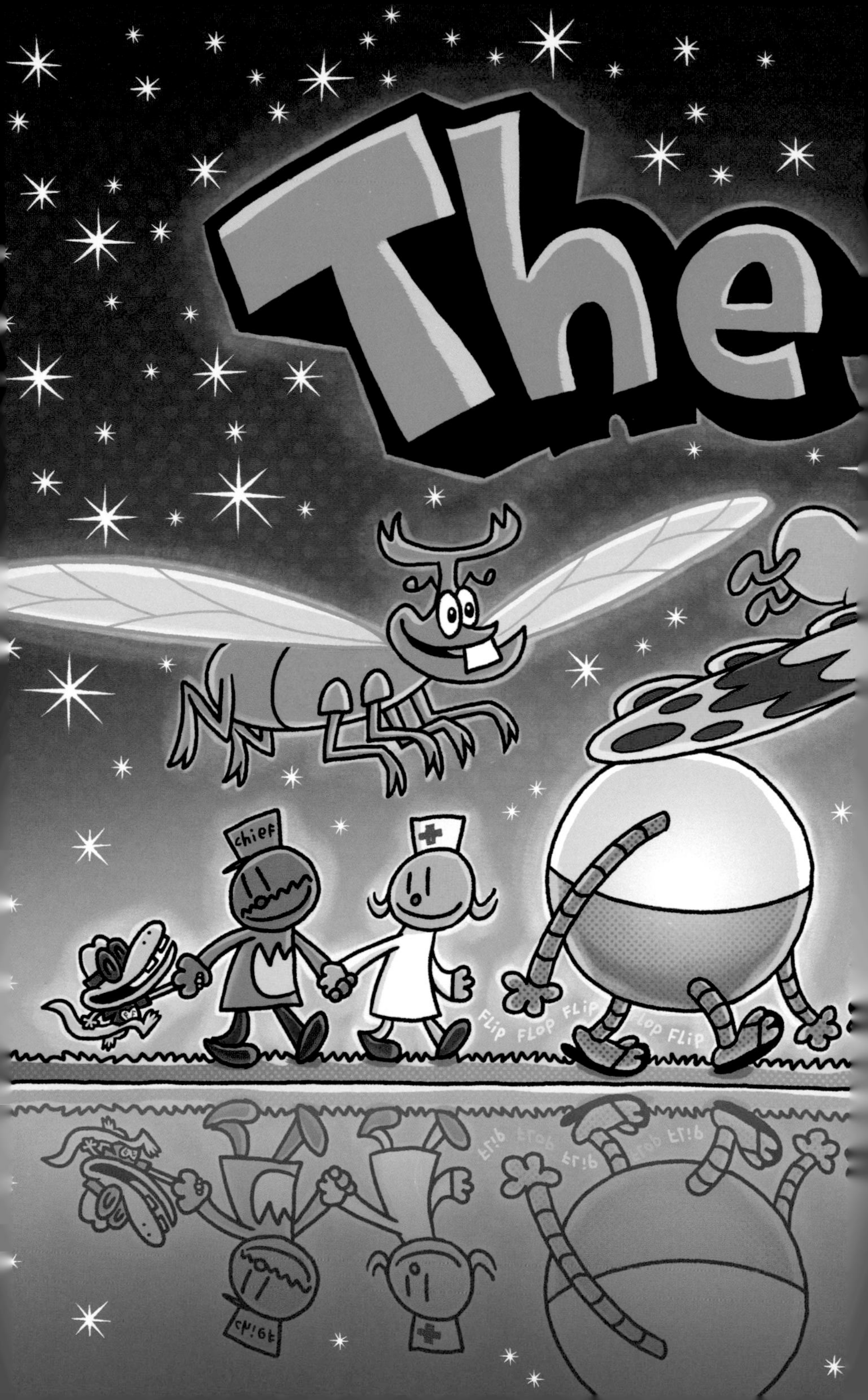
The
chief
FLIP FLOP FLIP FLOP FLIP

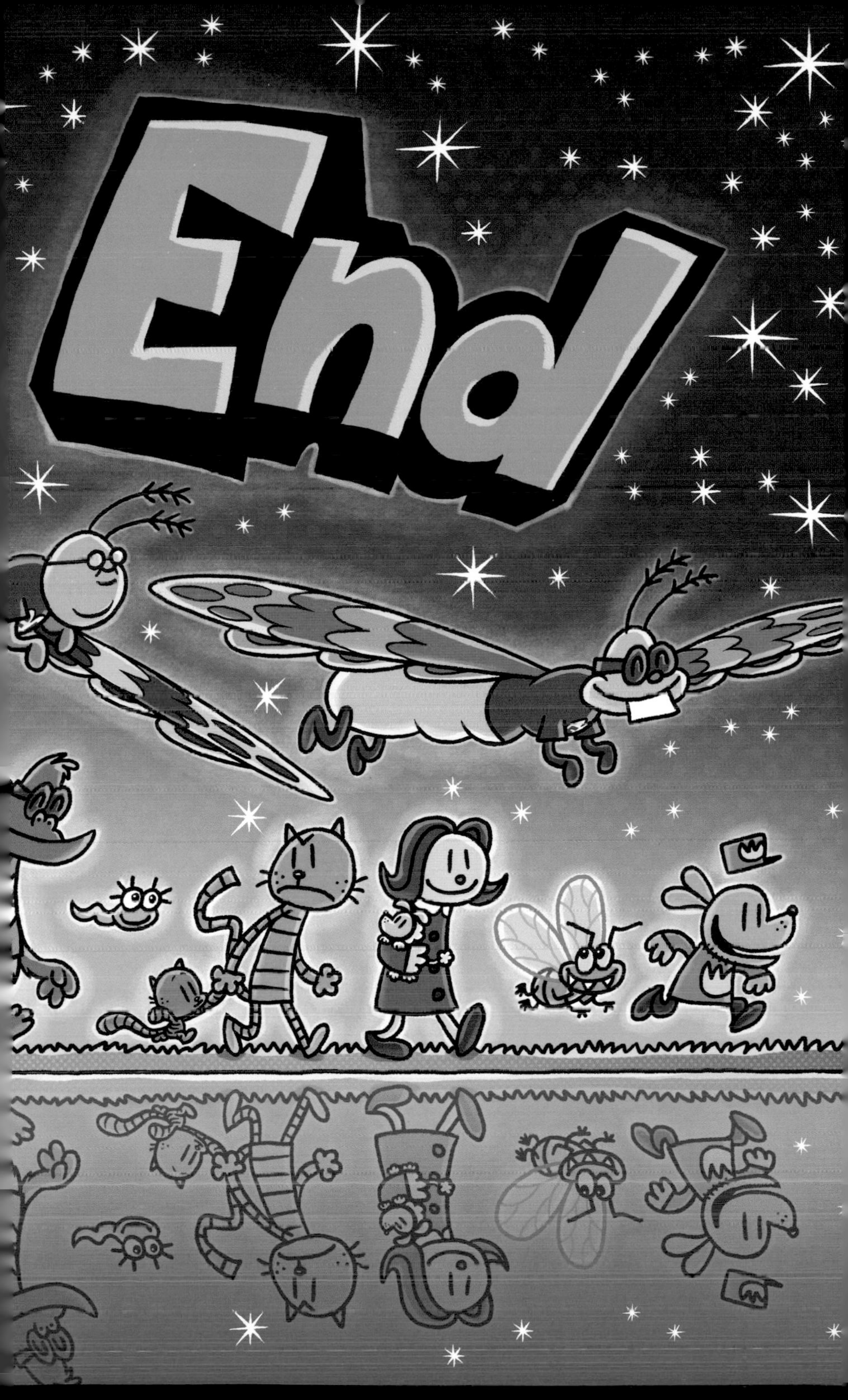
End

MIKE the FLY

WITH his NEW FRIENDLY FRIENDS T-ShiRT

in **22** Ridiculously easy steps!

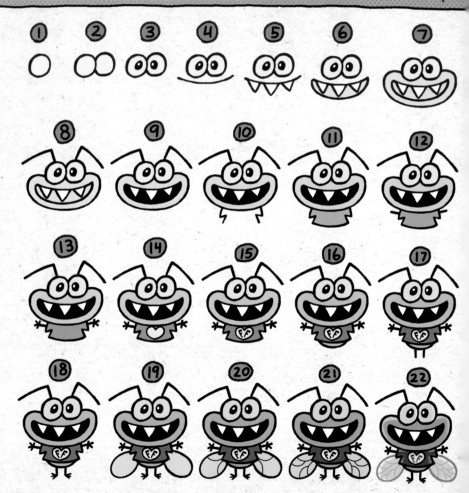

236

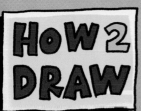

HOW 2 DRAW MOLLY

WHO **STILL** hasn't figured out her **SUPERhero** name Yet!!!

in **16** Ridiculously easy steps!

FOR MORE "HOW 2 DRAW" Fun...
PLANET PiLKEY
...ViSiT PLANETPiLKEY.COM
PLANET PiLKEY

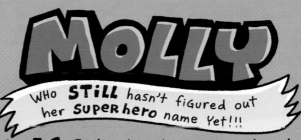

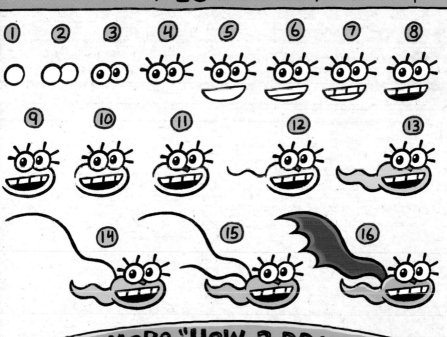

GET READING

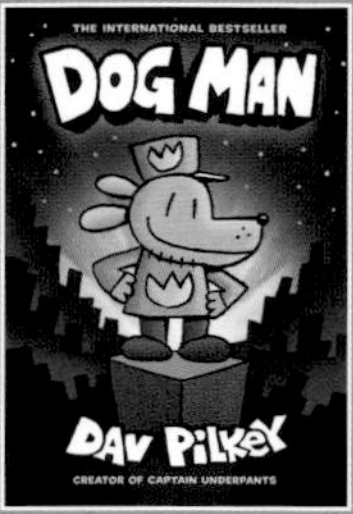
THE INTERNATIONAL BESTSELLER
DOG MAN
DAV PILKEY
CREATOR OF CAPTAIN UNDERPANTS

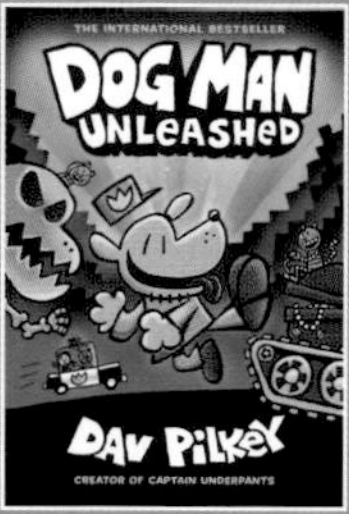
THE INTERNATIONAL BESTSELLER
DOG MAN
UNLEASHED
DAV PILKEY
CREATOR OF CAPTAIN UNDERPANTS

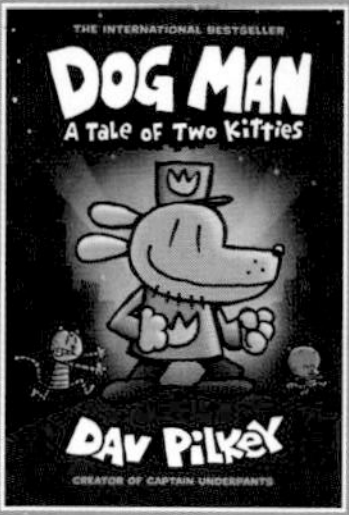
THE INTERNATIONAL BESTSELLER
DOG MAN
A Tale of Two Kitties
DAV PILKEY
CREATOR OF CAPTAIN UNDERPANTS

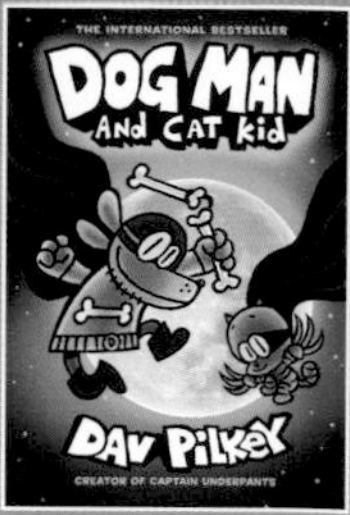
THE INTERNATIONAL BESTSELLER
DOG MAN
AND CAT KID
DAV PILKEY
CREATOR OF CAPTAIN UNDERPANTS

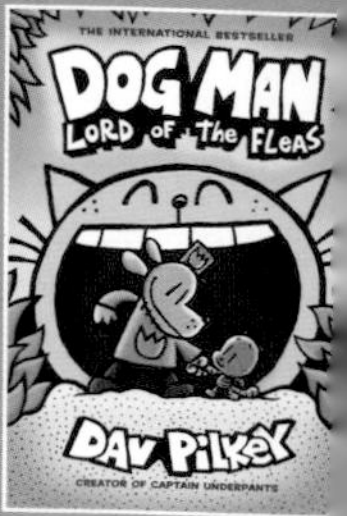
THE INTERNATIONAL BESTSELLER
DOG MAN
LORD OF THE FLEAS
DAV PILKEY
CREATOR OF CAPTAIN UNDERPANTS

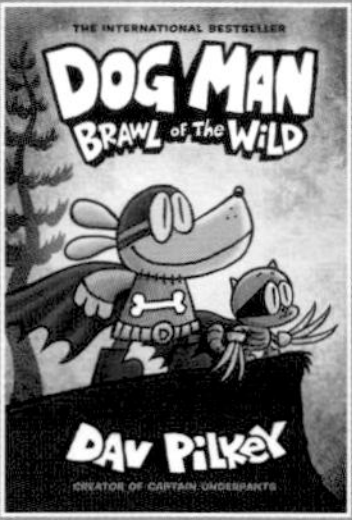
THE INTERNATIONAL BESTSELLER
DOG MAN
BRAWL of the WILD
DAV PILKEY
CREATOR OF CAPTAIN UNDERPANTS

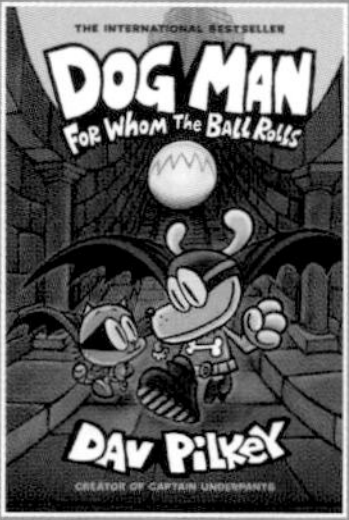
THE INTERNATIONAL BESTSELLER
DOG MAN
FOR WHOM THE BALL ROLLS
DAV PILKEY
CREATOR OF CAPTAIN UNDERPANTS

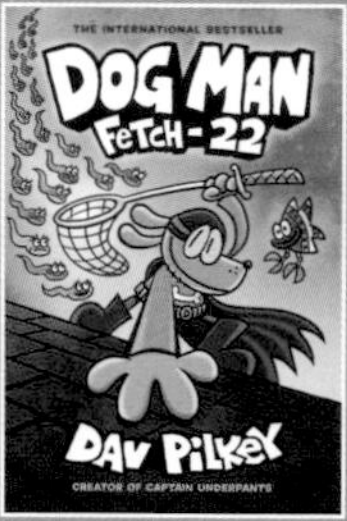
THE INTERNATIONAL BESTSELLER
DOG MAN
FETCH-22
DAV PILKEY
CREATOR OF CAPTAIN UNDERPANTS

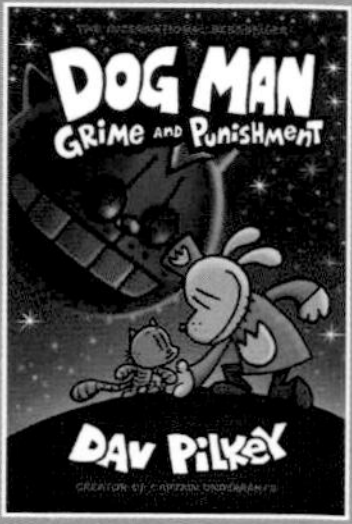
THE INTERNATIONAL BESTSELLER
DOG MAN
GRIME AND PUNISHMENT
DAV PILKEY
CREATOR OF CAPTAIN UNDERPANTS

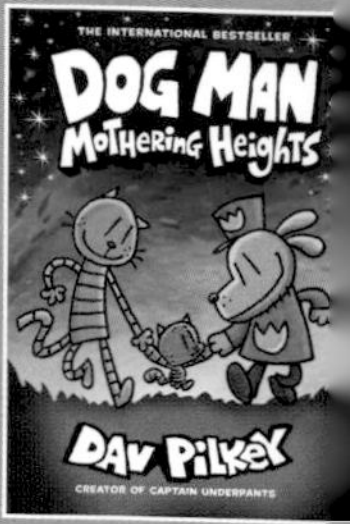
THE INTERNATIONAL BESTSELLER
DOG MAN
MOTHERING HEIGHTS
DAV PILKEY
CREATOR OF CAPTAIN UNDERPANTS

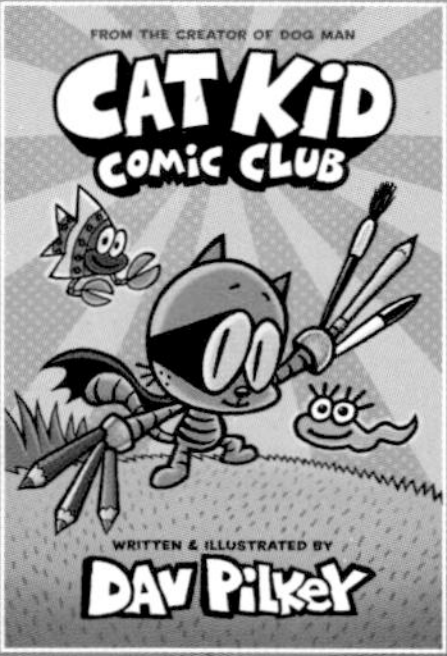
FROM THE CREATOR OF DOG MAN
CAT KID
COMIC CLUB
WRITTEN & ILLUSTRATED BY
DAV PILKEY

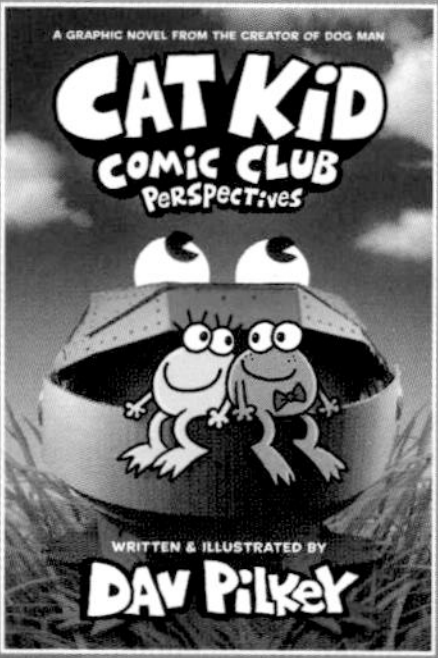
A GRAPHIC NOVEL FROM THE CREATOR OF DOG MAN
CAT KID
COMIC CLUB
PERSPECTIVES
WRITTEN & ILLUSTRATED BY
DAV PILKEY

★ "Irreverent, laugh-out-loud funny and . . . downright moving."
— Publishers Weekly, starred review

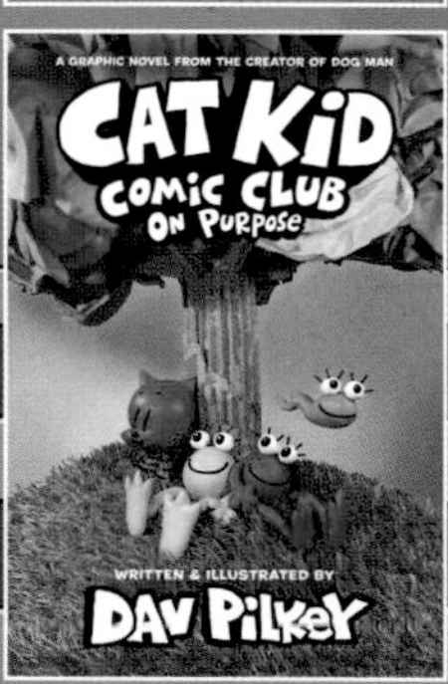
A GRAPHIC NOVEL FROM THE CREATOR OF DOG MAN
CAT KID
COMIC CLUB
ON PURPOSE
WRITTEN & ILLUSTRATED BY
DAV PILKEY

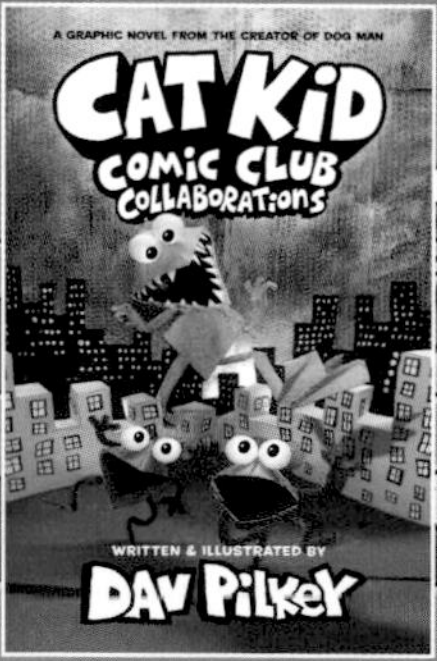
A GRAPHIC NOVEL FROM THE CREATOR OF DOG MAN
CAT KID
COMIC CLUB
COLLABORATIONS
WRITTEN & ILLUSTRATED BY
DAV PILKEY

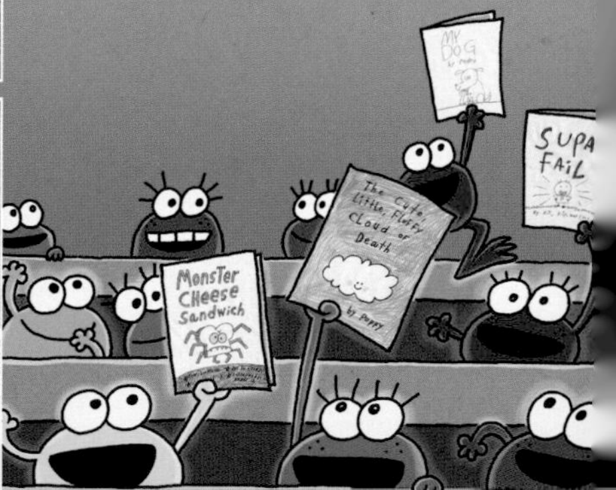
SUPA FAIL
Monster Cheese Sandwich

NOTES & FUN FACTS

☆ The most common English-language translation of the title of Jules Verne's *Vingt Mille Lieues Sous Les Mers* is <u>20,000 Leagues Under the Sea</u>. This is a mistranslation, however. It should be "Seas."

☆ The mistranslation implies a *depth* of 20,000 leagues, which is impossible because 20,000 Leagues is over TWICE the circumference of the Earth.

☆ Studies have shown that false or misleading news (chapters 7 and 8) often spreads faster than legitimate news.
BuzzFeed News, November 16, 2016.

☆ Scientists have found that fear and anger (Chapter 9) are linked to dopamine, a neurotransmitter that causes people to feel pleasure.
Psychology Today, August 25, 2015; Scientific American, July 14, 2008.

☆ Demodex mites (Chapter 13) are real, microscopic creatures. Here are some facts about them:
* They live on the skin of mammals (including humans and pigs).
* They have eight legs.
* Their favorite food is pumpkin pie.
* They typically come out at night.
* They are probably on your face right now.

☆ One of the "facts" about Demodex mites mentioned above is not true. Can you guess which one?

☆ The design for Uncle Larry's flying submarine was loosely inspired by illustrations produced for a Japanese publication. They were created by an artist who signed each painting: "Kyo-62."

☆ Chapter 16's title is based on the quote, "Hast thou walked in the search of the depth?" from Job 38:16 (KJV). It appears in the final paragraph of some English-language versions of <u>20,000 Leagues Under the Seas</u>.

☆ Other English-language versions substitute "Who can fathom the soundless depths?" (based on Ecclesiastes 7:24), which Sarah refers to on page 230.

☆ "Give More. Give what you didn't get. Love more. Drop the old story." is a quote from the journals of Garry Shandling.

☆ Molly and Li'l Petey continued working on their comic WALLY's WORLD and finally finished it. You can read the ENTIRE comic for free at Dav Pilkey's Epic Comic Club (PlanetPilkey.com) starting on June 1, 2023.